The Maiden

The Maiden

Dynasty 8

Cynthia Harrod-Eagles

W F HOWES LTD

This large print edition published in 2010 by
W F Howes Ltd
Unit 4, Rearsby Business Park, Gaddesby Lane,
Rearsby, Leicester LE7 4YH

1 3 5 7 9 10 8 6 4 2

First published in the United Kingdom in 1985
by Macdonald & Co (Publishers) Ltd.

A CIP catalogue record for this book is available
from the British Library

ISBN 978 1 40745 947 9

Typeset by Palimpsest Book Production Limited,
Falkirk, Stirlingshire
Printed and bound in Great Britain
by MPG Books Ltd, Bodmin, Cornwall

FSC
Mixed Sources
Product group from well-managed
forests, controlled sources and
recycled wood or fiber
SA-COC-1565
www.fsc.org
© 1996 Forest Stewardship Council

For Cassandra
for her sixteenth birthday

BOOK I

THE CASTLE

Loosn'd from the minor's tether,
Free to mortgage or to sell,
Wild as wind and light as feather,
Bid the sons of thrift farewell.
Call the Betsies, Kates, and Jennies,
All the names that banish care;
Lavish of your grandsire's guineas,
Show the spirit of an heir.

Samuel Johnson: *One-and-twenty*

CHAPTER 1

One fine October day in 1720, the first dry day for a month, James Edward Morland came riding home to Morland Place from Leeds. He had been staying with Sir John Ibbetson, a master-clothier, a visit which his father had arranged in order that he should learn something of the business; Sir John was unusually indulgent towards the young, and had two pretty daughters, and Jemmy had managed to pass his time most agreeably, despite the weather, which confined them indoors.

It was a relief to be away from Morland Place, a relief which he believed his father, Matt, shared. Jemmy's mother was dead: she had hanged herself in her bedchamber when Jemmy was a child, leaving behind her the confession of a series of adulteries which had broken her husband's heart. Matt had adored her, and had trusted her implicitly. After her death he grew morose and gloomy, and for a long time he had refused to acknowledge even the existence of the six sons she had left behind her.

Time had brought Matt to accept that Jemmy,

3

the firstborn, was probably his own, and he had acknowledged Jemmy as his heir. But he remained a solitary and uncommunicative man, and Jemmy felt that the frequent absences from home his father arranged for him were as much to take him out of his father's sight as to educate him. Of Jemmy's brothers, only the two youngest, Tom and Charles, remained at home, educated by the chaplain tutor and kept strictly out of their father's way. The other three had been sent away to be educated, Robert and Edmund at Christ Church, Oxford, and George at Eton.

There had been a time when it had seemed that Matt's sad life might be redeemed. The 1715 rebellion, though it had been tragic for the Morlands as a family, had brought Matt the return of his childhood friend Davey, and a second wife, his cousin Sabina, who had loved him since childhood. Sabina had survived terrible ordeals to escape to Morland Place with her sole remaining child, Allen, having lost everything in the rising. Matt had devoted himself to her, and they had married, and had been happy for a while. But a difficult pregnancy and a perilous delivery of a stillborn child had left Sabina bedridden, virtually a cripple, and her suffering, for which Matt blamed himself, had sent him back into his dark cave of solitude.

Jemmy was very fond of his step-mother, but he had been in no hurry to end his visit to Leeds. However the change in the weather could not be

4

ignored, and he had set off before dawn, as every good traveller should. No curtain of the Ibbetson house twitched as he clattered out of the yard on his horse, Auster, with his servant Jack slouched gummy-eyed and yawning on his own horse behind him. The young ladies were evidently not so in love with him as he had thought, not enough to rise from their beds early to see him go, at any rate.

As they rode, the sun began to rise in the pale sky, glancing off the pools of standing water on every side, glittering dazzlingly on the droplets that hung from every leaf and twig. It was fortunate that Jemmy had ridden this way many times before, for the road had virtually disappeared. In wet weather, the centre of the road became rutted and sunken, and gradually filled with water; it was impossible to drain it, for the continuous process of scraping layers of mud away on cartwheels and sledgerunners left it lower than the surrounding land. So travellers would begin to strike out their own line on the higher, drier ground on one side or the other, until that, too, became a morass. The present wet weather had lasted so long that where the road had once been there was now only a twenty-foot-wide quagmire, eating deeply into the unfenced fields on either side. Jemmy made no attempt to use the road, but went straight across country, heading for Wetherby and the Crown Inn, where he meant to break his fast. Auster was glad to be out after his long confinement in the stable, and laid down his feet with a will, while Jack kept up a *sotto voce* stream of complaint at the speed and the rough travelling. Kick his horse as he may, it would never break into a canter, but only trotted faster and faster, shaking Jack's teeth in his head where, in any case, they were none too soundly embedded.

In Jemmy's opinion, the Crown Inn served the best ale in Yorkshire, as well as good food, which was free if you drank enough ale. Besides that, the landlord had a pretty daughter of seventeen, and Jemmy was nineteen and unwed. He lingered with pleasure in the parlour, which he had to himself until a large grey cat stepped delicately in through the open casement, and sat in the patch of sunlight on the windowsill, its eyes half-closed in bliss at the blessed warmth, its bushy tail curled tightly around its forefeet as if to stop them escaping.

Rose, the landlord's daughter, brought his breakfast, but declined to be drawn into conversation, and Jemmy guessed from her muted voice and lowered eyes that her father had warned her not to linger. Jemmy had been wild in his youth, and at one time would have regarded that as a challenge, but at nineteen he was more philosophical, and Rose's reticence only made him shrug. He drank a quart of ale, and ate the best cut off a round of beef, a wedge of sweet, crumbly Wensleydale cheese, and enough fresh hot bread to have caused an older stomach considerable unease. Then he finished off his meal with a couple of small, crisp pearmains, stretched his legs and stared past the dozing cat at the sunlit world with contentment. Indeed, he had little enough in life to vex him. He was young, healthy, handsome, and the heir to a valuable estate. If his father's temper made his social life a little restricted, why, he had horses and hounds and coverts to hunt, and there was always something to do to take him out of the house.

When finally he went out to the stable to fetch Auster, he found Jack leaning against the doorframe and staring moodily at the sky, which had deepened from its pale beginnings to a perfect bluebell shade.

'Ready now, Jack? Did you get something to eat?' he asked cheerfully. Jack shook his head gloomily.

'Naught but new bread, master, and no doubt that'll give me the gripes before long. And hossler says the glass is going back, and it'll rain again any moment.'

Jemmy glanced again at the cloudless sky, and said, 'The ostler wouldn't be a cousin of yours, I suppose?'

'And the roads,' Jack went on remorselessly, ignoring the pleasantry. 'The mire'll be enough to drawn a man. If we get through it'll be a miracle, and if we sink, there's not a soul knaws where we are to come and fetch us out.'

'We'll go over the moor, and stick to the causeway,' Jemmy said soothingly.

'Aye, if t'causey's not broken all to bits, for it's

no man's care to mend it as I can see.' He sniffed. 'You'll not be the only one to think of sticking to t'causey.'

Jemmy made no answer, busying himself with tightening Auster's girth. Jack was right, of course – the stone causeway down the centre or the side of the road was meant for foot-travellers or single horsemen, but when the mud was bad, everyone stuck to it, even the heavily-laden pack-horses, and the stone surface soon broke and crumbled under heavy traffic. But he would not give Jack the satisfaction of agreeing with him.

When they got past Bickerton and onto Marston Moor, they found things even worse than expected, for the Sike Beck had overflowed, making a sheet of water to either side of the causeway, which itself was entirely blocked by a train of packhorses, standing inexplicably stationary.

'Now what's to do?' cried Jemmy crossly, flicking at the rump of the end horse with his crop. The packhorse did not even flinch, standing head down, burdened by its huge, bulky packs. Its legs were thick with grey-brown mud, its tail was lank with it; the long hair on its belly was so festooned with it that it hung down like strange stalactites; even its packs were splashed with it.

'Why aren't they moving?' Jemmy said, standing in his stirrups to try to see ahead. It was a long train, stretching seemingly for ever, and though he could see men moving about up ahead, he could see no cause for the holdup.

'We s'l have to strike our own path, master,' Jack said with gloomy satisfaction, eyeing the water to either side. 'Most like we s'l drawn, and that'll be the end of that.'

'If you go in over your head, Jack, I promise I shall erect a stone monument on the place,' Jemmy said tersely, and Jack was silenced, wondering whether or not this was a tribute to his loyal service. 'Come on.'

Auster was extremely unwilling to leave the safety of the causey, and Jemmy had to use spurs and crop before he could make him take the first leap. They went in girthdeep, and Jemmy shuddered as the water ran cold and clammy down inside his boots. He drummed on Auster's sides, and the horse proceeded, eyes bulging, in a series of snorting lunges, sending sheets of brown water up on either side as they went past the stationary pack beasts. Jemmy soon identified the trouble: the train was in fact two trains, of perhaps seventy animals in each, which had met head-on on the narrow track, and the packmen and their boys were apparently arguing over who should give way to whom. It was an amusing scene, for while the men were in hot altercation, with much shouting and waving of arms, the two lead horses in their belled harnesses had leaned their muzzles together like old friends and gone to sleep.

'Holloo!' Jemmy yelled as soon as he was near enough. 'What's to do? You can't stay here all day, you know.' The two men looked round. Jemmy knew

9

them both: one, Ezra Pyke, was a familiar figure around York, a brogger of the old school; the other, a clothier called Scotney, Jemmy had seen once or twice at market in Leeds. They both knew him, of course, and their faces brightened as they discovered an authority to appeal to. They both began speaking at once.

'Nay, master, it's my road. He won't give me past, damn his eyes.'

'I come this road same time every week, everyone knaws that. I'll not shift for him nor no man.'

They stared at each other.

'Why, you black-hearted villain!'

'You damned son of a thief!'

'Peace, peace, be silent both, I pray you,' Jemmy cried, lifting his hands. 'One at a time, gentlemen, please. Now, Ezra, you first.'

'Like I said, master, I come this road same time, same day, every week. Yon villain Scotney knaws that well enough. He comes of a Tuesday. He's no right taking my road. I'll not shift.'

He folded his arms righteously, and Scotney spread his hands to Jemmy in appeal. 'Nay, young master, it's true Tuesday's my day. But wi' beck overflowing, naught but a train of eels could have got by yesterday—'

'Then you should ha' waited til next week,' Pyke interrupted him. Scotney continued to address Jemmy.

'I couldn't hold off a week, master. The boat's

waiting at King's Staith, and I've to get this lot to York by tonight, or it sails without. And his horses aren't loaded. He ought to give me road.'

That was a telling point. Jemmy nodded wisely, thoroughly enjoying himself. Pyke was scowling furiously, but both men were still looking at Jemmy, appealing to his authority as 'the young master'. He never had such consequence at home.

'That's true,' he said at length, judicially. 'Master Pyke, you must give road.'

Scotney beamed and rubbed his hands, and Pyke looked from one to the other grimly.

'All very well, young master. But you nor no man will get my beasts to step off t'causey into that lake o' water, not when they're faced from home.' The unwillingness of packhorses to leave the causey was aphoristic, as Jemmy very well knew, but he smiled placatingly at Pyke.

'There's no need for that. The flooding does not go on for ever. There is firmer ground back there.' He nodded over Pyke's shoulder.

'Aye, master, but—'

'All you have to do is to untie each packhorse, turn it round on the spot, tie them all up again, and lead them back the way you came until the ground is firm enough to step off and let Master Scotney past. Scotney and his boys will help you with it, I am sure.'

Scotney nodded eagerly, and made admiring murmurs about Jemmy's cleverness, but Pyke only looked the sourer. 'Aye, and then I s'l have the

11

whole blessed business to do all over again, and Scotney will be long on his road by then, I warrant you, and leave me to do it all.'

'By no means,' Jemmy said patiently. 'All you'll have to do is untie your bell-horse, bring him round to the front of the train again, and off you go.'

Neither of them had thought of that, and Jemmy was hard put to it to hide his laughter. He beckoned to Jack and set off, and Scotney waved and called out, 'A judgement of Solomon, young master! God bless you!' Jemmy waved back, biting his lips determinedly. Behind him Jack rode in his own private cloud of gloom, and Jemmy thought ruefully how good it would be to have a friendly, cheerful manservant with whom he could share life's little amusements.

Shawes was a new house, within an easy walk of Morland Place. It was faced with the stone of the old house on whose site it stood, so that it looked as though it had always been there. That had been the design of Sir John Vanbrugh, who had built it for Annunciata, Countess Dowager of Chelmsford. It was a small house, in comparison with Vanbrugh's other masterpieces, and was therefore often called 'Vanbrugh's little gem'.

Henry Wise, who had been Queen Anne's gardener, had laid out the grounds, dammed the stream to form a small lake, planted a mixture of saplings and mature trees, and created the formal parterre, which was just now coming into its beauty. The trimmed hedges were of box, lavender, rosemary and yew, and encompassed gemoetrically-shaped beds of such small flowers and herbs as attracted the bees and butterflies. This parterre was the favourite resort of the Countess's daughter, Aliena. It reminded her of the Palace of St Germain where she had spent most of her life with King James III and his sister Louise-Marie.

She was walking with her three-year-old daughter, Marie-Louise, named after that same princess, and they strolled along the gravel walks in silence, the child having for once run out of things to say. It was hot in the sunshine, and the nurse, walking at a discreet distance behind them, doubted the wisdom of having left the shelter of the house, but they had been so much indoors that year that Aliena could not resist the beckon of the Indian summer. The dog Fand ran on ahead of them, burying his nose ecstatically in every bush he passed, drinking in the delicious multitude of smells. In his short life he had been bitten and stung so often that his muzzle was scarred and hardened, and Aliena was not surprised when he suddenly jerked his head back and froze. Then his ears cocked, he broke into a frenzy of barking, and rushed away, and Aliena saw that it was a visitor that had startled him.

'Jemmy!' Marie-Louise cried as the tall figure came round the corner of the house to receive the excited dog full in the chest, and she snatched her hand from her mother's grasp and ran towards him.

13

Jemmy thrust the excited dog down and walked to the edge of the terrace to wait for the little girl, but his eyes were on Aliena. She was so beautiful, tall for a woman, graceful with a kind of artlessness which he supposed her upbringing amongst the nuns had given her. Her dress of grey silk was barely hooped, her cap and scarf were of untrimmed white lawn, and she ought to have looked as plain as a Quaker; yet in the sweet expression of her face and dark blue eyes, and the natural fall of her soft dark curls, there was a beauty that tightened his throat.

Marie-Louise was very different. At three she was so precocious as to drive her nurses to despair, especially as her grandmother insisted on having her educated like a young gentleman, rather than concentrating on maidenly virtues such as sewing and modesty and silence. Jemmy had taken care of her riding lessons since she was eighteen months old; Father Renard, Annunciata's priest, who had taken Jemmy in hand in his wild youth, had been entrusted with the care of her mind. To the scandal of the servants, Marie-Louise had had a fencing master as well as a musicmaster; Aliena had taught her French and Italian and Court etiquette. It had been left to her grandmother alone to spoil her and pet her, and to fill her mind with tales of her illustrious forefathers and the glory of the Stuart cause.

Marie-Louise was well-grown for her age, and already beautiful, with tawny hair and white skin and large brown eyes flecked with gold, that would turn pure gold when she was in a rage. Her dress today was a perfect miniature of her mother's down to the small silk apron embroidered with a border of daisies, which Jemmy was willing to bet was not her own work. But where on Aliena the silvery grey brought to mind images of peace and cool water, on the child it was like a silver lamp to hold the flame of her face and eyes and hair. Beautiful and precocious she certainly was; she was also passionate, vain and imperious.

'Where have you been so long?' she cried now as she rushed up to Jemmy, seizing his legs in a hard embrace. 'You have been gone away for ever and ever, and it has never stopped raining, and I have been so *bored*!'

'Oh, I have been away on business,' Jemmy said easily, smiling down into the fiery golden eyes.

'What business?' she demanded. Fand, still circling, licked her face in passing with a swipe of his tongue, but she did not even notice. She was always single-minded about things, and now she gripped the fabric of his breeches so tightly her knuckles whitened, and shook at them to enforce his attention.

'Grown-up things. Very boring things,' Jemmy said.

'I don't like it when you are away,' she said deliberately, as if she had only to speak for her preferences to be fulfilled. Aliena and the nurse had now caught up with her, and it was to Aliena that Jemmy addressed his answer.

15

'Well, to say true, neither do I, but that is the common fate of us all. Being grown-up often means doing things you don't like to do.'

'You lie!' Marie-Louise cried, shaking him again. Aliena stooped and loosed her hands in a way that must have hurt her, though the child did not permit it to shew.

'How dare you speak so?' Aliena said. 'You will do a penance for that. You shall apologize at once.'

Marie-Louise barely gave her mother a glance, and her 'Sorry, Mama', was perfunctory. She was frowning at Jemmy, engaged in some thought process of her own. 'But I have to do things I don't like *all the time,*' she said with great emphasis. 'And if being grown-up is not any different, then what is it *for?*'

Jemmy was laughing into Aliena's eyes. 'I don't know, chuck. No one ever told me,' he said. The nurse stepped forward and reached for Marie-Louise's arm.

'Now then, miss, that's enough chattering. Come with me, and let your Mama speak privately to the gentleman.'

Marie-Louise snatched her arm away and whirled on the spot, glaring at the nurse. '*Don't* touch me! And don't call me "miss". Jemmy, tell her she must not call me "miss". I want to stay with you. I won't go away, just when you've come back.'

The nurse rolled her eyes, as if to say, there, you see what I have to endure from this unnatural child. But Jemmy stilled both women with a glance,

16

and went down on his haunches to look into the child's face.

'My love, you must learn to be obedient to your mother, and to those that your mother puts in authority over you. That is your duty, and if you fail in it, God will not love you, and neither shall I.'

Marie-Louise looked defiant, and something in her eye told Jemmy that she valued Jemmy's love more than God's.

He kept his face stern and said, 'Go now, without argument, and I shall come and see you later, I promise you. You shall have me to yourself.'

'For a whole hour,' she conditioned. She could no more have gone without arguing than fly.

'For the half of an hour, but only if you are a good girl, and do as you are told.'

She glared at the nurse, torn between the promise of having Jemmy to herself in the future, and the reality of sharing him in the present. 'But she shall not call me "miss",' she reverted. Jemmy looked stern.

'It is quite sufficient title for such a little girl,' he said. Her golden eyes filled with tears of hurt.

'But it's *not*,' she said desperately. 'It's *not*. You don't call me miss.'

'Sweetheart, your titles are between us, for love, not for public use. You have had that explained to you so many times.'

But she gazed at him, the tears overflowing onto her cheeks, and he did not know, as he never did, how much was politic, and how much her pride

17

really was touched. So he put his mouth to her ear, and whispered,

'Just between us, then. You are the Princess Marie-Louise Fitzjames Stuart, Countess of Strathord. There, will that do?'

She flung her arms round his neck and hugged him hard, and he could feel the hot wet tears on his neck. Then she released him, nodded, and smiled radiantly, and allowed the nurse to take her hand and lead her away, only turning back for a moment to say:

'Remember, you *promised*!'

'She is terribly spoiled,' Aliena sighed when they were out of sight. 'I'm afraid it is my fault. My mother indulges her, but I am too strict, and the nurses say they could manage her if I would leave her in the nursery as a mother should. But I should not care to see her once a day, for five minutes, as they wish me to. It was not so at St Germain.' She smiled apologetically for bringing up that subject again. 'She will never do anything she does not want to, but it seems only you have the knack of persuading her to virtue.'

'It is only because she is so young,' Jemmy said comfortingly, drawing her hand through his arm and walking with her along the gravelled path. 'I, too, was wild when I was a boy, as Father Renard will tell you. She will grow steadier as she grows older.'

'I hope so, if you are to be away for such long periods,' Aliena said teasingly. 'You have been back from Leeds these three weeks and never a visit.'

'I would have come sooner, as you must know, but there has been so much to do at home, with my father away. You know that he has gone to London? He went in my absence – this South Sea Company business must have unnerved him mightily.'

'My dear Jemmy,' Aliena laughed, 'you need not sound so surprised. The whole of England is unnerved. Thousands of people have been ruined, and lost all they had – not just the gentry, but the common people as well. Everyone who could lay his hand to a sovereign or two invested it in the Company, and now they want to know where the money has gone.'

'Oh, I know, there is talk of corruption and bribery and all sorts of villainy. But why should my father be troubled? You know he sold his shares months ago, when your mother sold hers, and made a very handsome profit by it. She made him do it. She said it could not last.'

Aliena smiled. 'My mother was not moved by some mysterious foreknowledge of doom, I'm afraid, but by plain superstition. She feels that gambling, except on horses, is wicked, and she began to be uneasy about getting so much for nothing, and sold out to avoid attracting God's attention.'

Jemmy laughed at this accurate portrait of his great-grandmother, the Countess Annunciata, and went on, 'Very well, whatever her reasons, she saved my father a deal of loss, and I hope he is grateful. But it does not explain why he has gone up to London.'

'Because, my dear Jemmy, the business life of the country has been in chaos, and anyone who has any concern in it is naturally anxious to be on hand and to see what is to come of it all. My mother is gone too, to stay with my brother Maurice at Chelmsford House. Maurice has contacts at Court, and at Leicester House where the Princess Caroline dotes on him. He is one person who can come and go freely between the two royal establishments. He says it's because he's a musician, and no one suspects him of listening to political gossip. If anyone ever says to him, 'What's your opinion of this, Morland,' he gives a great start and says, 'Why, I beg your pardon sir, I had not attended. Were we speaking of the new opera?''

Jemmy laughed, and said, 'Very well, your mother stays at Chelmsford House, which is after all her own property, and Maurice visits the Royal family. What then?'

'At Leicester House,' Aliena explained, 'Maurice bumps into Lord Newcastle and Sir Robert Walpole and their friends. I think my mother would not be averse to making their acquaintance.'

'But they're Whigs!' Jemmy cried in horror. Aliena's teeth shewed very white when she laughed.

'Oh the monsters!' she mimicked him. 'Well, perhaps my mother thinks that a Whig out of office

20

is the next best thing to a Tory in office. If this South Sea Company scandal destroys Stanhope, as seems likely, Walpole may be the next to rise to power. I think mother would like to have a friend in power.'

'Even a Whig?'

'Truth to say, I think she cannot get used to being out of the game,' Aliena sighed. 'She has spent all her life in and around Court, and she feels uneasy without her finger on the pulse, even if the pulse is now a minister's rather than a King's. And though she will never reconcile herself to the Elector, she quite likes Princess Caroline, though she finds it hard to call her Princess of Wales. When Princess Caroline is Queen, she might find it in her to return to Court.'

Jemmy considered all this, and then rejected it. The Countess Annunciata had been his mentor and confidante, and he knew the depth of her fidelity to the Stuart cause, and of her rejection of the Hanoverian usurpers. It was she who had encouraged him at the age of fourteen to run away from home to join the Jacobite rising in Scotland; and only last year she had corresponded with Jacobites in Spain who were planning an invasion. She had spent many years in exile with King James II, and her son, the earl, had been condemned to death for his part in the 1715 rising, though he had escaped the Tower with his life.

Would this great lady, with the royal blood of the Stuarts in her own veins, now be content to be wooing squire's sons and new-made peers, whether Whigs or Tories, whether in or out of office? Jemmy did not think so.

'She's plotting something,' he said, and Aliena shrugged and changed the subject.

On the last day of December, in the Palazzo Muti in Rome, Queen Clementina, the consort of King James III, gave birth to a healthy son. He was christened Charles Edward Louis John Casimir Sylvester Maria Sobieski Stuart. The news reached London within days, and not long afterwards was known in Yorkshire and in Morland Place.

Neither Matt nor Annunciata had yet returned from London, and Jemmy had been thoroughly enjoying his regency. That Christmas was one of the best Jemmy remembered, and the happy atmosphere so filled the house that his step-mother Sabina rose from her bed to join in the fun, and even Jemmy's brothers, home from their educational establishments for the season, were less disagreeable than usual. Jemmy had appointed himself Master of the Revels, since Robert was too pious and Edmund too sulky to make a good job of it. Robert complained that the servants were slack and that the religious observances were but slightly attended to; and Edmund complained that he was always given the worst old screw in the stable when he went out for a ride; but by Twelfth Night the food and drink and fun had thawed them considerably. George, of course, was always happy as long as he could keep eating.

The culmination of the madcap Twelfth Night celebrations was the Masque of Antony and Cleopatra, and Jemmy considered it a great triumph that he had persuaded his brothers to take part in it. Indeed, Edmund, his face darkened with lamp soot, made such an impact as Cleopatra's black slave that one of the servants got a stitch from laughing too much and had to be carried out to recover in the kitchen. Jemmy's hardest task had been to convince Marie-Louise that she could not, at three years old, play Cleopatra, the role which Jemmy had set aside for Aliena, to his Antony.

'But I am the only person with royal blood,' she protested again and again. 'I ought to play the queen.' In the end Jemmy had to quiet her by letting her play Cleopatra's daughter, Princess Selene. He had to write in a part for her, and let her make a grand entrance upon a litter, wearing the most lavish of all the costumes.

The night ended splendidly with a supper and ball at Shawes, arranged by Aliena as her contribution to the festival. It happened to be full moon that night, so all the invitations were accepted, and the long gallery at Shawes saw fifteen couples standing up to dance, reflected in the long mirrors, dazzling in the light from the crystal chandeliers and silver sconces. Aliena was reminded of the New Year Ball at Versailles in the Galerie des Glaces, when she had danced with King James III and her brother Karellie. It all seemed so far away now, a dream or a fairytale, for though most of her life had been spent in France it was the grey and green of Yorkshire which had now become her reality.

The ball was a tremendous success, in spite of her worries about what her mother was up to in London, and what new troubles the birth of a Prince of Wales would bring on them all. Jemmy danced every possible dance with her, until she was obliged to force him to dance with someone else, lest he make a scandal of her.

A week later, on his own authority, Jemmy ordered a service of thanksgiving for the new prince in the chapel at Morland Place. Aliena doubted the wisdom of it, for not all the servants were necessarily trustworthy, but she did not refuse to attend it. The chaplain, Father Andrews, spoke fervently, but obliquely, about the gracious gift from God, and the new hope that had come with the new year, and his references to the King and the Prince of Wales were so couched that an outsider would have been hard put to it to prove which King and which Prince of Wales he meant. Aliena, looking about her, was sure that some of the stupider servants did not know why they were there.

She loved the chapel, with its beautiful fan-vaulting, the tapestries and the marble monuments and the dark wood, the candle-light glowing on the silver altar furniture and catching the gilding on statues and decorations. The smell of incense carried her back what now seemed like a lifetime, to Chaillot, so that she almost believed she could hear the pure voices of the nuns as they sang their strange French Latin. She knelt in the place reserved for the family, and prayed for the son of her King, of the man who had been her lifelong companion. Beside her, in the Master's place, was Jemmy, his dark head bowed reverently, his long curls – for he wore no wig – falling forward to hide the clear, tender line of his jaw. On her other side knelt her daughter, unwillingly, restless as always at being confined. She fidgeted and looked about her, but repeated automatically the words she had been taught since her infancy; praying for the health and safety of the infant prince who was her brother.

CHAPTER 2

April had gone before Matt returned from London. The overwintering beasts, stalled since St Luke's day, were let out, gaunt and blinking, to feast upon the new grass; the pigeon house had been cleaned out and the precious dung carefully spread and dug in where it was most needed to fertilize the ground; the low-lying ings had been fenced off for hay. The spring seeds had already been sown: beans in late February – beans had to go in between St Valentine and St Chad – and the oats two weeks later; and now there was only the barley to be sown, drage barley for pig- and chicken-feed, and two-row-headed barley for drink, to go in at Hoke-tide.

Jemmy, proud in his new authority, had given the orders, made the decisions, settled the disputes, ever since his father went away. He had even held the annual meeting of the tenants to decide on the farming policy for the year, though in fact he found out there was little deciding to do. Farmers, he discovered, were the most conservative people in the world, and what was good enough for their fathers was good enough for them, especially as

most of them were holding land that their forefathers had held before them time out of mind.
There might be fewer tenants, each holding more
land, than in the olden days, but the names were
all the same, and as he looked round them, gathered in the great hall that day, he thought that if
a previous Master of Morland Place had been able
to cross Time and be there, he would probably
have recognized most of the faces too.

At all events, Jemmy discovered that there was
no use in his trying to change anything. The old
rotation of winter seeds, spring seeds, and fallow
had served them well in the past, they said, and
they saw no reason to change it now; and the allo-
cation of the strips was just as traditional, so that
it seemed to Jemmy like religious ceremony that
had to be gone through purely as a matter of form.
The only point where discussion entered into it was
in deciding what to do with the odd pykes and
corners, and over the commutation of road-labour.

The 'lord of the manor' was responsible for the
roads in his own area, and his tenants were obliged
to give a certain number of days' road-labour every
year for that purpose. But everyone hated to do it,
and like many another landlord, Matt had been
accustomed to allow them to commute their service
for a cash sum. The trouble was that the sum thus
raised was never sufficient to pay labourers to do
the work needed, and so the roads got worse and
worse. Matt himself did not care very much about
the roads, and the most that was ever done to them

under his authority was to have the mud shovelled from the sides where it accumulated back into the middle, and a load of broken stones, or cinders, or rubbish thrown over it and carelessly tamped down. Jemmy would have liked either to refuse the commutation, or to raise the fee, but it was far beyond his present authority to do either, and the tenants began to mutter and look dangerous when he even hesitated, and so he could only yield to pressure and set the commutation at the same rate as last year. But while he did it, he silently promised himself that things would be different when his day came and he was master in truth. For the time being, it was all useful experience, and gave him the chance to observe and get to know the men whose lives he would one day rule.

It was in the middle of the spring castration – a boring, bloody and dangerous business: last year one of the grooms had lost an eye to the kick of a particularly spirited long yearling – that Matt came home to Morland Place, having travelled up from London with the Countess. A servant brought the news to Jemmy at Twelvetrees that the master was on his way, which just gave him time to dash back to Morland Place and wash himself, put on a clean shirt and a decent coat, and assemble the senior servants in the great hall. After such a long absence, it was necessary to provide a formal welcome. Sabina waited in the hall with the younger children, Tom and Charles and her own little Allen, while Jemmy went out into the courtyard with Clement and Davey. It was a pleasant, breezy day, and the warm air was filled with smells, both delicious and pungent, and the sounds of reviving life: sparrows quarrelling in the gutters, pigeons courting, jackdaws chattering amongst the chimneys, the monotonously repeated crowing of the young cockerel; and far away, a background noise like the murmur of a stream one ceases to notice, the chorus of ewes with their new families.

At last the dogs began barking, and Matt rode in through the barbican. Davey stepped forward to take the reins, and Clement, the steward, positioned himself to help the master dismount and to take his cloak and gloves. As Matt came up the steps, Jemmy's first thought was that his father should not be so tired after a journey which, as he had travelled with the Countess, must have been performed in easy stages. Then he realized with distant shock that it was not just tiredness. His father's face was white with more than an indoor pallor; his cheekbones seemed too prominent; harsh lines had etched themselves from his nostrils to the corners of his mouth, which was shut in a grim line, grimmer than Jemmy remembered it. Most of all he walked with the stooped, difficult gait of an old man, or an invalid.

Matt stopped in front of his son and looked at him with eyes so deeply shadowed that they seemed expressionless.

'Welcome home, father,' Jemmy said, and went automatically down on one knee for his blessing.

It was a long time in coming, a time during which Jemmy waited anxiously, thinking perhaps his father was angry with him and would refuse to bless him, fixing his eyes on the sword hilt and the hand that rested on it. A phthisic hand, blue-veined, clenched too tightly, so that the knuckles were white. Then at last the hand moved forward and up, and Jemmy felt it rest lightly on his hair.

'God bless you, my son. I am glad to be home.' Jemmy heard the weariness in the voice. He rose quickly and ushered him in, and while Matt was greeting Sabina and the children Jemmy, with a quick nod and gesture, dismissed the servants, and then sent the children away before they could become a bother to his father. Only Clement lingered, waiting for orders. Matt turned to him, and their eyes met in understanding, like old friends.

'Is there wine in the steward's room?' he asked.

'Yes, sir, and a good fire,' Clement said. He had seen to those things personally, knowing his master better than anyone.

'That will suffice. I will need nothing more until dinner.'

Clement went away, and Matt, seeming to forget the presence of his wife and son, walked away towards the steward's room. One of the hounds got up from the hearthside and ran towards him, and Jemmy jumped forward to catch the hound's collar and hold it back, suddenly afraid that his father could not have borne the weight of an excited dog. He seemed so frail. He exchanged an anxious, puzzled glance with Sabina, who shrugged and gestured with her head that they should follow him.

Matt stood just inside the door of the steward's room and looked around. When he heard the others behind him he said quietly, 'You cannot think how often I have thought of this room while I have been in London. More than any other, it seems to me *my* room.'

Neither answered: it was too strange a thing for him to reveal anything about himself for either to feel comfortable with it. He turned and looked from one to the other, and addressed himself impartially to the air between them.

'You will have heard the news, I suppose. Stanhope and Craggs are both dead. Lord Townshend and Lord Carteret are become Secretaries of State. Walpole is Chancellor of the Exchequer, and First Lord of the Treasury. England's fate has a new arbiter.'

He seemed to expect some answer, and after a moment Sabina said, 'He is an able man, I am sure, sir?'

'An able man,' Matt repeated, and Jemmy wondered if he meant it, or if it was said in irony. Sabina made a movement as if to touch him.

'Are you well, sir?' she asked. Matt looked sharply at Jemmy.

'You should not suffer your mother to stand for so long, on any account. See how she pales. Help her to a chair at once. My dear, you must sit down and take a little wine.'

'I am very well, sir, pray do not alarm yourself,' Sabina said, though she suffered Jemmy to seat her in the fireside chair. 'Indeed, sir, you are looking tired yourself.'

'A little wine will do us both good,' Matt said and it was an obvious effort at civility, when he would sooner have snapped at her to leave him alone. Jemmy longed to be away from them both, out in the fresh air, back with the horses, in a world where he did not feel so threatened. He handed his mother her cup, and when Matt began to pour wine for himself Jemmy began backing to the door, bowing himself out. But as his hand behind him took the doorknob, Matt straightened abruptly.

'No, Jemmy, I wish you to stay,' he said. He drank off half the wine, and put the glass down, and then absently removed his hat and his travelling wig and threw them both down on a chair. His own hair was cropped close to the skull, and Jemmy noticed for the first time that the growing stubble no longer gleamed darkly against his skull, but was grey like frost. He looked about him vaguely. 'Where the devil is my cap?' he muttered.

'I'll go and find it, sir,' Jemmy said eagerly, beginning to open the door.

'Stay here,' Matt said sharply, and Jemmy let his hand fall reluctantly from the doorknob, and took a step forward into the room, his heart sinking with apprehension at what he might be about to hear.

'I have something to say which concerns you,'

Matt went on. 'In fact, my absence in London this winter has largely been on your account, and it is only right, now that my negotiations are concluded, that you should know what I have determined upon for you.'

Jemmy had been a frequent visitor at Shawes these last months, and had often come informally as one on terms of intimacy might do. In the Countess's absence, the household moved more easily. But his arrival that day, unannounced, uninvited, in great haste and in a state of obvious agitation, caused the servants to stare and whisper amongst themselves. He asked for the young mistress, and was told she was upstairs, in the Countess's room. It approached the hour of dinner, he was told, and as the Countess had just arrived back from a long journey and would be disinclined for company, perhaps Master Morland might consider postponing his audience until a more favourable and convenient season. But no, Jemmy insisted, he must see the young mistress. It was important. The servant sighed his reluctance to disturb the Countess with such a message, and went away up the stairs with reproachful slowness.

Jemmy paced up and down the hall until she came, calm and beautiful as ever, drifting down the stairs as though her feet did not touch them, a smile of welcome and enquiry on her lips that held no hint of reproach. Jemmy went impulsively towards her.

'Aliena!'

'Why, Jemmy, what is it? No one is ill, I hope?'

'No, no, but I must talk to you. There is a plot—'

She cut him off with a look and a shake of her head, there being servants within earshot.

In a quieter voice he said again, 'I must talk to you. Please. It is important.'

'Very well. We will go to the gallery, and walk up and down there. I have been sitting these two hours with my mother, and need the refreshment.'

It was all Jemmy could do to keep silence until they reached the gallery, and as soon as they were inside and the door was shut he whirled on her and cried out, 'Cousin, my father is come! He is returned from London, and he has told me – there is a plot afoot, a monstrous plot, to marry me.'

Aliena nodded gravely. 'Yes, my dear, I know. I have heard about it.' She took his hand and drew it through her arm, and made him walk with her along the gallery, hoping that the movement would calm him. He came with her like a man beyond noticing what his feet were doing. 'I have been talking about it with my mother. She has been helping with the negotiations. But why should you call it a monstrous plot? It seems a very good match to me. Lord Newcastle's sister—'

'Lord Newcastle is a Whig,' Jemmy cried, staring in astonishment that she should ask such a question. 'A Whig, a courtier. Friend of Walpole,

34

a Hanoverian to the heart. Anti-Jacobite, anti-Catholic – do you forget, cousin, that I fought for the King in the '15 rising? Or at least,' he added with an abrupt descent from rhetoric to honesty that both touched and amused Aliena, 'or at least, I tried to.'

'I should have thought that must be Lord Newcastle's objection to you, not vice versa,' Aliena said. 'But my mother says he and your father have come to a very good understanding. There is to be an election next year, and your father is worth twenty votes certain on the County, besides his influence with landowners and clothiers here about. In return, the Duke has a great deal of patronage to bestow which will be extremely useful to your father. Consider, he has six sons to settle.'

'But—' Jemmy waved his hands, frustrated by her calmness, and by finding her on the wrong side. 'My servant says my father's man saw her, and said she is a whey-faced, cross, sickly thing, small and plain, and never said a word the whole time she was in the room.'

'She has a large dowry, and excellent connections,' Aliena countered. 'Though her brother is only a new-made duke, her father was a gentleman and a baronet, and through marriage they are connected with all the best families in the country. You cannot be such a simpleton as to object to a wife because she is small and plain. And as to being cross, my mother says she has a good enough opinion of the girl, and that she is shy and modest, as becomes a young girl in company.'

CARDIFF
CAERDYDD

'Ah yes, your mother,' Jemmy said bitterly. Aliena looked grave.

'My dear, your father is quite decided, and whatever his reasons on his own behalf, I must tell you that my mother is anxious for the connection for reasons of her own, and there is no possibility that with such persuasion he will change his mind. So you must make the best of it.' They reached the end of the gallery and turned along the short side, and Aliena smiled at him and tried to lighten his gloom. 'Come Jemmy, accept it with a good heart. A man in your position does not marry for his own whim, but for the good of his family. The contract is signed, but it will not come about for a while yet. Lady Mary is only fourteen, and the match will not take place until she is sixteen. You will have two years more to enjoy yourself.'

Jemmy stopped abruptly as though goaded beyond endurance, and taking Aliena's hands turned her to face him.

'Aliena, you know my real objection to this match. I cannot marry this girl. How could I? It is you that I love – since the first moment that I saw you. It is you, and only you, that I wish to marry.'

'Jemmy!' Aliena tried to stop him, but he pressed her hands to his chest and went on, his face flushed and his eyes gleaming.

'Dear Aliena, I know of your love for the King, and I have grieved for you that he did not, or could not, return it as you wished. But you put

36

all that behind you when you came home here. You know that he can never be yours, and you are too sensible to grieve for ever, to waste your life on a hopeless dream.'

'You forget that I have borne a child,' Aliena said.

'Forget? Far from it! I love her dearly, as dearly as I could my own child. And she loves me, and respects me – this you know. You have often said that I can do more with her than anyone else. What could be more suitable than that the man who has a father's feelings towards her should become her father? Only think how happy we could be, the three of us. Only think—'

'Jemmy, stop it. You must stop. It is not to be spoken of. What you ask is impossible. And – unsuitable.'

Jemmy's face reddened. 'Unsuitable? Why? Because my father is only a gentleman? Because my mother – my mother—' He could not finish it. Aliena pressed his hand, sorry to have grieved him.

'No, my dear, not that. Of course not that. But I have been mistress to another man, and have borne his child. That alone should – oh Jemmy, I am thirteen years older than you!'

Jemmy's face cleared. 'Is that all? Oh Aliena, how could you think that the difference in our ages matters, when we love each other? You know that I love you, with all my heart and soul. How could any man not love you, who had once known you? And you – you love me too, don't you?'

She shook her head, unable to speak. Jemmy drew her towards him.

'You do not?' he said gently, kissing her forehead. 'Say it then.' He held her closer and kissed her lips. 'Say it, swear it.' He had meant only to touch her lips lightly, but at the first touch such wonder and love rose up in him that he kissed her again and again, punctuating his words. 'Say it now – and now—'

Aliena's hands crept up, from his chest to his neck, from his neck to his face, and for a moment she abandoned herself to the feelings that swept through her. She felt the warmth of his hands and the strength of his arms, his closeness, the relief of doing, just this once, what she had longed for so many months to do. But in the end she broke away with a despairing cry and ran to the window, blindly, like a butterfly trying to escape. In the silence she could hear Jemmy's quick, light breaths and her own rapid heartbeat. She rested her hot forehead against the cold window pane, gathering her strength and resolve to do what she had to do, to turn calmly and tell him what must break his heart – and hers.

When she turned, the expression of tenderness and hope on his dear face almost undid her, but she steeled herself, keeping him away with a little shake of the head, for if he touched her again she did not know how she would endure it.

'Listen to me, my dear – no, be still, and listen. You and I cannot marry, however much we love each other. Do you remember when I first came home, you said that you would call me cousin, to save having to work out exactly what we were to each other?'

Jemmy nodded. 'Yes, I know, but—' he began, puzzled, but eager, and she held up her hand to stop him.

'*Please*, Jemmy, let me speak. It is not easy for me to tell you this, but I must do so, and I must bind you to secrecy. You must never divulge it, for reasons which will become obvious to you. You call me cousin, but that is not the truth. You and I are much closer kin than you think. I am your father's sister.'

There was a silence, and Aliena watched with pity the struggle in Jemmy's face as he tried to assimilate what she had told him.

'My . . . ? I don't understand. You are—'

'Your father's father, James Martin Morland, was also my father,' Aliena said sadly. Jemmy stared, aghast.

'You mean great grandmother was – she – with her own stepson?' He stopped abruptly, the horror of it sweeping over him. In the end, Aliena felt she had to break the silence.

'So you see, you and I could never marry. I beg you, Jemmy, to keep this a secret, for my child's sake, if not for mine and my mother's. Oh Jemmy, I'm so sorry.'

It shook him out of his reverie, and he took a quick step towards her and put his arms round her, but she held herself stiffly, not yielding to him.

'Sorry? Oh Aliena, it does not matter that we cannot marry. We can still be everything to each other. I love you, and we can—'

She broke from him almost roughly.

'*No*, Jemmy. It is impossible. You must put all this from your mind. You will marry Lady Mary, and lead a normal life, and be happy. To do what you suggest would be to torture both of us needlessly.'

'I will not marry her,' he said. She fixed him with a resolute eye.

'You must. You shall – yes, and with a good heart, or you will be laying up sorrow for us all.'

He met her stare obstinately for a moment, but then she saw his shoulders sink in a sigh, and he held out his hands to her.

'Oh, Aliena,' he said. She gave him her hands, and he looked down searchingly into her face, no longer a boy and a suppliant, but a man now, and a lover. 'Is that what you want?'

'It is what I want,' she said steadily. 'Jemmy, you must go now. I cannot bear any more.'

'Very well. I will go, and I will not speak of this again. But before I do, please tell me, just once, that you love me.'

'To what purpose?' she said helplessly, but he held her gaze until at last she said quietly, 'Yes, I do love you. You were right about that.'

His eyes flickered closed for a moment, and then he lifted her hand to his lips and kissed it, and left her without another word. Long after he had gone, she stood there, with the print of his lips still on her hands. In that simple homage had been all his life and devotion.

When she reached her mother's room, she found the Countess alone, sitting before her looking-glass brushing her hair. Aliena met her eyes in the mirror and looked away again, and took the brush from her hand.

'What is it?' Annunciata asked. 'You look pale.'

'Jemmy. He had just heard of the proposed match with Lady Mary,' Aliena said diffidently. 'He did not like it.'

Annunciata shrugged – his opinion was nothing to the point – but then seeing how upset her daughter was she bit back the retort she had been about to make and waited.

At last, still looking down, Aliena said, 'He asked me to marry him.'

'Poor young man,' Annunciata said carefully. 'I had observed how he felt about you, but I thought it was a young man's fancy, and would come to nothing.'

'I told him why we could not marry,' Aliena said abruptly. 'I told him about my father.'

Annunciata frowned. 'Was that necessary?'

'He would take no other argument.'

'Could you not have told him that you did not care for him?'

'He would not have believed it,' Aliena said.

41

Now she looked up and met her mother's eyes again, and reading the message in them, Annunciata groped for and captured her daughter's hand, and brought it to her cheek.

'Oh my darling, I'm so sorry,' she said. Aliena tried to smile.

'I don't blame you, mother. And if I ever had blamed you before, how could I do so now, knowing what you must have felt? The difference in age—'

'It never seemed to matter,' Annunciata said, and her dark eyes were distant as she looked deep into the past, beyond the grave, to the bright place where things that had been were still. 'Nothing seemed to matter, except that we should be together. But there were consequences which neither of us could have forseen.'

'Mother, I shall have to go away,' Aliena said abruptly. Annunciata's eyes filled with pain.

'Away?'

'Right away. Abroad.'

At last Annunciata nodded, accepting the necessity. 'We will all go. We'll go together.'

Aliena knew what it had cost her mother to make the offer, and she shook her head and said gently, 'No, mother. I was born here, but I have lived all my life in France, and to me it would not be exile. But for you—' Exile, the word which for Annunciata had spelled living death. 'I am not like you. My pleasures in the world are many, but they are not binding, and I have nothing more to hope for. I shall go to France and enter a convent.'

'A convent!'

Aliena almost smiled at the shock in her mother's voice. 'It is what my heart longs for. I would not do it in a spirit of self-sacrifice. A little of me has always been homesick for Chaillot.'

'And Marie-Louise?'

'I should like to leave her here with you, to be brought up with her inheritance.' There was a silence, and to ease it with movement, Aliena took up the brush and began to brush her mother's hair, curling its harsh heaviness round her fingers. Her own hair was soft and fine, her father's hair, she had been told. She wished she had known him. His influence came to her daily, here in Yorkshire. It was one of the reasons she wanted to leave, one of the reasons she could not ask her mother to leave.

'Mother, what you did—' she said hesitantly. Annunciata looked up. 'What you did – tangled the thread. Someone must untie it.'

'But why must it be you?' Annunciata asked bitterly.

'Because I can do it,' Aliena said simply. She put down the brush, and laid her fingertips against her mother's hair, wanting to comfort her somehow. 'Let it end with me. Let my daughter grow up safe from it.'

Annunciata stood up and turned to face her.

'I love you so much,' she said. 'You look so like him. I wanted you, of all my children, to have everything, to be happy. Perhaps that is the greatest vanity of all, to think we can give our children anything.'

She moved away to hide her face, and after a moment said briskly, without turning round, 'You must do what is in you to do. But not yet. There will be much to arrange. And perhaps,' her voice faltered, 'it will turn out not to be necessary after all.'

'Oh mother,' said Aliena affectionately; and then Annunciata turned round, and Aliena ran to her, into her arms, and Annunciata held her close, one arm round her shoulders and one hand in her soft dark hair, as if they were lovers, and not mother and daughter.

It was almost three o'clock when Jemmy walked up the stairs to his room to dress. He had deliberately left it as late as possible to avoid having to meet anyone in the hall or on the stairs, and had almost been put to the indignity of being searched for, for when he came into the great hall Clement was hovering looking anxious, and at once disappeared in the direction of the kitchen, no doubt to report that all was well after all.

The hall was filled with flowers, and the niches on the stairs bore vases crowded with daffodils and sprays of young yellow-green beech leaves. That was partly because it was Easter, but mostly because there were house-guests: Lord Newcastle and his half-sister had come to visit, on their way north for the recess, so that Jemmy and his future bride could meet. There was to be a grand dinner, which had been put back to four o'clock, proof enough of the importance of the occasion, and Clement had borrowed the Countess's cook, or chef de cuisine, as he liked to be called, Monsieur Barry, to help prepare the feast. Jemmy had been hiding at the stables all morning, where Davey had told him of the ructions the volatile Frenchman had caused in the kitchen. He had argued with the Morland Place cook, Jacob, over the proper way to make oyster loaves, and when Jacob insisted that there should be a sprinkle of ground cinnamon added, Monsieur Barry had screamed 'Nutmeg! Nutmeg!' and begun pelting the unfortunate cook with nutmegs, following them up with the grater.

'They calmed him down in the end, and left him alone in the pantry making a riband-jelly in the shape of a castle,' Davey said.

'Why in the pantry?' Jemmy asked, leaning on Auster's rump.

'So that he could be alone,' Davey chuckled. 'But God help the first poor kitchen maid who has to go in to fetch something. The poor man is brooding over his desserts like a robbed hen. I should hate to be around when he starts spinning sugar for the clouds.'

Jemmy reached the top of the stairs and went quietly along the passage towards the bachelor wing where he had his temporary quarters, and was almost knocked down when the door of the first room was flung open and Robert flew out clutching a wig in his hand.

'Pard? Is that you? Oh—' He stopped with a

disagreeable frown when he saw it was Jemmy. 'I thought it was Pard creeping past, hoping not to be heard. Look at this wig! I told him to have it dressed and he hasn't touched it. How can I dine with the Duke wearing a draggled thing like this? I'll have him whipped when I find him. Do you know where he is?'

'No,' Jemmy said, looking at his brother with distaste. Robert's was not, in any case, an attractive face, since he had the kind of pale, freckled, wide-pored skin that tended to spots and blackheads, and his uncleanly habits did nothing to help the situation. His hair was wiry and red, and he grew it in long sideburns and little tufty whiskers on his cheeks and chin as if to hide as much of his face as possible, but it only drew attention to his bad skin and his rather protuberant, wide-spaced teeth. He had pale, bulging eyes like overripe gooseberries, and sandy eyelashes that looked almost white, like an aged horse's. Jemmy could have forgiven him all these things, as being his misfortune rather than his fault, if it had not been for his disagreeable expression, which Jemmy felt was a true indicator of his disagreeable personality.

'Oh, he'll be skulking about in Edmund's room, I warrant you!' Robert went on. 'What the devil does our father mean by making Edmund and me share a servant? It's intolerable. I tell you, we are the laughing-stock of Christ Church. You cannot conceive how ludicrous and unpleasant it is.' And then seeing the expression on Jemmy's face he added, 'Or perhaps you can. Perhaps you make good use of being the only one at home, and having father's ear to yourself. I suppose one will never know what poison you drop into it, day by day. And Edmund is always encouraging Pard to skulk off, and slight me, and do his clothes before mine. Everyone is against me. Edmund wants me to appear at a disadvantage before the Duke, I know he does. He thinks he will get preferment and cut me out.' Jemmy had watched his expression change from peevishness to self-pity, and knew what was coming next. 'I am so plagued you cannot conceive. If I had not the patience of a saint—'

Robert was intended for the Church, and one of the things Jemmy liked least about him was his self-satisfied piety and priggishness. He felt just for a moment the almost irresistible urge to hit Robert in the face and see what that could do to straighten his teeth.

'I'll find Pard and send him to you,' Jemmy said tersely and walked on as fast as he could, and gained his own room like a haven. Jack was there waiting for him, his face as long as a Scottish mile, and the three little boys, Tom, Charles and Allen, sitting in a row on his bed like starlings, chattering.

'Oh there you are, master,' Jack intoned. 'I made sure you met an accident, you did not come before. Well you will be late now, there's no doubt. And I could not get the stain out of this cravat, do what I might—'

Jemmy suddenly had a wonderful idea.

'Jack, go to my brother Robert with my compliments, and help him to dress. His own servant is busy and cannot go.'

'But, master—'

'My brothers here will be my valets, won't you, boys?' The youngsters gave a cheer and jumped up.

'Of course we will!'

'Hurrah, what fun!'

'Very good, master,' Jack said, even more gloomily, and went away, his back eloquent of ill-usage, closing the door with ostentatious softness.

'Now then, boys, bustle about,' Jemmy said, and they turned to with a will. Tom and Charles, who were thirteen and twelve years old, had sometimes helped Jemmy dress before, though never for so important an occasion, and they were handy enough with laces and buttonhooks. Little Allen, a solemn, chubby child of six, with golden curls of the false, buttery yellow that would turn dark before too long, was a nimble fetcher and carrier, and used his wits to have a thing to hand the moment it was needed.

'Four o'clock is so late for dinner,' said Tom, who had had his hours since. 'I hope the guests won't get too terribly hungry.'

'Perhaps they'll have some bits of bread hidden under their mattresses,' said Charles, giggling, thinking of the time their brother George had been beaten for that very crime. 'And they'll munch them and gobble them while their servants dress them.'

'And get crumbs inside their shirts,' Tom elaborated, 'and they'll wriggle about all through dinner because they'll be too polite to scratch.' He gave a realistic dumb-show of the action, and Allen gave a shout of laughter, and then hid his mouth behind his hand shyly. Jemmy ruffled his hair affectionately as he stepped into the stocking Charles was holding out.

'No, no, you forget they are people of fashion. They are used to dining late.'

'But how do they keep from rumbling?' asked Charles, kneeling to roll the stocking up over the end of Jemmy's breeches. He held out his hand for the ribbon, which Allen had ready.

'They don't breakfast until noon,' Jemmy said. 'They don't get out of bed until ten.' Tom was examining the cravat, holding it up to his eyes.

'I can't see any stain on this,' he said at last, passing it to Jemmy.

'I don't suppose there is one,' Jemmy said. 'That's just Jack's nature, to see bad where there is none.'

'Gloomy old Jack,' Charlie said carelessly, rolling the other stocking up Jemmy's calf. 'Maybe he ought to marry Lady Mary instead.'

Jemmy looked at him sharply. 'What do you mean?'

'Oh, nothing. Only Jack said – he said—' Charlie looked up at his brother's forbidding face and ended lamely, 'he said she did not smile much.'

'Jack has no right to say such things, and you have no right to repeat them,' Jemmy said angrily. 'Deuce

49

take this cravat, it has a will of its own. Now where is my pin – oh, thank you, Allen.' Allen's pale, bright eyes looked into his with an unexpectedly mature sympathy. Jemmy felt it was time to pull himself together. 'Now, Tom, my waistcoat. Did Jack put it out? That's right, the one with the silver embroidery.' Tom brought it, looking troubled. 'What's the matter, little brother?'

'Nothing,' said Tom. 'Only I was thinking – well, it's because of you marrying Lady Mary that I'm to join the navy, isn't it?'

'Well, that has something to do with it,' Jemmy said. 'Lord Newcastle spoke to the Earl of Berkeley, and he spoke to the Elector, and there was a vacancy aboard the *Agrippa* for a King's Letter Boy, and so it was decided it should be you. Why, Tommy, you aren't afraid, are you?' Tom looked surprised.

'Oh no! The *Agrippa*'s the best thirty-six in the navy, and everyone knows that the West India station is the best to be on, and Captain Wentworth's the most dashing captain on the list, and took a dozen prizes last year.'

Jemmy smiled inwardly at all this. Two weeks ago, Tom had known nothing about the navy, and cared less; but a fortnight's acquaintance with the Navy List had given him a multitude of firm opinions, vehemently aired.

'Well, then you are high good luck, a'n't you?' Jemmy said, pulling the end of his Steinkirk through his buttonhole.

'Yes, only,' Tom said uncertainly, 'Jemmy, you do *want* to marry Lady Mary, don't you?'

Ah, so that was it. Jemmy turned and put his hands on Tom's shoulders and gave him the most earnest and cheerful smile he could muster.

'Of course I do, Tom. There's nothing I want more.' Which in its way was true. 'Now then, give me my hat and my gloves – oh, my handkerchief! That's right. Now I must go downstairs. It would not do to be late.'

'Be sure and remember every single dish on the table,' Charles said. 'I want to know everything you have.'

'And taste them all,' Tom added, quite happy again now. 'Have a good time. You look like a prince.'

Little Allen only smiled and waved, and Jemmy waved back, and kept a smile stitched across his lips until he was round the corner of the corridor and out of sight.

As well as the oyster loaves, there was white soup in the first course, and fricassee of rabbit, red cabbage and peas, roasted ducks with celery sauce, and boiled ham with caper sauce. As far as possible, Jemmy concentrated on the food, in order not to have to be aware of the presence of his bride-to-be beside him and Aliena at the far end of the table. There was no call for him to speak, at least, for the Duke led the conversation, encouraged by Annunciata, who sat beside him.

51

He seemed much troubled by the ambitions of the Emperor of Russia, Peter the Great who, he said, was capturing seaports in the Baltic with the intention of dominating Europe. 'It is but a short step from the Baltic across the North Sea to Scotland,' said the Duke.

'Why should the Emperor of Russia want to visit Scotland?' Matt asked. The Countess's eye grew wicked and merry at the question.

'Why, sir, has not my lord Duke been talking about ambition? Julius Caesar, you remember, was assassinated for it.'

Lord Newcastle attempted to ignore this, and addressed himself to Matt sternly. 'Throughout our history, sir, would-be invaders of England have thought of Scotland as a convenient back-door. And it is no secret that the Emperor of Russia favours the Jacobite cause, and has offered aid and arms to the Pretender.' Now he turned to Annunciata again, and asked blandly, 'Did not your ladyship's son Maurice visit Russia last year? Perhaps he may know something of the secrets of St Petersburg.'

Was it Jemmy's imagination, or did the room hold its breath? He found himself staring very hard at the delicate morsel of fricasseed rabbit impaled on the end of his fork, suspended halfway to his mouth. There was a crack, he noticed, in the ivory handle, running out from the hood of silver acanthus leaves that hid the rivet. Someone must have dropped it at some time – a careless servant, perhaps.

But the Countess, who had once faced Titus Oates in court on trial for her life, met the Duke's look with one of her own just as bland.

'When I want news of my son, my dear Duke, I always apply to you, for I am sure you know everything that goes on within a hundred miles of London. And to tell you the truth, I have long since despaired of understanding Maurice's movements. Musicians are a law unto themselves, don't you agree? Music knows no frontiers, that is what dear Master Handel always says.'

The Duke could do no more than bow assent and change the subject. Implicit in the Countess's words was the reminder that Maurice Morland and George Handel were both favourites of the Elector, who admired their work, and that Annunciata herself was the Elector's cousin as much as the King's. The conversation flowed on, and the moment was past, but Jemmy was more sure than ever that the Countess was plotting something. He was also sure that plotting would not be as easy now as it had been when the Countess first developed her taste for it. Newcastle was already suspicious of Maurice and would have him watched, and no doubt the Countess's correspondence would be scrutinized. Would she be sufficiently on her guard? Jemmy wished he could warn her.

The first course was cleared, and the second was laid, and Jemmy tried to take note of all the dishes for Charlie's sake. He was reciting the green custard and the partan pies, the roast pigeons with fried marigolds and the lemon pudding, in his mind when he realized that Lady Mary, sitting next to him, was looking at him strangely. He felt his face grow hot, and he turned to her, searching his mind for some piece of polite conversation he could make.

She certainly was very small, and very plain, with no more figure than a child of nine. Her dress of pink brocade had an echelle bodice of large pink gauze bows, presumably to hide the lack of importance of her figure, and Jemmy thought the colour ill became her, for she was sallow-complected with dull brown hair and light brown eyes.

Jemmy smiled at her – a false, ill-at-ease smile he knew it was – and said, 'We are honoured by your presence here at Morland Place, madam. I hope you find yourself comfortable?'

Lady Mary did not smile. After a while she said, 'Thank you, sir,' and that was that.

Talk at the table revolved around politics and paintings, architecture and the army, always with the Duke and the Countess leading the way. Tom's good fortune in being taken into the *Agrippa* was touched on – Captain Wentworth's reputation praised – the good chance of prizes on the West India station mentioned. The conversation flitted like a butterfly from the navy to the army – a comparison of the strength of each – the army in Hanover, and the Elector's annual visit there – the valuable contracts for providing cloth for uniforms which Yorkshire clothiers had won – uniforms for the Russian army – Peter the Great – and at that point it took alarm and flew right away to the safety of food and drink and the comparison of different wines. The dinner being consumed was amply praised, and there were kindly murmurs of future benefits that might be bestowed upon the Morland family following its connection to that of the Pelham-Holles; and then the second course was cleared, and the desserts were brought on.

Whatever Monsieur Barry's temperamental disadvantages, he had certainly produced an impressive display, and the servants laid it all out in the most elegant manner. The centrepiece, on a high china dish so that it was raised above the rest, was the jelly-castle, striped in four colours, its turrets disappearing into a cloud of spun sugar. Around it was a ring of dishes raised to an intermediate height, on which were syllabubs, flummeries and possets; and the outer and lowest circle of dishes displayed ratafia cream, chestnuts, cheeses, celery, butter, oranges, elderflower fritters, naples biscuits, apples, orange cream, and pistachio nuts.

Whatever the Duke and his sister were used to in fashionable society, Jemmy thought, they could not but be impressed by such a wonderful spread. He turned proudly to Lady Mary and said, 'May I help you to anything, madam? Do you see what you like?'

Lady Mary surveyed the table in silence, and

eventually her chaperone, Lady Dudley, the hard-faced widow of an impoverished knight who evidently resented her dependence, leaned forward and answered for her.

'Lady Mary will have a small dessert apple. I will peel it for her.'

They sat so long over dinner that it was almost time for the tea to be brought when Sabina finally nodded to Matt that they should rise.

The Duke, intercepting the look, said, 'We have not yet drunk the King's health, sir.' Matt nodded gravely.

'Of course, Your Grace. I was just about to propose it.'

They all stood and raised their glasses, and Jemmy instinctively looked towards the Countess, as he felt the Duke must also be doing.

'The King!'

'The King.'

Jemmy drank, concealing a smile. Beside the Countess's place was a silver fingerbowl filled with water, and as she repeated the toast, she held the glass above the fingerbowl so that she was drinking the health of 'The King over the Water'. It was an old Jacobite trick, and Jemmy inwardly shook his head. Oh great-grandmother, he thought, do you think it will pass unnoticed, in *this* company?

CHAPTER 3

Leicester House was one of Maurice Morland's regular resorts in London. It was the home of Prince George and Princess Caroline – the Prince and Princess of Wales, as Maurice had no objection to calling them when he was away from his mother – who had set up house there in 1718 when Prince George had quarrelled for the last time with King George, and had been forced to quit St James's Palace, leaving his children behind. Father and son had always hated each other, and when the open breach finally occurred, King George made it known that anyone who was a friend of his son was no friend of his. This meant that anyone out of favour at St James's, or unable to gain a foothold on the ladder, was naturally attracted to Leicester House, where soon a rival and much gayer Court flourished, under the aegis of Princess Caroline.

Princess Caroline was a great patroness of the arts and all intellectual pursuits. She was fat, handsome, witty and shrewd, and Maurice liked and admired her enormously: she reminded him in many ways of his great-aunt, Sofie of Hanover.

Around her gathered many of the wits and rakes and artists, as well as out-of-office politicians such as Walpole and Townshend, and of course all the ambitious young women to whom the Court of St James's, lacking a Queen, could offer no position. Whenever Maurice strolled in, which he liked to do on most days, for it was here he gathered the most topical news and the spiciest gossip, there was sure to be someone amusing, chattering, flirting, and drinking endless bowls of chocolate.

Maurice was one of the few men in London who was welcome at both Courts, and he cultivated the image that made it possible, that he was vague, brilliant, improvident, utterly devoted to his music, and perpetually on the verge of bankruptcy. He lived in his mother's house, Chelmsford House in Pall Mall, for which he paid no rent; he had a small pension from King George, and otherwise earned his living from his playing and conducting and composing; he had a wife, Nicoletta Scarlatti, the youngest daughter of the composer, his old friend, and three small children by her, together with a grown-up daughter, Alessandra, by his first wife. Much of the house was left shut up and gathering dust, and it was assumed that Maurice could not afford to run it, for they had few servants and his wife often did the cooking. He had an enormous acquaintance, travelled a great deal, dressed eccentrically, and gave the best and most popular supper-parties in London.

It was in Leicester House, in April 1722, that

Maurice first learned of the Jacobite Plot. Secret information had been sent to Sir Robert Walpole, who had tried to keep the matter quiet, but it had leaked out nonetheless, and within an hour panic had spread and the streets were filled with crowds, and the Bank of England was besieged by people anxious to withdraw their assets in portable gold.

Maurice had been at Leicester House all morning, enjoying the company of the Princess's two most attractive and acerbic ladies, Mary Lepell and Mary Bellenden, who were eating apricots and complaining of the boredom of a maid-of-honour's life. The poet Pope was there, leaning against the back of Lepell's chair and looking as though he wished to take notes, as was Ashe Windham, a common friend of his and Maurice's, who owned an estate at Felbrigg in Norfolk and was Lord Townshend's nearest neighbour.

Mary Lepell, who at her birth had been made a cornet of horse in her father's regiment, said, 'When I tell you, dear Maurice, that the most amusing part of our day is when we ride upon decrepit and hard-mouthed hirelings for an hour or two in the morning, you may conceive how boring it really is.'

'I wish all those women who envy us might be forced to change with us for a week,' Bellenden agreed. 'Then they would see how fortunate they really are.'

'Even the wives of country squires, with a new child every year and a new gown only once in two years?' Maurice asked.

'Even those,' Bellenden said, running her fingers across the back of his hand. 'If you are thinking of retiring to the country, I should be glad to come with you to try the experiment.'

'Are you tempting him to bigamy?' Ashe Windham said, trying to look shocked. Mary Bellenden shrieked with laughter.

'Lord, no, I was thinking we'd poison his little wife first.'

'Not possible,' said Lepell. 'Don't forget she's an Italian. They know all about poison.'

'Besides,' said Maurice, 'I could never afford to live in the country. It's only because I pay no rent that I can afford to live at all.'

'Ah yes,' said Pope, 'I noticed last time I was in your house that those great mirrors were missing from the hall. Who did you sell them to?'

'Grafton,' Maurice smiled unconcernedly. 'He's the only rogue in London who never quibbles over a price.'

'One day,' Windham said severely, 'your mother is going to enquire after her furnishings. Still, Morland, if you ever get around to selling her Rembrandts, be sure to give me the first refusal.'

'You have no chance,' Pope said. 'Walpole would be sure to outbid you.'

'I think the Rembrandts are safe,' Maurice said. 'My new opera opens next week, and it is sure to be a success. I expect you all to be there at the opening performance,' he added severely. 'Ah, here's Burlington. He's looking devilish flustered

60

about something. Burlington! Over here! Where have you been? Campbell was here looking for you an hour since, with the plans of your little school in his hand and an anxious look on his face.'

'What, are you all sitting here so calmly?' Lord Burlington said in amazement. 'Have you not heard the news?'

'What news? We have heard nothing interesting this hour, but Morland's state of finance,' Ashe Windham drawled.

'There are such crowds in the street, I thought I should not get through,' Burlington said, dropping onto a brocaded sofa whose inadequate legs trembled at the shock. 'There's talk of calling the Guards out, and closing the Bank.'

'What, has the South Sea Company revived itself?' Mary Lepell said. Lord Burlington mopped his brow.

'Not a bit of it. It is a Jacobite plot, to seize power and execute the King and all his ministers. It is supposed to come about in June, when the King goes to Hanover, but of course the mob have got hold of the idea that it is all happening now, and they are out to save their skins and their fortunes at any cost.'

Maurice did not go straight home, but wandered around the streets for a while, enjoying the stimulating atmosphere of mingled panic and excitement, and then he went to the St James's Coffee House, a Whig stronghold, to hear what was being said.

61

Reports were amusingly conflicting. Troops and arms were to be supplied, he learnt, by the French, or as one man said, the Spanish, and the Bank, the Tower, and the Royal Exchange were to be seized. The Pretender was to lead the attack, and to join the troops in London when it was all over. It was to happen in May, before the King left for Hanover, and in June, when he had gone; and the King and the Prince and Princess of Wales were to be executed, imprisoned, and given a safe passage back to Hanover.

From there Maurice went down to the Cocoa Tree to get the Tory version of the story, and then strolled thoughtfully home. He found Chelmsford House in chaos, and was just in time to witness a collision in the great hall between a footman with his arms clasped round a marble statue of Mercury and a maid staggering under a blanket filled with most of the silver that had not yet been sold.

'What the deuce is going on? Put that down at once. Careful! Stand still, all of you! Now, where is the mistress? What is happening here?'

The surprised servants froze at the sound of his voice, and Nicoletta came running in from the dining room, with Rupert and Apollonia clinging to her skirts like kittens enjoying a game, and two-year-old Clementina tucked under her arm and bawling deafeningly.

'Oh Maurice, Maurice, thank heaven you have come home!' Nicoletta cried. 'There is the most terrible news, and the streets are full of people, and they say that the Guards are being marched out of the Tower this very minute to arrest the conspirators. Oh Maurice, what shall we do?'

'My dear Nicoletta, calm yourself,' Maurice said, detaching Apollonia from her mother's skirt and lifting her into his arms. 'What on earth is the matter? There is no need for all this panic. What is Mary doing with the silver?'

'But Maurice, we must leave at once. If we can get down to the coast, we may be able to get a boat for Italy. We can go to my father's—'

'Hush my dear, we are not going anywhere. Go back to your duties, all of you. There is nothing to fear. Sam, bring us some wine in the drawing room. Come, Nicoletta, my dear, there is no need for all this. Come and sit down and take some wine with me, and we'll talk about it quietly.'

Under the soothing of his voice, order was restored, and Nicoletta went upstairs with him to the drawing room where he sat her on a sofa with the children and gave her a glass of wine and petted her like a child.

'You must not allow yourself to be agitated,' he said, stroking her hair gently. 'Remember you are with child.' She sipped the wine and spluttered a little and sipped again, looking up at him with frightened but trusting eyes. He had married her, against his own better judgement, for this quality of innocence, just as he had married twice before. He had a fatal propensity to fall in love with child-madonnas, pure and perfect little models of his mother. But of course their perfection never lasted. He discovered all too soon that they were human and faulty, and that his possessing them marred their purity. After the death of his second wife he had sworn he would not do it again, but he had not been proof against his own absurd longings.

He had once said to his mother that she had ruined him for ordinary love, and it was at least partly true. Well, now he must take care of this flawed madonna he had stolen from Italy, as Burlington and Ashe Windham, and all the other young men on their Grand Tours stole paintings and statues to bring home. Nicoletta was silly and young and ignorant, and was therefore all the more entitled to his protection and at least the outward appearance of his love. He wished that she still had Alessandra to help her, for Alessandra had grown up into a sturdy and sensible young woman, and would certainly have prevented this absurd and dangerous panic. But when Aliena had left Shawes to enter a convent in France, Annunciata had taken Alessandra home to be a companion to her and a governess to Aliena's daughter. Maurice had objected, of course, but what his mother wanted, she got, and Maurice, living free of charge in her house, was in no position to argue.

'Now I will tell you all about it,' Maurice said when Nicoletta was calm again. 'There has been news of a plot just uncovered, to remove the Elector and restore King James to the throne. Walpole has been to see the Elector, and he has closed the Bank, to prevent everyone from trying to take their gold away at once, and he has marched the Guards down to Hyde Park in case the crowds get out of hand. Now what is there in all that to make you so afraid?'

Nicoletta clutched Clementina closer to her bosom in an automatic gesture and said in a low voice, 'I wish your name was anything but Morland. They are bound to suspect you, and then they will come and take you away.'

Maurice laughed aloud. 'Suspect me? My dear girl, what nonsense! Do you know where I have been all morning? Why, at Leicester House. I am a favourite of Princess Caroline's. The Elector pays me a pension. I am Maurice Morland the musician, that's all. Why should anyone suspect me of plotting against my own best patrons?'

'We live in your mother's house. They are bound to think we knew about it all along.'

'Knew? Knew about what?'

Nicoletta stamped her foot. 'Oh Maurice, don't be so stupid! You know perfectly well what she was doing while she was staying here the winter before last. Why else did she stay so long? What about all those strange people she saw? It will all come out, and we will be accused. At the very least, of concealing the plot.'

Now Maurice did not smile. 'My dear, you must not say such things, not even to me. Why should you think my mother is involved in this plot? She was here in London on business, as everybody

65

knows, as were a great many other people at that time. If you say otherwise, you are endangering us all.'

'But –'

'Listen to me,' Maurice said firmly, 'it is Atterbury they want, Atterbury, Bishop of Rochester, friend of King James, darling of the Tories, figurehead of the English Jacobites. They are already calling it the Atterbury Plot. They have no evidence yet but hearsay, but I promise you it is his head they are after. My mother had nothing to do with it. Trust me, we are quite safe, unless you let the servants think we have something to fear. Servants are the worst gossips in the world. And now, let us send the children back to the nursery and see what there is for dinner. I have been walking about the streets, and it has given me quite an appetite.'

He went to the door to pass the word for the nursery maid, while Nicoletta smoothed the children's dresses and hair with an automatic hand. Three-year-old Rupert, a stout, handsome, high-coloured little boy, scowled furiously and sidled away from the hand that brushed at his skirt.

'I don't want to go back to the nursery,' he cried. He had been having the most wonderful morning, and the thought of the nursery and the horn-book charmed him not at all. 'I want to stay here.' A thought crossed his mind and he sidled back to his mother and smiled winningly. 'I want to stay and protect Mama from the soldiers.'

Nicoletta beamed at him with love, but Maurice regarded him with an indifferent eye. 'There are not going to be any soldiers from which to protect her. And I am not in the least interested in what you want. Ah, nurse, take the children away.'

The little nurse had come running in and curtseyed, and now took Clementina from her mother and held out her hand to Rupert. Under his father's stern eye, Rupert could only allow himself to be led away, but as soon as the door had closed behind them he avenged himself by kicking the nursemaid's shin as hard as he could with his small boot. She flinched, but suppressed her cry. She was often black and blue from Master Rupert's rages, but it was a good job for a girl of her background, and besides she was terribly in love with the Master.

Maurice refused to be alarmed, and under his calming influence the household returned to normal and Nicoletta felt she had been foolish indeed and that there was nothing to worry about after all. But underneath his calm exterior, Maurice was anxious. He was not, and had not wished to be, in his mother's confidence, but he had no doubt that she was involved with the plot, and that Nicoletta was right in assuming that that was why the Countess had come to London and stayed all winter.

He knew they were in danger, for his mother was a Jacobite of known pedigree, and his brother Karellie, the Earl of Chelmsford, had been convicted

67

of treason for his part in the last rising. If any evidence could be found to link his mother with Atterbury, it would be hard to convince anyone that he, Maurice, had been innocent.

And of course, he had never been entirely innocent, as Walpole and Newcastle perfectly well knew, though they had no proof. He had been at pains to establish himself as being neutral in the Hanoverian-Jacobite argument, as being an apolitical artist, interested only in aesthetic things. His frequent visits to Italy – Venice, Florence and Rome – and his recent trip to Russia; his constant correspondence with his brother, and with his brother's mistress, the opera-singer Diane di Francescini, 'the Divine Diane'; his sale of plate and furnishings: these things could all be reasonably explained, but would nevertheless arouse suspicion if attention were ever directed towards him.

He had been careful, yet he had also been a fool. He had carried letters, he had raised sums of money, and he had asked no questions, and part of him despised himself for becoming involved with the sordid and temporal business of politics, the absurdities of who had the right to what title. The eternal beauty and universality of music ought to have taught him better. Yet though his intellect knew it was folly, and condemned him for it, his heart had driven him on. He was a Morland, and his blood would not be denied.

★　　★　　★

In May Atterbury's secretary was arrested, and in August there was deemed to be enough evidence to arrest the Bishop himself. Others soon followed him to the Tower, and in October when the new Parliament met, Walpole persuaded it to suspend the law of *habeas corpus* and to impose a severe penal tax on Roman Catholics. The trials were to be held in November. Maurice continued to live normally, dropping in at Leicester House, and his three favourite coffee houses, visiting Handel and Burlington and Vanbrugh and his other friends, conducting concerts at the Vauxhall Gardens and the opera house, playing for a few rich patrons who could afford him – and behind his casual mien he listened, and watched and waited.

He knew Chelmsford House was being watched, and he surmised that his letters were being intercepted and scrutinized before delivery, and as the same thing would certainly be true of Shawes, he had no way of getting in touch with his mother, nor she with him. Still there was no word of her implication or arrest, and there was no sign of his being shunned by anyone who might be supposed to know what was going on in the inner circle of government, and he began to hope that they would escape after all.

At the end of October, Jemmy came to stay for a few days on his way home to Morland Place. He had been sent abroad eighteen months ago, on Annunciata's advice, for an abbreviated Grand

Tour, in order to take his mind off Aliena and his betrothal, and to cure his natural restlessness. Annunciata's chaplain, Father Renard, had accompanied him. Maurice had been surprised that she felt willing to be parted from her priest, and had naturally suspected ulterior motives, though it had been said, and with truth, that she could more easily spare him than Matt could spare Father Andrews, who had Charles and Allen still in his care, as well as the accounts of the whole Morland estate to keep – along with all the other numerous duties a domestic chaplain was expected to undertake.

Maurice was much interested in Jemmy's recital of his adventures, and amused that he bore all the marks typical of the returning traveller – the tanned skin, the ultrafashionable clothing, the cosmopolitan manners, the sprinkling of foreign words and phrases in the speech. He also had the inevitable trunk full of art treasures, purchased at miniscule prices from the uncaring Italians who had so much they could never care about a quarter of it. But as well as his Madonnas and Roman Gods and Greek Horses, Jemmy had gained a maturity in his year-and-a-half absence. He listened in attentive silence as Maurice told him what had been happening, his face growing graver by the minute.

At length he said, 'I see. I understand a number of things now. This was the cause of great-grandmother's desire for us to be connected with the leading members of the Whig party. And that she has not been arrested suggests that it is that which is protecting her now.'

'Protecting us, too,' Maurice reminded him. 'As long as she is safe, so am I, and my family, and yours.'

'Oh yes, that too.' Jemmy was silent a moment, and then said, 'I saw your brother, the Earl, in Venice. He said that he had visited Aliena at Chaillot, and that she was very happy.'

Maurice nodded. In one way and another, he had learned the whole story of Jemmy's unfortunate passion. He said gently, 'She was always a nun at heart. I always felt she was too good for the world.'

Jemmy looked at him gratefully. 'I was afraid she had done it—' He hesitated.

'To protect you?' Maurice suggested. Jemmy shook his head.

'To expiate. I hated great-grandmother for a while. Now—' He shrugged. 'I am so glad Aliena has found what she wanted.' He sounded so bleak that Maurice wished there was some way he could comfort him. Maurice had always been glad he was not the eldest son. It seemed a thankless row to hoe. 'So,' Jemmy said at last, 'have you heard anything of any evidence against great-grand-mother?'

'There was mention in the correspondence of a Mrs Freeman – obviously a pseudonym, like all the Joneses and Illingtons. Some think Mrs Freeman is my mother, because it was a name she used once before. Of course, so did every other woman going to an assignation in the days of King Charles, so

71

it means little. But I heard today that the judges have been directed to suppress any mention of Mrs Freeman at the trials next month.'

'Newcastle?'

Maurice nodded. 'I am sure of it. Of course, the Elector may also be protecting her. He has done so before, because she is close kin to him, and he knew her in his youth. He pardoned my brother, you know.'

'Perhaps,' said Jemmy, 'but one could not take the risk of it *not* being Newcastle. He has done a lot for my family. There's Tom in the navy, and Edmund's ensigncy – and in a popular regiment! And Father was able to buy Robert a living at a very favourable price, much less than it was worth. And now here's great-grandmother, not in the Tower. And what has he had in return?'

'Your father's influence in the county, to be sure,' Maurice said. 'The seats were not even contested.'

'Well enough,' said Jemmy, 'but I can see my duty. I must become Lord Newcastle's brother-in-law before he has time to repent of the contract.'

His words were sturdily spoken, but his face was bleak, and Maurice could do nothing but look his sympathy. Jemmy looked up, and seeing the kindness of the eyes – so like Aliena's! – he said in a low voice, 'Love is over for me now. I must shut that part of myself away. My family depends on my doing my duty.'

'There can be great satisfaction in that,' Maurice said. 'Perhaps you may find that it will be enough.'

He knew better than to suggest to this passionate young man that he might come to love and esteem his chosen wife in time.

The wedding took place at Whitsun, 1723, when Lady Mary was seventeen. It had been planned for January, but had been put off because of the serious illness of Jemmy's brother Charles, who had taken to his bed with a fever after the St Stephen's Day hunt. Everyone had thought that he had taken a chill, and would soon be well, but the fever had settled on his lungs, and for a time his life had hung in the balance. He had taken to growing in the last autumn – Sabina said that he had grown too fast for his strength – and he had certainly presented an overstretched appearance, being nearly six feet tall, and very thin.

The illness, of course, had made him even thinner. Even after it was certain that he would not die of the present fever, the doctor shook his head pessimistically over the chances of Charles reaching twenty. But when the spring weather came, he revived, and sunshine and better food restored both his spirits and his strength. He remained painfully thin, though the dark shadows had gone from his eyes, but the doctor spoke of him as still being delicate, hinted that his lungs must always be taken great care of, and recommended plenty of open air, always provided he avoided dampness and night humours, which could be fatal.

So Charles had spent every warm, dry moment

out of doors, and since his strength was not at first equal to much riding, he came to know the gardens very well, and began to take an interest in the plants. The gardeners, who had a sentimental affection for someone who had almost died, were very patient with him and answered all his questions, but he was soon probing beyond their knowledge, and sought further information from books. The walk across to Shawes was a pleasant and easy one, and the Countess's library was better than Matt's; and the Countess said in the most obliging way that he should come and go as he liked, and not trouble to present himself formally.

This suited Charles's rather retiring manners, and he did not suspect that the little maid, dusting away at the books, to whom he chatted, was passing back information to her mistress; nor was his delight touched by suspicion when he discovered that the Countess's library contained a number of books on gardening and botany, from Garard's *Herbal* and Stephen Hales's work on vegetable physiology, to a number of surprisingly recent pamphlets from the Royal Society.

During Charles's illness, Jemmy had discovered how much he cared for his youngest brother. There had also arisen a strong affection between Charles and his stepbrother Allen, and during his restless, feverish fits, it had been Allen he had called for, and Allen alone who could soothe him, sitting by him for hours, talking quietly and wiping his brow with cold cloths. When Charles was well enough to go out, and the garden seized his interest, he forgot about his stepbrother, and Allen receded quietly into the background again, but Jemmy honoured him, and determined that when he was Master he would reward the boy for his faithfulness.

The day of the wedding dawned bright and clear, a perfect May day, and even Jack, who came to wake him, could hardly predict rain. The most he could manage by way of gloom was to hint at the effects of an early drought on the crops, and to complain that his teeth were troubling him again. Jemmy managed to ignore all this as he dragged on his breeches and shirt. He had asked to be called very early, for he had decided that he would go out alone before the dew was off the grass and have one last, glorious, wild, bachelor ride on Auster before the prison gates closed on him. It was not long after five when he got to the stables, and the grooms were still mucking-out, watched from the eves by a flotilla of sparrows waiting to dart down for the treasures of spilled oats which the process revealed.

Auster nickered an excited greeting to him, and fidgeted about, all excited eyes and ears, as Jemmy tacked him up. He was a most gratifying horse to ride, because he always shewed such interest in his surroundings.

'Come then, old boy, we'll see how far we can get, and have one last gallop together. This time tomorrow I shall be a married man,' Jemmy said, clapping the glossy black neck as he led the horse out into the early sunshine. Auster made a noise that sounded like laughter, and Jemmy realized how gloomy and apprehensive he had sounded. 'As if I were going to the scaffold!' He put a foot into the stirrup and swung up as Auster started forward, and as soon as they were across the drawbridge the horse broke into an irrepressible canter.

They went out towards Hessay, rounding the Whin, and across High Moor, scattering the sheep. The lambs stuttered on their absurd knuckly legs in a panic, torn between flight and suckling, and eventually dived underneath their dams, butting for the udder as a safeguard against all ills, presenting a woolly rump and a fast-twitching tail to Auster's dancing hooves as he passed. They made a long loop, coming along the nearside of Wilstrop Wood, and then galloped across Marston Moor. Jemmy crouched forward over the neck and whispered in Auster's ear, and they flew, faster than Jemmy had ever gone before, the soft wind stinging past his cheeks and taking his breath away. It was a wonderful ride, and Jemmy came back in through the barbican at a sedate pace, feeling that all his restlessness had been burnt away.

Now the house was astir, crowded with strange voices and strange smells. George, Edmund and Robert were all home; Tom was still in the West Indies with the *Agrippa*; cousin Frances had come down from Northumberland with her ten-year-old son John, recently become Viscount Ballincrea on the death of his uncle; and of course the bride, with her chaperone, and Lord Newcastle were in the house. Maurice and Nicoletta and their children were staying at Shawes, and would arrive for the wedding with the Countess, but Marie-Louise and Alessandra were staying at Morland Place because Jemmy had asked permission for Marie-Louise to be Lady Mary's flower-girl.

Jack had a bath ready for him in his bedroom when he arrived, and while he soaped his master's back, he gave him the latest bulletin on the state of his teeth, and recounted the trouble there had been downstairs because Lady Dudley had sent for a number of obscure toilet preparations for Lady Mary, of which there were none in the house, seeing as the mistress was bedridden and there were no young ladies. Finally, one of the maids had had to be sent over to Shawes to enquire there, which had put everyone in a bad mood because the maid was wanted for other duties and the boy on duty outside Lady Mary's door had been sent down every five minutes to ask why the things hadn't arrived yet.

When he was out and dry, Jemmy said, 'I think it would be a good idea if I were to ask my brother Charles to dress me. I know it would please him, and it would be a reminder of other times past. Go and ask him, will you, Jack?'

'If you really think so, sir,' Jack began with deep offence. Jemmy clapped him on the shoulder.

'I do. He has been so ill, that I think he would take it as a kindness. I'm sure you will be generous enough to give up the honour.'

'It isn't so much the honour, master, but will he

be able to manage the laces? Ten to one but he'll put your sword belt on upside down.'

'I'm not such a cuckoo I don't know which way up my own belt goes. Go, now, run and ask him, there's a good fellow. And then you can see if my older brothers need any help.'

'Very well, master,' Jack said, in a tone that suggested no one should blame him if the whole wedding was ruined, and went. Jemmy grinned to himself, and when the coast was clear, sent the boy outside for toast and hot chocolate. Charles arrived before the breakfast with Allen in tow, both of them delighted at this change of plan, and the three of them set about transforming Jemmy into the bridegroom with the greatest good humour.

In the West Bedroom Lady Dudley had been working for an hour on Lady Mary's face with white lead and Spanish paper and kohl and a battery of brushes and tweezers and scissors which Rachel, the depressed and timid maid, handed to her like a reluctant jailor's assistant handing over instruments of torture. The only voice to be heard during that hour had been Lady Dudley's, and she had been giving Mary advice and warnings about the state of marriage which had increased the younger woman's apprehension to a dull terror. She wished she could have gone in happy ignorance to her wedding, for it was bad enough having to wed at all, without all Lady Dudley's gloomy and savage prognostications, as she wrenched rogue hairs from Mary's brow with a chastising zeal. Lady Dudley's husband had done her the double disservice of going bankrupt and then dying, obliging her to fall back on the charity of distant relations, and his perfidy had left her with a poor opinion both of men and of matrimony.

'Being a young man, he will probably want to trouble you that way a good deal at first. But if you endure it, and shew your disapproval as a gentle-woman should, simply in your bearing towards him, I daresay that you will gradually be able to lead his mind towards better things. Most importantly, you must never cry out, however much it hurts. It would be exceedingly improper to make a sound of any sort at such a time, and it is a woman's fate to endure pain in silence.' She wrenched another hair away, and Mary bit back a cry, and blinked the tears away. Lady Dudley peered at her suspiciously, and then said, 'There, it has bled! I knew it would be so. Mary, my dear, you really must try to sit still. It is extremely ill-bred to wriggle about in such a fashion, and it makes my task so much harder.'

'I'm sorry,' Mary said. She caught Rachel's eye and looked away again quickly, lest sympathy should overcome her control of her tears. She and Rachel shared their fear of Lady Dudley, but Rachel was too timid and Mary too shy to express it, and they could do no more than give each other silent and unacknowledged support.

At last Lady Dudley finished, and whipped the cloths away. Now there was only her hair to powder, and the wedding-dress to put on. Lady

Dudley had chosen it. It was pale pink, a colour Lady Dudley loved, but which Mary knew did not suit her, with her sallow, yellowish skin and dull brown hair, and the things that Lady Dudley had done to her face seemed to make her look only more clownish and not at all less plain.

'There, now you may look at yourself.' The mirror was held up before her, and Mary struggled not to allow herself to cry.

'I wish I were pretty,' she said, the words bursting forth from her against her will. Lady Dudley raised an eyebrow.

'Physical beauty is a matter of no importance. It is not for that your husband will value you.'

'He doesn't like me,' Mary said in a small voice. The eyebrow climbed higher.

'Like you? Why should he like you? I hope, Mary, you have not been reading books. When I was a girl, such sentiments would not have passed my lips. It was not considered at all proper for a husband and wife to be affectionate towards each other. Marriage is a contract, remember that. Remember also that your husband has much the best of the bargain in this case, and should be grateful and respectful towards you. You should not encourage intimacy from him. Why, the whole family bases their pride on their kinship with the Countess of Chelmsford. Dreadful woman! Her title came from King Charles, and for what services we can only surmise. No, Mary, I hope I shall never see you demeaning yourself to be friendly towards your husband. Let him do his duty, and be grateful for the connection you bring him.' She snapped her fingers at Rachel for the shoes.

'Yes, Lady Dudley,' said Mary. Rachel scurried over with the pink satin high-heeled slippers, and knelt to put them on her. Her little, workworn hands were warm on Mary's instep, and when Mary looked down, Rachel glanced up for a moment, and Mary saw in her blue eyes the tears that she was not allowed to cry for herself.

The chapel was so beautiful, filled with banks of fragrant white flowers, ablaze with candles and with every piece of plate, silver and gold, it possessed. Marie-Louise walked before the bride scattering white rose-petals and lilac florets in her path. Marie-Louise was dressed in a pale pink replica of the bride's dress, and looked exquisitely beautiful in it with her red-gold curls and her brilliant eyes. It seemed to Mary one more strand in the plot to make her look ugly on her wedding day. And when she saw Jemmy, her rout was completed. His coat and breeches were of sapphire blue satin, his stockings and waistcoat were of white silk, the latter embroidered with blue and gold and scarlet threads. He was tall and elegant and so handsome that she was frozen with a shyness that rooted in her soul. He smiled at her tentatively, but she was too overcome to smile back, and she saw his expression change to one of remoteness, and her heart sank.

★ ★ ★

The rings were exchanged, the vows made, the Communion taken: they were man and wife. Now Jemmy must take her hand on his arm and walk with her down the aisle, receiving the bows and curtseys and smiles and nods of congratulation from the family and close friends who crowded the chapel. Out into the hall, where the servants were assembled to give their congratulations. Bow, smile, shake hands. To the door, to stand at the top of the steps and look down into the courtyard where a deputation of the tenants and villagers in their best clothes waited to give three cheers for the young master and mistress, and to present their gifts and their blessings.

Jemmy did his duty, and his smiles for the servants and tenants were genuinely warm, for he had known most of them since his childhood, and there existed a firm affection between him and those who would one day be his people. But he was horribly aware of the woman on his arm, and when he, for form, turned to smile at her, the smile was a frozen falsity. She had done something horrible to her face, presumably to make herself look prettier; the powder in her hair only made her face look yellower; and why in the world had she chosen pink again? But worst of all was her expression of haughty disapproval. If she would only smile, if she would only be agreeable! It didn't matter so much from his point of view – he was well aware that she regarded the match as beneath her – but he was angry on the tenants' behalf, that they should be so snubbed by a stranger. Their goodness of heart and generosity was amply proved to him in the words he over-heard from two of them as they turned to go in.

'A very proper, pretty young lady indeed,' one said.

'A pity she's so shy – but there, it's only proper feeling in a young lady,' said the other. Shy! Jemmy thought. Well, it was kind of them to attribute it to shyness.

Things got worse at the banquet that followed. For one thing, Jemmy's own hair was too luxuriant to wear a wig with any comfort, but on the other hand, if he powdered it, it took days to get the powder out again. In the end he decided, since they had to powder, he would wear a wig over his own hair. He was regretting it now. He grew so hot under his double thatch, and the hotter he got, the more he drank, and the more he drank, the hotter and crosser he got. And then his bride sat beside him in the place of honour and barely ate or drank a thing, turning everything down with that sneering expression of superiority that he was coming to hate, and when he spoke to her, answering in monosyllables as if it wearied her to have to acknowledge his existence. A fine time he was going to have of it, with such a wife, he thought.

Mary felt as if she was trapped in a nightmare that would never end. The wedding dinner went on and on, until she wondered how people could go on eating and drinking for so long without falling unconscious. Her agonies of shyness, heightened by being the centre of attention, and by the awareness of her own grotesque appearance (she had said, not pink, to Lady Dudley, not pink, but Lady Dudley had gone ahead and ordered pink just the same) made her feel nauseous, and she was unable to do more than taste a morsel of the delicious delicacies that were being pressed upon her. Her tight busk was filling her stomach with acid bile, and she knew what agonies of diarrhoea that would mean tomorrow. Her face seemed to have gone rigid in her embarrassment, and whenever she tried to smile she could feel it contorting into such a grimace that she found it safer not to make the attempt. It was terribly hot, and the sweat running along her scalp was mingling with the hair powder and depositing a sticky kind of mud on her forehead.

Worst of all was her handsome, glorious husband (her husband!) sitting beside her, evidently enjoying himself, eating and drinking with a will, and occasionally flinging questions at her which she would still be groping to answer when his attention was distracted again. He would think her such a fool, she thought miserably, as well as ugly. He was getting rather drunk, she noticed. Later on would come that ordeal that Lady Dudley had warned her so fully about. Anxiety made her feel more nauseous. And there was another worry that she could not tell anyone about. Her monthly flux was due in only two days and she knew that anxiety could sometimes make it come early. Supposing the tension of this day brought it on – what would happen then?

She longed desperately to urinate, but had no idea how one would excuse oneself from such a public situation.

The ceremonies were all over. They had been put to bed, and given the loving cup, and the priest had blessed them. The bridegroom's brother had undressed Jemmy and ushered him in, and he exchanged a whisper as he took the cup back that made the bridegroom smile – not a smile of levity, but a charming smile of affection. The bride thought that it must be wonderful to have him smile at one like that.

The bride's chaperone had undressed her, with a further repetition of her warnings and advice, and her last whisper as she left was, 'Remember all I have told you.' Would that I could forget it all, Mary thought. Then they were alone.

It was a long, long silence. Mary listened to Jemmy's breathing – the slightly thick breathing of a man well-primed with wine, as she was to come to recognize – and the tension in her was such that when he hiccoughed, she almost leapt out of her skin. It is the worst pain you have ever felt, Lady Dudley had told her, like being torn with red-hot pincers. It is a woman's lot to endure such things. Why? she wondered. It seemed strange, if it were so horribly painful, that people went on doing it – not married women, who had to, but sluts and prostitutes, who could presumably choose.

Jemmy stirred and touched her, and she flinched – she simply could not help it. At once he withdrew his hand. Her relief was only momentary.

'You do realize, madam, that it is a legal requirement?' he said. She did not know how to answer such a question. After a moment he went on, 'However, I will certainly keep the secret, if you will. I have no wish to do what is so obviously distasteful to you. If you wish to be left alone, I will not trouble you.'

The silence lengthened itself again. Her fear was beginning to recede a little, partly the result of being alone with him, and in the dark, away from the glare of all those eyes. Perhaps Lady Dudley was wrong. Perhaps it was not so bad. After all, some people apparently enjoyed it; and besides, if it had to be done, as indeed it did, better sooner than later. Perhaps it would make him like her a little better. It would be wonderful, she thought, if ever he would smile at her in that way.

Timidly she cleared her throat. 'Sir, I think that—' She stopped. He had made a sound. It was not a sound of response. It was – it definitely was – a snore. Fuddled with a great deal of wine, he had fallen asleep.

Lady Mary lay very still, struggling not to cry, and after a while she succeeded. Then she realized that there was wetness on the inside of her thigh. Her flux had started.

86

CHAPTER 4

At first it was not so bad. The wedding of the heir to Morland Place was evidently an event of great importance in the locality, and there was a long round of festivities attached, visits to be made, visits to be received, dinners and balls and supper parties and picnic parties, which kept everyone occupied, and which meant that Lady Mary never had to get to grips with her situation. One of the worst things was the continuous presence of horses in her life. She had not properly grasped beforehand how devoted to horses Yorkshire people were. To her, horses were things which pulled your carriage and made the streets dirty. But to her new family and their neighbours, horses were almost like people, just as important and, apparently, a great deal more beloved.

They talked about them all the time, about their rival merits, their abilities, their diseases and, endlessly, about breeding them. Lady Mary was taken on a visit to the stables at Twelvetrees, much as, when she went to stay with Lady Cooper in her house in Kent, she was taken on a tour of the house to admire the paintings and statuary. There was a great deal of talk about the provision of a riding horse for her, and it was evidently a matter of such first-rate importance to her father-in-law and husband, a matter for earnest debate and endless comparison of equine candidates, that she did not like to suggest that it was hardly necessary. Lady Mary was rather afraid of horses, and would far rather never have to mount one. But such an idea was evidently akin to heresy, and she looked forward with anxiety to a future of riding and hunting. Her only hope was that they would never manage to decide between themselves on which animal was to be hers.

Even in the house one could not get away from the beasts, for there were almost as many portraits of great stallions and prolific mares as there were of ancestors on the walls. The marble-topped table in the great hall was generally littered with crops and spurs and odd riding gloves, and if ever a male member of the household sat down for a moment, he was almost sure to be occupied with mending a piece of harness or working out a horse's genealogy.

She was never alone with her husband during the day, although he sometimes went out without her, on business or for some pleasure he did not ask her to share. At those times she would be left in the company of her mother-in-law and the cousin from Northumberland, Frances. These two women were always very kind to her, and she felt that, had Lady Dudley not been there, she might have been able to make friends of them. But the presence of her chaperone – although she could no longer be called chaperone, but was a sort of lady-companion – made conversation stilted, and often when one of the ladies addressed a remark to Mary, Lady Dudley would answer for her before she could speak.

'Perhaps you would like to walk in the garden a little?' Sabina might say, thinking that the poor child looked pale.

Lady Dudley would immediately interject sternly 'Thank you, madam, but it is a great deal too hot at this time of the day for Lady Mary to be walking out of doors.'

Or Frances might say kindly, 'Would you like a piece of work to do, my dear, to keep you occupied?' Whereupon Lady Dudley would retort:

'Lady Mary does no close work. Her eyesight is too delicate.'

So the two ladies tended to chat pleasantly to each other, leaving Mary out of it, sitting with her hands in her lap, waiting for the next thing to be demanded of her. It was better when Alessandra joined them, for she would play on the spinnet and sing, and that was very pleasant. But sometimes she would bring her charge, the red-headed child from Shawes, and that was not so pleasant. Lady Mary thought the child passionate, spoiled and rude, and she had obviously conceived a dislike for Lady Mary which she evinced by being extremely polite and affectionate to everyone else in the room.

Mealtimes were better, for while Maurice was

there there was always music while they ate, which excused her from the necessity of making conversation, and which she found calmed her and made eating easier. Her husband continued to drink more than everyone else every evening and was therefore generally well foxed when they went to bed. She had at first dreaded the approach of bedtime, but it had been no ordeal since the first night. Her husband let her retire first, and came up the chapel stairs to the dressing room later on, where he spent so long preparing himself for bed that she was able to pretend to be asleep by the time he came to bed. He made no further sexual approaches to her, and she was thus saved the anguish of having to tell him about her flux, although in the way of shy people, it was long before she stopped torturing herself with trying to decide how she would have done it.

Although it was south-facing, the drawing room was pleasantly cool that hot August day, for it had thick stone walls, and its small, diamond-paned casement windows were thus set so deep in the thickness that they let in the light but were shadowed from the direct beams of the high sun. Lady Mary sat on the long window-seat, officially to get the best light on her work, but really for the pleasure of being near the open window. The air that came in through the casement when the wind stirred was fragrant with roses, blowing as it did from the rose-garden across the moat, and it brought a multitude of sounds which she enjoyed identifying. Sometimes a bird would land nearby and call for a while before taking off again; sometimes a bee would settle on the windowsill in front of her to comb its fur and take its bearings. Butterflies, too, liked the sunny sill on which to rest for a moment, opening and shutting their wings. She stitched her hem by feel, watching the jewel-bright colours of the admiral and peacock and painted lady, the tawny skippers, the bright brimstone, the delicate silver-washed fritillary, and the piece of fallen sky that was the chalkhill blue. And when there was no butterfly to watch, there were the swans, passing slowly in their circuits of the moat, their feathers dazzlingly white against the reflected blue of the sky. Seeing her at the window they always paused a moment and drifted to her side of the water, in case she should have something for them. On the other side of the moat there was a small, low window in the kitchen wall on which they would tap with their beaks in the morning to be fed.

A small sound within the room made her turn her head, and she glanced round to see that Lady Dudley, sitting in the shadowed corner of the room, had fallen asleep over her embroidery. Mary smiled to herself; it made her feel somehow more private when her companion dozed off. She let her hands idle in her lap and gazed dreamily out of the window. It was such a perfect day that she felt almost happy. The household had been in a ferment of excitement for days at the approach of race-week, and amid all the frenzied preparations, Mary discerned that however much Lady Dudley forced her to keep aloof, there could not but be some enjoyment to be had for her from the festivities. There was to be a grand ball at Beningbrough House, and the invitation which had come for her had been couched in the most flattering terms. Sabina had recommended a dressmaker from York, who had come to Morland Place with samples for the women to choose from for the new gowns essential to such an important ball. Mary had already resigned herself to whatever Lady Dudley would choose, but Sabina – whether by chance or deliberate design Mary could not tell – had sent Lady Dudley out of the way while the dressmaker was in the house by asking her to do a task for her that, she said, she could only trust to someone of Lady Dudley's experience and delicacy. The result was that Sabina, who would look wonderful in it, was to have the pink silk. With Sabina's help, Mary had chosen a delicate harebell-blue silk for her gown; the underskirt was to be quilted with silver rosettes, and the stomacher was to be embroidered with a pattern of purple pansies with silver leaves.

In such a gown, and if she could resist Lady Dudley's ideas about cosmetics, she might look almost pretty. She daydreamed for a moment, about coming down the stairs in her ball-gown to where Jemmy waited for her in the hall; he turned to look at her, and was frozen in amazement at her unexpected beauty. In her dream, he came slowly towards her, his hand outstretched, with a tender look in his beautiful eyes and that smile on his lips . . .

A sound in the hall broke her reverie, and a moment later the dog Fand padded in through the open door, trotted up to thump his chin down onto Lady Dudley's knee for a second, and then came over to Mary, tail swinging, pink-frilled tongue dripping. She caught his head in her hands and roughed his ears ruefully, for he had woken the dowager who was now stitching busily away to pretend that she had not been asleep.

'Mary, dear, make sure that the dog does not sully your gown,' she said.

'Yes, madam,' Mary said vaguely, for she was listening to the sounds in the hall. Now she heard Jemmy shout to a boy for cold buttermilk, and Fand pulled his head away from her caressing fingers and ran to the door as Jemmy came in, looking deliciously hot and ruffled, dressed only in breeches and shirt, and smelling of sweat and grass and animals, his long black curls tied out of the way at the nape of his neck. Mary's palm grew damp just at the sight of him, and she thought how wonderful it would be if they were two ordinary people and able to fall in love. The dog Fand ran back and forth between her and Jemmy, head low, smiling his delight – he was very fond of Mary, a thing which she knew had puzzled Jemmy. Jemmy was looking at her now with a slightly quizzical expression, and she felt her cheeks grow hot. She had thought she looked prettier today than usual, wearing a light green dress which made her skin look better, and a dark-green ribbon in her hair.

'Well, madam,' he said, and his voice was kinder than usual. Lady Dudley was straightening in her chair and bristling at his effrontery, in coming in such a state before her lady.

'Perhaps you would like to seek the services of your valet, sir, before you enter the drawing room,' Lady Dudley said. Mary glanced anxiously at her, willing her to be silent. Jemmy frowned slightly. 'It is hardly fitting—'

'Thank you, madam,' Jemmy interrupted her, 'I shall seek my valet in a moment, when I have cooled myself on the window seat and drunk my – ah, here it is. Thank you, boy. Is Clement in the house?'

'Yes, master,' said the boy, carefully passing the tall cup of buttermilk to Jemmy.

'Tell him I'd like to speak to him in the steward's room before dinner.' The boy nodded and left, and Jemmy came and sat down on the window seat beside Mary and drained off half the buttermilk.

Mary could smell its coolness mingled with Jemmy's sweat. The action of sitting with her seemed unexpectedly kind. She plucked up her courage to say, 'Have you amused yourself this morning, sir?'

'Why, yes,' he said, looking at Lady Dudley. 'I have been down to Clifton Ings – where we hold the races, you know – to help drive the grazing animals off.'

'Surely there is a common herdsman to do that,' Lady Dudley said, scandalized. Mary could see that Jemmy was enjoying teasing her.

'Why, of course there is, madam. But the beasts are accustomed to being driven out at dawn and in at sunset, and they resist any change in their routine. It takes as many men and dogs as may be to round them all up and keep them together. It is the greatest amusement, I assure you. The beasts run about, and the dogs bark, and the men shout, and there is a terrible din. One man was knocked clean into the river by a panicking ox, and was almost drowned before anyone noticed and fetched him out.'

'I should have thought that the commoners would have provided all the labour necessary,' Lady Dudley said icily.

Mary interposed gently, saying, 'Why, madam, I am sure Mr Morland had some reason other than enjoyment to be there.'

She felt Jemmy looking at her again, though she hid her face from him, concentrating on the thorough scratching of Fand's head and ears. The hound closed his eyes in utter bliss, resting the weight of his head in Mary's lap. It was not often anyone went to these lengths to discover the delicious places in the hollows of his ears and jaw.

'You are right, madam,' Jemmy said. 'It is a good opportunity to check on what animals are using the common grazing, to make sure that each man is grazing no more than the proper number, and to see that there are no serious diseases. Sometimes my father sends the bailiff to do it, but this year he asked me to go. It is as well that I should see these things for myself at least once in my life.'

Mary admired the subtlety of the speech, by which he reminded Lady Dudley that his father was arbiter of all their fates, and that one day he would be Master. Lady Dudley had nothing more to say. She gave a kind of muted snort, and went back to her work. Jemmy finished his buttermilk, and then studied Mary again, covertly. She had supported him against her duenna; the dog certainly loved her; and she looked very well this morning. Perhaps there might be some way of making contact with her. They had been married almost four months, and had hardly spoken to each other. As he continued to look at her, she looked up from under her eyelashes at him, and he could swear she almost smiled. He had an idea.

'Madam,' he said gently, 'If I could tempt you to leave down your work for a moment, there is something which I would like to shew you.'

Before Mary could answer, Lady Dudley said sharply, 'Lady Mary cannot possibly go out in the heat of the day. I wonder you should suggest it, sir.'

Jemmy smiled pleasantly. 'I do not, madam, I assure you. I intend to take her only to the stables, quite in the shade.'

It would have to be the stables, Mary thought,

with a sinking heart. Of course it would have to be something to do with horses – he probably wanted to shew her one of his racing-horses, a huge and snorting, unpredictable beast, with teeth like a crocodile and hooves like a ploughman's beetle.

'The stable, sir!' Lady Dudley quivered, managing to make five inflections of disapproval in one word.

Mary decided it was time to act and, her heart beating at the enormity of her own defiance, she jumped up and said, 'Indeed, sir, I shall be glad to come.' She gazed at the dowager with a mixture of beseeching and defiance.

Jemmy jumped to her aid, standing up and saying, before Lady Dudley could open her mouth, 'There is no need in the world for you to disturb yourself, madam. We shall be gone but a few minutes. Come, Mary.'

He had never called her by her name before. Without looking at Lady Dudley, she hurried after her husband, the dog Fand jumping about them, butting at their knees. Mary could feel her heart beating with a mixture of fear and excitement. I will not shew my fear of the horses, she told herself over and over. I will appear interested and pleased. They passed through the great hall, out of the open front door, across the briefly blinding heat of the court-yard, and in by the cool dark mouth of the stable building. There, the strong smell of horses and clean straw assailed Mary's nostrils, and she dug her nails in her palms for courage.

The long, cobbled passageway that ran behind the stalls was swept spotlessly clean, and there was no need for her to fear for her dress, as of course Jemmy had known. But most of the stalls were occupied, and a row of gleaming rumps and swishing tails presented themselves, a gauntlet of hooves to be run. Jemmy was leading the way unconcernedly along them, and the dog was nudging at her hand, and there was nothing to be done but follow. A brief daydream crossed her mind, of one of the creatures lashing out and stunning Mary, of Jemmy running to her, lifting her in his arms, crying, 'My darling, my darling, what have I done to you? How can I ever forgive myself?' and of Mary forgiving him, of course . . .

The last stall was not open, but enclosed by moveable bars so that the animal within could move about freely. Here it was that Jemmy paused, looking back at Mary, picking her terrified way along the passage, until she reached the safety of the corner of the building where she tried not to press herself against the wall. In the last stall was a horse, not a very big one; it was delicately built, with a pretty head, and its coat was golden, its long mane and tail a shade lighter, and there was a white mark roughly star-shaped on its forehead.

The horse whickered a greeting as Jemmy appeared, and Mary, despite her fear, noticed that it had large, friendly-looking eyes, and that when Fand ran under the rails the horse lowered its nose to greet the dog.

'This is Leppard,' Jemmy said, putting a hand under the horse's neck to scratch its further ear. 'We called her that because she was a great "lepper", as well as being very fast. Unfortunately, she strained herself trying to jump out of a paddock, poor old girl, and now she's no use for racing. But she's perfectly all right for gentle exercise, provided she's not overtaxed. She'd make a fine riding horse for a lady.'

Mary began to have an inkling of what was coming. Jemmy pulled the mare's head towards him and rested his face against hers for a moment, and she made a chuckling sound through her nose. 'It's time you had a riding horse of your own,' Jemmy went on. 'Would you like to have Leppard?'

It was decided that the cool of the later afternoon, in the hour before evening prayers, would be a suitable time for Mary to try her new horse. Mary spent an uncomfortable afternoon, for nervousness always went to her stomach and brought her face out in itchy patches, and she had a very poor appetite at dinner. Lady Dudley was deeply offended by the whole business, and treated her with a lofty distance which normally would have upset her deeply, but on this occasion she could only be thankful not to have to talk. Though she had been but once or twice on a horse before, Mary had a riding habit, for in London it was what ladies wore to walk about the park. Sabina, who was more or less the same size, lent her a very handsome pair of soft leather riding boots, her riding gloves, and a hat which only wanted retrimming to be very smart.

When the hour came, a number of people had gathered to see the sport. The servants, in their usual mysterious way, had gathered a good deal more about t'young mistress than her husband had, and they knew that she was terrified of horses, and there were consequently a number of them lingering near by, industriously picking up kindling or investigating the soundness of the fence-posts or gathering moss for the kitchen. Matt, looking strangely shrunken in the open air and daylight, for Mary normally only saw him at night by candle-light, had strolled down to watch, and Charles and Allen had arrived good and early and got them-selves seats on the paddock fence where they were swinging their legs and peeling withies. To Mary's distress, at the last moment Marie-Louise appeared, towing a nursemaid and followed by Alessandra.

'They brought a message to say Jemmy couldn't give me my lesson because you were going to try your new horse,' she said as soon as she was within earshot, 'but I thought if I came down there might be time for him to teach me when you've finished. I don't suppose you'll want to be up very long, will you?'

Mary nodded nervously, knowing perfectly well that the little fiend was hoping to point up the contrast between them by springing lightly into the saddle as soon as Mary had fallen out of it.

'You are lucky,' Marie-Louise went on, 'having Leppard. She's a marvellous horse. So *spirited*. Before her accident, only Davey was allowed to ride her, she was too difficult for the boys to handle.'

Just then Jemmy arrived, followed by Davey leading the chestnut mare, already bridled and wearing a sidesaddle.

'Here we are, then. If you like her, we'll get a saddle made for you, to fit both of you. It makes a deal of difference, having your own saddle,' Jemmy said cheerfully to Mary. Davey, noticing her pallor and the pinched look around her mouth, spoke with a deal more sympathy.

'Why don't you take her around once or twice first, Jemmy, so that her ladyship can see how quietly she goes? I'll just slip the saddle off, and you can jump up bareback.'

'Good idea,' Jemmy said. In a moment the mare's golden back was naked, and with the beautiful ease of the expert, Jemmy had taken the reins and vaulted lightly astride her, his long legs dangling below the level of her belly. 'Come on then, lady, shew your paces,' he said to the mare, and wheeled her round and trotted her into the paddock. Round and round they went, walking, trotting, cantering, circling one way then the other, and finally halting true and square before Mary and backing neatly four paces. 'You see,' Jemmy said triumphantly. 'She's so light in hand, she almost hears your thoughts. Now you try her.'

101

The mare was saddled again, and Mary approached. She seemed very tall, even when Mary stood on the mounting block that two of the boys had dragged out. But Davey was close beside her, giving her a look of mingled sympathy and reassurance, holding the rein very tightly.

'She's as gentle as a kitten, my lady,' Davey murmured to her. 'She'll do whatever you want.'

Mary gritted her teeth and mounted. Now she was a long way from the ground, swaying in the open air, with nothing but the pommel and the reins between her and disaster. 'You take hold of a good piece of mane, my lady, then you'll feel safer,' Davey whispered kindly. Then he let go of the reins and clicked to the mare, 'Giddap. Walk on.'

They walked forward, and made a slow circuit of the paddock, while Mary tried to accustom herself to the strange movement. The mare walked quietly, her head nodding as if she were reassuring Mary. 'Yes, yes, it's all right.' As they passed the group by the gate for the first time, Jemmy called, 'She's wonderful, isn't she?'

Mary nodded grimly. After the second circuit, she began to feel she might survive the ordeal. After the third circuit, Marie-Louise said, 'It's like a funeral procession. Why doesn't she try a canter?'

'Good idea,' Jemmy said, 'try a canter now, Mary!'

Mary opened her mouth to suggest enough was enough, but Leppard, hearing the word canter spoken in the master's voice, obeyed and sprang lightly forward. Mary jerked backwards in the saddle, and was only saved from falling off by the lock of mane clenched between her fingers. She lurched forward, dropped the reins, fumbled for them, and hung on as if her life depended on it. Leppard, enjoying herself, cantered round and round the paddock, passing the gate again and again. The reins were lying loosely on her neck, for Mary had no thought other than to stay on at all costs. Every time they passed the group of onlookers she hoped the horse might stop, but round she went again. Mary had the impression they were calling to her, but she could not have distinguished their words, or obeyed any instructions they might have been giving her. At last the mare tired of the game and, coming back to the gate for the seventh time, she skidded abruptly to a halt and Mary lurched forward again, banging her nose painfully on the mare's neck.

Slowly her breath came back. Through the tears in her eyes from the bang on her nose, she saw Marie-Louise smiling with malicious glee, Davey looking anxious, the stable boys amused, and everyone else talking unconcernedly amongst themselves about the mare's good qualities. Jemmy came up and took the rein.

'You must have liked her,' he said. 'I thought you would never stop. Have you had enough now, or do you want to go round again?'

His face was innocent of guile. He evidently thought she had been cantering round in sheer delight. Breathlessly she shook her head, and was so eager to dismount that Jemmy was not ready for her and almost dropped her. Davey came and took the mare from Jemmy, and gave Mary a look of sympathy in passing.

'She's a lovely ride, isn't she?' Jemmy was saying in honest pleasure. 'Do you like her? Shall she be yours?'

Safe on firm ground again, Mary could afford to dissemble. 'She's lovely,' she said firmly.

'Then she's yours,' Jemmy said. Marie-Louise pouted in disappointment. She had hoped that Mary would fall off, and Leppard would be given to her.

'Can't I have my lesson now, Jemmy?' she cried. 'There's still plenty of time, and I've come in my habit all this way.'

Jemmy glanced towards Mary apologetically. 'Do you mind?' Mary shook her head. 'Very well, then, Princess, let's go and find you a horse.'

'Can't I have Leppard, since she's here and ready?'

'Leppard is Lady Mary's horse now, child,' Jemmy said sternly. Mary tried to smile. She had found her legs were trembling, and she was afraid they might give way under her.

'Oh, that's all right. I don't mind.'

'Just this once, then,' Jemmy said.

The party broke up, some to stay and some to go back to the house or about their business. Mary walked back with the gratefully silent Matt, and after

104

a while Davey caught them up. He walked beside Mary for a moment, and then murmured so that only Mary would hear, 'It's largely a matter of practice, you know, my lady. She really is a very gentle horse.' Mary nodded, grateful for the sympathy. He went on, 'If you like, my lady, I could give you a few lessons. You'd soon get the hang of it.'

She looked at him, startled. He smiled gently. 'We could arrange it so that the master didn't know,' he said.

'Oh thank you, Davey,' she said, then, hesitantly, 'how did you know?'

'Through being frightened myself,' he said. 'When I was a boy, they looked so big and strong. But I soon learned they're like big stupid children. I'll shew you too, if you like, my lady.'

'Thank you, Davey,' Mary said again. He nodded and strode on.

Lady Mary was almost gay that evening. She put on her pale green gown again for supper, though Lady Dudley said the carnation-coloured satin would be more appropriate. For once Mary, to the silent admiration of Rachel, insisted on having her own way, and Lady Dudley retreated into a baffled and furious silence. Over supper everyone was in very good humour; for once Sabina stayed down for supper, and even Matt was almost chatty. The talk was all about horses and the forthcoming race-week, and though Mary as usual said very little, for once she did not feel left out of things.

She was able to eat a good supper, and Sabina said pleasantly, 'My dear Lady Mary, you see the exercise and fresh air has given you an appetite. We must encourage you to ride regularly.'

Jemmy smiled at her with something like approval, and in spite of the close and icy presence of Lady Dudley, looming at the end of the table like a monument of disapproval, Mary said, 'Thank you, ma'am, I think I shall.'

After supper everyone retired to the long gallery, which was more pleasant on summer evenings than the drawing room, which seemed rather dark when fires were not lit. Matt and Father Andrews set up the chess-board – the ivory and rosewood table with matching chessmen which had been in the family for over two hundred years – and Sabina said, 'I think I must seek my bed, if you will excuse me. But why do you not play to the young people, Lady Mary? I am sure it would amuse them. There is plenty of music in the cupboard there.'

Mary blushed deeply, but was pleased to be asked, for music was one of the few things she excelled at. Before when music had been proposed it had been because Alessandra or Maurice had been present to provide it, and no one had ever enquired whether she could play. Jemmy now looked towards her with surprise and approval.

'Do you play, madam? I am astonished!'

'Why should it surprise you, sir?' Lady Dudley snapped. Jemmy bowed in her direction.

'I beg your pardon, madam, I meant only that

I am astonished she has never mentioned her talents during our musical evenings.'

'Lady Mary is not accustomed to parade herself like a public performer. She has been used to playing only for intimate friends and close family.'

The tone of her voice was so insulting that there might well have been unpleasantness, had not Matt looked up at that moment and said abruptly, 'Play, child, if it will not weary you?'

'With pleasure, sir,' Mary murmured. His abruptness did not offend her, since she knew it was not directed at her, but the result of his unhappy temper and the constant pain she suspected he bore. She walked over to the spinnet and opened it, and Allen leapt forward obligingly to place a chair for her and fetch out the bundle of music. At nine he had grown into a slender, wiry, handsome boy, with a sensitive mouth and an air of strong quietness about him. His eyes were grey-blue, large and rather beautiful; his butter-gold curls had darkened to a golden-brown. He spoke rarely, and kept himself in the background, as was suitable to his position, but he had a way of making himself silently useful which made people look about vaguely for him when he was not there.

'What shall I play?' Mary asked when she had seated herself. Her voice was so quiet that only Allen heard, and so he answered her, by silently placing a piece of music before her. At the first notes Fand yawned noisily and came and flopped down at her feet, and she suppressed a smile and played on.

After the first piece Charles came and joined Allen in leaning against the spinnet, and when after the second piece Jemmy joined them, Charles said, 'Can you play madrigals or glees? Then we could all sing.' Mary obliged, and in this way they spent the rest of the evening.

Mary went up to bed later than usual, where Rachel was waiting sleepily to undress her. She was in her shift when Lady Dudley came in, simply to say, 'I hope I do not need to warn you, Lady Mary, against too frequent a repetition of this evening's activities. The way to retain the respect of these people is not, I think, to match them in vulgarity.'

Trembling all over, Mary said as firmly as she could, 'These people, Lady Dudley, are my family.' Lady Dudley stared at her, nostrils quivering, for a moment, and then went away without another word.

Rachel undressed her, put her into her bedgown, brushed her hair, and helped her into bed, and went away silently, leaving the candle burning. Mary lay for a while, smiling at the flickering shadows on the bedcurtains. Rachel's silence had been as expressive as three hearty cheers. She had only just blown out the candle when Jemmy came in and after a moment got into bed beside her. It occurred to her that this was the first time since their marriage that they had spent the evening doing anything together – the first time, too, that he had come sober to bed. After a moment she felt him turn over and place an arm across her. This time she did not flinch.

'Mary,' he said softly, 'I think it is time for us to become husband and wife in truth, don't you?'

Her mouth dried, and she felt her body tense with apprehension, but he seemed waiting for her answer, and she was sure if she said no, he would turn over and leave her alone. At last all she could manage was to say in a very small voice, 'Will it hurt?'

'I will be very careful,' he said. He had not said 'no', and she appreciated his honesty.

'Very well,' she whispered, bracing herself. He laughed, silently, and she felt his warm breath on her cheek.

'Oh, not that way,' he said, and she could hear from his voice that he was smiling. 'I'll shew you.'

And he took her in his arms and began kissing her. It was an extraordinary experience and, she found, very pleasurable, and she was glad to discover that there was some part of the process, at least, that she could like. It was quite a long time before he came to the difficult part.

It *did* hurt, and she was hard put to it not to cry out with the pain. But it was not anywhere near so bad as she had expected, or as Lady Dudley had told her, and after some time the pain went away, and it began to be pleasurable. It was all rather baffling, but eventually she gathered that it was over, and that Jemmy was satisfied. He took her into his arms and cradled her on his shoulder, and that part she found very agreeable.

'There,' he said, kissing the top of her head with affection. 'Now you are my wife, and nothing can ever part us. And I promise you that it will never hurt like that again. The next time, you will like it much more.'

He understood! Gratitude swept warmly through her, but she was very sleepy and very comfortable, and she could not rouse herself to answer. Her last thought before falling asleep was, if I am with child, I won't have to go riding any more.

For the whole of race-week, Mary was happy. A shyness as deep-rooted as hers did not melt away all at once like spring frost, and she still smiled and spoke very little, and was dumbfounded by company or too much attention. But Jemmy looked kindly on her, and at night led her gently through the stages of intimacy. She still did not quite understand it all, and the doors of pleasure did not open for her more than a tiny crack, but it certainly did not hurt, and Jemmy's enjoyment and kindness were quite sufficient for her to think that it was a pleasant thing.

By day there was all the excitement of the races and the dinners and balls. Every day she drove down to Clifton Ings in an open carriage, from which she had a splendid view of the races. Jemmy himself placed her bets for her, advising her which was the best horse, and after one or two races she became so taken up with the excitement that she chose a horse for herself and even shouted out with excitement when it came near to winning. Everyone behaved in a very friendly and informal manner during race-week, and etiquette was almost set aside, and only the disapproving presence of Lady Dudley prevented Mary from being taken quite into the bosom of local society. As it was, they looked kindly on her, and were as friendly as the dowager's frozen looks permitted.

On the first morning after race-week, Mary woke feeling especially happy, for Lady Dudley had left early that morning to visit a friend in Harrogate, an elderly lady to whom at least so much respect was due. Jemmy was, as always, up and gone before she awoke, and she lay stretching comfortably in the bed and thinking about him until Rachel came in to wake her. She was in a fair way to being in love with him, which she knew Lady Dudley would think scandalous. But I shall hide it from her, Mary thought, ignoring for the moment the fact that she had never been able to conceal anything from her stern duenna for long.

Rachel almost smiled when she came in, so much did the atmosphere lighten when Lady Dudley was absent. With great cheerfulness she helped Mary dress, and then the housemaid came in with a tray containing Mary's breakfast — toasted cheese, and a pot of chocolate. Mary sat down to it by the window with a great appetite.

'Where is Mr Morland – my husband?' she asked the departing maid.

'He's over to Twelvetrees, m'lady,' the maid said, curtseying. 'I heard him tell Davey he would be back in an hour, though.'

'Thank you,' Mary said, and the maid departed. Rachel came behind her to dress her hair while she ate. 'I think I shall go for a walk in the gardens, until Mr Morland returns,' she said.

'Yes, m'lady,' Rachel replied, understanding that it was to be imparted to the other servants, so that when Jemmy came back and asked, he would be told his wife was walking in the gardens waiting for him. She hoped so much that Lady Dudley would stay away for a few days, so that her mistress might have a chance to be happy with her husband, but knowing Lady Dudley, she thought it unlikely. Lady Dudley had only gone with the greatest reluctance, and had left at an unholy hour that morning with the intention of returning the same day if possible.

Fand joined Mary in the rose garden, and trotted along by her side, leaving her every now and then to bury his nose perilously in a bush or flower. She was glad of his silent companionship, and began to see how a man could take such pleasure in horse and hounds. She was even growing fond of Leppard as her fear decreased. During race-week she had managed to have two brief, secret lessons with Davey, and his patience had helped her greatly. She passed two gardeners, an old man and a very young boy, and they bowed respectfully to her and then returned her cheerful greeting with pleasure and faint surprise.

A little while later she sat down on a stone bench under a tall hedge to rest, and heard their voices on the other side of the hedge from her. She listened idly to their conversation for a moment before she realized what they were talking about. They evidently had no idea she was there.

'T'dog seems to 'ave taken to 'er, any road,' said the boy. The old man grunted.

'Aye, well, he allus was a woman's dog. He were supposed to be for the little girl, but he pined so when his mistress went away, that the master took him back.'

'He seems right fond of the little girl,' the boy said.

'What, t'young master? Well might he be.' A silence, and then the old man spoke again. 'I reckon he loves that dog for *her* sake, and the little girl as she's the only thing left to him of the woman he loved.'

Mary got up quickly and walked away, more puzzled than upset. There was a great deal she did not understand. Fand trotted along at her side, and when she stopped to look down at him thoughtfully, he smiled up at her with his wolfish yellow eyes and butted her hand impatiently. When she got near the house, she saw Clement coming out on some errand, and called him.

'Yes, my lady?'

'Clement, whose dog is this?' she asked. Clement looked puzzled. 'I mean, whose *was* he?'

'He belonged to Mistress Aliena, the Countess's daughter, over at Shawes, my lady. When she went to become a nun, the dog pined for her, so the young master took him in.'

'I see,' she said thoughtfully. Clement was watching her alertly. She asked with apparent casualness, 'Is my husband returned yet?'

'Yes, my lady, he's in the stable with Davey. I heard his voice as I passed.'

'Thank you,' Mary said, and walked on. As she went into the courtyard, Fand left her, running ahead into the stable where, she supposed, Jemmy must be. In fact he was in Auster's stall, leaning on the horse's black rump, and talking to Davey, who was grooming the horse.

'She's been getting on much better with everyone since I gave her the horse,' Jemmy said. 'Do you know, I think all her coldness and aloofness might have been shyness after all.'

'I wouldn't be surprised,' Davey said, pushing Auster's face away as he tried to chew Davey's hair. He was keeping Mary's riding lessons secret, of course. Better Jemmy should think she liked horses than that she had learnt to bear them.

'It seems to me,' Jemmy said, 'that much of the trouble is that lady companion of hers.'

Davey grunted agreement. It was at that point that Mary came near enough to overhear them.

'I hate her,' Jemmy was saying. 'Haughty, frozen-faced creature. She thinks herself too good for us. When she gives me one of those sour looks of hers, I wish to God I could send her away.'

Outside Mary stood rigid in the sunshine, feeling the words sear her, feeling her cheeks burn with shock and shame.

'You know that's impossible, sir,' Davey answered.

'Aye, I suppose I must do my duty, and put up with her. All my life seems to have been spent doing my duty.'

Mary's feet unfroze, and carried her towards the house at a stumbling run. Like a hurt animal she sought privacy, running up the stairs to the bedchamber. Well was it said eavesdroppers heard no good of themselves! She had lived in a fool's paradise, but thank God she had found out soon enough, before she had made too much of a spectacle of herself. Lady Dudley had been right to warn her not to be friendly with her husband. How could she have been such a fool as to think she could love him, or him her? He had loved someone else, and had married her out of duty. He 'put up with' her, that was all, and put a good face on doing his duty.

She lay down on her bed, and hot tears coursed helplessly down her face, though she struggled against them. She must not cry so much as to be unpresentable at dinner time. She must do *her* duty. But she would never, never again risk her heart, her affections. She longed for Lady Dudley, the only safe rock in a stormy sea; Lady Dudley who had known her since earliest childhood, and would never leave her, who had her best interests at heart all the time.

In the stable, unaware that his words had been overheard, Jemmy had continued by saying, 'Besides, I am sure my wife is fond of her, and I would not grieve her. Hey-day, here's Fand. What have you been doing, old fellow?' He rubbed the hound's head between his hands. 'Where is your mistress, then? It is wonderful, isn't it, Davey, how Fand has taken to his new mistress.'

A message came down that Lady Mary had a headache from walking too long in the sun, and would stay in her room, and later another message came for Jemmy, asking whether he would be kind enough to sleep in the bachelor's wing, as Lady Mary felt a little feverish and needed an undisturbed night. Jemmy sent an obliging message back, asked if he might see her, and was politely denied. That night the servants discussed what appeared to be a lovers' tiff, and laid odds on its being resolved before the next day's ending.

Indeed, the misunderstanding might well have been resolved, had not Lady Dudley arrived back the following morning, heard the news of Mary's 'indisposition', and rushed upstairs in alarm. It did not take her long to discover the true state of affairs, and though her heart rejoiced, she wisely hid her glee, and managed not to say 'I told you so', which would have lost her Mary's confidence. Instead she was kind and sympathetic, and only said, 'You know that you have me to rely on, child. I am always here, whenever you need me.'

Jemmy was puzzled, when he met Mary, at her coldness, and thought it was the result of her illness, compounded by Lady Dudley's return. But Mary insisted on sleeping apart for the rest of the week, saying she still did not feel well, and when they met during the day she treated him with a coldness that at last roused his anger, and the breach widened until it was impassable.

At the end of that week, Mary's flux was due, but did not appear, and she was sure she was pregnant. She told Lady Dudley, who concurred: her fluxes had sometimes been early, but never late. When Lady Dudley went away to fetch her some cold buttermilk, and some Elsham ginger against possible nausea, Mary buried her face in her pillow and cried; but after a while her tears stopped, and she began to feel rather pleased about her pregnancy. For here, at least, would be a creature who was bound to love her, and whom she could love without fear of rebuff, at least while it was small. A son or a daughter – it would be someone of her own, of her very own. Perhaps if it was a daughter, it might grow up to be a friend.

CHAPTER 5

In the stone barn at the far end of the orchard, the cider-making was in full flow, and every boy in the neighbourhood had been pressed into service to gather up the apples and bring them in, sound and windfall together, to be thrown into the apple-crusher. The red-and-white spotted ox trod patiently around his circular track, blindfolded so that he would not get dizzy, his breast against the outer end of the long pole that turned the crushers' blades in the huge oak hopper, into which the boys tipped their basketloads of cider-apples. The boys had to perch on the raised waist of the hopper to reach its mouth, and if they were still balanced there when the pole came round, they had to jump over it. It was a favourite game of the older boys to wait until a younger one was perched precariously, holding on with one hand while he heaved the basket up with the other, and then whack the ox with a stick to make him break into a trot, so that the pole would come round too soon and knock the young boy over.

Jemmy had done it himself when he was younger, and he watched, grinning secretly, from his adult fastness, wondering if there was any adult pleasure to compare with those forbidden sports of childhood. He was at the other end of the barn, where the press was. The process had always fascinated him, and though there was not the least need in the world for his presence, he told himself he ought to look in. The press was hand-carved of oak by some longdead estate carpenter, and was a thing of beauty, its long handle decorated with an ambitious pattern of leaves, flowers and fruit in raised relief, only the hand-hold being left smooth, and polished to a deep patina by generations of hands. Onto the base of the press had been laid a foundation of oat straw, on top of which had been spread a six-inch layer of crushed apples. Then came another layer of straw and another of apples, and so on until the pile was three feet thick. Then the top of the press was lowered into position, and the handle put in place.

Knowing his preferences, the bailiff, Cradoc, who was supervising the business, offered Jemmy first turn at the handle, and Jemmy, smiling sheepishly, pushed at his sleeves, and stepped forward to take it. At the first turn the pressure came on and the first of the golden apple-juice went trickling noisily into the stone cistern below. The men let out a cheer, and after a moment the first of them came gently to take the handle from Jemmy, and under his more vigorous action the trickle increased to a splashy flow. When no more could be wrung out, the press would be opened, and the cake of pressed straw and apple-pulp would be taken out and a fresh one built up. This straw-and-apple leaving was given to the dairy-maids, who chopped it up and gave some to the milch cows and some to the poultry. Geese were particularly fond of the confection, and at cider time it was wise to see they were shut up somewhere, for they were not above coming into the cider-shed and demanding it with threats and menaces. No man can concentrate on his work with an angry goose biting his calf.

When the cistern was full it was drained by a spigot into buckets and the juice carried to the brew-house, where it was emptied into open barrels to ferment. Starlings nested in the roof of the brew-house, but it was reckoned that the odd bird-dropping or piece of nest-litter – even a fallen fledgling or two, or an inquisitive mouse – helped the fermentation along and gave the final result 'a bit of body'. When the fermentation was finished, the liquid was strained through muslin into clean barrels and plugged, and that provided drink for the household for about six months. The 'rack' – what was caught in the muslin – was fed to the pigs, along with the used grain left after the brewing process. Morland Place made about half of its own ale, as well as wines from fruit and flowers. Elderflower wine was much prized, and the servants regarded plum brandy as a sovereign remedy for toothache, influenza, green-sickness, rheumatism, palpitations – indeed, almost anything except the gout and the stone.

Sabina had always overseen the wine-making,

following the receipts from the Household Book, vast and leather-bound, which was added to and handed down by every mistress of Morland Place. This year, Jemmy supposed that the housekeeper would see to it, for it was mortal sure that Mary would not do so, and Sabina was dead. She had died in February, in the depth of the coldest part of winter, while a blizzard blew around Morland Place, soughing in the chimneys and blowing gusts of snow down them to fizzle abruptly against the glowing logs. Jemmy missed her, far more even than he had expected to. She had been the spirit of the house, and without her there seemed a lack of something, no sense of community within the household; for what she had provided, Matt would not and Mary could not. Father Andrews had spoken her funeral mass, she had been buried in the crypt, and Jemmy had worn mourning for her for three months, and that was that.

He had been still in mourning when Mary had given birth to her baby, two days before her birthday. Jemmy always thought about it as her baby, rather than his, or theirs. Since the child's conception, he had had little to do with his wife. Sometimes he shared a bed with her, but only in the formal sense. Quite often he slept in the dressing room or in the bachelor wing, taking advantage of her frequent headaches, which he was sure were politic. They met at mealtimes, and in the evenings after dark, and spoke, when they had to, with great politeness to each other. Often they did not even spend the evening in each other's company, for she retired early to her bedchamber, like a mediaeval lady, to work there, and he often sat at night in the steward's room, either working, or pretending to. At first Jemmy had been puzzled by her attitude, and angry at her rejection of him; now he had become so used to it that he did not think of it at all. He avoided her automatically, like a man stepping round a known and permanent hazard.

The baby had been born, he gathered, without undue difficulties, and was a boy, and was healthy and bonny. Mary had named it Thomas, after her brother the Duke, and Jemmy had written to the Duke to that effect, and had asked him to be Godfather. The other Godparents were Maurice, Sir John Vanbrugh, John Bourchier, the squire of Beningbrough, and Annunciata, Countess of Chelmsford. Mary had looked disapproving of this last choice, but had not spoken against it. The baby had been given a grand Christening, with all its Godparents present, as well as the best society of York and all the Morland tenantry; a banquet and ball had followed, with a whole roast ox and country dancing on the lawns for the servants and tenants. Then the baby had disappeared into the nursery and the care of nurses, and though Mary was very fond of it and apparently spent a great deal of time in the nursery, Jemmy forgot for most of the time that he had become a father.

Matt, oddly enough for one who had been so

notoriously careless a father, had been delighted to become a grandfather at last, and had smiled more and spoken more at the Christening celebrations than Jemmy could ever remember.

When everyone was retiring to bed after the ball, moreover, he had asked Jemmy to come with him to the steward's room, and there he had given Jemmy a glass of wine and made him drink the child's health once again, and then had said, 'I could not feel easy while the inheritance hung by the thread of a single life. Now there are two generations. But you must not be complacent either. You must not rest until there are three or four. I know well the problems attaching to being the sole heir. All my childhood, I bore the weight alone. Well, I have done what I can. Now it is your responsibility.'

Jemmy had thought afterwards that it was a distinctly odd speech, but had put it down to his father's state of health, which had been bad for some years. After the baby was born, Matt seemed to get rapidly worse, as if he had been holding back the tide of dissolution in anticipation of that very event. Almost from the following day, he had seemed to shrink and grow feebler, and it was plain to everyone that he was suffering from some wasting disease, though used as he was to autocracy, he refused to consult anyone of the medical profession, or to take any remedies other than simple herbal mixtures to relieve certain of his symptoms. Jemmy had gradually to take over more and more of his father's duties, but that was no more than a speeding-up of the process that had been going on for years, and was certainly no hardship.

The men were unwinding the wooden screw of the press now, the first pressing being finished, and removing the flattened straw-and-apple cake.

'You two can take that down to the dairy,' Cradoc directed, nodding to the men who had lifted it off. Jemmy had a thought.

'How are the pigs coming along?' he asked. 'I wonder should it be given to them? It lacks but three weeks to the killing. Only three weeks left to fatten them up.'

Cradoc nodded. 'They are well enough, sir, but they'll always eat more if they're given it. You know pigs. But it's as you please, sir.'

'I'll come down now and look at them,' Jemmy said. 'They're on the fallow by the windmill, aren't they?'

'Yes, sir. I'll walk down with you. Carry on here, you men.'

Jemmy and the bailiff had not gone more than fifty yards, however, when there was an outcry behind them that halted them, and they turned to see one of the house servants running clumsily towards them over the uneven turf.

'Master, master, wait!'

The man reached them and stood panting, one hand to the stitch in his side, the other waving in the effort to communicate before he had breath to do so.

'Take your breath, man, be easy,' Jemmy said,

wondering what minor crisis demanded his presence this time: with Sabina gone, everything seemed to get referred to him. 'No news is worth choking for.'

But the man waved his hand again in distress, and his face was white with strain. 'Master,' he panted, 'you must come quick. It's your father, sir – he's been taken very bad.'

Jemmy stood beside his father's bed in the West Bedroom, staring down at the shrunken figure that lay propped against the mound of pillows. Clement had got him to bed and sent a servant for the doctor and another to fetch Jemmy, and he had kept watch by the bedside, along with Matt's new body-servant, a young boy named Pask, who was a distant cousin of Clement's, until Jemmy arrived.

Matt's face was dark and suffused with blood, and his breathing was laboured and rattled distressfully in his chest. His hands, resting on the counterpane, twitched, as did the skin of his face, and his eyes moved about under his eyelids as if he were trying to see through them. Jemmy was aware of how bare and fleshless his father's face looked without the frame of his usual wig. The nose looked sharp and pinched, the teeth shewed faintly through the lips and the cheekbones were too prominent, as if the face were rehearsing its final appearance. Clement, in his haste, had put on the nightcap crookedly, and Jemmy reached out to straighten it, for the clownish angle was grotesque in conjunction with the cadaverous aspect.

'What's happened?' Jemmy asked quietly. Clement looked at Pask, but the boy was wringing his hands, evidently too upset to speak, and the older man finally answered for him.

'It was quite sudden, sir. Master hadn't long been downstairs. Pask dressed him, and then he went up to the nursery, sir, and—'

'The nursery?' Jemmy interrupted sharply. Clement nodded, unsurprised.

'Master went up to the nursery every day, sir. He didn't stay long. Then he came downstairs, and he'd just got to the hall when he suddenly cried out and fell down. Pask called for me right away.'

'Had he eaten? Had he taken anything?' Jemmy asked. Pask looked frightened – in cases of sudden illness, talk of poison was commonplace.

'Only what he usually had, master,' Pask whispered. 'Bread and small beer. I brought it before I dressed him.'

'I don't suppose it could have been that, then,' Jemmy shook his head. Pask began to cry, but silently, and Clement murmured to him to fold up the master's clothes, in order to keep him occupied. Jemmy took the flask of wine from the bedside and, with his fingertips, wet his father's lips and tongue with wine. Matt seemed to feel it. He frowned and muttered, and his hands jerked as if he wanted to touch his face. Jemmy trickled a few more drops of wine between his lips, and then bathed his father's face with the cloth and water Clement had had brought up.

126

After a moment or two, Matt's eyes began to flicker open, and he stared up at Jemmy, frowning.

Jemmy leaned forward and said gently, 'Father? It's me, Jemmy. How do you feel?' His father did not answer, frowning as if in thought. 'You are in bed, in your own room, father. You fell ill. We have sent for the doctor, and he should be here soon. Is there anything you want?'

His father's lips moved, though he made no sound, and he closed his eyes again. Jemmy caught Clement's eye, and between them they propped up Matt's head and put the wine cup to his lips. The wine spilled over, running down his chin and staining the sheets like blood, but Jemmy thought he had swallowed a little too. They laid him back down on the pillows, and Jemmy took his father's hand and held it between his own, not knowing what else to do.

Suddenly Matt's eyes opened again, and he looked at Jemmy with recognition. His lips moved again. Jemmy leaned closer, and Matt's hand clenched suddenly and painfully. Jemmy could feel the whisper of Matt's breath on his face, hear it rattle as it was dragged in and out with such effort, but the words were hard to distinguish.

'Jemmy – promise me—'

'Yes, father,' Jemmy encouraged him. 'Anything, anything I can.' The hand gripped his tighter. For a long time there was only the gasp of laboured breathing.

'Promise – me—' A long pause. Don't – break – up—'

But the rest was indistinguishable. Jemmy waited, but the fingers gripping his began to relax, and when he drew his head back a little, he saw his father's eyes were closed again.

There was no more. His father did not again shew signs of consciousness. A while later Matt gave a convulsive jerk and gasp, as though he had been struck heavily in the back; drew one short breath; and one more; and then there was silence. Jemmy stared, pressing the hand he still held. Surely that could not be all? He looked up at Clement, who shook his head, but Jemmy could not believe it, and stared into his father's face, willing him to breathe again. He could not be gone, not just like that, so simply between one second and another, leaving without saying goodbye. But Pask and Clement had slipped down onto their knees, and Jemmy felt a terrible sense of loss and abandonment wash over him. I am Master now, he thought, and the idea was grief and loneliness. His father was gone, and Jemmy was the ultimate authority, and he wished passionately that he could tell his father that he understood now. It was too late ever to make up to Matt for all the love he had never given him.

A little while later the doctor arrived, and then Father Andrews, who unluckily had been visiting a sick weaver in the village. The priest laid a hand on Jemmy's shoulder and spoke to him comfortingly.

'It's all right. I have heard his confession daily,

and I can give him the last rites now, while his spirit is still hovering near. It will be all right, don't worry.' He busied himself with his impedimenta, and Jemmy, feeling suddenly in the way, wandered out into the corridor. A number of servants were gathered there, their faces sombre, and at the sight of Jemmy's face they crossed themselves, and one or two sank to their knees to pray for Matt's soul. And then Mary arrived in a flurry of skirts from the nursery wing. Her face was white, her eyes wide.

'They have just told me your father is ill,' she cried before she took in the scene, and came to a halt, her hands rising to clasp each other at her breast. Through the open bedroom door she saw the priest bending over the bed, saw Clement and Pask still kneeling in prayer, and then her eyes came back to Jemmy. 'He's dead?' Jemmy nodded. She stared for a moment, and then her face hardened. Why didn't you send for me?' she cried. Jemmy shook his head vaguely.

'I – didn't think,' he muttered. 'There wasn't time.' She stared for a moment longer, and then whirled around and ran back the way she had come.

There was a great deal to be done. The women who had laid out Sabina so recently came to do their work, to wash and bind and dress the Master, and the estate carpenter and his mate hastily knocked together a temporary coffin and a trestle on which to stand it in the chapel. The black cloth, embroidered with the Morland arms, was got out to cover the bier, and by dusk James Matthias Morland was lying in state in the chapel with candles burning all around him and the first of the watchers kneeling in prayer at his head and foot.

Jemmy spent the rest of the day giving orders and writing letters. People had to be told, friends, family and tenants; mourning had to be arranged – fortunately, if one could use such a word at such a time, the mourning livery made for Sabina's death could be used again, and the lower servants only needed weepers. Dark drapes for the windows, black hangings for the beds. Arrangements for the funeral, the feast, the procession, the doles, the flags, the guests to be asked, Pobgee, the lawyer, sent for. There was no dinner that day, for Jacob the cook was so grief-stricken that he let the fire go out, and Jemmy did not go into the dining room for supper – what there was of it. Clement brought him bread and cold meat and wine, in the steward's room, and he stared at it in amazement, and said he could eat nothing. But he was thirsty, and drank the wine, a little watered, and then found he was savagely hungry, and cleared the tray. The household routine was going on, albeit a little dazedly. Fires and candles were lit, and the house bell was rung to signal that the outer gates were about to be shut. And like an echo came back the sound of Great Paul, the tenor bell of St Stephen's in the village, ringing the nine tailors for the passing of a man, and then forty-one single strokes, one for each year of Matt's life.

Jemmy thought again about that one, slender, unremarkable second that had divided the forty-one years from the rest of eternity. Time to go to the chapel: instead of the normal evening prayers, there would be prayers for the dead, and tonight there would be no absentees.

As was only right, Jemmy took the first watch, from eight until midnight, and Charles asked to take it with him. When they were relieved, Jemmy was so exhausted he hardly said goodnight before dragging himself up the chapel stairs, the short way to the bedchamber. To his surprise, he found the candle still burning, and Mary sitting up reading, evidently waiting for him.

He had not seen her all day, since that one moment outside his father's room; seeing her now reminded him of that moment, and he relived the reality of his father's death, and the loneliness. He was glad she had waited up for him. His heart suddenly warmed to her for understanding that he would need comforting. They had not been close of late, but perhaps now they might make a new start, now that they were Master and Mistress of Morland Place, and would need each other all the more.

'Mary,' he said gently, 'you waited up for me—'

She turned to look at him, and he saw that her eyes were red with weeping, but also that they were angry.

'There did not seem to be any other way that I could get to speak to you,' she said harshly. 'I have sometimes wondered whether it would not be better for me to write you a letter from time to time. It might be quicker to trust to the post boy than to hope to pass you in the house somewhere.'

Jemmy frowned, puzzled. What was it she was saying? Was she angry with him? What had he done? 'I have been busy all day, you must know that. There were so many things to be done—'

'Things which, of course, only you could do,' she said.

'Well, yes – I could hardly leave them to a servant,' Jemmy said. Mary's mouth set in a grimmer line.

'And it did not occur to you to trust any of them to your wife,' she said sarcastically. Jemmy's mouth opened but she did not wait for him to speak. 'But of course, you find it very difficult to remember that you have a wife, don't you? If anyone had challenged you to say what I was wearing today, would you have been able to answer?'

'Mary, on such a day—'

'On any day! I wonder if you would even be able to describe what I look like? After all, you never see me. On some days I do not speak one word to you – no, not one word, not even, "Good-day, Master Morland", "Goodday, Mrs Morland".' She performed a parody of a bow and curtsey. 'No, it's all too easy for you to forget that you are married. Or that you have a child. When did you last see the baby? I'll wager you cannot remember.'

'I can,' Jemmy said, stung. 'It was – it was yesterday.'

'It was not yesterday or the day before, or the day before that. It was on Monday, when the nurse brought him down to the drawing room and you happened to look in because you had forgot your pen-knife. Nurse presented him to you, and you looked at him and gave him back very quickly, as if he were a snake.'

'As I remember, he began to cry as soon as I came near him—' Jemmy said in self-justification. Mary reddened.

'Of course he did! You are a stranger to him. Do you know, when your father picks him up he smiles—' She stopped abruptly as she realized what tense she had used of the verb. Tears filled her eyes. 'Your father loved him. He never cried when your father was near.'

'Clement told me today that my father used to visit the nursery,' Jemmy said gently. 'I had no idea before—'

'You knew nothing of your father, just as you know nothing of your son,' Mary cried angrily. 'Jemmy was good enough for Jemmy. Nothing in the world was so fascinating as the life and concerns of James Edward Morland. Your father came up to the nursery every day, sometimes twice. He and I used to walk and talk in the garden, and in the evenings I would play to him, or he would read to me while I sewed. All this you knew nothing of, because you were too interested in yourself. And today, today when he lay dying, *you did not even send word to me!*' Tears sprang from her eyes in a painful burst. 'I had to wait until one of the servants told me in passing, and when I got there it was too late. He died alone, because you did not call for me.'

'He was not alone. I was there,' Jemmy expostulated.

'That was as good as alone. What use were you to him – you never cared for him at all!' She was weeping with sorrow and rage, and the tears clotted in her throat and made her gasp. Jemmy went to her and took hold of her arms and she struggled against him.

'I did love him, Mary, you're wrong,' He said. 'He was *my* father, after all. I never had a mother, and he was everything to me. He was never an easy man to know. You have only seen him in his mellower years. When he died, I felt – I felt—' He swallowed. 'I was glad when I saw you were still up. I thought you could comfort me.'

Mary beat ineffectually at his chest, gasping against her sobs for the words. 'I – comfort *you*! You think only of yourself! Who is to comfort *me*?' He still held her, and she stopped struggling, exhausted, and he gathered her into his arms. She did not resist, but her body was brittle to him. 'You are a selfish, selfish, callous, hateful creature,' she wept. 'I wish I could divorce you. Maybe I will. Maybe I will ask my brother.'

'You know that is not possible,' Jemmy said.

'Not possible – no!' she flared up again, and with a sudden access of strength thrust herself away from him. 'Because you need my protection, you and your family, Jacobite traitors that you are! But we shall see what my brother says when I tell him. I'll not sleep with a traitor again, that's for sure!'

And she ran towards the door. Jemmy, stinging from her words, caught her in two strides and whirled her away from the door, and as his grasp slipped she staggered across the room and fell against the bed. For a moment they were both silent, aghast, and then Mary began struggling up.

'How dare you!' she hissed. 'How dare you handle me thus. Do you forget who I am?'

But now Jemmy, too, was angry. 'I remember well enough. You are my wife – and as you seem to have forgotten it, I will have to teach you.'

'Don't you dare to touch me,' she cried, but he seized her and flung her on her back across the bed. He had not intended anything in particular, but when he saw by the expression of her face what she expected him to do, he decided that was the only way to revenge himself on her for the things she had said that still smarted in his mind like new wounds.

'I'll touch you all I like,' Jemmy growled, climbing up after her. 'You forget your duties as a wife. You forget that I keep you here. I have been kind and patient with you – more than any other man would be – let you have your own way – but now I shall teach you who is dependent on whom.'

'Don't you dare touch me!' Mary cried again, struggling madly. 'I am—'

'I know who you are – no one ever has a chance to forget that! Ever since you came here you have treated us all like beggars, sneering at us as if it was beneath you to eat at the same table. But I tell you, you cold, proud bitch, that my forefathers bore a coat of arms when yours were cattlegraziers. You may despise me, but I can tell you I am just as sorry to be wed to you as ever you can be.'

He began to drag up her bedgown, and she struggled like a lunatic, trying to kick and even bite him, in such a rage that she had no fear. But she was a small and undersized woman, and Jemmy was tall for a man, and had no difficulty in pinning her down.

'I'll kill you for this!' she gasped. 'I'll poison you!'

'You can try,' Jemmy snarled. 'One look from you would sour the milk.'

In the silence, Mary began to weep quietly. Jemmy heard the sound, and it wrenched at his heart. He lay as if dazed, appalled at what he had done, at what had been said on both sides.

'Mary – Mary – I'm sorry,' he whispered. 'Please don't cry. I'm so sorry. It was – like a kind of madness.' The steady weeping went on. He eased himself from her, and she gasped with pain and wept the louder. 'Did I hurt you? Oh God, I never meant – I don't know what came over me.'

'I'll kill you for this,' she said again, but the voice was heartbroken, not angry. He stroked her hair off her face, and she tried to jerk her head away from him. 'Don't touch me, you brute.'

136

'I've never done anything like that before,' he said gently, puzzled. 'I'm not like that – anyone would tell you so. I don't know what came over me. You made me angry—' At such a time, too, when his father was lying dead in the chapel below them, only a few yards away. Mary turned away from him, hunched over on her side, and wept into the pillow, and Jemmy lay still and did not speak or try to touch her until he heard the weeping slow and ease. Then he pulled out his handkerchief and reached over and thrust it into her fingers. He got up, careful not to touch her, and undressed himself on the far side of the bed, put on his bedgown and got into bed. He leaned across and gently pulled the covers from under her, straightened her bedgown and covered her up. She was quiet now, still hunched away from him, making no sound.

'Do you want a little wine?' he said as tenderly as he could. She made a small, negative sound. He brushed the hair from her face and settled the covers around her shoulders, and she let him do it, quiescent like a child exhausted from a storm of weeping.

'Sleep, then,' he said. 'I'm sorry, Mary. I will be good to you, I promise. I'll never hurt you again.'

He blew out the candle and settled down, but though he was tired, he could not sleep. He thought that Mary had fallen asleep, but after a while she said quietly into the darkness, 'From tomorrow, I want my own bedchamber. I do not want to sleep with you ever again.'

Jemmy sighed. 'If that's what you want,' he said, believing she would change her mind in the morning. A night's sleep, he hoped, would diminish the outrage in both their minds. After all, it could not really be termed a rape, could it, when they were man and wife?

All Jemmy's brothers came home for Matt's funeral. Tom was still with Captain Wentworth, had transferred with him from the old *Agrippa* into the *Laconia*, and as she was lying at Portsmouth, still being refitted, Tom was able to get leave without much trouble to travel up to Yorkshire. Charles and Allen were overjoyed to see their old playmate again, and Jemmy was interested to see the change and improvement in him. He had filled out, though he was no taller, and had a dignified, manly bearing that suited him, and an air of authority which mingled pleasantly with the humour in his bright blue eyes. His face was very much tanned, and at first he had difficulty in pitching his voice low enough for the drawing room, but otherwise he was not obviously the sailor. He had done well in the *Agrippa*, as was proved by Captain Wentworth's thinking so highly of him as to take him with him on his new commission; and Tom evidently thought well of Captain Wentworth, by the number of times that name came up in his conversation. He had twice seen action, and though it was but against guarda-costas of inferior force, the boys were wild to hear about it. As soon as the formal greeting had been exchanged, Charles and Allen towed Tom off to the old schoolroom to hear his adventures.

George was by this time home from Christ Church permanently. He had done his time at University, but had not taken his degree, which marked him out for a gentleman. While at University he had learned a great deal about wine and cards and clothes, and the pedigrees and future incomes of all his contemporaries at Christ Church, and he had summed up his University career with the sentiment 'that Oxford had been well enough, but he was glad to be back home, because the hunting was so much better in Yorkshire'.

Robert, of course, had only to come from his living, which was but five miles away. Indeed, he had never been averse to exchanging his own house for Morland Place at any invitation, and it seemed to Jemmy that the only thing that had ever tempted him to dine at his own table was the dislike of his father, which Matt had never troubled to hide. He came in complaining mood.

'How can one live even tolerably like a gentleman on such a pitiful income? What an irony to call it a living! Well, a poor parson who keeps a pig and tills his garden for beans and cabbages might possibly just scratch through, provided he were as hardy as a farm labourer. The house is as small as a coffin, and needs so much doing to it to make it habitable that I cannot tell where to begin. The tithe is pitiful, and my income so small that by the time I have paid the servants' wages and keep, and the keep of my horse, there is nothing left over for my own food and drink. Indeed, my servants live better than I do, since I am obliged to buy them new clothes every year. I cannot remember when last *I* had a new coat.'

He was so determinedly cross that Jemmy did not like to point out that the wages of Robert's manservant, Pardric, had always been paid from Morland Place, or that his horse had been a gift from Matt, or that Robert had had all his oats and hay from Morland Place for nothing by the simple expedient of ordering the head lad at Twelvetrees, in Davey's absence, to send it over. When Edmund arrived, Robert needed all his determination to be heard, for Edmund was even more complaining than he had been, and waxed almost lyrical about the iniquities of the army system.

'It's all very well for the colonel, indeed,' Edmund concluded. 'There's no end to the ways *he* can make money, what with the bounties for recruiting, and dealing with army contractors, and the men's clothing, and rationing. Our colonel has even worked out a way to make money out of the men that fall sick – he doses them himself, and charges them for his own patent medicines.' His voice was filled with admiration for the colonel for having thought of it, but then it sank back into discontent at the contemplation of his own plight. 'But for a poor ensign, all he can hope for is what he can scrape off the men's billeting allowances, and there, by my cursed luck, I have to be

140

stationed at one of the only three barracks in the country, so there's no billeting allowance to be scraped! And the Tower is the devil of a place to live, not even the most primitive comforts, and so far from the Court, where one might at least shew one's face and gain a little credit, that it might as well be in China. If it weren't for what I have managed to make at dice and cards, I should not be here now, for the food is nothing short of poison, so one has to have it sent in from cookshops as often as possible, just to keep body and soul together,' he said pathetically.

Jemmy regarded the handsome beginnings of a paunch filling out Edmund's breeches and forbore to comment. 'I wonder you can bear it, brother,' he said.

'Well, I have worked out one scheme,' Edmund admitted. 'I let the men who are due a flogging buy themselves off for a lighter punishment. That has worked quite well. But then, they do not always do anything one can flog them for; and their pay is so pitiful that sometimes they cannot afford to buy themselves off, once the senior officers have been over them. You can't shear the same sheep twice. And whatever I do manage to get, all goes on my own expenses day to day. At that rate, with commissions the price they are, I shall never save enough. I shall die the oldest ensign in the army,' he concluded gloomily.

With Robert and Edmund complaining endlessly, George alternately eating and sleeping, and Tom

141

always away somewhere with Charles and Allen, Jemmy found himself more than ever alone. Mary had not changed her mind, and they now had separate rooms. She treated him with perfect politeness whenever they met, which was not often, and the only thing he seemed to have to be grateful for was that she evidently had not told Lady Dudley about his brutality towards her, for if she had, Jemmy was sure Lady Dudley would have had plenty to say to him about it. Davey, who had often been a friend to Jemmy, had been gloomy and morose since Matt's death, for he and Matt had grown up together, and Matt had been Davey's only friend in the world. Jemmy had kept on his father's servant Pask to be his own valet in place of Jack, but Pask was still too young, too shy, and too upset over his master's death to be a companion to Jemmy.

His only comfort had come from Shawes. The Countess had sent a very kind letter as soon as she had heard about Matt's death, a letter extolling Matt's many virtues and ignoring his shortcomings, and speaking of her lifelong acquaintance with him and affection for him. Matt was, of course, the only child of the Countess's daughter Arabella, and the Countess had been present at his birth, and for some time after the disappearance of his mother and the exile of his father she had been Matt's sole guardian and protectress. The letter spoke of how much Matt would be missed, and hinted at how isolated Jemmy must feel. Such informed sympathy was exactly what Jemmy needed, and though he had not often been able to get away from Morland Place since his father's death, he had paid one or two informal visits to Shawes, where the warm understanding of Annunciata, the calm kindness of Alessandra, and the imperious adoration of Marie-Louise, had warmed him a little, and suggested that life might still be worth living.

Pobgee, the lawyer, was a small man, so unfashionably slender that one might have thought he was unsuccessful in his profession, had not his clothes spoken of a degree of elegance that only a rich and successful man could have sustained. He eschewed any appearance of business, or even busyness, wearing an enormous full-bottomed wig, rather than the tie-wig or even pigtail-wig that was more usual amongst professional men, and travelling in a coach rather than on horseback, as if to emphasize his leisure. He always assumed that his reputation would go before him, and as it rested largely on charging higher fees than anyone else, it generally did. He was, however, a keen racing man, and Jemmy had known him for many years, for he had a small but select stable of horses, many of which came from Twelvetrees, and he gambled enormously but often successfully. He also had a fine nose for claret, and it was after an excellent meal which he praised lavishly that they gathered the family together in the drawing room at Morland Place to disclose the secrets of Matt's will.

'The will is essentially a very simple document,'

he said after a preamble on his friendship with, and admiration for, the late James Matthias Morland of Morland Place in the County of Yorkshire and Emblehope Manor in the County of Northumberland. 'There are a number of small bequests to servants and pensioners, a pension payable for life to Davey Shepherd, in acknowledgement of a lifetime of friendship and service. There is an amount of money set aside for a memorial in the chapel and commemorative gifts to various churches, and a bequest to St Edmund's School and Hospital.'

Pobgee's eye gathered up the attention of his audience with an actor's skill. Robert was sitting very upright on a hard chair by the door, looking bored; Mary and Lady Dudley were in the fireside chairs like two heraldic supporters, rigid and unbending; Edmund was lounging against the chimney-wall looking peevish; Charles, Tom and Allen were seated in a row on the windowseat looking expectant; George was in a comfortable chair looking somnolent; Jemmy and Father Andrews were seated on the sofa, Jemmy looking tired and the priest anxious.

'Apart from those small matters,' Pobgee continued, 'James Matthias Morland leaves all his property, whatsoever and wheresoever situated, entirely and without condition to his son, James Edward.'

There was a moment's silence, and then Robert cried out in disbelief, 'What, all of it?'

'All of it,' Pobgee said gently, 'unconditionally.' He

seemed to be enjoying the situation. Jemmy heard the words without shock. Somehow it did not surprise him, though he foresaw endless trouble for himself because of it. Edmund had jumped to his feet.

'Surely he has made some provision for us?' he said, and waved his hand vaguely as if to indicate his brothers. 'He must have mentioned some part of the estate to be divided amongst his other sons? Or some money set aside for our advancement. Damn it, sir, commissions cost dear these days!'

'I beg your pardon, sir,' Pobgee said, ever more gently, 'but you and your brothers are not mentioned at all, neither by name or by implication. The only one of his children mentioned is James Edward.' He nodded politely towards Jemmy, who bowed automatically in response. Now Robert was on his feet too.

'It's outrageous! It cannot be so! Am I to understand, sir, that you allowed my father to draw up this unspeakable travesty of justice, that you actually aided him in the perpetration of this – this—' He was lost for words.

Pobgee replied mildly, 'The document is perfectly legal, sir, I do assure you, and the property was his to dispose of as he wished. It would have been most improper for me to have expressed any views upon it – indeed, to *have* any views upon it – other than those concerning its legal viability.'

'He must have been insane,' Edmund now said,

having thought his way through everything else. 'When was this will drawn up?'

'Some four years ago,' Pobgee said. Edmund looked towards Robert.

'He was already ill then, was he not, brother? The nature of his illness was no secret to the doctor who attended him. He will testify that it was a painful illness. No doubt my father was deranged by the pain he suffered, and it was because of such derangement that he drew up such an insane disposition.'

'The will, sir, reflects his wishes as they have been fixed for many years,' Pobgee said, standing his ground like an expert fencer parrying the thrusts of a pair of overeager schoolboys. 'This document is the last in a series of wills I have drawn up over the years for your late father, and I assure you it does not differ materially from any of its predecessors.'

Now Robert sniffed a different trail. 'The latest, you say? But how do you know that, sir? You say it was drawn up four years ago – ample time for my father to have changed his mind and made a new and fairer disposition.'

They had forgotten already, Jemmy thought dully, that they had agreed he was insane. Edmund grasped eagerly at the straw. 'Yes, of course, that must be it.'

'There is no other will bearing a later date,' Pobgee asserted. Robert sneered.

'However eminent you are, sir, you are not the only lawyer in England. My father might well have asked a different man of your profession to aid him. Someone from London, no doubt.'

'Yes, of course, a London lawyer,' Edmund echoed.

'But why should he do that?' Mary said, startling everyone by her unexpected entry into the argument. Robert was not halted.

'He knew Pobgee's views on the matter, and did not wish to have to argue with him.'

'As I have already mentioned, sir, I could have no views on such a subject. But in any case, I have, as a matter of normal business, checked that there is no other disposition lodged with any other man of law. I should have done that in any case. You do not have to take my word for it, however. The will has to be proved before it can be enacted, and I think you will find yourself satisfied by the process.'

'I will never be satisfied,' Robert said, glaring at him. Father Andrews intervened.

'Gentlemen, please, do not wrangle in such a manner and at such a time. And remember, I pray you, that Master Pobgee is the instrument and not the instigator.' Pobgee bowed his thanks to the priest. Jemmy had had enough of hearing his father abused. He had not forgotten Mary's accusations, and knew how far short he had fallen in love and duty to Matt, and he felt guilty about it, and deeply regretted there was no means of redress now available. But if he was guilty, how much more so were Robert and Edmund. It enraged him to hear them and see them. The younger boys merely sat quietly and listened; Allen, of course, had had nothing to hope for from the will, and Tom and Charles, being the youngest, could not have hoped for much. George was probably not even listening: his eyes were half closed, and he seemed to be pursuing the last of his dinner around his teeth with his tongue and a forefinger. They were probably all indifferent about the late master, and it seemed that was the best Matt could ever have hoped for. It was Robert and Edmund that Jemmy addressed.

'You know why the will is the way it is,' he said harshly. Father Andrews made a movement of his hand as if to restrain Jemmy, but Jemmy ignored it. 'You know that because of our mother's frailties—'

'I don't think this is the time to speak of them,' Father Andrews said quickly. Jemmy shook his head.

'She broke his heart. Great-grandmother says she ruined his temper too, that before he found out about our mother he was a kind and happy person. Well, that wasn't our fault, but we all know what he thought, how he felt about us. At first he did not regard any of us as his children. Eventually he came to accept that I was his son.'

'Really, sir, I hardly think—' Lady Dudley began. This time it was Mary who interposed. She simply lifted her hand towards her companion and said, 'Madam, be silent.'

Jemmy shot her a look of surprised gratitude, and went on. 'It is not for my virtue I am chosen as heir, nor for your demerits you are excluded. It is simply a reflection of my father's beliefs about our parentage. The Morland fortune was his to leave as he wished, and he wished to leave it all to me.'

'Of course, you would be bound to agree with him,' Robert said nastily. Jemmy looked angrily at him.

'It doesn't matter what I think or want. As a matter of fact, in many ways I would much rather not be the inheritor, except that I know I will make a better Master for Morland Place than you would. But it is not my wishes that signify.'

'You don't know what my father wanted. You only know he left everything to you,' Robert said. 'Perhaps he meant you to divide it up, so that we could all have a share. As he died suddenly, there is no knowing, is there?'

'After all,' Edmund added, 'he did not leave the estate entailed, did he?'

'Just before he died,' Jemmy said, 'my father regained consciousness for a few moments. He called me to him, and made me promise something.'

'Promise what?' Robert asked.

'I could not understand all of it. It was hard to hear him. But he did say very clearly the words 'Do not break up'. The rest was indistinguishable, but in the light of this will, I believe he asked me to promise not to break up the estate. And I shall not do so.'

'We'll contest the will,' Robert said angrily.

'Do so if you wish,' Jemmy said indifferently. 'Pobgee will advise you whether it is worth doing so.'

And Pobgee shook his head gently. 'There are one or two things I should like to discuss with you,' he added to Jemmy, 'if we could obtain a measure of privacy? If the ladies would excuse us?'

'Of course. We'll go to the steward's room,' Jemmy said, and the meeting broke up. Jemmy led the lawyer to the steward's room in silence, and once safely inside with the door shut, he asked, 'Master Pobgee, you probably knew my father's mind better than any of us. What do *you* suppose his wishes were?'

'I cannot say that I knew your father well. There must be others who knew him better. But in the matter of the estate, I think I understood his wishes, and they were just as you supposed. I am sure that you have interpreted his last words correctly. His desire was that the Morland Estate should pass wholly into the hands of a Morland, and that no part of it should go to the sons of his late wife whom he did not believe to be of his blood.' He paused reflectively, and went on, 'I did not mention it in the drawing room as the atmosphere was already rather, shall we say, explosive, but there is a residuary clause in the will. In the event that you had died before your father, the provision was that the whole estate should have passed to John McNeill, Viscount Ballincrea. As the grandson of his sister Sabine, McNeill was his nearest Morland kin, after you.'

It was not until much later, when Jemmy was alone and able to think collectedly, that he realized the lawyer was wrong. His father, too, had been wrong, for he was acting on insufficient information. After Jemmy himself, assuming that Jemmy's brothers were excluded, Matt's nearest kin had been Aliena, his half-sister, and after Aliena, her daughter Marie-Louise. It gave him pause for thought. If he were to follow his father's wishes, as he intended to, he must not break up the estate to provide for his brothers; but Marie-Louise, ah, that was different!

CHAPTER 6

When they reached Ten Thorn Gap, Jemmy split off from the rest of the hunting party in order to escort Marie-Louise and Allen to Shawes. It had not been a particularly good hunt, for the snow was deep and crisp on the ground, and the air too cold for scent under a brilliant dark-blue sky, but after having been confined to the house by the falling of that same snow, everyone had been too glad to get out of doors to care much. The sun was distant and bright, and now that it was well up, Jemmy could feel just a little heat from it when he turned his face up to its rays. The whiteness was everywhere, relieved from monotony by the deep blue of its shadows and the stark black where snow-slips had revealed dark branches underneath; and by the bright colours of the hunting-party and their horses and hounds. Jemmy smiled as he pushed Auster to catch up with the children, for Marie-Louise was the brightest spot of colour in the landscape. Her riding habit was of deep crimson cloth trimmed with grey squirrel-fur; Annunciata had designed it herself, basing it from memory on the habit the Dauphine had given to Marie-Louise's namesake and aunt, the Princess Louise-Marie, at St Germaine. Marie-Louise wore her wide-brimmed, grey beaver hat tilted well forward, shewing her glossy auburn ringlets gathered to the back of her head, with the long white ostrich feather curling round them like a cat's tail.

She was as pretty a sight as could be imagined, Jemmy thought, and he noticed that Allen could not take his eyes off her. Just before Christmas Jemmy had conceived the idea that Allen and Marie-Louise ought to be brought up together and share their lessons under Father Renard, and he had approached Annunciata about it.

'You see, I notice a great difference between my brothers who were brought up by Father Renard from a young age, and those who had less of his influence,' he said, 'and though I have nothing but good to say of Allen's temperament, I should like him to have the same education as I did.' Annunciata had nodded judiciously and, encouraged, Jemmy had continued, 'Besides, now Tom and Charlie are grown up, it must be lonely for Allen. He and the Princess are about the same age, and would be company for each other. I think it would do him good to be around someone lively. He is a fine boy, but tends to be rather solemn. And it would do Marie-Louise good to have a little competition.'

'I have nothing to say against that,' Annunciata laughed. 'But would he provide competition? Would he not rather become her unquestioning admirer

153

and slave? She does not, emphatically, need more adulation.'

Jemmy cocked his head. 'He is quiet, but he is very clever, and very determined in his own way. Naturally he will admire her beauty – who could not? – but I don't think he will allow a girl younger than him to put upon him.'

Annunciata said doubtfully, 'I don't know. Marie-Louise has a way of – but there, I see in your eye another plan suggesting itself, you wicked boy. You are thinking that it would be no bad thing for the children to grow so accustomed to each other that they cannot do other in adulthood than wed.'

Jemmy smiled sheepishly. 'Well, it would be no such bad thing, would it? He is a well-born and well-principled boy – all he lacks is money.'

'Which she has in plenty,' Annunciata finished for him. 'And do you think I should consider him a good enough match for a girl who will not only inherit a large estate but is a Countess in her own right?'

'I should have thought, great-grandmother, that you would have lived long enough by now to have changed your views of what constituted a good match.' Jemmy went cold when he had said it, for it came close to being insolent, and was a criticism of Annunciata on many deeply personal levels.

For a moment there was an ominous silence, but then she said only, 'I see you have not lived long enough to learn to curb your tongue.'

At all events, she had agreed to the scheme, and Allen had gone with some apprehension to take his lessons at Shawes, and had very soon come to like it. He was a very quick and intelligent boy, and soon came to admire Father Renard deeply, in a way that was impossible for him with the less intellectual Father Andrews. Marie-Louise quickly went through a variety of behaviours from haughtiness to petulance, but finding that Allen was a true challenge to her in their lessons, and that while he adored her from first sight, he would not be put upon, she soon settled down. Father Andrews was glad to be released from the task of teaching Allen, who was now frequently asking him questions he could not answer, and to have more time for his numerous other duties. Apart from that, Mary's baby, Thomas, was approaching two-years-old, and almost ready to come into the schoolroom; and now it seemed there was to be another addition, for Mary was pregnant again.

She had told him at Christmas, had come to him abruptly one morning when he was alone in the steward's room working on the play for Twelfth Night. Looking up at the sound of the door being shut rather hard, he had noticed that she looked unusually pale, and that her lips were set in a grim line.

'Madam, are you unwell?' he said, getting up quickly to go to her, in case she fainted. Fand, who had been lying by the fire, was as usual circling her knees in delight, jabbing at her hand with his muzzle.

She caressed the dog automatically as Jemmy came to her. 'Please, won't you sit down? May I get you some wine?'

'No,' she said comprehensively. 'I have come to tell you – tell you—' She swallowed, and then blurted out the words, 'I am with child again.' Jemmy did not at first know quite how to react, but it was the accusatory tone that warned him. He composed his features into a neutral gravity and said only, 'I see.'

'You see,' she almost snarled. 'Yes, you see now the consequences of your actions – consequences that I have to bear.'

'Madam, I am sorry that you are unhappy, and more than sorry that the child should have been conceived in the way it was; but marriage means childbearing, and you cannot surely have expected that Thomas would remain your only child.'

'I know not to expect anything pleasurable from my life,' Mary said bitterly, and Jemmy was suddenly piercingly sorry for her. He tried to take her hand, and though she pulled it away he took it again and held it. It was very cold and very small. He said gently.

'Mary, I am truly sorry that you are unhappy. It is not my desire to make anyone unhappy, much the least my own wife. You and I have been brought together against our will for the sake of duty, and part of that duty is to have children.'

'An easy duty for you! The pains are all mine.' She pulled her hand away from him. Jemmy shrugged.

'That is true, but there is nothing that I can do about that, is there?' he said reasonably. She looked at him for the first time.

'I suppose not,' she said unwillingly.

'When is the bairn due?' he asked.

'The end of June. You could work that out for yourself,' she said sharply.

'Yes, of course,' he said contritely. 'Well, well.' There was an awkward silence, and then Jemmy said, 'Mary, if there is anything that you want, or anything I can do for you, I will try to arrange it for you. Please try not to be unhappy. We are married, come what may, and we have to try to make the best of it.'

'The best you can do for me is to leave me alone,' she said, turning to go; but at least she did not speak sharply or angrily. Jemmy caught back Fand as he went to follow her, and thought that a first step, be it ever so small, had been taken.

As they approached Shawes, Fand, who had been trotting behind Jemmy to take advantage of Auster's footprints, suddenly rushed off to one side in a series of huge leaps, barking joyfully, and looking round. Jemmy saw Annunciata also approaching her own house on horseback, with her maid Charley and her man John behind her.

'You look surprised, Jemmy,' the Countess said when they were near enough. 'Did you think you were the only one to crave fresh air after these storms?'

157

'Of course not, but I wonder that you did not come with us, or even mention it.'

'I am too old to enjoy the sort of hunt you would have had this morning,' Annunciata said, falling in beside him. Her horse Phoenix touched noses with Auster and then jerked his head away, making the coral and ivory decorations on his bridle clink and ring. 'With such scent as there would have been, you must have spent more time standing around near the coverts than running. Ah, child, don't look so surprised! I have spent a lifetime hunting. I can judge the scent better than your huntsman, I warrant you. The arrogance of the young! You think the world was new-made the day you were born! Marie-Louise, the riding has given you a fine colour at least. Ride on ahead, children, and see that the grooms know we are coming, and send word that I will have a pot of chocolate waiting for me by the hall fire.'

Marie-Louise and Allen kicked their ponies into a canter, and Jemmy checked Auster, who thought that was a much better idea than pacing through the snow at walking-speed.

'Well, and so what had you to tell me?' Annunciata said to Jemmy when they had gone. Jemmy raised an eyebrow. 'It was not at all necessary for you to accompany the children, was it.'

Jemmy smiled. 'The will is proved. I had word from Pobgee this morning.'

'Ah! And so you are now Master of Morland Place, and all Robert's machinations were in vain.'

'Robert's and Edmund's,' Jemmy said. He frowned and turned a lock of Auster's mane back the right way. 'Great-grandmother, do you think I was wrong? Sometimes I wonder if I did what I did through greed. After all, my father did not leave the property entailed.'

'It is much too late to begin doubting, Jemmy,' Annunciata said. 'Besides, you must look back at the history of Morland Place before you judge. It never has been entailed, but generation after generation, the Master has passed it on intact. It has never been divided, and even the Northumberland estate has been given away only for the lifetime of the recipient, to return to the Master on his death. Matt was doing what everyone has done before.'

'But my brothers—'

'You know what your father felt about them.'

'Yes. But whether or not they were kin to my father, they are without a doubt my brothers.'

Annunciata smiled. 'The blood is more surely passed through the female. My mother took the precaution of having only one daughter, and no husband to confuse matters. She left the property to me. I will do the same. Worries about the male line are needless complications. But what of your brothers? Surely it is only Robert and Edmund who are troublesome, and they already have their careers. I am sure Matt intended them to get on by their own exertions. Robert ought to be able to do that. He learned the art early in life, and I hear he dined with the bishop only last week.'

'Yes, but for Edmund it is more difficult. Commissions have to be purchased, and I do not know where he will get together the money to do that.'

'There are ways,' Annunciata said soothingly. 'Court sinecures, for one thing. Your brother-in-law ought to be able to help there. And long nights at the Groom Porter's – if Edmund is any hand at gambling, he will make his fortune. But what of the others?'

'Tom came to me before he left to rejoin his ship, to say he thought I was quite right, and that he was very happy in the navy and would make his own way. At least in the navy one can get on by merit, and his captain thinks the world of him.'

'A little patronage you know, never goes amiss. There I may be able to help. Through Prince Rupert and King James I learned a great deal about the navy, and Berkeley, the First Lord, is a friend of mine. But what are you going to do with Charles? It is time that boy went away from home. How old is he now?'

'Eighteen.'

'Then you must get him a career, or send him to University. I do not think that would be against your father's wishes; he did as much for the others.'

'I have spoken to him, and he wants to go to University. When he was ill, that time, with the lung fever, he got very interested in plants, you know—'

'Yes, I know,' Annunciata said with a quiet smile.

'Well, it seems a regular interest with him, and

160

he says now that he would like to study botany at University.'

'Oxford?' Annunciata said with a frown. She was not aware that anyone studied botany at University – or, indeed, studied anything. But three years or so at Oxford were important to a young man in developing his taste and acquainting him with the right people amongst his contemporaries.

'No, Edinburgh,' Jemmy said. 'Yes, I was surprised, too, but it seems that Charles has been corresponding with James Sherard, you know, who has the garden at Eltham that everyone talks about; and Sherard advised him to go to Edinburgh as they are much more advanced there, and much more serious minded.'

'*That* I can believe,' Annunciata nodded. 'But you know they are all presbyters and dissenters up there, very gloomy, savage people, devoted to their dreadful religions and with horrible manners.'

'Charles really does want to go,' Jemmy said, concealing a smile. 'He is quite determined. And you know, great-grandmother, a good upbringing can withstand most influences.'

'I hope you are right,' she said. 'But be sure to tell him to keep his religion secret, for I am sure they still hang Catholics north of the border. And tell him he must not on any account apostasize. If he feels at all tempted, he must come home at once, botany or no botany.'

They had reached the yard and a servant had come forward to take Phoenix's head.

'I will tell him, great-grandmother,' Jemmy said solemnly.

Annunciata dismounted and straightened her dress, and said, 'Come in, will you, and have some refreshment with me.'

'Thank you, but I must go home. Now I am Master, there is always so much for me to do.'

'What a poor liar you are. You have no more to do now than you had before Christmas. But be off with you. An old woman's company, I know, holds no charms.'

Jemmy smiled. 'May I dine with you tomorrow?'

'Perhaps,' she said loftily. Jemmy grinned and saluted, and turned Auster away. Annunciata called after him, 'George, what of George? We did not mention him. What will you do with George.'

'To be frank, I do not think there is anything one *can* do with George,' Jemmy replied. 'But he is very little trouble. Most of the time I do not even remember he is in the house.'

'That is exactly what I would expect of anyone with such a name,' Annunciata said with some satisfaction, and turned away towards the house.

Mary's baby, born in June 1726, was another boy. The birthing was not so easy this time, and Mary was rather ill afterwards, too ill to care about naming the baby, which was thus left to Jemmy. He named it Henry, after the second child born the year before to King James and Queen Clementina in Rome. He did it mainly to please Annunciata, whom he asked to be Godmother to the child. During Mary's illness, Marie-Louise took a great interest in the new baby, whom she insisted on pronouncing was named after 'my brother, the Prince'. Jemmy was worried that Annunciata seemed to encourage Marie-Louise in this sort of talk, and that it would lead her into trouble. Since the Atterbury Plot, Jemmy was fairly sure that the Countess had not been involved in any more Jacobite action or correspondence, but she seemed to be making up for it by being more and more openly Jacobite at home, where there was no longer even any pretence at drinking the health of King George rather than King James. Those in power in London might have decided that the Countess of Chelmsford at the age of eighty-one was no longer a threat to Hanoverian government, but Jemmy was not so sure what their reaction would be if they learned that the Countess's granddaughter was openly acknowledged as King James's bastard daughter.

The new baby flourished, and his older brother, now two, began his lessons with Father Andrews, and Mary recovered her health and strength and seemed delighted with both her children. Her relationship with Jemmy settled down into a distant politeness, although from habit they still did not share a bed, and his estate kept him so busy that he spent very little time in her company. As to his two children, his feelings were ambivalent towards them. He was glad that he had been provided with two legitimate heirs for Morland Place, and was happy to here them pronounced handsome, healthy children, but he felt completely detached from them, as if they were a neighbour's children and not his own. He generally saw them once a day, when they were brought to him for his blessing, and he would ask Thomas if he had been a good boy, and peer obediently into Henry's crumpled face to verify that his rash had disappeared, and as soon as they were taken away out of his sight, he forgot them as completely as if they did not exist.

His fatherly interest was much more involved in Marie-Louise's progress, and of the little leisure time he had, he spent a great deal, one way and another, at Shawes. His brothers were now all settled. Charles had gone to Edinbugh University, from which he sent regular letters speaking content. Robert continued to ingratiate himself within his profession, and at the end of 1726 he was able, by the favour of his bishop, to add another small benefice to his income, which pleased him so much he began to talk about looking for a wife.

At the beginning of 1727 Edmund's regiment was transferred to Hull, which meant that once again he was stationed in barracks, without the chance to make money from his men's billeting. He began to absent himself a great deal from duty, and when, on finding him always about the house like a discontented ghost, Jemmy asked if he was on leave, Edmund merely shrugged and said no one would miss him. It was clear that he, at least, was going to need further help, and Jemmy began to think of trying to purchase a lieutenancy for him, if only to get him out of the house.

Tom, on the other hand, evidently needed nothing more from Jemmy. He was made lieutenant in January 1727, and transferred into the *Veronica*, 75, flagship of the fleet that was to be sent to the Baltic as soon as the ice melted. Tom had done very well in his lieutenant's examination, passing with the highest marks of his group, and the difference between his career and Edmund's was sadly marked.

In June 1727 the Elector, George Lewis, left for his usual summer visit to Hanover, and there died, suddenly and unexpectedly, in July. His son George and Princess Caroline were at Richmond Palace at the time, but though Jacobites all over the country pricked up their ears and held themselves in readiness, nothing happened. Within days George and Caroline were installed safely in London as King and Queen, with the faithful Walpole in close attendance.

Karellie wrote to his mother that King James had set out at once for Lorraine, in readiness for the expected recall to his throne. After three weeks in Lorraine he was expelled, and travelled to Avignon, where he waited again, hoping for help from France.

But only the year before the seventy-three-year-old Fleury, former tutor of the young King Louis, had succeeded as first minister, and Fleury favoured peace with England. Maurice, as always lounging innocently around the new King and Queen Caroline, reported that George had written to Fleury demanding that James should be forcibly expelled, backing it up with similar demands of the Pope, who owned Avignon. In October they agreed, and King James was forced to return to Rome, the only place in the world where a home would be provided for him.

For Maurice, the change of kings meant only an increase of comfort, for now he did not have to divide his time between St James's and Leicester House, nor make himself agreeable to two men who were deadly enemies. George II continued and even increased the pension his father had paid Maurice. Although Maurice now had five children to support, he found himself better off than he had ever been, for there were no longer any Jacobite plots to draw the gold out of his breeches' pockets. For George II's coronation his friend Handel wrote an anthem, *Zadok the Priest*, and Maurice wrote a series of fanfares, for which both were amply rewarded; and in the same year Maurice had a new oratorio, *Magdalena*, performed at the Haymarket, and rewrote and revived on stage an early opera, *The Martyrdom of St Apollonia*, which took advantage of the upsurge of interest in Italian opera which followed the arrival of Buononcini in England.

Annunciata had been indifferent to the death of her cousin George Lewis, whom she had always disliked, but she had not considered that he was affording her protection until, shortly after the accession of George II, she found herself heavily fined for hearing the Catholic Mass, and her priest, Father Renard, imprisoned for saying it. Annunciata, like her forefathers, was an Anglo-Catholic, and except in times of severe persecution was left alone; but Aliena had been brought up a Roman Catholic, and Father Renard, though the Mass he spoke was a modified version, was a Roman Catholic priest. For a time the situation looked very unpleasant and even dangerous, until Maurice was able to come to her aid, by persuading Princess Caroline to point out to her husband that George Lewis had protected Annunciata only out of a sense of duty to his mother, and that he had actually always disliked her intensely. Father Renard was released from prison, and life at Shawes returned to normal.

In 1729 both Robert and Edmund got married. Robert's choice fell on the daughter of the rector of a parish north of York, a man who had developed pluralism to a fine art, and was therefore able to supply a very acceptable dowry and the promise of patronage to the man who was willing to wed his rather plain daughter. Rachel Goode was two years older than Robert, and had long resigned herself to spinsterhood, so the fact that Robert had only two small livings troubled her not at all. She pronounced herself delighted with the shabby rectory that Robert was offering her as her home, and was even more delighted when she discovered that her husband spent far more time at Morland Place than at Shelmet Rectory. Robert was also hoping for some kind of interest from the Countess at Shawes, who despite her Jacobite leanings seemed to know everyone. Rachel was more than willing to ingratiate herself with the Countess, but being more clear-sighted and much less conceited than her husband, she soon acknowledged to herself that Robert had less chance of succeeding at Shawes than he had of becoming a cardinal before he was thirty. The Countess openly mocked Robert: a married priest, she said, was an abomination, and that was that. She was, however, oddly kind to Rachel, who could not at all account for it. It was in fact for a wholly inconsequential reason, which Annunciata only admitted to her priest: that Rachel, tall, bony-faced and with coarse gingery hair, reminded Annunciata guiltily of her long-lost daughter Arabella.

Edmund was married towards the end of 1729 to one Augusta Pratt, the exceedingly pretty and empty-headed daughter of his colonel. Jemmy had bought Edmund a lieutenancy in '27, and part of Augusta's dowry was the offer of a captaincy at an attractively reduced price, which Edmund assured Jemmy he could not afford to miss. It seemed plain to Jemmy that Edmund could not afford to support Augusta on a lieutenant's income, and that if he did not want Edmund and his wife forever hanging around Morland Place, like Robert and *his* wife, he had better get him made a captain.

Meanwhile, Jemmy himself was becoming an important figure in York society, not least because of his involvement with the races. He had for a long time been unhappy with the site of the annual races, Clifton Ings, for being so close to the river the course was often swampy, and sometimes even flooded, and in 1730, when Robert and Rachel were preparing to have their first child born at Morland Place, Jemmy got together with one or two other interested parties to look for a more suitable site. Just outside the city, alongside the great south road, was a large stretch of open land called Micklegate Stray which was common grazing land. Part of the Stray, more or less opposite St Edward's School, was a bog called The Knavesmire, useless for any purposes other than cutting turves, and it was on this that their choice fell. It proved easy to drain, and was ready for the first race of that year's race-week.

Annunciata proposed holding the grand culminating ball at Shawes, which caused some unpleasantness, as several other ladies, including Mary, wanted to have the honour of holding the ball. The fact remained that Shawes had the biggest and best room available for such a social event, and that the long saloon at Morland Place was pitifully inadequate for an entertainment of any size.

'What we need,' Jemmy said to Annunciata, 'is a set of public assembly rooms, so that we could avoid this sort of rivalry. The Bourchiers will be bound to say they ought to hold the ball, but the fact is that Shawes is much nearer. If we had proper assembly rooms in York, there would be no question about it.'

'The answer, my dear, is simple,' Annunciata said. 'You must build some. The need has long been felt. Now you have the new race-course, you must have some proper rooms to go with it. Speak to them, Jemmy – strike while the iron is hot.'

So Jemmy got together with the same men and published a broadsheet, proposing the matter and pointing out the advantages. There was an immediate and enthusiastic response, and subscriptions began pouring in. For choice of architect, Jemmy naturally applied to Annunciata, who said that since dear Van was dead, the commission must go to her friend Burlington. He had designed the new building for the Girls Charity School of St James, of which Annunciata was a trustee, having taken over the interest from her former brother-in-law Clovis. Lord Burlington had been mightily impressed by the Palladian style which he had seen in Italy on his grand tour, and he had published Palladio's books in England and built himself a villa at Chiswick in the style. The design he drew up for the assembly rooms in York was based on Palladio's Egyptian Hall, and was distinguished by no fewer than forty-eight Corinthian columns supporting the frieze. The clearing of the site began at once, and it was hoped to have the building ready in two years.

★　　★　　★

In 1731 French troops occupied Lorraine under the command of those two old friends, the Marechal Duc de Berwick, and the Marechal Comte de Chelmsford, both aged sixty, the two tallest men in the French army. It was Berwick, the Bastard son of the late King James II of England, who wrote a few days later to inform the Countess Dowager at Shawes that her son had been killed in a minor skirmish at Commercy.

Annunciata had survived a great many things in the course of her long life, including trial for treason, long exile, and outliving seven of her ten children, but Karellie's death hit her hard, and she took to her bed in a state of shock and grief which Jemmy feared might kill her. He and Marie-Louise kept constant attendance on her, nursing her, talking to her, encouraging her to respond, but for many days she would only stare in misery at the wall, her hand clasped in Father Renard's as if she expected to be snatched away at any moment. But on the day two letters with royal seals came, she began to revive. Jemmy read the letters to her, and saw the response in her dark eyes. One was from the King of France, young Louis XV, who wrote to commiserate over the death of the Comte, and to praise his long and loyal service to France. The other was from King James in Rome, who expressed his grief over the loss of one who was a dear friend as well as a loyal servant. He spoke of Karellie's courage and love in leaving his home-land to follow King James II into exile, of the unswerving devotion he had shewn to the royal family ever since, and the many valuable services he had performed for them. He added that he was putting his whole household into mourning for the Earl, and would be holding a memorial service for him, at which he himself would speak the oration.

Annunciata's eye filled with tears as she listened – the first tears she had been able to shed since she heard of Karellie's death. She nodded and said, 'It is no more than he deserved. Father Renard—'

'Yes,' said the priest, 'I understand. You wish me to hold a memorial service here, at Shawes?'

'More than that,' Annunciata said. 'I want you to bury him.' She turned her head towards Jemmy, speaking with difficulty. 'Jemmy, I want you to get him back. I want him brought home.'

It proved a task of immense difficulty, and it needed not only all the influence of Maurice, who had now succeeded to the title, and Berwick himself, but of Lord Newcastle and Sir Robert Walpole as well. It was fortunate that Walpole had succeeded in negotiating a state of peace with the wily old French first minister Fleury, for had the two countries been in a state of hostility, the task might well have been hopeless. But Maurice and Queen Caroline worked upon King George, Newcastle upon Walpole, and Walpole and Berwick upon Fleury, and at last things were arranged. Karellie's body was shipped to England in an immense lead-lined casket, brought

hear, to sit with Jemmy, alone with him, to have him look at her with those suddenly gentle eyes, to have all his attention, and his respect, and perhaps, even, his love. Hers had been a lonely life, always, and though she loved her two sons, their love and company could not replace a husband's. 'Yes,' she said. 'You shall tell me. We will order the mourning, and you shall tell me what to put in my letter to my brother.'

'Lady Mary, I warn you!' Lady Dudley began indignantly, but Mary turned a cold eye upon her.

'Madam, you have leave,' she said firmly, and held her disbelieving stare unwaveringly. After a moment, the dowager withdrew with icy dignity.

In the May of 1732 Lady Mary lay in the great bedchamber at Morland Place struggling to give birth to her third child. It had been a difficult pregnancy, and for the last two months of it she had been virtually confined to her room. Alessandra and her maid Rachel attended her, with Edmund's wife Augusta looking on: Robert's Rachel was still confined to her own bed after the birth of her second son a week before, or she would certainly have been there as well. Lady Dudley was no longer at Morland Place. She and Mary had quarrelled even more seriously when Mary had become pregnant, and Mary had invited her to seek a home elsewhere, and the atmosphere had been the lighter for her going.

Now as the midwife wiped the sweat from her brow and she writhed again with the racking pain that had been going on already for ten hours, she thought how happy the months had been since Karellie's funeral, in comparison with her life before. She and Jemmy were still not very intimate with each other – her reserved nature and his continual busyness prevented it – but they met now on terms of calm friendliness, occasionally deepening into affection, which once or twice had expressed itself in physical terms. He took her into his confidence a great deal more when Lady Dudley was not there to come between them, and she had sometimes wondered how much of her life's isolation had been caused by her duenna.

She groaned as another pain tore through her. She was sure she would not survive this childbirth, but she was glad she had known at least a little love, and that she would die regretted by her husband. She sought Alessandra's face through the mist of pain and gasped.

'If I die, tell him – tell him—' Alessandra pressed her hand firmly and bent nearer to catch the words. 'Tell him I love him,' she managed to finish. Alessandra nodded wordlessly, catching the midwife's eye. She did not believe Mary would survive either.

Below, in the drawing room, Jemmy paced up and down, followed by the anxious Fand, and by the faintly amused eyes of Marie-Louise who, with all the confidence of being fifteen and never having experienced a day's illness in her life, was sure that

Jemmy was worrying about nothing. She had come over with Alessandra in order to shew off to Jemmy her new riding habit, which was of emerald green cloth, and in which she knew she looked enchanting, with her red-gold hair and tawny eyes. Alessandra had gone upstairs to the birth chamber, bidding her stay below and keep Jemmy occupied; but Jemmy simply walked about muttering to himself and casting anguished glances at the ceiling whenever Mary let out a louder cry than usual, and hadn't noticed Marie-Louise at all.

'Oh God! It's all my fault,' Jemmy cried now, putting his hand to his head. 'If only I had – I should never have—' He looked at Marie-Louise and away again, conscious only of her youth. Marie-Louise tapped her fingers irritably against the chimney-piece.

'Really, Jemmy, people have babies all the time. It's nothing to worry about. Why, Lady Mary has had two already, and there was nothing to it. And only last week you know Rachel had her boy, and there was nothing to that. You mustn't fret so. Why don't you come out for a ride with me, and when we get back, it will all be over.'

Jemmy groaned at the words, and tore at his hair. 'All over! Dear God!'

'Oh do come,' she wheedled. 'It's a perfect day for riding, and it really is too ridiculous to stay here when there's nothing we can do. I'm sure Lady Mary would wish you to go,' she added with what she thought was cunning.

Jemmy stared at her, and then with an odd grimace said, 'Marie-Louise, go upstairs, there's a dear girl, and see if there's any news. They won't let me anywhere near.'

Marie-Louise pouted. 'Oh very well. But I must say you are a great disappointment to me. I put this on especially to divert you, and you have not even noticed it. I might as well have come in sackcloth.' She got up to go to the door, and at that moment it opened to shew Augusta's frightened, pretty face.

'Oh dear, Mr Morland, I think you ought to send for the doctor. The midwife says we ought to have the doctor. Oh dear, poor lady! I vow and swear, I shall never have another after this! Oh!' as a scream rent the air, 'I do think the doctor ought to be sent for very soon.'

She had to step back very quickly to avoid being knocked over by Jemmy.

The silence, when it came, was more unnerving than the cries of distress had been before. Jemmy was sitting alone in the steward's room with one guttering candle. Even Fand had deserted him, to seek the comfort of the hall hearth and the other hounds. Marie-Louise had gone home before sunset, and it was now nearly four in the morning. At last he heard the doctor's footsteps coming across the hall, but he was too tired and afraid to get to his feet, only looked up dully as the doctor appeared in the doorway. She's dead, he thought, and the idea filled him with a hollow pain.

The doctor's eyes were red-veined with weariness. He had not left his patient for over twelve hours.

'Both alive,' he said economically. 'God knows how. She must never have another, do you hear me? Not on any account.'

Jemmy nodded, and slowly the understanding seeped through him, warming his cold heart. 'And the child?' he said at last.

'A girl.'

A girl! Somehow he had not thought of that. A foolish smile began to spread over his face. A daughter! 'I never had a daughter before,' he said foolishly. 'Can I see my wife?'

The doctor shook his head. 'She's sleeping now, and she must not be disturbed. Sleep is the best healer for her at the moment. Tomorrow, when she wakes of her own accord, you can see her. But you can see the child if you wish. It's healthy.'

Jemmy followed the doctor up the stairs, and waited outside the great bedchamber until Rachel brought the child out, firmly wrapped in its shawl, and placed it in Jemmy's arms. It was so tiny and light – he always forgot how tiny newborn babies were – and he stared down into its crumpled, rosepetal face with wonder. His heart was full, and a strange jumble of images tumbled through his mind as he looked at his daughter. For some reason, he found himself thinking of Aliena.

Mary won't want to be troubled about naming the babe he thought, not when she's been so ill.

I had better give her a name. Jubilance and a strange, fierce possessiveness surged through him. *I* shall name her, and she will be mine; mine and named for me. He touched the baby's cheek with a fingertip, and she frowned in her first, determined sleep. I shall call her Jemima, he thought.

BOOK II

THE AXE

Sound, sound the clarion, fill the fife!
Throughout the sensual world proclaim,
One crowded hour of glorious life
Is worth an age without a name.

Thomas Osbert Mordaunt: *The Call*

CHAPTER 7

Jemima pricked her finger for the fourth time, and sighed for the eighth time, and cast a longing glance towards the window of the drawing room and the sunlit day outside. It seemed so unfair to her that she should be shut up here to do embroidery on such a day, when everyone else in the world, she firmly believed, was out enjoying themselves. She looked surreptitiously around the room. Her mother, sitting very upright in one of the chimney chairs, was reading, her spectacles balanced on the end of her nose so that she did not have to bend her head to see the words. Jemima did not have to see the title to know that it was a book of sermons that she was reading, for Lady Mary was a Protestant, and very pious. Jacob, the cook, who was Jemima's best friend, had explained to her that Protestants, like her mother, were very pious but not at all religious, while Catholics, like him and Jemima's father and most of the people at Morland Place, were religious but not at all pious. Jemima did not entirely understand, being only eight, but it confirmed her in her belief that she did not like Protestants, which was founded on the fact that she

183

did not like her mother. Her mother did not like her, either, as Jemima very well knew. Her mother blamed Jemima for the fact that she had to walk with a stick and got pains if she did anything very active; she loved Jemima's brothers, Thomas and Henry, and had no room in her heart for anyone else except her freckled spaniel, Spot.

In the other fireside chair was her uncle George, who also held a book but was not reading it. He was asleep, as he always was at this time of day, but he was so fat that his bulk wedged him upright in the chair and his chins were propped up on his cravat, and unless he snored, a stranger might easily believe he really was reading *Robinson Crusoe*, which rested open at page sixteen on his large knees. Uncle George rose early every day and rode or hunted vigorously until dinner-time. After dinner, replete with food and wine, he slept until supper time, and after supper he went to bed. Lady Mary despised Uncle George and had once in Jemima's hearing called him a parasite. Jemima had asked Jacob what a parasite was, and he had said it was a flea. This had puzzled her, for she could not see any resemblance in Uncle George to a flea, until she remembered that when he was out hunting he was quite fearless and would often jump extremely high hedges. She supposed this was what her mother was referring to, although it seemed strange that Lady Mary should disapprove of it. Jemima rather liked Uncle George, who was kind to her in his silent way. Sometimes when they met on the stairs, he would smile shyly at her and give her a sweetmeat from the little enamelled box in his coat pocket.

Looking down at her work again, she saw that she had got another bloodspot on the linen from her pricked finger. With so many rusty marks, the shirt she was embroidering was beginning to resemble her mother's dog. She sighed again. This time Lady Mary looked up from her book and said, 'Do stop puffing and blowing in that way, Jemima, it is most unladylike. And sit up straight. You slouch like a dairymaid. Really, Chort, you must instruct Miss Jemima in better deportment, or I shall have to see about replacing you.'

'I beg your pardon, milady,' said Jane Chort, Jemima's governess, humbly, and when Lady Mary looked down at her book again, she gave Jemima a savage frown, which meant, 'Now see how you have got me into trouble.' Jemima gave a grimace of contrition, and managed to stop herself only just in time from sighing again. It *was* unfair, however, for it was only she that was suffering in this way. Aunt Augusta had gone over to Shelmet Rectory to visit Aunt Rachel, and had taken with her little Augusta and Caroline, who would normally have been sharing Jemima's imprisonment. The boys, Aunt Rachel's Robert and Frederick, and Aunt Augusta's William, who would normally be doing lessons in the schoolroom with Father Andrews, had been let off that afternoon because, with Quarter Day approaching, the priest had so much to do, and they had gone to help with the haying.

185

Jemima's brothers, who had attained the inaccessible heights of sixteen and fourteen years, were pretty much a law unto themselves, since Papa did not trouble himself with them, and they could wind Mama round their little fingers, and they were off somewhere, probably over at Twelvetrees or riding on the moors.

Jemima put the last stitch into the leaf she was embroidering, oversewed it, and cut the thread, and spread out her work to survey it. It was, to be sure, a very uneven and disagreeable-looking leaf, and no fit companion for the neat crimson rose that Jane had done before passing the work on to Jemima. Jemima stared at it and felt the frustration welling inside her. She hated to sew, and she hated to do bad work, and it seemed to her a piece of monstrous foolishness that she should be forced to go on and on doing something she was so bad at. If only she could talk to Papa about it, she was sure he would arrange things better for her; but Papa was always so busy, and she hardly ever saw him, and then never alone. At eight years old she did not, of course, take her meals with the grownups, and unless she met him by accident somewhere in the house, the only times she saw him were twice a day in the chapel, and on the occasions when she was brought down to the drawing room after supper to play to her parents. When there were guests, it was usually Augusta who was sent for to play, for although Jemima played better than her, Augusta was very good for her age, which was only five, and also with her plump pink face, golden ringlets and blue eyes, was very much prettier than Jemima. Jemima had dark hair that was always untidy, and her face was too thin, and her expression was usually thoughtful and earnest – disagreeable, her mother called it. She did not smile winningly at people as Augusta did, and tended to ask too many questions, and look at people too sharply.

She selected a new piece of silk, and began the tedious business of threading her needle, and then there was a diversion: a servant came in to say that the samples of silk had arrived from York and that Lady Mary's woman, Rachel, had taken them up to her room. Lady Mary put her book aside, took her silver-tipped, ebony cane, and with a final severe look at Jemima, which was a clear warning to her to work hard, she left the room. Jemima immediately felt happier, and managed to persuade the end of her silk to pass through the tiny eye. A few stitches later one of the nursery maids peeped hesitantly round the door and beckoned to Jane, mouthing some evidently urgent message. Jane went to the door and carried on a conversation *sotto voce* which Jemima could not catch, except that it seemed her presence was urgently required in the nursery. Jane looked across at Jemima doubtfully, and Jemima kept her head bent over her work and stitched away industriously, trying to exude trustworthiness.

She heard Jane say, 'Well, just for a moment, then. If Lady Mary should come back—'

187

'But she'll be hours with those silks,' the nursery maid whispered urgently. Jane gave one more doubtful glance over her shoulder, and then went with the maid, leaving the door open. Jemima listened for the footsteps to die away up the stairs, and then let out a sigh of relief. In his chair, Uncle George slept peacefully, his lips exploding in a soft puff at every exhalation. Jemima felt a surge of affection for him, dear, reliable Uncle George, and she blew him a kiss as she pattered silently out.

Outside she waited her moment and then scudded like a blown leaf across the staircase hall and the great hall, down the kitchen passage and into the pantry. A door led from the buttery into the courtyard, but there was always someone in the courtyard, and she would certainly be challenged if she tried to walk out through the barbican. But the pantry had a door into the inner courtyard, and she only needed to cross that to reach the brewhouse passage, which gave onto the back door. The back door was hardly ever used, because the bridge over the moat was rotting and unsafe, but it would take Jemima's small weight. A few moments more and she was out into the sunshine, and free, and her heart lifted with joy. She would probably get into very bad trouble for running out like this – she might even get a whipping, unless her father interfered on her part – but she didn't care. Just then all she cared about was the warm, sweet air and the grass and the great arch of sky above her and the mad carolling of the skylarks, so high in the blue that they were invisible.

She had no idea where Papa was, but she thought the most likely place was Twelvetrees. In any case, they would know his whereabouts at Twelvetrees. She pulled off her cap for the pleasure of feeling the hot sun on her head, and swinging the cap round and round by its laces, she set off at a run. She was soon much too hot, and slowed to a walk, and decided to cut through the bottom end of the orchard for the coolness. There was a place that William had told her about, where you could climb over the wall by the aid of an old thorn tree that grew outside. She reached through the slit in her dress and thrust her cap into the pocket which was tied round her waist under her skirt, for she would certainly need both hands for climbing.

She managed pretty well, despite her hampering clothes – how well she would climb, she thought, if only she could wear breeches like a boy – and it was not difficult to swing herself across onto the top of the orchard wall. But the wall itself was old and crumbling and slippery with moss, and she could not steady herself upon it. She heard her dress rip as it snagged on something, and with a stifled cry she half slipped, half jumped, landing with a thump on the orchard grass.

The first thing she saw was a pair of legs only a few feet from her head, and with a sinking heart she looked up to see her uncle Allen Macallan

189

looking down at her with mild surprise. He was stripped to his shirt, with the sleeves pushed up, doing something to a small, spindly tree. He was wearing a carpenter's apron, out of whose capacious front pocket protruded the handle of a pair of nippers, and the end of a ball of twine. Jemima watched him apprehensively. Of all her uncles, he was the one she knew least – of the uncles at home, that was: of course Uncle Thomas, who was a captain in the navy, had been away at sea all her life, and she had seen him for the first time last Christmas when he had come home to recover from a wound, got at the capture of Portobello and exacerbated by the scurvy. Uncle Charles, the botanist, travelled round the world all the time collecting strange plants, and his visits home were so infrequent that Jemima could not even remember what he looked like.

But though Uncle Allen was at home, she saw less of him even than of her father. He was a quiet, retiring man, and he shared Papa's work, acting as a sort of deputy or assistant, and when he was not working he took a book to his own room and read or wrote letters there. Now Jemima surveyed his face as she rubbed absently at the various parts of her body that hurt. He was a small, slight man, with a small face, fair-skinned, and with large pale blue eyes and very long eyelashes like a girl's. He wore his own hair, which was dark brown, but had it tied back at the moment in a queue, presumably to keep it out of the way while he worked.

His nose and mouth and chin were strongly-marked and firm, and his hands looked strong and capable, but though he did not smile, there was nothing grim about him. Indeed, the corners of his mouth seemed to turn up slightly, as if only waiting for the right excuse to break into laughter.

'Oh, it's you,' he said. 'When I heard the scrambling about on the other side, I thought it was one of the boys.' He didn't seem much surprised at her presence, nor angry, but still Jemima held her silence, knowing how unpredictable adults could be. 'Are you hurt?' he asked her after a moment, nodding to where she was rubbing her elbow with her hand.

'Not much,' Jemima said. 'I banged my elbow on the ground. And I've cut my hand on something.'

'Let me see.' He hunkered down in front of her and took up her hand and spread it open, palm up. The mound of the thumb which had taken her weight as she landed was grazed and dirty, and he began brushing the grit away very gently with his fingers. His hand holding hers was warm and strong, the sort of hand that animals surely trust. She watched his face as he frowned over her injury, seeing his golden eyelashes fan down on his cheeks. Close to, he smelled nice, she discovered, like warm grass. The eyelashes swept up, the blue eyes looked for a moment into hers, and the concentrating tuck of the eyebrows straightened as a spot of colour appeared inexplicably in his cheeks.

'Do you always stare like that?' he asked, but not in anger.

'I'm sorry,' Jemima said. 'My mother says it is rude, but I can't help it. I don't mean to stare, I'm just—' She puzzled how to explain herself.

'You're just interested?' he offered. She nodded with relief. 'I see,' he said. He took out his hand-kerchief, moistened it and cleaned away the last of the dirt and grit. 'It's just a graze,' he said. 'Nothing to worry about.'

'I know,' Jemima said, hoping he would not release her hand, for it felt so comfortable in his; but he did. 'What were you doing to the tree?' she asked. He glanced back at it, and then sat down on the grass in front of her, drawing up his knees and clasping them with his hands. She had never seen an adult sit like that, and it enchanted her.

'I was grafting on a slip – a young shoot from a different sort of tree. As described in your Uncle Charles's book.'

'What for?' Jemima asked. He looked at her for a moment, as if gauging her interest or her capacity, and then said merely, 'To improve the stock.'

'Oh,' said Jemima.

'And what were you doing on top of the wall?' he asked. 'I don't suppose anyone knows you're here?'

'Not unless they saw me from a window,' she said, and explained how she had run away. 'I thought if I could find Papa—'

'That he would make it all right? But where were you going?'

'To Twelvetrees. I thought he would most likely be there.'

Now he smiled for the first time, and Jemima thought now nice he looked when he smiled. 'You would be right more often than wrong in assuming so, I grant you. But not today. Today he is over at Shawes, riding with the Princess.'

Jemima knew that this was her father's nickname for Marie-Louise, the Countess's granddaughter. 'Why do you say it like that?' she asked abruptly.

'Like what?'

Jemima was at an age when she often felt things she had no words for. She struggled now. 'As if he should not be. As if – I don't know. As if it made you angry.'

He cocked his head a little. 'You're a funny, noticing little thing, aren't you? But I don't think you'd understand. Tell me about you instead. I don't know anything about you. Wait – we must be comfortable first. If I am to be your host, I must provide you with refreshment. Come on.'

He got up and held out his hand to her, and pulled her to her feet, and, still holding her hand, led her across the orchard to where his coat was flung across a wooden bench. He took it off, dusted the seat with his hand, and bowed her to it with mock cere-mony which amused her. Then he seated himself by her and, out of his coat pocket, produced a horn bottle of water-and-wine, and a cloth which, when unwrapped, proved to contain some little cakes and a handful of ripe yellow gooseberries.

'Enough of a feast, so soon after dinner,' he said. 'Now, help yourself, and tell me about you.'

So Jemima told him about herself, about how her mother loved her brothers and disliked her, about how she hated sewing and reading sermons and learning to be ladylike, about how her father kissed and petted her on the rare occasions she saw him, but had no time to talk, about how Augusta was prettier than her, and how she was always in trouble for being untidy and disagreeable and asking too many questions and staring at people.

'I wish I was a boy, like my brothers,' she concluded. 'I like to be good at things, and I'd be good at being a boy. I'm no good at being a girl. I'm not even pretty.'

'No, I wouldn't say you're pretty,' he said judiciously, studying her, 'but one day you'll be better than pretty, you'll be beautiful. Then you may have the laugh of Miss Augusta.'

Jemima sighed, as if she would like to believe it, and then she said, 'Now you tell me about you. About why you mind my father being with – with the Princess.' She watched his face carefully. 'Is it because you are in love with her?'

Allen did not answer directly. He said, 'When I was younger, before you were born, I was sent to Shawes to be brought up with the Princess, because we were about the same age. Your father hoped we might fall in love with each other, and that we might get married, because she is very rich, and it would be a way of providing for me. I should have been rich myself, you see, but my father was killed in the rebellion, and all the property that should have come to me was confiscated.'

'But it didn't work,' Jemima suggested.

'Only partly. I fell in love with her, but she did not fall in love with me. Without my property, you see, I was no match for her. I'm completely unimportant.'

'Like me!' Jemima cried eagerly. 'I'm unimportant, because of my brothers.'

'I'm even more unimportant than that,' Allen said. 'You at least may be hoped one day to marry someone rich or influential.'

'I hope not,' Jemima said with a shudder. 'I don't want ever to go away from here. Still,' she brightened, 'perhaps I could marry and stay here, like my uncles Robert and Edmund. Though, of course, they are men. Everything's always different for men.'

There was a brief silence as they looked at each other, pondering over the unfair ways of the world, and then Allen said, 'I tell you what, shall we walk over towards Shawes? Perhaps we'll meet your father coming back. Because, you know, unless we can persuade him to speak for you, you're bound to be in trouble for running away.'

'Won't you get into trouble for not finishing your work?' Jemima said hesitantly.

He stood up and offered her his hand. 'I can finish it later,' he said.

★   ★   ★

Jemmy and Marie-Louise were walking the last half mile home, leading their horses to cool them off. They had the reins hooked negligently over their arms, while they strolled slowly, their other arms linked, through the long lush grass on the far side of Shawes' lake. Marie-Louise's horse, Sovereign, was one of the prettiest horses in the world, and had been chosen by Jemmy as a gift for the Princess for that very reason. He was a chestnut, but his coat was remarkably pale: if gold were such a liquid as milk, and could put up a cream, his coat was the colour that cream would be. His mane and tail were slightly darker, and his large golden eyes darker still. His bridle was decorated with gold medallions that glinted and chimed with the drowsy nodding of his head as he walked; round his ears hung a drooping crown made of daisies, which Jemmy had fashioned while he and Marie-Louise sat together in the grass of a secluded meadow.

But, Jemmy thought, as he strolled along, feeling the light pressure of her arm through his, and listening to her pleasant, sweet voice as she chatted to him and swung her hips so that her skirt would swish the grass as she walked, however pretty Sovereign was for a horse, he could never be as beautiful as Marie-Louise was for a woman. At twenty-three she was fully mature, her well-shaped body lithe beneath the snug-fitting habit of thin midnight-blue worsted, the severity of its cut lightened by the absurd froth of lace at throat and cuff. From out of the lace rose her slender throat, and her little chin, always poised so high and proudly, and her handsome face with its clear-cut features and those remarkable, lustrous golden eyes. Her vivid, coppery hair was drawn back from her face and fell behind in a long tail of glossy ringlets from under her broad-brimmed, feathered hat. Again and again Jemmy searched for her mother in her face, but the likeness was so transitory and so elusive that he sometimes thought he must imagine it; yet he could never have enough of simply gazing at her.

'Of course, no one is pleased about the higher taxes,' she was saying, 'but apart from that, I think grandmother is actually very glad about the war with Spain.'

'I shouldn't have thought she cared much about our merchantmen being attacked by the guarda-costas,' Jemmy said vaguely. 'Though of course, war with Spain has been building up for years—'

'Of course she doesn't care about that sort of thing,' Marie-Louise said robustly. 'But she says that France is bound to side with Spain, because of their family ties, and that will mean King George is France's enemy while King James is France's ally, and then France will be bound to help King James regain his throne. And when the people discover that the war is costing them too dear, they will blame King George for biting off more than they can chew, and turn against him, and welcome back King James so that they can have peace again. And besides, there's bound to be war soon over the Holy Roman Empire, and King George will go rushing off to protect his precious Hanover, and the people won't like *that*. Grandmother says that two wars at once will see the Hanoverian off.'

'She's very optimistic,' Jemmy said. 'It sounds a slender hope to me.'

Marie-Louise shrugged. 'And to me; but grandmother ought to know. She's been intriguing all her life. And now Maurice is furious because she's started writing letters again, to the Scottish lords and to the King in Rome.'

'The Scottish lords?'

'Seven clan chiefs, who can raise a good number of men, and want French aid. Of course Cardinal Fleury likes peace, but if he has to go to war because of his compact with Spain, he might well back the Scottish lords for an invasion.'

'And Maurice is worried for your safety, I suppose?'

'Not entirely,' she said with a grimace. 'Maurice has financial worries. His friend Handel isn't doing too well, with all the competition from Buononcini's Italian school, and though Maurice always managed to keep a foot in both camps, one foot is slipping now that Queen Caroline is dead. King George never entirely trusted him, you know.'

'I'm surprised that Maurice didn't make friends with the Prince of Wales when he set up in

Leicester House,' said Jemmy. Prince Frederick, who had quarrelled with his parents over finances, had caused a scandal three years ago by quitting St James's Palace with his wife, Augusta, when she was actually in labour, and setting up a rival Court at Leicester House, just as his father had done before him in competition with the Elector George Lewis. Whatever the King and Queen liked and supported, Frederick and Augusta hated and opposed, and vice versa. While the King and Queen loyally attended the Haymarket Theatre and Handel's entertainments, the livelier rival faction crowded round the Prince and Princess of Wales at the opera house to listen to Buononcini's works.

'He left it too late,' Marie-Louise said. 'Besides, he did not like to offend Queen Caroline. She hated Frederick, you know. She called him a monster, and said if she saw him roasting in Hell, she'd help to stoke the fires.'

'Still, Maurice can't be too badly off. At least he still lives rent-free in Chelmsford House; and he has the title. That must be worth something.'

'A little credit, but not much more. He has written a new opera, in the Italian style, which he hopes will recoup his position, but it takes money to stage it with all the effects people like, and he's afraid if grandmother starts plotting again, she'll come to him for money. About the only thing left to sell is Chelmsford House itself.'

'She would never sell that, surely?'

'No, but she might want to rent it out, which would mean evicting Maurice and his family. Well, Maurice got Nicolette off his hands, marrying her to that Russian Prince, and grandmother's negotiating for a marriage between Clementina and John Ballincrea, but that still leaves Maurice with his wife and Apollonia and the boys to support, and I believe that Rupert is already very expensive. Ever since he became Baron Meldon, he's been running up dreadful debts on the strength of it, which Maurice has to pay. So Maurice has written to me to ask me if I mind if he tries to persuade grandmother to give him Chelmsford House. She has always promised to leave everything to me, you see.'

'Of course,' Jemmy said gravely. She spoke of it so easily, as if the fortune in question were no more than a few pieces of furniture and old dresses. 'And do you mind?'

'I suppose not. After all, I'll have Shawes and everything else, and if she did leave Chelmsford House to me, I suppose I'd have to let Maurice go on living there, or else have him to live with me here. One does seem to be burdened with the necessity of looking after relatives, doesn't one? If she gives him Chelmsford House, I'll be let off lightly. I dare say you'd feel the same, wouldn't you? After all, you had to provide for all your brothers, one way or another.'

Jemmy nodded. There were times when he felt almost weighed under by his dependants. It was true that Thomas had been no burden on him, for although he was at home now, recovering from his wound, he had hardly been home nine months in all the nineteen years he had been in the navy. Merit had got him his promotion to lieutenant, and merit had got him his presentation at Court, which in turn, by the influence of Queen Caroline, had got him made captain in 1735. He had not been particularly lucky in the matter of prize-money but, being always at sea and having no wife or children to support, he had always managed to live on his pay and had never asked Jemmy for anything.

Charles, too, after his time at University was finished, had been no burden, spending a great deal of time abroad on 'herborizing' expeditions, financed by the Society of Apothecaries and the Royal Society and other interested bodies; and when he was not on those expeditions, he was as likely to be staying with his mentor, James Sherard, or with one of his botanist friends in Scotland, as at Morland Place. As to Allen, the work he did on the estate more than paid for his keep: Jemmy would have been lost without him.

But on the other hand there was George, who did nothing but wear out horses and eat and drink at Jemmy's expense. There was Edmund, who despite the fact that war had been declared with Spain nearly a year ago, was still more often at Morland Place than at Hull Barracks; and his wife, who only left Morland Place to visit Shelmet, and his children who were being brought up at

201

Jemmy's expense. And there was Robert, whose two sons were also living at Morland Place and being tutored by Jemmy's chaplain. Jemmy sometimes felt that he worked from morning till night to provide a living for a host of people he cared nothing about, with scarcely a moment for his own pleasure. It was for that reason that he sometimes ignored the clamour of duty and rode over to Shawes to take Marie-Louise out riding, or to converse with the Countess who, although she was now well past ninety years old, still had a clearer mind and a sharper memory than most people half her age.

'Morland Place is my duty, and Shawes is my pleasure,' he said now, 'and since I come here to be pleased, let us not talk about my brothers. Tell me instead about the ball you went to at Beningbrough last week. Who did you dance with? Did you have any flirting? Tell me what you wore, and how you dressed your hair.'

Marie-Louise pressed his arm and laughed, her golden eyes shining. 'There is nothing I should like more. But I fear we must talk about brothers after all. Look where one of them comes!'

Jemmy looked, and cursed softly. 'And my brat with him. Now what's to do?'

They waited for Allen and Jemima to join them, and when the greetings had been exchanged, Allen explained their presence, and mediated for Jemima's forgiveness. His words were addressed to Jemmy, but his eyes were continually straying, despite him, to Marie-Louise, and when the recital was finished, it was she who spoke.

'You must come back to the house for some refreshment, both of you, and I shall help you convince Jemmy that he must not be hard on the child. I remember so well from my own childhood how I hated to be shut indoors sewing on a fine day. Come now – and, yes, you shall stay to supper! Grandmother will like it, and I shall send a servant to Morland Place to say where you all are.'

Jemmy glanced from Allen, who could not take his eyes from the Princess, to Jemima, whose thin face was alight with hopeful excitement at the idea of taking supper at Shawes, when she had never eaten away from her home in her whole life, and he could not deny the pleasure to either of them.

'Very well,' he agreed, and they turned towards the house. Allen hurried to take the place at the Princess's free side, and took Sovereign's reins from her, though he was no trouble, following her as meekly as a well-trained dog; and Jemmy offered his spare arm to Jemima, who took it as though she had been offered all the treasure of El Dorado.

'May I lead Auster, Papa?' she asked, and Jemmy gave her the reins. Old Auster was twenty-three, and Jemmy had a new young colt, Pilot, for hard riding, but Auster so loved to go out that he almost broke his heart if Jemmy came to the stable and left him behind, so he used the old horse if it was to be an easy day.

'I wanted to speak to you, Papa, about something very important,' Jemima said breathlessly. Jemmy looked down at her. She was very plain beside the Princess's remarkable beauty: her face was too thin, her features too strongly marked, her expression too earnest, and her colourless skin and dark hair were not fashionable. But she was his little pet, named by him and for him, and he smiled at her eagerness.

'Of course, my pigeon, of course. We can talk later. For now, remember to be on your best behaviour. We are to see the Countess, and she is very particular. It was very kind of Marie-Louise to ask you.'

He smiled at the Princess as he spoke, and she received the smile with lowered eyelashes and then turned back to Allen. She did not care for the child, and emphatically did not care to have the men's attention divided in any way. However, she knew Jemmy was fond of the brat, and that he would approve her kindness in including her, and she had felt that Allen would not stay without the child, having brought her here, so this was the best way. She would work it to her advantage somehow.

The inside of Shawes was like a palace to Jemima, after the small rooms and low ceilings of Morland Place. The size of the rooms, the size of the windows, the glittering chandeliers, the mirrors, the gilded furniture, the cleverly created vistas through doors and along corridors: she gazed at it all almost open-mouthed.

Marie-Louise, with a hint of distaste, interrupted her reverie by saying, 'The child's dress is torn; and she has no cap. Smith, take Miss Jemima upstairs and make her presentable. I am sure there is something of mine put away somewhere that she can wear. Then bring her down to the drawing room.'

Jemima went upstairs with the maid, who was very stiff and formal and did not speak to her, as the Morland Place servants would have. She was taken to what was evidently the old nursery, where the maid brought her a basin and water and towel for her to wash, and then began rummaging in a large trunk pushed aside in a corner. Jemima delved into her pocket.

'I have my cap here,' she said hesitantly. The maid glanced at it, and sniffed.

'It's main crumpled,' she said disapprovingly, before turning back to the trunk. 'All Madam's things she had as a child are in here. I expect there'll be something to fit you, though you're right small and thin. How old are you?'

'Eight,' Jemima said guiltily. The maid looked ever more disdainful.

'Madam was twice your size when *she* was eight,' she said. They spoke no more. When Jemima had washed, the maid helped her into a dress of apple green linen which, with the aid of a tightly tied sash, fitted her nearly enough, and then brushed

205

her hair and led her downstairs again. Jemima went meekly, wondering what would happen to her dress. Would they keep it in exchange for the green one, she wondered? Or send it back? She hoped the former, for then she might never have to confess to tearing it.

In the drawing room there were yet more terrors to be faced, for the three adults were gathered around a tray of tea, on the other side of which, very upright in a tall-backed chair, sat the Countess. Jemima had heard a great deal about her, and had seen her once or twice at a distance, but now she was to see her close-to, and speak to her, and be spoken to by her. In a daze she heard herself introduced, allowed herself to be led forward, and then she was standing in front of the Countess, her face on a level with the old woman's. It was incomprehensibly old. Jemima had never known an old person before: Jacob, the cook, was the oldest man she had ever known, and he was fifty; the Countess was almost twice as old.

But though the face was thin and wrinkled, it was not repulsive, as she had momentarily feared: indeed, in some extraordinary way it was almost beautiful. Around her throat the Countess wore a collar of diamonds which glittered in the reflected light from the windows; but they were not more bright than the astonishing dark eyes that now looked at Jemima with a curiosity and interest equalling her own.

After a long time the Countess said, 'You are Jemima.'

It was not a question, but it seemed safer to treat it as one, and Jemima said, 'Yes, your ladyship,' and for good measure curtseyed again.

It seemed to be a good thing to have done, for the Countess suddenly smiled as if they had shared some secret joke, and said, 'Sit down beside me, child, and we will talk. You will have a dish of tea? But no, it is poor stuff, weak and indeterminate, fit for your aunts, no doubt, but not for women of spirit. We shall have wine, you and I. Charley, bring the Italian cups for Miss Jemima and me. Now Jemmy, you need not stare so. You have Marie-Louise to entertain you. Leave Jemima and me to talk in peace.'

Jemima sat down beside the Countess, feeling already much less overawed, especially after the jibe at her aunts and the suggestion that she and the Countess were somehow of the same make. The maid Charley brought two tall silver cups filled with wine, and the Countess lifted hers to Jemima as if to drink a toast.

'Yes, I see whose you are. You have his blood in you. *A tes beaux yeux, enfant.*' She drank, and then said, 'It is no use our speaking French to be private, for Marie-Louise speaks it better than English. We must hope love will make them all deaf.' For a moment they sat in silence watching the other three who, having handed about the tea, were now settling down to their own chatter,

Marie-Louise bending like a sapling in the breeze in her desire to captivate them both simultaneously. Jemima drank of her wine, injudiciously, for it made her choke, being far stronger than she was used to, and she felt herself blushing at her ineptitude; but the Countess did not seem to notice.

After a moment she turned her dark, curious gaze back to Jemima and said, 'Now, tell me about yourself. What brought you here today?'

Slowly at first, but with gathering confidence, Jemima talked. She had never had such a flatteringly attentive audience, nor one who seemed to understand what she wanted to say when the words were hard to find. In a short while she had told everything; then the Countess talked, and that was so fascinating that Jemima was sorry when the supper was brought in to interrupt them.

'We shall eat in the French style,' the Countess decreed. 'Jemima shall hand me my plate. Do not trouble about us. Go to the beaufet, child, and make a selection of food and bring the plate to me. Serve yourself in the same way. Charley, fill my cup. There,' when all was done, 'now we may be comfortable again. Are you comfortable?'

'Yes, your ladyship,' Jemima said, and then, feeling it was inadequate, added, 'It is very kind of you and her ladyship to invite me.'

The Countess smiled again. 'Marie-Louise did not do it to please you, so you need not be grateful. She is as selfish as the day is long, but such beauty as hers is justification in itself. They think you plain, do they not?' she added, studying Jemima's face. Jemima blushed and nodded. 'No matter. You have not yet grown into your beauty, but you will. You wonder how I know that? Because I know what you will look like. Do you see the bureau yonder, the black one with the gold dragon on the front? Go to it, and open the topmost drawer on the left. Inside you will find a lacquer box. Bring it to me.'

Jemima put down her plate and did as she was bid. The other three adults were so deep in their talk and laughter they did not even notice that she had moved. The Countess took the box onto her quilted satin lap and opened it, unfolded the black velvet cloth inside and drew out of it an oval miniature in a frame of twisted gold wires. She looked at it for a moment and then gave it to Jemima.

The face of the man in the picture looked somehow familiar. It was a brown face, with a long nose and a long, mobile mouth, beginning to smile, and dark blue eyes, deepset, and dark hair curling like feathers. She looked up.

'Your great grandfather,' the Countess said. 'You are very like him. You will be liker. And look, here, a piece of his hair.' She drew a long curl from the box and laid it across Jemima's palm. The cut end was tagged with gold to keep it together. It was very dark brown, almost black, and soft. The Countess reached out and picked up a lock of

Jemima's hair and drew it down against the cut curl. They were almost the same colour.

'You see?' Jemima nodded. Abruptly, the Countess seemed to change the subject. 'I am very old, you know, and I will not live much longer. When I am dead, all this will go to Marie-Louise. My mother left her estate to me, an old, damp, dark house it was. I pulled it down, and Vanbrugh built me this, his little gem, so beautiful. Each generation has its improvements. What will Marie-Louise do with it? She has a great deal of vanity and nonsense about her, as you see, but she has also a great deal of courage and sense. And she was educated – few men are better educated than she. I hope she will have a daughter to leave it to. Everything is so much surer through the daughter.' She looked sharply at Jemima, and Jemima was sure the Countess knew that she was thinking the words were an old woman's ramblings. She frowned and said aloud, 'I am tired, and you must all leave me. It is late enough. Jemmy, you must take this child home.'

When one is as old as the Countess, Jemima saw, one's wishes are instantly obeyed. Jemmy and Allen and Marie-Louise stopped talking at once and stood up, evidently preparing to leave. Jemima got up too, and at the Countess's gesture helped Charley to help her to her feet. For all the bulk of her clothes and weight of her jewels, the Countess was light. Jemima was reminded of a fallen autumn leaf, golden, dry and brittle.

'Jemmy, you must educate Jemima. Well enough,

all this sewing and sitting, but she has a brain, Jemmy, a brain, and you must feed it.'

'Mary won't approve of that,' Jemmy said smiling. 'She wants Jemima to be a lady.'

Jemima could see that her father was not taking the Countess's words seriously, and the Countess evidently saw it too, for she stamped her foot and said, 'Never mind what Mary wants. Ignorance is a prison. Let her learn Latin and Greek and mathematics. Would you have Marie-Louise any different? Then have Jemima taught as she was. And if Mary complains, refer her to our Princess. You would hardly say she is not a lady.'

Jemmy smiled wickedly at Marie-Louise, as if he was not entirely in agreement with the last words. But Marie-Louise looked gravely at him, and said, 'Come, Jemmy, the poor child came all this way and risked a beating to beg you for education. If it was a comfit or a new dress, you would not deny her, would you? Then grant her this – to shew you approve of me.'

Jemmy took her hand and bent over it, and laid his lips against it lingeringly, saying, 'Approve of you? My dear Princess, how could you ever doubt it? You are perfection. And you know that I can deny you nothing you ask of me. To please you, I will even risk Mary's wrath.'

'Then you will educate her?' the Princess said, smiling again, her hand still in his. 'Thank you, sir. You will not regret it.'

★　★　★

211

The carriage was got out for Allen and Jemima, but Jemmy decided to ride Auster home, and so they had it to themselves. For a while they sat in silence as the carriage jolted over the track, and then Allen said, 'You have what you came for; and you will not be beaten for running away. Why do you still look so sad?'

'Because it was—' Jemima frowned, seeing in her mind's eye how it had been, that the extraction of the promise had been a piece of flirting between Marie-Louise and her father, and nothing to do with Jemima herself; that her father, ruffling her hair as they departed, did not take her seriously at all, did not even see her as a person, and probably had no intention of keeping the promise. She felt sore inside, as she once did after a bout of vomiting, when she had colic, but she did not have the words to express all this to Allen. She turned her head, still frowning, to look at him, thinking, surely he must have seen it for himself. 'It was just a joke. Only a joke.'

'Yes,' Allen said, and she saw that he did understand. 'They make light of me, too.'

A week later, on 29 June 1740, Annunciata died. She was ninety-five years old, and her long and crowded life had spanned the reigns of eight monarchs, and she had many times faced violent death; but when the time came, she died quietly, in her sleep, in her own bed, in the exquisite house that Sir John Vanbrugh had envisaged as the perfect setting for her. The maid who dressed Jemima that morning told her the news in a hushed voice, and the same hush prevailed throughout the house. It seemed a monumental happening; no one wept, but no one would have been surprised at an eclipse, or an earthquake, or a sudden access of portents. Normal activities were suspended by common consent; the sun was veiled and hazy in a strange, colourless sky; the birds did not sing; and though the household dogs did not howl, they crept for hiding under tables with their ears down.

Though she had met her only once, Jemima felt bereaved, that she had lost a friend. All that day she relived the talk she had had with the Countess, remembering her words exactly, and the expressions of her face, and the way she had moved her hands. *She knew*, thought Jemima, and after a while, another thought came to her: that it was because the Countess new her time was close that she had tried to do something for Jemima. *I am to carry on for her*, she thought, and that did not make sense. She had Marie-Louise, did she not? Marie-Louise was her heir. She remembered the Countess saying 'I wonder what Marie-Louise will do with it?' *She does not trust her*, Jemima thought.

All that long day the strangeness and silence persisted, and the household went to bed early, bemused, avoiding each other's company. But the next day the sun rose hot and brilliant in a clear blue sky, and everything was back to normal. Jemmy ordered a month's deep mourning for the family and livery-servants, followed by two weeks' half mourning, and saddled Auster to go to visit Marie-Louise and ask if she wished him to help her plan the funeral. He felt that an era had ended, but inevitably the regret was mingled with a faint feeling of relief. He did not, as Jemima knew he would not, remember his promise to have her educated. As far as she could tell, he had never mentioned the matter to her mother at all.

The Countess's will was proved without contention. She had left Chelmsford House in London, with all its furnishings, to Maurice, and Shawes, its estate, the property in York, and her personal effects to Marie-Louise, who now openly styled herself Countess of Strathord. There were the usual small personal bequests to servants and friends, those she had not outlived. The gold locket containing a lock of her father, Prince Rupert's, hair she left to Lady Clementina Morland for a wedding gift for her marriage to John, Viscount Ballincrea, which was planned to take place in September: she must have known, Jemmy reflected, that she would not live to see it. To Alessandra, who had been her faithful companion since Aliena retired from the world, she left a pension, and the miniature of herself that Samuel Cooper had painted for Prince Rupert threequarters of a century ago.

It was some weeks later that Marie-Louise rode

over to Morland Place to fulfil the last bequest, and she did so with obvious puzzlement, handing the lacquer box to Jemima with an air of inquiry and also of reluctance, as if she had been wondering for some time whether to treat the matter as an abberation.

'My grandmother was most specific that you should have this box and its contents intact,' she said unwillingly. 'It is my duty to fulfil her wishes.'

Jemima looked up at her in the way that her mother objected to as being 'disagreeable', for it was a considering, too-seeing look. Marie-Louise was still in deep mourning, black crepe, white muslin scarf and cap with black ribbons, black chamois gloves, but the cut of all was fashionable and elegant, and the shining copper hair was revealed at the front by setting the cap farther back than was consistent with deep grief. She looked all the more handsome for the severe setting of black-and-white. Morland Place was now in half mourning, and Jemima knew that in her dress of dark grey tabby she looked sallow and dowdy, and far more like a mourner than the Princess. She saw in Marie-Louise's expression that she had thought long and hard before deciding to honour her grandmother's wishes; that she had examined the contents of the box and did not wish to part with them. Jemima wondered whether it had been some chance circumstance, such as the presence of a witness, that had finally made up her mind for her.

'Thank you, milady,' Jemima said, and glanced to her father for permission.

'Yes, chuck, open it by all means,' Jemmy said, his eyes going straight back to the Princess.

In the lacquer box lay two miniatures – the one she had already seen, of Martin Morland, and another painted on ivory and framed with gold, of the Princess Henrietta, sister to King Charles II, painted by Samuel Cooper. Underneath was the lock of hair tipped with gold, and underneath again, wrapped in more black velvet, the diamond collar. Jemima drew it out, and the stones flung rainbows of light across the room. She looked up at the Princess. This was the cause of her unwillingness.

'King Charles gave her that,' Jemmy said in awe. 'It's worth a small fortune.' He looked at the Princess and frowned. 'Surely it must be a mistake. Surely she did not know the diamonds were in there.'

'Alessandra doesn't think so. She is adamant that it was what grandmother wanted,' the Princess said. She took the diamonds from Jemima and looked at them. Against the dull black of her chamois gloves their brilliance seemed muted. She gestured towards the miniatures and the lock of hair. 'Apart from the locket she gave Clementina, those were her greatest treasures, though they are worthless.'

'Why should she give them to Jemima, then?' Jemmy said, still puzzled. But the Princess met

Jemima's eyes, and as an understanding passed between them, she blushed deeply.

'An old woman's fancy,' she said harshly, with a shrug to cover her sudden, brief shame. 'Here, child, take your own.' And she dropped the diamonds carelessly into Jemima's hand, turning away in such a manner that Jemmy was obliged to turn with her, presenting their backs to Jemima. Jemima put the diamonds carefully back into the box and closed the lid, holding it against her chest as if afraid she might drop it. Tears prickled, and she shut her eyes to hold them back, afraid that if Marie-Louise saw them, she might think she was the cause.

The diamonds and the two miniatures were locked away in the strong room with the family jewels and treasures. The lock of hair Jemmy had enclosed in a gold locket, which he gave to Jemima as a belated birthday present. The box, being of no value, she was allowed to have, and she kept it by her bed and put her locket in it when she was not wearing it, which was hardly ever. Sometimes when she felt lonely or discouraged, she would reach out and touch it, and think of the Princess's words, 'Those were her greatest treasures.' *I* am the real heir, she would think.

But still she spent her days in embroidering, playing the spinnet, learning the fashionable dances, and keeping a journal in which, since her mother read it every day, she could only record the permitted commonplaces. Nothing was said of education for her, and she had no opportunity to speak to her father again on the subject, even had she thought it of any use to do so. But there was one improvement in her lot: as often as his duties permitted, Allen began to accompany her on her morning rides, and as they rode along with the uncaring groom a discreet distance behind, he would tell her things: the names of the planets and constellations, the order and dates of the Kings of England, the names and histories of the Greek Gods and Heroes, the names of the countries of Europe and their principal cities, the history of the Pragmatic Sanction and the Austrian Succession, which were likely to cause war in Europe at any moment. And one day he brought along a slate and chalk in his saddlebag, and when they stopped and dismounted to breathe the horses and enjoy the view, he began to teach her the elements of mathematics and Latin.

It was a poor, piecemeal sort of education, but it was a great deal better than nothing, and Jemima absorbed it all frantically, and repeated everything over to herself at night in bed for fear of forgetting part of it. He could not ride with her every day; sometimes a week would pass without her seeing him; but sometimes other occasions would arise to compensate. The servants probably knew what was going on, but now that Jemmy was the Master, instead of the young master, they no longer told him everything; and if Jemmy noticed that Allen had a predilection for his daughter, he only thought it all of a piece with Allen's general kindness to those smaller or weaker than himself.

CHAPTER 8

In February, 1742, Walpole, whose grip on power had been slipping ever since, against his desire and his advice, England had declared war on Spain, was forced to resign. Maurice missed him more than he had ever thought possible. He had always cultivated a carefree, offhand, and even faintly cynical attitude to life, and had professed to maintaining only such friendships as were useful to his career. In this way, he had juggled with such success his relationships with George Lewis and his son, now George II. But Walpole's fall left him feeling flat, and aware of a strange lassitude. Queen Caroline, of whom he had been very fond, had died her painful and horribly undignified death four years ago, and without her Maurice found it hard to be interested in Court affairs, for he had never liked her husband, and had never managed to get on terms with Frederick, the Prince of Wales, and his wife Augusta.

Moreover his mother and brother Karellie were both dead; Vanbrugh and Wren were dead; Walpole, out of office and an old man, could not last much longer. Maurice was forced to realize that he was approaching seventy, and even by his own standards was past middle years. Greatness, having passed him by so far, seemed unlikely to visit him in the time that remained, and the Italian opera was, in any case, dying in London. Maurice's young friend Handel – not so young now, he had to remind himself – had abandoned the form for the more popular oratorios, for which he could still find audiences, but Maurice no longer had the energy to start any major new works. Recently, he had contented himself with rewriting old pieces, and composing the songs and entertainments for which he could find commissions.

Last year, 1741, had been particularly lean for him, beginning with the death of his daughter Apollonia in April at the age of twenty-three. Though he had claimed to have no favourites amongst his children, he had always had a marked partiality for Apollonia, the shy and grave one who had acted as second mother to her younger siblings. He had never troubled to arrange a marriage for her, but Apollonia had not seemed to mind staying at home with Papa. After she had become Lady Apollonia with her father's accession to the title, she had had one or two suitors, but never seemed seriously to consider the possibility of marrying any of them. Her death came suddenly and unexpectedly after a short illness, and left Maurice so low and shocked that he could not even exorcise his emotions with music, as he had done before in times of grief.

Without her, the big house, growing shabby after

the years of occupancy with insufficient money, seemed empty. Clementina was gone, married to Viscount Ballincrea and living in Northumberland; Nicolette was gone, married to her Russian prince, Nicholai Anosov, to whom she had just presented a daughter, Nicholaevna, and living in St Petersburg; even Charles, the 'baby', now thirteen, was gone, being a chorister at St George's Chapel school at Windsor, from which holidays at home were infrequent and short. His wife Nicoletta was past childbearing, so there could be no more additions to the nursery to fill up the silences. Maurice sat out in the garden under the cherry trees as often as the weather permitted, to avoid being in that tomb of a house.

His friends did their best to cheer him up and to persuade him to write again. In the heat of that summer, George Handel was occupied with a new oratorio, using some of his old operatic arias and a strange mixture of Biblical texts, and he tried to engage Maurice's interest by talking about it.

'It's to be a little different from my previous oratorios,' he said. 'The subject matter, to begin with.'

'But you have done religious oratorios before,' Maurice said. 'What about *Saul*? And *Israel in Egypt*?'

'Ah yes, but those were, shall we say, dramatic texts which told a story. This time it's . . .' he hesitated, evidently not sure how to describe his vision. 'I would say it's a statement of belief, a summary of the Christian code. Jennens has assembled various extracts and put them together, from both Old

222

and New Testaments. I don't suppose,' he added gloomily, 'that the public will like it. They did not like *Saul* and *Israel*.'

'It sounds rather – incoherent,' Maurice said. 'Are you sure you wouldn't be better off with some other subject matter?'

'It's something I want to do,' Handel said, 'and it seems there's no pleasing the public anyway, so I am not troubled about it. I've been bankrupt already, so there can be nothing worse to fear.'

'And I'm on the brink of it, though I suppose my title will keep me out of Newgate itself,' Maurice said with an attempt at cheerfulness.

'I think I shall not present this new work in London at all,' Handel said. 'The Lord Lieutenant of Ireland has invited me to visit again next year. Perhaps I shall take my piece over there, and see if Dublin society has better taste than London.' He cocked his head speculatively at Maurice. 'Why don't you come with me?' he coaxed. 'It would do you good to get away from here. It must have so many sad memories for you. You used to travel such a lot, and now you never leave Pall Mall.'

'What, impose myself uninvited on the Lord Lieutenant of Ireland?' Maurice opened his eyes wide with simulated shock. Handel snapped his fingers.

'The Earl of Chelmsford need not talk about "imposing himself", even if Maurice Morland the composer is out of favour. Besides, I am hoping you will give me some very material help with my

223

Messiah – that's what I'm calling this new piece. I want to have a trumpet obbligato part, and you are the best trumpeter in England, as well as the best composer for trumpet . . .'

'Aren't you thinking of Maurice Green?' Maurice said slyly. Handel refused to be baited.

'You are my friend,' he said, 'and I want to see you raised out of this slough of despond and interested in some work again. Look here, won't you give me your advice? This is the text – "The trumpet shall sound, and the dead shall be raised incorruptible, and we shall be changed". The bass sings the first phrase, and then the trumpet replies. This is my idea – what do you think of it?' In a few moments their heads were bent over the manuscript, and for a while Maurice actually forgot his woes in the old potent magic of creation.

The effect lasted long enough for him to search out and rewrite an old opera of his – *Herodias* – along oratorio lines, which he presented at the Ranelagh Rotunda in September. It coincided with the visit to London of the remarkable Italian female soprano, Karelia, who was the daughter of his brother's former mistress, Diane di Francescini, and therefore reputedly Maurice's niece. Karelia had sung at all the principal Courts of Europe, had been invited to sing for the King of Spain at the recommendation of the great Farinelli himself. For the past six months she had been at Versailles, where Louis XV had so loved both her beautiful voice and, it was widely rumoured, her equally beautiful body, that he had given her a title and a fabulously valuable jewel, and begged her to remain permanently in France. But in London her welcome was cool. King George would not receive her because she would be returning from England to the exiled Court of King James III, and though she consented to sing the title role in *Herodias* at the Ranelagh Gardens, the audience was small and unappreciative. Though Maurice would gladly have kept Karelia in London for his own pleasure, he could not pretend that she was likely to be fêted there, and she said that in any case she did not wish to miss another Carnival in Venice. So after a stay of only one month she took ship for France again on the first leg of her journey home. Maurice saw her off with great reluctance. She was his last link with his brother, and he thought it unlikely that he would ever see her again.

Money was becoming a pressing problem, for though he had now only one son, Rupert, Lord Meldon, at home, that one son was a considerable expense. Rupert was twenty-two, an extremely handsome young man, but with increasingly and alarmingly dissolute habits.

'It is your own fault, Maurice,' Nicoletta would rebuke him mildly. 'You never gave him anything to do, and you never loved him as you did your daughters. It has been long since I was able to restrain him, and now he is beyond mending.'

'I always intended him to go to Europe,' Maurice said. 'He should have gone on a Grand Tour with

Ashe Windham's son, but somehow I never got around to arranging it.'

'There are so many things you did not "get around to",' Nicoletta said with unaccustomed severity. 'You always believed tomorrow would do, and now tomorrow is come and gone, and it is too late. I wish you may not regret it.'

Maurice looked surprised. 'He is not so very bad, is he? Not worse than the rest of the Patriot Boys?' This was the name given to the young bucks who hung around the Court of the Prince of Wales at Leicester House. 'All young men get drunk – it is a part of growing up. It is his gambling debts I am really worried about. I don't know if he is unusually unlucky, or unusually stupid, but he seems to lose a great deal more at cards than any of his friends.'

'I'm sure he is not really bad,' Nicoletta said. 'Poor Rupert, he needs a father's guidance. But he is your son; I cannot help him.' And she would not be prevailed upon to say any more.

In October, therefore, Maurice gave a concert of popular vocal and instrumental music at Goodman's Fields to raise a little money, and, so that he should for once at least know where Rupert was, he obliged him to attend. The concert was divided into two parts, and between the parts was a performance of the *Tragedy of Richard III* by William Shakespeare. The part of Richard was taken by an unknown young actor called David Garrick, who had only recently come to the stage, having failed in his previous career as a wine-merchant. His method of acting was strange, even revolutionary, for he did not declaim and make grand gestures, but spoke the words in a normal tone of voice and moved about the stage so quietly and naturally that at times Maurice found himself forgetting that it was an actor he was watching. The audience, strangely enough, loved it, and applauded the young man wildly, and Maurice was intrigued enough to invite him to supper afterwards. It was the beginning of a rather unexpected friendship between David Garrick and Rupert – unexpected, because Garrick was such a quiet, dedicated young man, albeit friendly and cheerful. But Rupert seemed a changed person in Garrick's presence, leaving aside his oaths and heavy drinking and gambling, and as the months passed Nicoletta prayed that the friendship would continue, and that Garrick would not tire of being hero-worshipped by such a young reprobate as her son. For the time being, however, Garrick seemed happy enough to be a frequent visitor at Chelmsford House; though he had taken London by storm, he had many enemies amongst the jealous exponents of the Old School of acting, who were powerful and influential.

This was the state of affairs in February 1742 when Walpole finally relinquished office. In the middle of Maurice's depression over losing such a friend, George Handel came to tell him that he was definitely going to Dublin to stay with the Lord Lieutenant, and that he would be giving the first performance of his *Messiah* there in April. He asked Maurice, with the Duke of Devonshire's permission, to accompany him, and this time Maurice accepted.

Nicoletta was not pleased. 'To cross the Irish Sea at this time of year? No, Maurice, it is too much. I should be dreadfully ill. And you know I have been unwell lately. I cannot go. I will not.'

'Very well, my dear,' Maurice said peaceably. 'I have no objection to going alone. You shall stay here.'

'I shall do no such thing!' Nicoletta said crossly. 'Stay here alone, with Rupert? And how do you suppose I should keep him within bounds? And what should I do in this house day after day without you? No, Maurice, it is too much to bear!'

Maurice suddenly began to smile. She was so very Italian when she was in a rage, and the image of the tiny, crowded house in Naples where he had first been taken by her father, where her mother, Antonia, had ruled supreme always sprang to his mind at such moments. Nicoletta could have made just such an excellent wife and mother in just such a house, ordering the irrepressible servants, alternately hugging and chastising the children, abusing the tradesmen and berating her husband. She had always been out of her place here, in the great empty tomb of a house Maurice had blessed and cursed her with, where no voice was ever raised and no ear was ever boxed. He suddenly thought that she *was* indeed looking unwell, pinched and pale like a plant shut out from the light. He put his arms round her and hugged her suddenly and hard.

'My dear Nicoletta,' he said, kissing her brow. 'My poor, dear Nicoletta! What you have had to bear all these years as my wife is past telling. Can you ever forgive me?'

'Forgive you? Maurice, what nonsense is this?' she asked suspiciously. He pulled her closer still and rocked her a little, his face against her hair.

'It was cruel of me, cruel, to take you away for my own selfish pleasure. How brave and uncomplaining women are! Listen, *carissima*, would you like to go on a visit while I am in Ireland? Would you like to go and visit some of your relatives in Italy?'

'Italy?' she scolded. 'How could I travel to Italy, when I am too ill to travel to Ireland?' But her bird-thin body pressed against him for a moment, and he knew she was pleased. 'I *should* like to visit Alessandra, though. I have missed her very much all these years.'

'Then you shall go, *uccella mia*,' Maurice said. 'I shall write and arrange it immediately.'

Jemmy's hound Jasper had been working his way stealthily towards the drawing room fire for nearly a quarter of an hour, but when he covered the last few feet round the back of Lady Mary's chair and finally crept belly-low to the hearth, pushing Spot out of the way with his nose, he could not help letting out a sigh of bliss and achievement, which called the mistress's attention to him.

She put down her book, drew her skirt back fastidiously, and said, '*Will* you call this dog away from the fire! He smells abominable, and the heat of the fire makes it worse.'

Jemmy looked up from the chessboard, exchanged a silent glance with Father Andrews, and called, 'Jasper, come here.' Jasper came unwillingly, head low, tail clamped between his legs, and rolled his eyes tragically at his master. Jemmy gave him a grimace which might well have been of sympathy, and then ostentatiously seized the hound by his considerable scruff, and pulled him down beside his seat. 'Lie down. Good dog. Stay.'

Lady Mary did not seem satisfied. 'Why don't you keep him out in the yard with the other dogs? A creature like that has no business in the house.'

'You have Spot with you, mother,' Thomas said. He was lounging in the windowseat, idly paring his nails with a penknife.

'That is entirely a different matter, as I should have thought you could see. Spot is a house dog. Jasper is a hunting dog. And sit up, Thomas, do. I cannot bear to see you lolling like that. Have you nothing to occupy yourself with?' Thomas began to straighten himself with a great show of unwillingness which was designed to hide the penknife: his mother thought very ill of *that* habit . . . and Henry, seeing his brother was in trouble, came to his rescue as usual.

'Ah, but you see, mother, Jasper *thinks* he is a house dog too. He would like best to get upon father's lap, as Spot tries to get on yours, for in his heart he's no bigger than a cat. He comes in for the company and the warmth of the fire.' Henry was sharing the small table at the far end of the room, where he had been writing a letter. At the other side of the table, with her back to her mother, Jemima was writing something she was at pains to keep hidden. Jemima, Harry noticed with some sympathy, did not loll or lounge in her seat. Although during the mornings, when there were no visitors, she was allowed by her father's intervention to wear a frock and sash, her mother had insisted that she must change into adult clothes for dinner. The stiff boning of the bodice and the hoops in the skirt made it impossible for her to sit other than upright, and even leaning forward over her paper was something of an effort.

His letter being finished, he pulled the sealing-wax towards him, and picked up the candlestick to take it to the fire and light it, the action reminding him how light the days were getting now. 'I suppose it will soon be too warm for a fire this early in the day,' he said aloud as he walked to the hearth, 'and then Jasper will stay out in the hall with the other dogs.' He smiled at his mother as he spoke, and though she did not smile back, the grimness of her face relaxed a fraction. She loved Henry a little less than Thomas, and therefore scolded him less, but he could sometimes make her smile. Thomas, the first-born, was her darling; Thomas was handsome, looking very like his father, with curly dark hair and a straight nose and a beautiful, if sulky, mouth; Thomas was clever, and high-spirited, and destined to be a great man of politics like his uncle the Duke, for whom he had been named. Henry, on the other hand, was mediocre. He was smaller in stature than his brother, and not handsome, looking too like his mother; his hair was an ordinary light brown, and did not curl, his nose was not straight, his teeth were unremarkable, and he was good at his studies in a painstaking way without being brilliant. Harry, as his mother had conveyed to him since his childhood in many indirect ways, was destined to live in his brother's shadow, and his business was to help Thomas reach the greatness that was waiting for him.

To be placed thus second to a brother in every way more indulged would have made some young men bitter; but Harry loved Thomas no whit less than his mother, and a great deal more clear-sightedly, and his own inclinations to love, help and protect Thomas concurred with his mother's commands. He felt that Thomas was in need of protecting, as much from his mother's love as his father's indifference. Thomas, though full of love ready at any moment to spill over, was very proud and easily wounded, something his mother did not understand.

He lit the candle and then went to the door of the drawing room and opened it. The boy standing outside shoved something hastily into his pocket and tried to look as if he had been standing to attention for the last hour. Henry suppressed a smile. 'Run and ask Clement if anyone has gone for the letters yet. I have a letter to go.'

'Yes, sir,' said the boy, and ran. Henry went back to the table and sat down to seal up his letter. With wax in one hand and candle in the other, he had no hand free to hold down the flap of the letter which, being of stiff paper, was tending to spring open, and Jemima in her quiet, noticing way, reached across the table and pressed it down for him until it was sealed. He smiled his thanks at her.

The movement called her mother's attention to her, and Lady Mary said sharply, 'What are you doing there, Jemima? What are you writing?'

'Only my journal, Mama,' she replied.

'Bring it to me.'

Jemima, still with her back to her mother, looked up at Henry with alarm and dismay on her face, and he saw now that there were two writing-books, one concealed by the other. Her eyes and mouth opened in frantic appeal, and Henry gave an infinitesimal nod, and pushed his hand across the table towards her. Her eyes flickered shut with relief, and she pushed the smaller book under his hand, picked up the larger, and took it demurely across to her mother. Henry, amused, slipped the guilty screed inside his coat, wondering what quiet little Jemima could have been writing that was so shocking. He felt sorry for his little sister, who was plain in a world which valued only beauty in

233

women. Now that her governess had started curling her hair, she looked a little better, but she was still too thin, which even the adult cut of her gown could not conceal, and her features were too big for her face, her skin too colourless. He guessed that she led a life of stupefying boredom, but then it seemed to him that all women did. He could only suppose that they liked it.

He blew out the candle and remarked, 'How quickly the days grow light, once we reach spring. It seems only yesterday that it was dark at three or four o'clock.'

'Yes, and before we know it, it will be summer,' Thomas said, jumping up and walking around the room restlessly, 'and I will be a year older, and still have done nothing.'

Jemmy put down the knight he had picked up and with the air of one much goaded returned to the old argument. 'If you do nothing, it is entirely your own fault. I have tried again and again to get you to learn the business of the estate, and you shew not the slightest interest. You do not know the name of any or our weavers or spinners. I daresay you would not even recognize above half of our tenants. How you will manage to run the estate when I am gone I cannot imagine.'

'He will employ subordinates to do it, of course,' Lady Mary retorted. Jemima took advantage of the distraction to slip away back to her table at the far end of the room. 'He will in any case be too often in London to run the estate as you do, on a personal basis. His career at Court will be much more important.'

The vehemence of her voice woke Uncle George for a moment. He stirred in the other fireside chair like a basking whale, and said, 'Eh? What? Indeed, madam,' and sank back into slumber. Jemmy did not heed the interruption.

'Even if he does have a career such as you evidently long for, madam,' he said in exasperation, 'he must still learn the business of the estate, or how will he govern these paid subordinates? How can he see things are properly done, if he does not know himself how they *are* to be done?'

Lady Mary waved this away. 'He must have trustworthy subordinates. There are always such to be found, if one looks carefully enough.' Her glance strayed to Allen, sitting in an even more retiring position than Jemima, at the far end of the room, reading a book about improving sheep by breeding with choice rams. He appeared not to be listening to the conversation. Lady Mary went on, 'He will have Harry, at all events, and you have seen to it that he is growing up surrounded by penniless cousins. Surely he can make use of them.'

In the fractional silence that followed, Jemima looked at Allen, and saw his lips tighten. Whether the jibe was intended for him or not, it had hurt him. But Thomas had already broken in, waving his hands with frustration.

'But that's not the kind of thing I meant. I don't want to do things about the estate. I want to do something interesting. Why can't I go on a Grand Tour, like everyone else? Or go to University? Or join the army? I don't suppose you even remember that there's a war on . . .'

'How can I forget,' Jemmy said bitterly, 'when I'm paying for it? Land tax, house tax, excise – and all so that the Guelph can march our men out to defend his precious Hanover against his rival petty princelings. He makes it plain enough he cares no more for England than his father did – I think we ought to shew him what we think of him and his German duchy.'

Thomas saw the argument drifting away from him and towards the eternal debate of Jacobitism, and made an effort to recapture it. 'I would have thought, father, that you would at least have wanted me to see Italy, considering—'

Seeing that his brother was about to make a tactless reference to how much time his father spent at Shawes, always a sore point with their mother, Harry began coughing noisily, and Father Andrews, bent on the same mission of rescue, surreptitiously kicked Jasper so that the hound yelped and jumped up, knocking the chess-table so that Jemmy and the priest both had to grab for it to stop it turning over. Lady Mary drew in her breath to expostulate about the unsuitableness of having a hound in the drawing room, and the door opened to admit Clement with the letters and newspapers.

'The boy had already gone,' he apologized to

Henry. 'Your letter will have to wait until tomorrow, I'm afraid.'

'That will do just as well,' Harry said, relieved that the embarrassing moment had passed. 'Shall I take them? Thank you. Here's one for you, mother, and a note from Shawes, and the rest are for father. Oh, there's one here from Uncle Thomas, if I'm not much mistaken. Are you going to read that first? Then may I have the news-papers?' He thrust one of them into Thomas's hands with a sharp look enjoining to discretion, and retired with the other to his seat.

Lady Mary looked with dissatisfaction at the note from Shawes in Marie-Louise's outlandish, spiky hand, and said, 'Jemima, open the instru-ment and play to us while we read. The silence is so stupid.'

Henry smiled to himself, for only last week she had been complaining that there was always too much noise, and never a moment's silence, because the house was so crowded with people. This week the drawing room did seem strangely empty, for Robert and Rachel were away staying at the house of a bishop from whom Robert hoped for prefer-ment, taking their sons with them; Edmund's presence had for once been required with his regi-ment; his three eldest children were staying with their mother's brother in Scarborough; and Augusta herself was still confined to bed after the birth of her fifth child, a boy, Ernest, who was lying placidly in the nursery beside his year-old brother George.

Jemima went over to the instrument, and Allen jumped up attentively to pull out a chair for her and open the lid and arrange her music. Under cover of these manoeuvres he whispered, 'I can be free the whole of tomorrow morning. Would you like to do some Latin? If we start off early enough we can ride up to the Whin, and there will be time for some mathematics as well.'

Jemima flashed him a grateful look, and nodded, and began to play.

After a moment Jemmy looked up from his letter and said, 'Hey-day, here's some news. Thomas, my brother Thomas, is to be married.'

Lady Mary looked up sharply. Another brother to live at their expense and fill the Morland nursery with his own children, she wondered? 'That is very sudden, is it not? I hope she is not a blackamoor. I cannot imagine there can be many English girls in the West Indies.

Jemmy smiled at the idea, but said only, 'He is not in the West Indies. He got the fever again, and they took the excuse to send him home with despatches. He writes this from Plymouth. He says he is lucky to have been sent home ahead of time, for the men are dying like flies over there, and Admiral Vernon's in despair. He wanted a quick action, like the one that took Porto Bello, so that they could avoid staying so long in infected waters, but he could not agree with General Wentworth, and now things have dragged on too long.'

'And who is the girl he is to marry?' Lady Mary asked. 'A Plymouth beauty? An admiral's daughter?'

'Not a Plymouth girl at all, but yes, she is a sailor's daughter, though only a captain's, not an admiral's. He writes that he is travelling at once to Lyme Regis to stay with his friend, Captain Elliott, who has been invalided out of the service and has taken a house there, "to be near the sea", Tom says. It is Elliott's daughter Maria he is to marry. He met her at Portsmouth when he was on his way back to join Vernon's fleet after his last illness, and they came to an agreement almost at once.' Jemmy put the letter down and smiled around the room. 'How pleased I am for him! It is right that Tom should marry for love. I only wish he could be married here, instead of at Lyme. I have half a mind to travel down there.'

Lady Mary looked disapproving of the idea, but said only, 'I do not think you will want to go when you hear the contents of my letter. Here will be gaiety enough even for you, Thomas, I think. Lord Chelmsford's wife Nicoletta has come to stay at Shawes while he is in Ireland, and brought her son Lord Meldon with her. There is to be a house party, and everyone is invited to dinner on Wednesday, and to a ball on Thursday. You would not like to miss all that, would you?' she suggested to her husband. Jemmy could not tell whether she was pleased with the invitation or not. On the one hand, there were to be important and titled people to meet, and Lady Mary had a proper reverence for

239

titles. On the other hand, she hated Marie-Louise to the extent that she never mentioned her name, or referred to her even indirectly, if she could help it. Jemmy went across to her to look at the letter, and saw with amusement that Marie-Louise, perhaps out of wickedness, had signed it 'Marie-Louise Fitzjames Stuart, Countess of Strathord' instead of merely initialling it, which would have been sufficient on such an informal note.

'A dinner, and a ball,' Jemmy said. 'And then of course we shall have to have at least a dinner in return. How gay we shall all be. I think, Thomas, that you might postpone running away to join the army for a little while. Perhaps young Robert might give you a hint or two on how to pass your time in gentlemanly pursuits. He will have all the London gossip, at least. And there will be plenty of young ladies for you and Harry to dance with. But how pleased Alessandra and Nicoletta will be to meet again.' And I, to have an excuse to be more often there than here, he thought to himself. In the ensuing silence the sound of Jemima's playing was heard. He looked across at her with sudden pity.

'But why should not poor Jemima have some share in the pleasure? It must be dull for her with Augusta and Caroline away.'

'Oh no, papa,' Jemima said, pausing. She did not care for her cousins, and in any case, she was too happy at the thought of spending the morning with Allen tomorrow, learning Latin and mathematics.

Besides, she did not like him to draw attention to her in front of her mother. She knew that part of his pretended preference of her was to spite her mother and emphasize how little he cared for her favourites, his sons.

Her mother said, 'How can she have a share in the pleasure, as you put it? She is not invited. These are not social gatherings for a child of ten; they are for adults.'

Jemima actually saw the idea come to her father, saw his head go up and his eyes gleam with it. 'I did not mean that. But you know Jemima has not been looking well, since she had that cough during the winter. I think a change of scene and some fresh air would do her good, perhaps some sea air.' He turned to Jemima now. 'I cannot go myself, that is plain, but how would you like to take my place, chick, and go to Lyme Regis to Uncle Tom's wedding?'

The ball was as elegant and splendid as anything Annunciata had ever given at Shawes, from the size and excellence of the orchestra to the quantity and deliciousness of the white soup, which was, after all, made from Annunciata's own recipe, calling for quantities of chicken, almonds and egg yolks and gallons of thick cream. All the best York society was there, for though there were many who refused to acknowledge Marie-Louise's title, and even doubted her respectability, yet there were none who refused her invitations. Not least amongst the eager

241

guests were a number of unmarried men of various ages who hoped to persuade Marie-Louise to marry them. She was very beautiful, after all, and, more to the point, very rich, and though she reputedly had a temper, once she was married her property would belong to her husband, and she might mend her manners or find herself locked up in her own house. Jemmy worried from time to time that she might be foolish enough to marry one of these worthless creatures, but his friend and mentor, Davey, would shake his head and say, 'There are some mares you cannot breed from.'

She looked magnificent as she received her guests at the head of the stairs, and every inch a princess. Her gown was all of silver, silver tissue, opened over a silver brocade petticoat with scallops of silver lace gathered up by pale pink artificial roses. Her red-gold hair was dressed high in curls and ringlets, and she wore a pearl half-hoop head-dress, and her throat and slender arms were circled with pearls, too. Jemmy stooped low over her head, and then stood for a moment, still holding it, simply gazing at her, thinking how well she would have looked in the diamonds Annunciata had left to Jemima. He should have thought of offering them to Marie-Louise on loan, but it was too late now.

'Have you decided who is to open the ball with you?' he asked her. Her tawny-gold eyes looked directly into his, and widened slightly at the question.

'Why, I naturally intended that it would be you,'

she said, and he laughed as he kissed her hand again. Mary watched them with some bitterness, aware that they had entirely forgotten her presence for the moment, that they knew exactly what the other was thinking, that they were completely in accord. Now, belatedly, Marie-Louise turned to her with a charming smile which Mary distrusted entirely.

'Dear Lady Mary, how lovely you look tonight. Blue becomes you so. It is a thousand pities you cannot dance, but I hope you will enjoy yourself all the same. There are plenty of card tables.'

To play cards at a ball was the province of old ladies and old gentlemen and clerics, and Mary did not know whether or not she was being insulted. She could only smile tightly and move on, almost pushed out of the way as she was by Robert and Rachel, anxious to pay their respects. They had come back at full gallop from the disappointing bishop as soon as they heard of the proposed ball at Shawes, and Mary could not avoid hearing the first phrases of Robert's nasal drawl and Rachel's fussy fulsomeness.

'How delightful, your ladyship—'

'How very good of you to ask us, dear Lady Strathord, how very affable—' She hurried on as fast as her limp and ebony stick would allow her, to avoid hearing more.

There were a number of pretty young women present, for as Francis Drake had said of York in his book *Eboracum* a few years back, 'The women are remarkably handsome; it being taken notice of by strangers that they see more pretty faces in York than in any other place'; and Daniel Defoe had said in *his* book, 'The ladies of the north are as handsome and as well dressed as are to be seen either at the Court or the ball.' Henry hurried off as soon as he was in the room to take advantage of his name and his good-humoured countenance to fill a few blanks on the young women's cards. He may not have been as handsome as his elder brother, but he was very little less popular at balls, making half the looks go twice as far by the economical addition of charm. Thomas would have done the same, but Rupert, with whom they had been standing, did not seem at all inclined to move, and Thomas felt obliged to wait for his cue.

They had met yesterday at the dinner-party, and despite being expected to be friendly by their seniors, they had been sufficiently attracted to each other to have arranged to spend the morning of the ball together. Thomas was fascinated by Rupert, by his fashionable appearance, his languid elegance, and above all by his talk. He had hoped to repay the entertainment, and perhaps win a little admiration of his own, by taking Rupert riding that morning, for there was no doubt that Thomas was the best horseman in the county and that the Morland horses were the best, probably in the country. Lord Meldon accepted the invitation readily enough to flatter Thomas's hopes, but though he appeared at the arranged time, dressed in splendid style, and though he sat his horse well enough, he did not take any notice either of Thomas's horse or his horsemanship. Lord Meldon's idea of a ride, indeed, was quite different from Thomas's, being a leisurely amble at walking-pace through the fields, broken by a short and gentle canter over the most level ground. He did not wish to see any of the countryside, nor jump hedges, nor gallop over the moors, nor dare the quarryside or the river-crossing.

He did not talk horses, either, which puzzled Thomas, for in Yorkshire young men talked little else. All Rupert's conversation was the theatre, and 'my friend Garrick, the actor, you know'. However, the theatre was a new field to Thomas, and undeniably fascinating, especially when Rupert larded his talk with cant phrases and technical terms and flatteringly assumed that Thomas would understand them. Nevertheless there was something odd about him, Thomas thought, though he could not quite decide what.

Seeing Harry dash off, however, he thought it wise to give Rubert a hint.

'I say, Meldon, would you not like to speak for a partner for the first dance? I know there are the minuets first, but the best girls are snapped up so quickly, that we shall be left out if we delay too long. See, my brother has already asked Miss Nevill – she is considered quite a beauty at the Assembly Rooms.

Rupert looked around from under his half-closed eyelids and said languidly, 'There is not, my dear

Morland, a woman fit to be stood up with in the whole room except our hostess. Your Miss Nevill a beauty? Do not say it! The frightful hag your brother is talking to this minute? The creature with the bird's-nest hair? My dear, you cannot mean it.' He sighed. 'I did not at all want to come to Yorkshire, you know, but my father insisted upon it, and as he has control of my allowance I cannot say him nay. I hoped Lady Strathord might provide me with a little amusement, but of course even she cannot make bricks without straw.'

Thomas was looking a little puzzled. He had never come across anyone who talked like Rupert. He tried again, hesitantly. 'But the young woman over there, in the blue sack, with the golden hair?' he said, indicating Miss Pobgee, with whom he had hoped to dance the two first. 'Do you not think *her* handsome?'

Rupert bestowed the favour of half a glance on her, and turned his head away, closing his eyes. Thomas, aware that Miss Pobgee was watching him from behind her fan, blushed with embarrassment.

'Monstrous!' Rupert cried. 'But come, my dear Morland, we shall not harm our senses by looking at such creatures. Dancing is so stupid, as tedious to perform as to watch. Let us find something to drink, and a quiet place to drink it, and talk instead. I wish to tell you about the cruel, cruel satire that Foote has made on my friend Garrick.'

He walked away, looking for a servant to send for

wine, and Thomas trailed after him, half admiring anyone who could so despise the best society of York, and half disappointed, since he had looked forward to the ball for days. Yet there was no resisting Rubert's fascination.

Despite the horrors of the journey across the Irish Sea, Maurice was well pleased with his visit, and wondered that he had never gone before. Dublin was not at all what he had expected: it had public and private buildings of great beauty, and a society of wit and learning whose taste for the arts, and especially for music, was voracious. It was a small society, of course, and everyone knew everyone else to an even more claustrophobic degree than in London; the gossip was wittier and also more cruel; the women seemed to enjoy a greater degree of freedom than at home. There was a strange mixture of native Irish nobility and gentry, and English pensioners and placeholders, and one or two eccentrics who, having once lived in Dublin from necessity, simply refused to live anywhere else. Maurice was also aware that outside the glittering circle of the society was the mass of silent, poverty-stricken aboriginals, just as outside of the architecturally acceptable centre of Dublin lay the mean streets and squalid hovels that he had anticipated and was now able to ignore completely.

He and Handel were staying at the Castle with the Viceroy, and on the day after their arrival a reception was given for them, at which they met the people whose faces were to become so familiar in a matter of days. Handel was greeted rapturously, for this was not his first visit, but Maurice was amused and flattered to find that he, too, was a hero, and the degree to which his music was known and, at least professedly, admired amazed him. He expressed his surprise to one of the leading lights of Dublin musical circle, a Mrs Estoyle. Despite the obviously French origins of her name, she pronounced it with a heavy emphasis on the first syllable, as if it were completely Irish. She was a widow of around thirty, beautiful in a ripe, Roman way, evidently extremely rich, to judge by her diamonds. She had glossy red hair and long green eyes, which gazed into his with unmistakable promise, and long white fingers which seized his arm to keep him close by her, and a magnificent white bosom at which he found it difficult not to stare. Her salons were famous, and she was reputed to have had a hundred lovers. Maurice was not at all sceptical.

'But my dear Lord Chelmsford, I assure you we know all about you here. I wonder, do you underestimate yourself, or us?'

'As I cannot, in politeness, confess to the latter, I must admit the former,' Maurice said, amused. She pouted a little, and her bosom lifted towards him invitingly.

'I do not believe you. Your music – so heavenly! So absolutely what one likes! And I believe Karelia herself sang your *Herodias*? Wonderful, wonderful woman! We invited her here, you know, but she would not come. No, I'm afraid she had the same thoughts, the same unworthy thoughts, about Dublin society as I see plainly you had, despite your denials. Well, my dear Earl, let me tell you, a few, only a few years ago, you would not have been so very wrong. Why, when George I came to the throne, Dublin was nothing but a dirty, ill-built little town with nothing to recommend it.' Maurice made polite noises of disbelief. She smiled coquettishly.

'But it is true, I vow and swear. Do not, now, be disbelieving me, or I shall have to be angry with you! Yes, hardly a house fit to be visited. But we have pulled down, you know, and built up. Whole streets demolished, others widened, hovels torn down and such a multitude of lovely mansions erected in their place, for all the best people in Ireland. The Duke of Leinster, and Lord Tyrone – there, you will meet them all, may dear Lord Chelmsford, and think me impertinent for wishing to inform you. But my dear sir, may I hope that while you are here you will favour us with a performance?'

'A performance?' Maurice said, wondering for a wild moment whether she was making a gross sexual advance to him. She widened her already wide green eyes.

'Why yes! We know that you are the greatest exponent of the trumpet of our age, and we are hoping so much that you will give a recital.'

'Madam,' Maurice laughed, 'you must spare

my years. I have not given a public performance for years. I play only in private for my own and my friends' amusement.'

'I am sorry, Lord Chelmsford,' she said with pretended gravity, 'but I do not believe you. I think you are afraid for your dignity. But I assure you in Dublin, music is all. Lord Mornington does not disdain to perform in St Stephens or St Patricks. We take a collection, you know, for the hospital. But you have lived in Venice, where the noblest in the land perform in public, and you are merely playing with me, I know it. You will perform while you are here.'

'Madam, I can only say I have no intention of doing so,' Maurice said. She inched even closer, her marbled bosom heaving.

'And you must promise me that as soon as the official parties are over, you will make mine the very first house you visit. I insist upon having the honour. I wish to present you to everyone, all my dearest friends who love your music so much. And afterwards, when they have all gazed their fill, I shall send them away, and then you and I may have a little private supper and talk,' her voice became liquid, 'and talk to our hearts' content. About music, you know.'

Maurice had much ado to keep from laughing. It was very flattering to be found so attractive at his age, by a woman of half his years. When she finally left him for some other conversation, he sidled over to Handel, who was sorting through some music in a quiet corner of the room.

'*Who* is that extraordinary woman?' Maurice asked, shaking his handkerchief out of his sleeve to wipe his brow. Handel glanced up.

'Oh, Mrs Estoyle. She's very rich. And very musical.'

'*Is* she? She asked me to her house in the most extraordinary manner.'

'Nothing extraordinary about it. She has a salon. I've been on a number of occasions. All the best people go. She is a very generous patroness – subscribed a score of tickets for my *Messiah*. You won't be required to sing for your supper, you know.'

'I'm not so sure about that,' Maurice said. 'Were you one of her fabled hundred lovers, George?'

Handel looked no more than mildly surprised. 'My dear Morland, that sort of thing is not in my line at all. My attractions for her are entirely artistic.'

'I wish I could say the same,' Maurice murmured.

The performance of the *Messiah* was to be given in the Music Hall in Fishamble Street on 13 April, and there had been a remarkable seven hundred subscribers. 'Two hundred more even than last year,' Handel said in delight. 'I can't imagine how they are all going to get in.'

It was indeed a problem, as Maurice appreciated when he had seen the size of the hall. Eventually it was decided to ask the subscribers to help by coming to the concert, the ladies without hoops to their dresses, and the gentlemen without swords. Having regard to the relentless fashionableness of society,

Maurice wondered if the appeal would have any effect, but in fact almost all complied, leaving at home the very symbols of their gentility in the cause of art.

Handel was as nervous as a novice before the performance, and begged Maurice to accompany him up until the last minute, which Maurice was only too delighted to do. He was worried about the reception the piece would get, for it was certainly very odd, though some of the music, which he had only seen in manuscript, was ravishing. The Lord Lieutenant's coach left them down at the back door, and as soon as they entered, the continuo player rushed up to them waving his hands in panic and telling a tale of woe. In a moment he had led them to the back-stage room where the musicians were assembling, and there they found the trumpet-player who was to perform Handel's special obbligato sitting in a sorry huddle, a bloodstained handkerchief to his face.

'It was an accident, I swear to God it was,' cried the timpanist. 'I didn't see him bending over there.'

He had been bringing in one of his great drums, unable to see much over the top of it, just at a time when the trumpeter had been bending down to fasten his shoe, and had walked straight into him.

'The lip isn't split, thank heaven,' Handel said, having examined the man's swollen mouth and nose, 'but he can't play today, that's clear. Well, we shall have to manage without the second trumpet part, and second trumpet can play the first trumpet part. Where is he?'

A thin, pale boy of fifteen was shoved forward by his fellows, who were, in the way of all flesh, enjoying the disaster. He turned paler still and said, 'I couldn't, sir, I really couldn't. It's too hard for me, that part. Patrick there, he's the only man in Dublin could play you such a piece, and no man in the world could do it on sight, without a bit of a practice beforehand.'

Handel turned to Maurice, and the two men read each other's thoughts and began slowly to smile. 'Not so, lad. I know one man who could play it on sight,' Handel said. Maurice raised his hands in a gesture of surrender.

'Don't overawe the lad, George. Remember I've seen it before.'

'You, sir?' gasped the boy. Handel put an arm over his friend's shoulder.

'This is the great Maurice Morland, boy,' he said.

'There, and I thought he was only a nobleman,' said the child innocently. Handel raised an eyebrow at Maurice.

'Well, Lord Chelmsford? Will you?'

Maurice gave his most Italian shrug. 'I don't see how I can refuse. But for God's sake, don't announce it, and try not to tell anyone. I hate to think how Mrs Estoyle will gloat.'

On the day after the ball, Nicoletta did not get up. She had been feeling very tired for the last

253

few days, and now she had a headache, and odd pains in her back. Alessandra came at once to see her, and sat by her, holding her hand in concern.

'I had better call for the doctor to come and see you,' she said. 'My poor Nicoletta, you look quite flushed. I think you may have a fever.'

'Oh no, it is nothing. Too late a night, too much excitement, too much dancing,' Nicoletta said. 'Do not trouble anyone, please, *cara*. I shall have a lazy day in bed, and I shall be well tomorrow. What is that noise outside?' They both listened.

'It is Rupert, going out riding with Thomas again,' Alessandra said. 'I'll tell them to be quiet.'

'Oh, no, please ask Rupert to come and see me for a moment; I want to see him in his new coat. It is so good for him being here, away from London and all those actors. I am sure they are not respectable. Thomas is such a nice boy.'

Alessandra gave a curious grimace, and went to bring Rupert in. Thomas came with him, looking pink and shamefaced, and apologized for making a noise. Rupert went over and kissed his mother on the mouth like a lover, which Thomas thought odd – but then so much that Rupert did was odd. Nicoletta smiled and pushed Rupert's hair from his face.

'How nice you look, my darling. And did you have a good time at the ball?'

'Oh yes, very nice,' Rupert said, curling a lock of her hair round his finger.

'But you did not dance with anyone, my darling. I made sure you would dance a little.'

'I did not care to. You are the only woman I love, madonna. Besides,' he looked over his shoulder at Thomas, 'I had a *much* nicer time talking – didn't we, Morland?'

'Oh – much,' Thomas said awkwardly. Nicoletta smiled at him kindly.

'And you take my Rupert riding again today. How kind you are. Well, I won't keep you. Come and kiss me too, Thomas. Goodbye. I hope you have a pleasant time.'

'We will, mother, we will. Come on, Morland, don't dawdle,' Rupert cried, and grabbing Thomas's hand, hurried him out. Alessandra watched them go thoughtfully.

'He didn't dance at all, did he?' she said. Nicoletta brought her thoughts back with an effort.

'No, not at all. But then,' she brightened, 'nor did Thomas.'

By the afternoon, the headache was worse, and she had begun to have shivering fits, and was obviously feverish. She ate no dinner, but Alessandra persuaded her to take a little gruel at tea-time, which she vomited up soon afterwards. She still insisted she would be better the next day, but in the morning the fever was worse, and Alessandra called for the doctor. He came in the afternoon, and shook his head gravely.

'I cannot tell what it is. It could be any one of many different things, which all display the same symptoms at first. In a day or two we shall know. But in the meantime, she must be kept in isolation, and nothing must go out of this room unless it is thoroughly scrubbed and fumigated.'

Alessandra's hands clenched nervously. 'What – is it you fear?'

'Smallpox,' the doctor said. 'It is the most infectious disease known to man.'

CHAPTER 9

On the third day of her illness, Nicoletta woke feeling better. The fever had abated and the pains in her back and the headache had gone.

'You see,' she said triumphantly to Alessandra, 'I told you I should be well again.'

'But, my darling,' Alessandra said in concern, 'your face is so flushed. Surely you cannot be right about the fever having gone?' She leaned forward to examine Nicoletta's face more closely, and then said, 'Shew me your hands.' Nicoletta spread them forth, and they both stared at them as a slow horror spread over Nicoletta's face. Her hands, like her face, were covered in a rash of tiny red spots, so close together that they had at first resembled a blush. Nicoletta gave a terrible cry.

'What is it? *Christe Maria,* what is it?'

Alessandra placed a firm hand over her wrist and said, 'I will send for the doctor at once. Be of good heart, dearest. Perhaps it may be nothing.' Her voice wavered as she said it, betraying her fear.

The doctor came two hours later, examined his patient gravely, bled her from the toe, and then drew

Alessandra outside to speak to her. She looked at him in mute appeal, but he only shook his head.

'It is as I feared,' he said.

'Smallpox?' she whispered. He nodded. 'What can you do?'

'Madam, there is no cure for smallpox. There is nothing I can do.'

'Then . . . she will . . . ?'

'Many die from smallpox. Many survive. It is impossible to tell at this stage whether the attack is light or serious. All that can be done is to keep her warm and quiet, try to get her to take some nourishment, and above all keep her isolated. You would be advised to leave the house as soon as possible, and fumigate the clothes you have been wearing in the sickroom.'

'Leave?' Alessandra said with a puzzled frown. 'How can I leave?'

'There is nothing that you or I can do,' the doctor said. 'She must be nursed, but that is no task for a lady. I can find you a professional nurse willing to take on a smallpox case, if you offer her enough money.'

Alessandra hesitated. 'I should have to meet her, to see if she was suitable.'

The doctor's smile was grim. 'Madam, anyone who would take a smallpox case would not be the sort of woman you would wish to meet. Do you not understand that whoever nurses that sick woman in there will almost certainly catch the sickness herself?'

Alessandra drew herself up. 'Give me your instructions. I shall nurse her myself.'

'Madam, have I not made myself clear . . .' the doctor began in expostulation, but Alessandra cut him short.

'You have made yourself very plain,' she said. 'I cannot abandon that woman to a stranger's hands. If nursing is the only thing that can help her, she shall have it from one who cares enough to do it well. Give me your instructions.'

'No one owes such a debt,' the doctor said, and then shrugged. 'Well, I have warned you. I can do no more.'

When the doctor had gone, Alessandra went back into the bedchamber. Nicoletta turned her head on the pillow to look at her, and Alessandra saw that she already knew, that the task of breaking the terrible truth to her was unnecessary.

'You will come through,' Alessandra said, holding her gaze steadily. 'You and I together will see to that. We won't let you die.'

The rest of the household withdrew to the other end of the house, isolating the sickroom, and Alessandra prepared as if for a siege, with enough water and food for days, candles and firewood, ointments and dressings.

She tried to persuade Marie-Louise to leave the house entirely, but she refused. 'As long as you are here and in danger, I will not go,' she said. 'Do you think I do not know what I owe to you, who have cared for me for so long, since my mother left?' Alessandra thought of the doctor's words, 'No one owes such a debt', but she could not insist when she herself would not leave Nicoletta. Rupert, however, did go away, to stay at Morland Place with Thomas, which he seemed not only willing, but eager to do. Alessandra made up suitable messages from him to his mother, but Nicoletta smiled sadly at them. She adored her son, but any illusions she had about him were entirely wilful.

On the fourth day of her illness the rash, which had spread from her face and hands over her entire body, changed its appearance, and any remaining hope that it was not smallpox quietly died. The pocks became raised up, and filled with a clear fluid, with a slight depression in the centre of each. Alessandra and Nicoletta regarded them with horror, and Nicoletta broke into a storm of weeping which lasted for almost half an hour. Alessandra comforted her as best she could, and when the tears were over, she tried to keep her occupied by reading with her and playing cards and chatting. It was in some ways the worst part of the illness for Nicoletta, for the fever was almost entirely gone, and she felt normal enough to be rational and therefore to have all a rational person's fears and dreads.

On the sixth day the fever returned, and with it came another change in the nature of the rash. The pocks grew in size, and the fluid in them changed into yellow pus, and each was surrounded by a ring of inflamed and swollen skin. Nicoletta tossed irritably on her pillows, her eyes glazed with the fever, her tongue swollen, and as the inflammation grew worse it distorted her features. Alessandra could do nothing for her but to give her sips of water and try to keep her quiet, but as the fever increased and the irritation of the rash grew less bearable, it became difficult.

On the seventh day she was evidently very much worse, and a new complication revealed itself. The rash was not only on her skin, but also on the inside of her mouth and throat, and though Alessandra propped her up on a number of pillows, it was plain that she was finding it hard to breathe. After watching her for an hour, gasping for breath, tossing her head back and forth, and snatching with her hands at her swollen throat, her eyes squeezed almost closed by the inflammation of her face, Alessandra sent again in desperation for the doctor. But this time he did not come, sending instead a note which regretted that there was nothing he could do for the patient, and again recommending that Alessandra leave Nicoletta to the care of a professional nurse. When she read the note, Alessandra wept; having wept, she dried her eyes, rolled up her sleeves, and used her own wits. Since the doctor evidently despaired of Nicoletta's life, it seemed to Alessandra that she would try to make her more comfortable. She let the fire die down, and opened the sickroom windows so that the fresh April air blew in. She tied back the bedcurtains, and stripped off most of the bedclothes, bathed Nicoletta carefully and put a clean bedgown on her, brushed her hair, and brewed up a herbal febrifuge from the recipe in Annunciata's Household Book. All these things had the effect of quieting Nicoletta. She seemed to breathe more easily, and became less restless, as if the fever and irritation had declined; and so Alessandra felt she had been justified.

During the night she seemed to sleep, but on the next day, the eighth of her illness, Nicoletta grew worse again. It seemed that the blebs that covered the membranes of her mouth and throat were swelling to the extent that they were suffocating her. Alessandra sent again for the doctor, and while she waited, she sat beside Nicoletta, fanning her face in the vain effort to give her more air. Nicoletta lay propped up, her face turned towards the open window, her mouth open, dragging in painful, hoarse breath after painful, hoarse breath. Her eyes were open now only a slit, and though Alessandra could see the dark gleam of her eyes moving behind the swollen lids, she had no way of knowing if Nicoletta was conscious or recognized her.

The breaths grew more and more laboured, and Alessandra fanned more and more desperately. The moment finally came when Nicoletta's hands went up, scrabbling feebly towards her face, her body heaved upwards in the vain effort to draw air into her tortured lungs through the suppurating throat, and she fell back onto her pillows. Her feet kicked once under the bedclothes, and then she lay still. In the silence Alessandra became suddenly aware of the birdsong outside and the maddeningly sweet smell of the spring air. The doctor had not come, had not, this time, even replied to the message. It must have been a quarter of an hour before Alessandra realized that she was still fanning Nicoletta's swollen and deformed face.

It was several more days before anyone realized the smallpox had not been confined to Shawes, but had transferred itself to Morland Place. In the more confined and crowded spaces there, it wreaked more havoc. It revealed itself first of all in one of the servants, the boy who took care of Thomas's clothes, and as soon as the rash made its appearance, Lady Mary went in hysterical fear to Jemmy, to demand that Rupert be send forthwith back to Shawes.

'It is he that has brought this horrible sickness to our house,' she cried. 'You must send him away at once, before he infects us all.'

Jemmy tried to calm her. 'It is possible, of course, that he has brought the sickness. But you know, we were all at Shawes for the ball – any one of us might have been the carrier.'

'But that was weeks ago,' Lady Mary said. It did not seem worth Jemmy's while to explain to her that smallpox took time to reveal itself. 'Besides,' she went on, 'the boy has been taking care of Rupert's clothes as well as Thomas's while he has been staying here, and it is plain enough that it was from those clothes he took the sickness. If you don't send him away, I shall.'

'Very well, Mary, but—'

Mary rounded on him furiously. 'He has been sleeping in the same room, in the same bed as Thomas! Do you wish *our son* to catch this horrible disease?'

'I will send him back to Shawes at once,' Jenny said pacifically.

So Rupert went back to Shawes, and justified Mary's outburst by immediately developing a rash. Alessandra, who so far had escaped the infection, nursed him, and this time did not consult the doctor at all, but used the methods she had used, towards the end, with Nicoletta, keeping him cool and giving him fresh air. The attack he had was a light one, and either because of that or because of Alessandra's nursing, he recovered quickly and emerged barely marked.

But his removal from Morland Place did not save its occupants. Ten of the servants took the sickness, including the nursery maid who had been wet-nursing both of Augusta's babies; and despite the removal of Rupert, first Thomas and then Harry fell sick. Jemmy did what he could to isolate the victims and sent away as many of the healthy people as he could. Mary at first declared that she would nurse her sons herself, weeping hysterically and cursing Lord Meldon and Nicoletta and, by association, MarieLouise, swearing revenge if anything should happen to her boys. Jemmy restrained and calmed her, and forbade her to go into the sickroom. 'You cannot help them, you who have a mother's feelings – it would be too much for you.'

'But I want to see my sons,' she cried. 'A mother's care, a mother's love shall heal them.'

'Nursing is no task for a lady, particularly this sort of nursing,' Jemmy said firmly. 'You can help them best by staying away and remaining healthy. How could it help them for you to catch the sickness too? And how could that help me?' She looked at him sourly, with a look that said she knew he had never cared for her or for her sons. He went on gently, 'Let them find you healthy and unblemished when they recover, Mary dear. Let me arrange for you to go to Scarborough, away from this infected air, until they are well again.'

He knew what she thought of him, but it could not be helped. Jemmy had been to the sickroom, he had seen the boys and he knew she must not be allowed to see. Thomas had the type of the disease called confluent smallpox, a more severe form, in which the pocks were so numerous and close together that they ran into one another. His face and body were disfigured by huge, running, suppurating sores.

He had his way, for once exerting his right to command as Master, and sent Mary, with Rachel to attend her, to Scarborough along with Augusta. He also prevailed upon Marie-Louise to leave Shawes for a while, and pay a visit to Harrogate until the danger was past, and with a happy thought sent Allen along with her as escort. They all left on the morning of the day that Augusta's babies died. After the flurry of the departure came the sad business of the deaths, and it was well past dinner time when Jemmy at last came down to the drawing room with the intention of sitting quietly for a moment and composing himself. To his astonishment he found his brother George, whom he had entirely forgotten in all the confusion, standing by the empty fireplace, waiting for him.

'Ah, there you are,' he said cheerfully, 'I thought you'd be down soon. Must be dinner time, or past.'

Jemmy only stared. He had sent away Mary and Augusta, Jemima was safe in Dorset, Robert and Rachel had made their escape at the first whiff of sickness, but he had quite forgotten George.

'Dinner time?' he said vaguely. George nodded.

'Quite an appetite today. I've been out shooting at Wilstrop. Got a few birds for the larder. Make nice eating.'

'Don't you realize there's sickness in the house? And you talk of dinner and birds for the larder?' Jemmy said, amazed at his callousness.

'Got to keep your strength up, or you'll fall sick too,' George said. Jemmy looked at him with distaste.

'I think you'd better make arrangements to leave as well. You could go with Robert and Rachel, or to Scarborough with Mary, if you prefer.'

Now George looked surprised. 'Leave?' he said. He took a step closer and laid a meaty hand on Jemmy's wrist. 'I'm not leaving. Someone's got to

266

stay here with you, help you and so on. Can't leave you here all alone. Come on now and get some dinner. Things always look worse when you're hungry. The boys'll be all right, you'll see.'

Tears came to Jemmy's eyes at the unexpected sympathy. 'I didn't even think you realized they were ill,' he confessed. George did not look offended.

'You give me a home here – do you think I'm not grateful? I know there's not much I can do, but anything I can, you just say the word.'

Later, when Jemmy mentioned it to Father Andrews, the priest gave a wry smile.

'If prayer can help the boys, they'll certainly recover,' he said. 'Your brother has been spending two hours a day in the chapel on his knees – and with his figure, that takes some doing.'

Maurice was having an affair with Molly Estoyle – at least, officially. He drove with her in her carriage, dined with her publicly, shared her box at the theatre, supped alone with her, and frequently stayed the night. As far as society was concerned, he was her lover. As far as Maurice was concerned he had reached an age where sex was theoretical rather than physical, and he had in any case never been attracted to matronly charms, being a lover of child-madonnas.

Molly Estoyle was, however, an amusing companion, witty, well-educated, and flatteringly devoted to him, and he was perfectly happy to become one of her fabled century, especially when

267

it became obvious that she was equally content with a communion of the minds only. Mere pride had compelled Maurice to consummate their relationship on the first few occasions, but when he desisted, she had not insisted. The daughter of a clergyman, she had been brought up in genteel poverty and had married a rich but uncultured merchant much her senior, who had let her have her own way and then died leaving her in possession of his fortune while she was still young enough to enjoy it. She revered society, fame, gentility, and especially nobility, and devoted her life to being associated with it. She must give the best dinners, mix with the best people, be talked about in the best circles. Anyone who was the current talk must appear at her table before anyone else's; any man who was much admired must be reputed to be her lover. She was rich, charming and beautiful, and she had never yet failed, not even with George Handel who, though he would not become her lover, was happy enough to accept her patronage and her invitations to dinner.

She had wanted Maurice for his reputation before she ever saw him, for he was not only famous on his own account, but also for being the son of one of the most notorious women of the age, and he was also an Earl. Molly Estoyle had a proper respect for titles. When she saw him, however, she wanted him for himself, for Maurice had the looks and the charm of the Stuarts whose blood ran so interestingly in his veins. She was not, despite her reputation, a passionate woman – possession was what interested her – and since it was men she wished to possess, because men held the power in the world, and she was a woman, she used the most obvious means at her disposal to possess them. A man whom society knew to be her lover was hers in a way that no amount of mere friendship or patronage could ensure; but the sexual act did not interest her in itself, and provided the indecencies were observed, she was perfectly satisfied with the fact rather than the act.

So she and Maurice got along famously, especially as, now she did not need to entrap him, she behaved more naturally with him, and allowed her considerable intelligence to emerge from behind the battery of her physical charms. This morning, for instance, they had been awake and talking for more than an hour before her maid and her man brought in their breakfast to them in bed. While Maurice, resplendent in scarlet silk dressing gown and night cap, sat up lordlywise in bed, Molly wandered about the room in her drifting draperies of sky blue, that made her tumbled hair look redder and more glorious than ever, and amused him with the story of how she had tried to ensnare Handel.

'Oh it was too ridiculous! There I was, doing everything a woman can do, to get him into my bed, and all the time he thought I wanted him to write me an opera! He did not in the least understand what I was about, and I was so stupid that

I did not see for weeks that the way to ensnare him was to praise his music.'

'George is a very devoted musician,' Maurice said gravely. 'He married his muse long ago, and he is a faithful lover. While I – I am a very different proposition.'

'You certainly demanded different tactics,' Molly said thoughtfully.

'Oh, I am the merest sensualist,' Maurice said lightly. 'A child of this world, subject to all its vices and vanities. I make my way by writing music just as a cobbler makes his way by making shoes – it is my trade.'

Molly came across to the bed and sat on the edge, picking up one of Maurice's hands, turning it over in hers and running her fingers over his palm.

'What beautiful hands you have,' she said softly. 'Not a cobbler's hands at all. Yes, you like to make-believe you are a simple, worldly man. I have seen you play-acting at my salons, and you convince a great many people—'

'But not you?' Maurice smiled.

'I know you a little better than they, my dear Earl. What I do not know is why you do it? Why you are at such pains to make your talent seem ordinary?'

Maurice looked into her face for a moment, into the bright, rather protruberant green eyes, so full of considering intelligence, and said, 'Perhaps for the same reason, my dear Molly, that you are at pains to seem like an ordinary woman.'

270

She laughed. 'Do not use your tricks on me! I shall not be diverted by flattery. No, you know very well that I use what weapons I have to hand to get on in the world. Where it will not pay to seem intelligent, I hide my wit – and there are many who do not like wit in a woman, though thank God Dublin is less prone to that fault than elsewhere. But you—'

Maurice lifted her hand to his lips and said, 'I will tell you my secret, my dear madam, if you promise to pretend to believe that I am jesting. All my life, I have been afraid of the consequences of hubris.'

Molly looked at him for a moment, her face still framed for laughter; but the sadness in his dark eyes defeated her at last, and she turned her face away awkwardly.

It was at that moment that the servants entered with the tray and the welcome smell of coffee and hot bread, and they were both glad of the interruption. The tray was set down, and the manservant handed the letters, saying with a delicate cough, 'There is one for his lordship, madam, which was sent on from his lodgings, on account of being marked urgent, and them not knowing when his lordship would be back.'

Molly smiled a small private smile of satisfaction that it was so well known where Maurice was spending his nights, and dismissed the servants with a nod. She sorted her letters and passed the one mentioned to Maurice. It was sewn into canvas for the sea-crossing, and was much stained by its long journey. He opened it while she poured coffee, watching him from under her eyelashes. She saw his face grow still with shock and pain and her heart sank.

When he had finished it, he handed it to her to read without a word.

She read it and looked up, wondering what to say, whether to speak sympathy or be silent. He was staring into the distance, and in his gravity she saw for the first time that he was old.

'I never loved her,' he said sadly, as though that were an explanation of everything. 'I wanted her once, but I never loved her. I think she knew it.'

In silence, Molly laid her hand over his, trying to express understanding and concern. Behind her carefully composed face, her mind was busy; he had called her no ordinary woman, and now he was a widower. How would it be if she were to become the next Countess of Chelmsford? She could give him companionship for the rest of his life, which was not likely to be long. She had married one old man, who had left her his fortune; perhaps now she had been sent another who would leave her his title?

From the first day Jemima was happy at Lyme. Captain Elliott's house was a tiny cottage right down by the sea's edge, so small that none but a lifelong sailor could have thought it large enough to invite so many guests. However the weather was so fine that they were a great deal out of doors, and the outdoors came to seem an extension of the house, so that after the first day or two Jemima never noticed its smallness.

Captain Elliott was kindness itself, a cheerful, untutored but naturally gentle man, whose care for everything that lived meant that he never turned anyone away from his door, be it sly old sailor asking money for drink, beggarwoman with a child at her breast, lame outcast dog, or seagull with broken wing. He was not a wealthy man, having nothing beyond his half-pay but the house and a small annuity, both of which he had purchased with his prize-money, but he was a great contriver, and could make almost anything with his hard-palmed but surprisingly nimble hands. And he had a great many friends, and he and his guests dined as often at other tables as at his.

Jemima found her uncle Tom little changed from her memories, though the harsh life and the fever had aged him and greyed his hair. His bride to be, Maria Elliott, was a sensible, cheerful girl, plumply pretty, with brown curls and brown skin and merry brown eyes, and she treated Jemima with such flattering consequence that she was at first almost embarrassed, not being used to having her wishes deferred to. Jemima, along with Maria's sister Ann, who was twelve, was to be bridesmaid at the wedding, and the three girls spent much of their time choosing the material and pattern of their dresses, and then making them.

But there were plenty of outdoor pursuits, too. Jemima missed her riding at first, for there were no horses for her at Lyme, and nowhere to ride them had there been any, but after the first few days she almost forgot about horses. The town itself was so charming: having lived all her life at Morland Place, Jemima was fascinated by the teeming, precipitous little town, balanced precariously down the side of a hill so steep that it seemed designed to send houses, people and carriages rolling down into the sea. Many a time when they were walking along the streets Jemima clenched her hands in anxiety at the sight of a team of horses slipping on the cobbles of a road that seemed almost vertical.

Then there was the sea itself, which was so extraordinary, so enthralling and exciting, that Jemima felt she could never have enough simply of staring at it. Every day brought its walk along the sea-shore; she scrambled over rocks and collected shells and wet her shoes and stockings examining seaweed. When the weather was fine Captain Elliott sometimes took the ladies out in a boat, so that she found herself actually, perilously, floating on the top of this magical medium that was like a living thing. And at night in her tiny attic room she would fall asleep to the sound of its voice, murmuring incomprehensibly but somehow compellingly to her, so that she was in a perpetual happy trance like a girl in love for the first time.

And as if all this were not enough, there was

society too, for in the pleasantly informal atmosphere that surrounded Captain Elliott, Jemima and Ann were included in all the entertainments, and not sent away as children to be shut up in a nursery or schoolroom all day, brought out only to curtsey to the adults or to play the spinnet. And finally, of course, there was the wedding itself to look forward to. Maria's Godfather, who was a senior captain and a baronet, was paying for the wedding and the wedding-breakfast which was to be held at the Three Bells, and it looked as though it would be a very grand affair, as well as a very merry one. Jemima was particularly happy to see how much Uncle Tom and Maria loved each other: she had not grown up with an example of marital bliss before her, and it had hardly occurred to her before that marriage might be contracted for reasons of mutual affection. The idea, once in her mind, blossomed there, and as she drifted off to sleep at night with the sound of the sea rocking her heart, she dreamed of a day when, like Maria, she would pledge herself for life to a man who looked at her the way Uncle Tom looked at Maria.

Two days before the wedding the dresses were finished, and the three young women shut themselves up in the largest bedroom to try them on. All three were of satin, with echelle bodices and skirts opened over quilted petticoats; Maria's was of primrose yellow, the colour which suited her best, and she was to have her hair dressed in the Dutch style, with yellow ribbons and freshwater pearls. Ann's and Jemima's dresses were of a pretty harebell blue shade, and they had round-eared caps to go with them, trimmed with blond and bows of darker blue ribbon.

Jemima was enchanted with her dress, and turned before the mirror which Ann held up for her, viewing herself in sections and wishing just for one moment for one of the huge mirrors at Shawes so that she could see herself all-of-a-piece.

'It's lovely! Oh thank you, Maria, for asking me to be your bridesmaid, and for giving me such a pretty dress!'

'It suits you very well,' Maria said. 'You will be very pretty one day, Jemima, do you know that?' Jemima blushed and hung her head, and Maria went on, 'Tell me, do you like it here at Lyme? Are you happy here?'

'Oh yes!' she cried ecstatically. 'I like it more than anything!'

'And you are not homesick?'

'Not the least bit,' Jemima said, and then wondered if perhaps Maria were trying tactfully to prepare her for leaving. 'Why do you ask?' she said in a small voice.

'Tom and I were talking last night,' Maria said, 'and we wondered if you would like to stay on after the wedding and spend the summer with us. We won't be going away for a honeymoon, but my Godfather is to lend us his carriage as often as we want it, and there are many interesting places within reach of Lyme, which we could visit.

We would do our best not to let you be dull, if you would care to stay.'

Jemima was speechless for a moment, and then she flung her arms round Maria with joy, and then whirled and hugged Ann too. 'Oh please, please, may I? I should love it so. I do like being here with you, much more than at home. Of course,' she added dutifully, suddenly realizing how it must sound, 'of course I miss Papa and my brothers and everyone, but—' her perfunctory duty done she allowed herself to shine again, 'but everything is so much nicer here.'

'Then you shall stay, as long as your parents permit. Tom will write this very evening.'

'Oh I'm sure they'll let me,' Jemima said. 'They'd never miss me at Morland Place. They have Thomas and Harry, you see, and I'm only a girl.' It was said entirely without resentment. It was a state of affairs she was accustomed to, and for the first time she could see that it might even have its uses.

It was on the following day, the eve of the wedding, late at night after Jemima and Ann were in bed, that the express arrived from Morland Place. Maria and Tom were sitting up alone in the little parlour, enjoying a last communion before retiring to their separate beds, when the letter was brought to them. Tom opened it. It was from Jemmy, with the news that Harry and Thomas were dead of the smallpox; he requested that Jemima be put immediately into deep mourning, and that she should be sent home to Morland Place at the first possible opportunity.

Tom and Maria exchanged a long glance.

'Poor young men,' Tom said at last. 'And poor Jemmy. Both his sons – and Mary cannot have another.' He pondered for a moment. 'It will make a deal of difference to Jemima.'

But Maria's thoughts were nearer home. 'Only a few more hours,' she said with some bitterness. 'If it had been delayed only a few more hours! She has looked forward so much to the wedding, that to miss it will break her heart. And what of us? It will spoil the whole occasion.'

Tom nodded. They looked into each other's eyes, reading each other's thoughts. She was not callous, he knew; if sadness could have brought back the two boys, she would have been sadness itself. Her concern, like her father's, was with the living.

'Maria, what if it were delayed?' he said slowly. Her bright eyes watched him consideringly. 'No one knows of this yet, except you and me. No one knows that the letter came except us and Joshua—'

'And Joshua will hold his tongue, if he has good reason,' Maria said. 'Oh Tom, do we dare? Is it right?'

'I think so,' Tom said firmly. 'Nothing can help poor Thomas and Harry—'

'Let's do it then! Oh Tom—'

'I'll go and find Joshua. He can deliver the letter to us tomorrow night, when it's all over.'

Maria nodded. 'Poor Jemima – she was so looking forward to spending the summer here. But at least she'll have the wedding.'

Tom put his arms round her and drew her towards him, and kissed the end of her nose. 'Poor Jemima indeed! I am extremely glad you are not an heiress, my darling, or your Papa would never have let you marry a penniless, weather-beaten old tar!'

Maria giggled. 'But then I should have run away with you, and what fun that would have been. Perhaps Jemima will run away with her love one day.'

Tom shook his head sadly. 'I don't think they will ever give her the chance,' he said.

CHAPTER 10

Jemmy held the door for Marie-Louise to pass into the vine-house, and followed her, closing it carefully behind them. They were enclosed at once in a warm, damp, and growing silence, a green silence and a privacy secured for them by the canopies of pale green leaves that pressed themselves against the glass walls and ceiling. The bunches of grapes, still green, hung down like tight-packed translucent beads, making Jemmy think of chandeliers. He touched one, and its unripe integrity rebuked his hand like the innocent eye of a maiden. When they were ripe and black, they invited touch, yearned for the mouth; but not now.

The Princess turned and waited for him, the green light making her hair look more coppery and her skin whiter. She stood very still, her gold eyes impassive, like an animal in its own habitat, wondering if its prey would be good to eat.

'Mary – she seems almost dazed with grief,' he said, continuing where he had left off. 'She sits all day long with her hands in her lap, not speaking. If she would weep it would not be so bad. And if I try to speak to her, she just gets up and goes away, to another room. It isn't so bad for me – I have things to do, things I have to do, to keep me busy. While I'm busy I can forget about it, but even then, when I finish a job, it suddenly comes back to me, like waking from a happy dream – Thomas and Harry. I can't think of them dead. It surprises me every time. Handsome, clever Thomas, always doing, always complaining – he wanted to go on a Grand Tour. I keep thinking, now Thomas will never see Venice. And Harry – gentle Harry, always clowning. He reminds me of myself at his age. *Reminded* me – you see, for ten seconds together I can't remember it. Why is death so *surprising?*'

Marie-Louise did not speak, only nodded, to make him go on.

'But for Mary, it's so much worse. She has nothing to do, she can't forget even for a moment. And besides—'

'And besides, she loved them more than you,' Marie-Louise said, her voice perfectly neutral. Jemmy frowned.

'Not really *more*. Anyone would think so, I suppose. She was devoted to them, yes, in a way I never was. But I don't think she ever saw them as people. They were not separate from her, they were an extension of her.'

'All the worse then, for her.'

'Yes. I suppose so. She blames me, you know, that I wouldn't let her see them before they died. But how could I? How could I let her see her precious Thomas looking like that.' He shuddered at the memory. 'That handsome face, so disfigured by those horrible sores—'

'Perhaps you should have,' Marie-Louise said abruptly. 'Perhaps then he would have been real to her. Perhaps his death would have been real to her.' Jemmy stared in surprise. 'You treat her like an idiot, like someone incapable of rational thought, and then complain that she behaves irrationally.'

'But – you don't like her,' he protested.

'No, I don't like her. I despise her, but I can see her as a person. You only see her as an extension of yourself.'

Jemmy backed away from the accusation. 'She doesn't like you either. I never understood why.'

'Because she's jealous – *fool*!'

'Jealous? Of you?'

'Oh Jemmy! Because you love me more than her, because you spend more time with me than her. Because I am handsomer and richer and cleverer and freer and do what I want and have everything I want and everyone admires me, but most especially because *you* admire me.'

'I don't think you can be right,' Jemmy said painfully.

Marie-Louise gave him an exasperated smile. Her eyes were very bright now, glowing, ferally, golden in the green shade. 'Come here,' she commanded. He obeyed her without question, taking the step that separated them, and stood close, looking down into her upturned face. He began to smile irresistibly – he always smiled, looking on her beauty – and when he did she put her hands up to his face and held it still while she went on tiptoe and kissed him. Her hands were cool and soft, and their touch soothed him, but the touch of her lips on his mouth was electric. For the briefest of moments he struggled against the excitement, thinking she was kissing him in jest. But then as she leaned her body against him, and he felt her lips part invitingly under his, he realized that she meant it, and his blood leapt in response.

His arms went round her, pulling her harder against his avid body. It was a long, long time since he had known the release of passion, and in this moment he discovered that the love he had always had for Aliena's daughter had changed without his knowing it from a fatherly affection into this burning desire. His mind whirled with it, with images of her laughing, beautiful face, of her white body, of himself conquering, possessing – he crammed his tongue into her mouth, forcing her head back, crushing her against him almost savagely.

It was only a moment's madness; the fit passed almost as soon as it came. Marie-Louise released herself and stepped back from him, panting, her eyes brilliant, her cheeks red, her lips parted. He stared at her, dazed by the surging tides within him.

'You see?' she said simply. He shook his head, as if he were shaking water out of his ears.

'I'm sorry,' he said after a while.

'Don't be,' she said. 'It is better that you should

know yourself. *She* knows it, though I think not with words, not with the front of her mind.'

'But I should not have – Princess, I am sorry. You must understand that it has been a long time since – since I—'

'Jemmy!' She silenced him with a lifted hand, and came close again. She did not touch him, but he could feel her closeness like heat, and it made him tremble. He wanted to tell her to move further off, lest he forget himself entirely. She looked up at him intently. 'Jemmy, don't be sorry. I made you do it.'

'But I should not have so forgotten myself.'

'I intended it,' she said. 'It was what I wanted. Now do you understand?'

He stared at her, and her words ran round his brain like madness. 'No, no, you mustn't,' he whispered.

'Why not?' she said, and now her body was touching his, lightly, all down the front of him. 'Why not?' She raised her hands to his shoulders.

'It would be like incest,' he gasped.

She laughed at the word. 'Incest? We are cousins. That is not incest.'

'No, you don't understand,' Jemmy said, trying to break away from her, hampered by the fact that his arms were round her. In his confusion he thought she was holding him. 'Your mother—'

'My mother was your aunt,' she said with a triumphant laugh. 'So we are cousins.'

'How did you know that?' he said in astonishment. She only laughed again.

'Oh Jemmy! Kiss me, kiss me again.'

But he broke from her, taking her hands gently but firmly from his shoulders and folding them together at her waist, and then pushing himself away, one pace, two paces backwards.

'I cannot. I dare not. You are like my own daughter to me.'

'Not any more. I love you, Jemmy. I have always loved you, and I mean to have you. I *shall* have you. And it is what you want too, if you would only be honest with yourself. But for now, I permit you to go. You have leave, sir,' she bowed her head, parodying her royal title. 'Go to your wife, and comfort her if you can.'

Jemmy fled, as if devils were hounding him.

On his way to his room that night, he saw that there was still a light shewing under Mary's door, and he paused, knocked hesitantly, and when there was no answer went cautiously in. Mary was alone, sitting in a chair beside her bed, dressed in her bedgown and cap, with a wrapper round her. Jemmy gained the impression that she had been sitting like that for a long time.

'Mary?' he said carefully. He went across to her, and sat down on the edge of the bed near her, looking at her with concern. At last she moved her eyes from contemplation of the empty air before her and looked at him.

'What do you want?' she said coldly. 'I should not have thought even you would suppose I had anything else to give you. You have had my dowry and my two sons.'

'Mary, please don't be so unhappy,' he said gently. 'Just think that—'

'You have what you wanted,' she went on as if he had not spoken. 'The girl is all yours now.' For one horrible instant he thought she meant the Princess, but she went on. 'You did not waste any time in calling her home, did you? I know you never loved my sons, but I did not think you would go so far as to kill them.'

'Mary, dear,' he said, 'you cannot know what you are saying.'

'*I know!*' she shouted suddenly, her eyes flashing. '*You* killed them, *you* did, with your horrible infatuation with that terrible house and all its inhabitants. I know you never loved me – I know you wanted that other woman – Aliena – I heard the servants talking about it. Well, I forgave you that. But you have spent your life running around after her daughter, spending your time there, with her, doing her bidding, like a foolish dog, forcing us into intimacy with her. Princess, I have heard you call her. Princess! She is not even honourably born! She is a bastard! And when her horrible relations came, bringing that foul disease, you let them infect my sons! My sons! It's all your fault. I shall never forgive you for it, never.'

Jemmy was silent. There seemed nothing he could say. After a moment she went on more quietly.

'You never wanted to marry me, I understand

286

that. Well, I never wanted to marry you. But I was willing to make the best of it, to love you and be a good wife to you. But you treated me with contempt, you slighted me and ignored me for the sake of that other woman and her child, except when it suited you to make use of me. I gave you your daughter at the cost of my own health, and don't think I don't know why you made a pet of her, rather than loving your sons as you should have. And even now they are dead, when you should be in mourning for them, you still can't keep away from Shawes. You were there today.'

'I had to, Mary, I had business—'

'I know what your business is. Well, you have what you wanted. Now leave me alone. They were all I loved, and you killed them. Don't tell me not to be unhappy.'

'Mary please—'

'Leave me alone,' she said, calmly and coldly. 'Go away and leave me alone.'

St John's Day – midsummer – was an important day in the year's calendar. It marked the end of the hay-harvest, when the ings which had been fenced since Candlemas were opened up for pasturage; it was the end of sheep-shearing, too, with all its concomitant festivities. It was by ancient tradition a time of merry-making, and though the Church frowned upon such pagan jollifications, it could no more stop them than stop the sun in its course. St John's Day was also quarter-day, when the rents fell due, and the tenants came up to the Big House to pay them and to lay any problems or complaints before their Master for settling, and to discuss and decide the farming policy for the second half of the year.

Busy though he had been overseeing the haying and shearing, Jemmy had not failed to ensure that the midsummer festivities would be as splendid as ever. A huge bonfire had been built, and a cook-pit dug, in which a whole ox would be roasted; there were tents and canopies and coloured flags, and space for various stalls which were to be let to enterprising tradesmen from the city; there was to be a wrestling booth, and all the usual games, and a team of tumblers, a fire-eater, and of course the morris-men, and any number of roving musicians. There would be plenty to eat and drink, and then dancing, and when it grew dark enough at last, on that longest of days when the magical green twilight extended itself almost until morning, there would be fireworks.

All those things were to take place from midday onwards: in the morning there was the quarter-day business to take care of, and Jemmy had passed the word to his tenants that he wished to address all of them formally before the festivities started. So at eleven o'clock they all found themselves assembled in the great hall, hats politely doffed, a gentle murmur of speculative conversation rippling amongst them. The senior house-servants also drifted in, gathering in doorways wherever they could find room. At one end of the hall a makeshift dais had been placed, and around this the family began to gather, some looking curious, some interested, some resentful. They presented a sad group, being still in half-mourning for the 'poor young gentlemen' as the tenants had dubbed Thomas and Harry. Silence fell as they gathered, a silence that breathed a sentimental sigh at the sight of Lady Mary, who eschewing the lighter greys and whites permissible at the end of the half-mourning period, was dressed all in crow-black silk, even to her black lace gloves and the black ribbons on her cap.

The Master's brothers were all there, together for the first time in many years. Captain Morland was paying his wedding-visit with his bride, a comely lass, the tenants thought, and looking like to breed well, though it was sad to see a bride so newly wed in mourning clothes. The Reverend Robert Morland was there with his gaunt wife and two stout sons; Captain Edmund, elegant in his red coat even though it had black 'weepers' sewn to the sleeves, supported his pretty wife, who looked pale and likely to faint away at any moment, poor lady, she who had lost two babies to the pox, though she had the boy and two pretty maids left to her, thank the Lord. There was Master George, a hale and stout man indeed, his great belly and red face making him look a proper gentleman. Everyone liked Master George, for he rode well to hounds, was affable, and always tipped a man a shilling if he opened a gate for him. And causing a great deal of interest and excitement, there, too, was Master Charles, tall as a maypole and looking sadly brown from his travels, back from one of his trips to the New World. He had brought back a strange new plant from the pine forests of Mexico which the Aztecs called *cocoxochitl*, which he was busy trying to cultivate in the kitchen garden of Morland Place. It was said that it had a root like a potato, and Master Charles hoped it might be a new kind of vegetable.

All these thoughts drifted about the minds of the tenants as they stood waiting for the Master, and a new buzz of conversation was beginning to rise when Jemmy finally appeared, pushing his way through to the dais from the staircase hall, followed by his step-brother Allen and little Miss Jemima, who took their places to the side of the dais as the Master sprang up and began to address them.

'I called you all here because there is something I wish to tell you which affects you all in one way or another,' Jemmy began, 'something which I thought you had better hear from me, so that you know the truth of it.' At that point Lady Mary flicked her husband an irritable glance, which would have told the intelligent observer that she had no idea what he was going to say, and that she thought is most improper for her to be addressed thus as part of a public meeting, instead of being informed privately and beforehand.

'As you know,' Jemmy went on, 'God has seen

fit to take to His bosom my sons Thomas and Henry.' He paused to allow the expected murmur of sympathy to die down. 'He has also seen fit to deny me any more sons to take their place, and it is not for us to question His judgement.' Many eyes turned towards Father Andrews, who thought it proper to nod in assent to this proposition, though he doubted whether many of the stubborn and contentious folk that made up the Yorkshire community could have refrained from questioning anyone's judgement, even God's, if it went contrary to their desires.

'Many of you must remember my late father, James Matthias Morland, and all of you know that when he died he left the entire Morland estate to me alone, disregarding any claims which the world might have considered my six brothers' – he moved his hand in a gesture to encompass them, and Robert and Edmund exchanged a sour glance – 'my six brothers had to a share in it. His reasons for doing so are not our concern here today; his intention in doing so is, however, quite clear. He did not wish the estate to be broken up.'

A buzz of comment was irrepressible, and again Jemmy waited for quiet before continuing.

'His intention I feel bound to honour, and I would do so from filial duty even if I did not think, as I do, that it is in the best interests of you all that the estate should be kept intact. God, as I said, has seen fit to take my sons from me; but he has left me a daughter, Jemima, whom I present to you all here today as my sole heir. Gentlemen, the future Mistress of Morland Place.'

His last words were almost inaudible over the talk which broke out. Jemima was staring up at her father with huge, surprised eyes, and when he smiled down at her and held out his hand, she could not move until Allen gave her a gentle, friendly shove. Jemmy helped her up onto the dais, and turned her to face the assembly, keeping his hands on her shoulders in reassurance. It was a reassurance she needed, for she had never been the object of so many eyes before, and nothing in her sheltered childhood had prepared her for this public exposure.

The sea of faces seemed to ripple and blur before her terrified gaze; the eyes seemed to burn her skin; she saw the mouths moving though the roaring in her ears prevented her from hearing what they said, and they seemed like the mouths of predators, ready to devour her. Her legs trembled, and tears prickled her eyes; but her father's hands were warm and strong on her shoulders, holding her down and bearing her up all at the same moment. She was too terrifed to smile, but the upturned faces studied the solemn, sallow, large-eyed face and saw what they wanted to see. Someone shouted out, 'God bless the little Mistress!' and at once others took up the cry, and there was cheering and applause, and caps were waved in the air. It was an excuse for celebration at the very least, and outside the smell of roasting ox was beginning to scent the air, reminding them that now business was over they could all go out into the sunshine to eat and drink at the Master's expense. And if the Master – their *good* Master – wanted to give everything to his little girl, why, that was his business. Morland Place had been ruled by a woman before and no harm, so God bless her, she'd like to do as well as a boy.

Jemmy nodded to Allen, who alone had been party to his confidence and plan in this business, and he came to the front of the dais and lifted Jemima down, and escorted her towards the great door, through the passage that opened up automatically before them. Jemima, with Allen pressed close behind her, walked in bewilderment through the crowd, looking to left and right at the grinning, cheering faces, nodding to those who bowed or curtseyed, hearing a confusion of blessings and kind words, feeling hands touch her arms or shoulders as she passed. When she reached the great door and passed out into the yard, Allen quickly took her hand and led her towards the stable.

'There are horses ready,' he said. 'Come quickly, and we will get away from the crowd before they follow. It's all right, your father commanded it. He thought you would be best away from it all for today.'

Bemused, Jemima allowed herself to be led, but her brain, though lagging behind, caught up with her before they reached the stable, and she stopped short to say, 'You knew about it? He told you?'

Allen nodded, and in reply to the implied rebuke said, 'Yes, but only this morning, when Pobgee came with the will and he asked me to witness his signature. He had to tell me, to arrange for me to get you away quickly, but he swore me to silence, so I could not have told you anything, even if there had been time. Speed and secrecy were his object.'

He led her horse out and linked his hands for her foot. She began obediently to mount, then paused.

'But why?' she said. Allen gave a rueful grin.

'Knowing your uncles, knowing your mother, you ask that? There's only one more unpopular choice he could have made for sole heir, and that's me. Come on, they're after us already.'

He flung her into the saddle, and slapped her horse on the rump, springing up onto his own mount even as it started forward in pursuit. They clattered under the barbican and over the drawbridge even as the first of the tenants began streaming out of the great door.

'Foxed them!' Allen called cheerfully as they pushed their mounts into a canter along the track, skirting the field where the tents and stalls were laid out. 'A pity we shall miss the fair, but it can't be helped.'

'We'll miss the feast, too,' Jemima said, beginning to regain her wits now they were away from the house. Allen gestured to the large saddlebag behind him.

'All taken care of. I have a cold collation in here

that I think won't disappoint you. Jacob himself put it up, and he was very secretive about it, and you know what that means.'

Jemima smiled suddenly. 'Anyway, I'd sooner eat with you than with a crowd,' she said, and Allen was touched, even if he didn't wholly believe her.

The outraged commentary and argument could not be avoided, but Jemmy's plan had been to delay it until tempers were perhaps a little cooled and arguments blunted. Thus he had arranged for Allen to spirit Jemima away, knowing that she would otherwise be overwhelmed by it all. While all eyes were on her, he slipped quietly from the dais and out by way of the kitchen passage and a buttery door. The public nature of the day's festivities meant that none of his family was able to speak to him privately at any time, and it all went on until such a late hour that he was able to go straight from the fireworks to his bed without having had to talk about his will at all.

But the next day, after first Mass, there was no avoiding it. Robert, in his nasal pulpit voice, was the most vocal.

'Outrageous – preposterous – impossible – impious—'

'Impious?' Jemmy questioned mildly. 'Impious to carry out my father's last wishes?'

'You don't know what his wishes were,' Edmund protested angrily. 'He left you the estate, that's all

295

you really know. The most likely thing is that he meant you to divide it up between us.'

'That's right,' Augusta nodded. 'Between us all.'

'Probably didn't like the trouble himself,' George rumbled slowly. 'Can't say I blame him. But you know how he used to shut himself away.'

'That's true,' Edmund seized on it eagerly. 'Towards the end he was doing very little of the business of the estate. He left it all to you. So it's only reasonable to suppose that he meant you to take on the task of dividing the estate amongst us.'

'Only reasonable,' Augusta nodded.

Mary listened to it all in painful confusion. Much as she did not wish the estate to go to Jemima, still less did she want it to go to Jemmy's brothers. She had determined not to involve herself in the vulgar wrangling, but to speak to Jemmy privately on the subject, but Augusta's foolish, sheep-like bleat annoyed her so much that she found she had said 'Nonsense!' very clearly and cuttingly before she could stop herself.

'That's right – it is nonsense,' Robert agreed loudly. Rachel looked at him in surprise, but he gave her a warning frown. He had been most vociferous in the past for dividing the estate, but that was when Jemmy's boys were alive. Now he saw a more rosy prospect before him, and he didn't want anyone to jeopardize it. But before he could expand his comment, Thomas, although mildly, had entered the argument.

'I must say, Jemmy, it does seem rather hard on

us all, to take this attitude. Naturally you wouldn't want to break up the actual land here, but I can't see anything against selling off the other properties and assets, to give us each a little something. I know I've got my pay, and Edmund's got his, and Robert has his living – but times are hard, and I've got Maria to think of now. She can't live at her father's house for ever, and if we should be fortunate enough to have children—' he glanced towards his wife, who blushed and lowered her eyes, 'Well, as I say, I've got my pay, and I don't want to be greedy, but he was our father as well, and we ought to have *something*—'

'Was he?' Jemmy said quietly. Edmund flung his hands in the air in exasperation.

'Now don't bring that old story up again. No one really believes it. It was just malicious gossip.'

'My father believed it.'

'*Your* father?' Edmund sneered. Jemmy nodded.

'I know he had doubts about me, too, but in the end he made up his mind to acknowledge me, and he did so, and left me everything.'

'You're all missing the point,' Robert said, cutting through the debate as firmly as he could. 'Our father left everything to Jemmy, it's true – not because he didn't acknowledge the rest of us, but because he wanted it kept intact by passing it to one person.' There was a silence of utter astonishment which encompassed even Jemmy, who could not believe that Robert was arguing his case for him. 'Obviously,' Robert added as a sop to Edmund, 'obviously he expected Jemmy to make some provision for the rest of us out of that estate, but his intention was evidently to keep the government of matters in the hands of one person, *his eldest son*. Now while Jemmy's sons were alive, I would not have questioned his decision.' Here Allen and Jemmy both stared at him in amazement. 'But I'm afraid, brother, that you are going wrong now. You are right to want to honour our father's wishes, and now that your sons are, most sadly, no longer with us, the estate must and shall pass to the next proper heir, my eldest son.'

A fractional pause, and then the storm of protest.

'Nonsense!'

'You can't just make a decision like that on—'

'Naturally, you would say—'

'Why *your* son, for Heaven's sake?'

Robert raised his voice above the roar. 'I am the next oldest. In the failure of the eldest son to provide a male heir, the natural line of succession is to the second son and his male heirs. Fortunately,' he added smugly, 'I have not one, but two sons—'

There was another babble of protest, and when Jemmy could make his voice heard again, he merely said quietly, 'The estate was not entailed.' The noise died down and everyone looked at him. He went on, 'Had my father wished things to go as Robert describes, he would have left the estate entailed—'

'But you don't know that for sure,' Robert began, but Jemmy held his hand up for silence.

'Pobgee was quite clear as to my father's intentions in willing his estate as he did. It was to prevent any of you, or your heirs, from ever having part of the estate. There is no use in your arguing or protesting. My mind is made up and my will has been drawn up and I am satisfied that I am carrying out my father's wishes.'

It was useless to hope that the argument would stop there, but Jemmy felt, looking from face to face, that he had convinced them, and that they were arguing for form's sake rather than in the hope of changing his mind. Robert and Edmund had met each other's eyes and looked hastily away again. In each of them was born a new thought, that Jemima was an important heiress, and that she must marry one day. Robert had two sons, Edmund one, and what could be more natural than that she should marry a cousin with whom she had grown up?

The talk began to break up into small conversations, and Jemmy took the opportunity to walk away from the centre of the room to the window where Allen was standing, an onlooker. He had nothing to hope for or to lose: he was the merest pensioner, but he had also taken on so much of the day-to-day running of the estate that whoever inherited it was likely to want him to remain and continue the task. He gave Jemmy a look of sympathy as the latter sighed wearily, staring morosely round at his wrangling brothers.

'There's one advantage in leaving the estate to

a woman that my father would certainly have approved of,' he said *sotto voce* to Allen. 'At least when she has children, there will be no doubt that they *are* her children.'

Allen smiled a little at the wry jest, and then said, 'I suppose, now that you have definitely made her your heir, you will want to do something about her education.'

'Jemima's?' Jemmy said in surprise. 'I hadn't thought about it.'

'Then you should,' Allen said firmly. 'It is a tremendous responsibility you are burdening her with.'

'You don't need to tell me that,' Jemmy said. 'But after all, I shall still be doing the running of it—'

'You will not always be here,' Allen reminded him.

'And then there's you,' Jemmy added. 'I venture to hope that you will not desert her.'

'Again, I may not always be here. She must marry one day, and unless she is educated, and understands her business, she is likely to lose control of the estate to her husband, and *that* surely cannot be your intention.' He was watching Jemmy's face, as he had watched it all through the preceding argument. 'I doubt whether you are really leaving everything to Jemima to please your father's ghost, but you ought at least to see she is equipped for the heavy task.' Jemmy turned to look at him with a raised eyebrow, and Allen, reading his thoughts, smiled and said, 'Yes, but Lady Strathord was educated from childhood for the business, as was her grandmother before her. *That's* why they do it so well.'

And Jemmy grinned. 'You're right, of course. Well, I shall consult Father Andrews about drawing up a plan of education for her. Provided she has the ability to learn such things.'

'She has the ability, and the desire,' Allen said. 'I have been teaching her the rudiments for some time past.'

Jemmy stared in astonishment. 'The Devil you have! And I thought you only took her riding.'

Maurice thought it wise to send Rupert a day's warning that he was returning to wind up his affairs, for Rupert had been alone at Chelmsford House for over a month, and there was no knowing what or whom he might have installed there. The journey from Dublin was tedious and uncomfortable, and to be greeted by Rupert's sulkiness might have annoyed Maurice, had not his righteous indignation at the news amused him.

'You cannot be serious, father! I simply refuse to believe it. To marry this woman – such a woman! – and my mother hardly cold in her grave. It's indecent. I simply cannot believe that you are not making a horrible jest.'

'A jest? What can you find to amuse in it?' Maurice asked mildly, examining his son's make-up minutely, and trying not to breathe too deeply because of the heavy perfume he was wearing.

'Amuse? Well, father, that is the kindest reaction one can have to such a scheme, and really, such a woman as Mrs Estoyle—'

'But Rupert, my dear, you have never met her,' Maurice smiled.

'I do not need to, so fast her reputation runs before her.'

'Oh, you must not heed gossip, my son, especially gossip that originates in Ireland.'

'Nevertheless, father,' Rupert said firmly, 'I must point out that this woman is not of gentle – hardly even of respectable – birth, that she is known to be vulgar and mercenary and to have lived a life of great intemperance. They say she has had a hundred lovers—'

'Oh it must be more than that by now. It was a hundred before me,' Maurice said. Rupert pursed his lips angrily.

'You may joke about it, but for the life of me, father, I cannot see what you can hope to gain from this marriage. You cannot love her. You cannot believe she loves you. Are you infatuated? What can you be about.'

'Truly, Rupert, I am not entirely sure myself,' Maurice said, sitting down rather wearily. 'I do not love her, and I don't *think* she loves me, though I may be wrong about that. I have frequently been wrong about women's feelings. I have nothing to *gain* from the marriage, if you mean materially—'

'Then why?'

'Perhaps,' Maurice said slowly, 'I wish just for once to marry a woman for *her* advantage instead of my own. Molly would dearly like to be Lady Chelmsford, and in return she will certainly pretend to be in love with me for the little time I have left.' He looked up, and seeing that Rupert had not understood any of that – and indeed, why should he? – he added with his more usual expression of wry cynicism. 'Or perhaps it is that I wish to go out with some eclat, end a reprehensible life with one last resounding piece of scandal. My wife dies mysteriously, and I contract a hasty and disgraceful marriage with a woman of evil repute. That will give them something to gossip about, eh, boy?'

Rupert rolled his eyes. 'Oh it's no use talking to you when you're in this sort of mood. Well then, if you are quite determined to make a spectacle of yourself, may I know what you intend to do about me? I have to live, you know, and I'll be damned if I will go and live in Dublin. One might as well be dead.'

'Your friend Garrick has a very good opinion of Dublin,' Maurice reminded him, 'but don't worry. I should not at all like to have you there witnessing my amours with disfavour. You shall stay here. I shall continue to pay your allowance. This house is far too big for you,' Maurice went on, looking about him sadly at the evidence of decay. 'I shall rent it to some rich merchant, and you shall have enough of the rent to take a good apartment for yourself wherever you wish – Drury Lane, I imagine, would be your choice.' Rupert was silent, not being sure how to take the last remark, for Drury Lane was the site of the theatre, of course, but was also a street famous for prostitutes. 'You may have any of the furniture you want for your new home. The rest I shall rent with the house, or sell, if it is not wanted.'

'Won't you be taking anything?' Rupert asked.

'Molly's house is fully furnished, and it would not be worth the trouble of taking things all the way to Dublin. Only one thing I want – that portrait.' He nodded towards the picture over the fire, the wedding portrait taken of him with his first wife, Apollonia, more than forty years ago in Naples.

'And where will you stay when you come back?' Rupert wanted to know. Maurice shook his head.

'Oh, I don't think I shall be coming back,' he said.

When his affairs in London were dealt with, he drove down to Windsor to see his other son, Charles, who was fourteen.

'I feel rather guilty about you,' he confessed, 'since I have sold your home without even telling you. We shall have to decide what is to become of you now, Karellie.'

'I am very happy here, father,' Charles said sadly, 'but of course now that my voice is breaking I shall not be able to stay on as a chorister.' Charles was the image of his mother, and Maurice found it difficult to look at him without the tears coming to his eyes. 'I suppose if they thought I was good enough, and if you could speak for me, I might be able to become one of the gentlemen of the chapel.'

'Is that what you want? Or would you like to go to University? Or have you some other life in mind? The law – you could train for that, you know, or go into the church. And I need hardly say that you have a home always with me and your step-mother. I don't,' he added with a frank smile, 'expect you to love her, you know, but she is a pleasant woman, and not in the least difficult to share a roof with.'

Charles smiled shyly at being included in his father's confidence in such a way, and he said, 'Music is really all I care about, Papa. To sing, and play music, perhaps one day to write it, like you and my grandfather – that is what I want.'

Maurice nodded, pleased. 'It is in your blood. I am glad it is also in your heart. Well, Karellie, if you want to be a musician, you must go to Italy.'

Charles nodded, not yet old enough to oppose his father's opinions, though he knew that the idea that the only good music came from Italy was old-fashioned, and that many people were opposing it nowadays.

Maurice went on. 'That will be very easy to arrange, I am glad to say. You could go to Venice, to the Palazzo Francescini, or to Naples, where your cousins live, or I could write to the King, in Rome, and have you attached to his household, just as you please. Yes, I think perhaps that is the best idea. You are a little young still to be out alone in the world, but the King would take care of you, and in a royal household, even an exiled royal household, you will learn many things besides music. And you will grow up with the young Princes, which is important. I shall write to the King and ask him to appoint you to the bedchamber. King James is very musical you know, and will be delighted to have one of your talent. Will that suit you?'

And Charles, whose best friend was going to Prague to study, and who had had his heart set on Prague or Leipzig if he could not stay in England and study with Dr Arne or William Boyce, nodded and smiled gratefully. He worshipped his father, and not for worlds would have admitted even to himself that he found his music hopelessly outmoded and limited.

CHAPTER 11

In the July of 1743, the magnificently aged Cardinal Fleury, first minister of France, died, to be replaced in office by Cardinal Tencin. The news was received at the exiled Court in Rome with great joy, for Tencin owed his cardinal's hat largely to King James's good offices, and could be expected to be grateful. Only a month earlier, it had been reported with great glee that English Foreign Minister Carteret's policies were making George II ever more unpopular, for the tax-payers resented financing expeditions to protect the Duchy of Hanover against France. The leader of the politicians out of office was the vociferous Pitt who made vitriolic and widely-reported speeches of condemnation. George himself had not helped matters, for when he led the combined English and Hanoverian troops to victory at Dettingen in June, he chose to do so in Hanoverian rather than English uniform which, it was said, had caused deep disgust and anger amongst the English people.

The pace of the plotting picked up, and letters and messengers came and went in an atmosphere of restrained excitement. Young Charles Morland observed it all with a mixture of puzzlement and exasperation, yet he could not remain unmoved himself. His year at the Court of King James had affected him in many ways. He had always been puzzled at the vehemence of the Jacobites in England, for he had been born into a world which seemed so securely Hanoverian that the desire to change it seemed as unrealistic as a desire to make the sun rise in the west and set in the east. Now, though he still thought it unrealistic, he could understand their longing. King James had received him kindly, had pressed him courteously and eagerly for news of England, and had frequently asked his opinion of the veracity of various reports he received. Was the Usurper really so unpopular? Charles was forced to admit that he was, but could not bring himself to add that he did not think the unpopularity would bring the people to rebellion. King James, he could see, was a man of all the virtues: noble, truthful, just, generous, high-minded, selfless, pious and hard-working. King George, as far as he knew by report, had no detectable virtue of any sort. It would be wonderful to have a King such as James, to have a country inspired by his example to emulation, to live in a world where truth and honour inspired men to beautiful thoughts and noble deeds.

But the world simply was not like that any more, and Charles knew it in a way he could not express in words. The atmosphere of the exiled Court, however, affected him until he was aware that his mind and his heart were believing exactly opposite things. James was King of England, and that was a fact, unquestionable and unalterable. He had been taken from England as an infant, and had never seen it since; his father was half-French, a quarter Danish and a quarter Scots, while his mother was wholly Italian; yet he never thought of himself as anything but completely English. And though he had never been crowned or annointed, he was King in a strangely holy way which impinged itself upon Charles whenever he was in the King's presence. Strip George II naked and turn him out into a strange street, and you would have thought him at best a wealthy country farmer. Strip King James naked, and anywhere, amongst any people, you would have known he was a King.

And that, Charles knew, was as outmoded as all the rest. The world simply was not like that any more, and it frustrated him almost to the point of screaming that he could not tell anyone so, even while another part of him was slowly but surely being absorbed into the extraordinary, dreamlike assumption that it was. After the first Christmas he no longer struggled against the enchantment, and apart from the cool, practical observer who stood aside in his mind and judged everything almost with cynical amusement – a faculty he had surely inherited from his father – he was the King's man of life and limb. The King had been very kind to him, had made him a gentleman usher, had arranged for him to continue his musical studies, and had praised and encouraged his performances. The King always had music played during meals, and often it was Charles who was asked to play to him. But he also kept Charles by him at other times, to ask his judgement of letters and sometimes of men, to question him minutely about life in England and particularly at Court: Charles, as a chorister at the Chapel Royal at Windsor, had had frequent opportunities to observe King George and his immediate circle. Charles also had a number of useful contacts: his father in Dublin, his aunt Aliena in Paris, and his many relatives in Italy, all of whom were sympathetic towards King James, and many of whom were willing to help, by carrying letters or raising funds.

The most active of them, Charles soon discovered, was his cousin, the opera singer Karelia. He met her the first autumn, when she came to Rome to sing for the Holy Father, and was afterwards a guest at the King's table. She greeted Charles with interest, openly acknowledging their kinship, speaking kindly of his father, and Charles was quite prepared to talk music with her – he had heard her performance before the Pope, and was deeply impressed – but soon discovered that politics interested her more.

'My father fought in the '15 rebellion,' she said simply, as if that explained all, but after some time in her company Charles formed a different opinion. It was the excitement she wanted. She had conquered the musical world: there could be few people who would not acknowledge her the world's finest soprano, and so there was no challenge left for her in that sphere. She was certainly a very useful tool to the Jacobite cause, for it was the most natural thing in the world that she should come and go, travelling from one Court to another, visiting St Petersburg and Versailles, and who would dare attack her or search her baggage or question her movements? She was in Rome again shortly after the news of Fleury's death, and was going from there to Versailles, where she was to persuade Tencin to talk to King Louis about an invasion of England – and talk to Louis too, if the occasion arose. She spoke to Charles alone before she left.

'I have been in Dublin again – in May – and seen your father. He continues well, I am sure you will be glad to know.'

'Thank you,' said Charles, a little bewildered, as always, by her beauty and energy.

'More especially he is being active, my dear cousin, and he is very sure the time is coming soon. He charges me to tell you so, and bid you do everything you can to aid the endeavour. He and Lord Clare have been making friends with the shipowning community – there are many of them who use Dublin to avoid English port taxes – and there is one in particular, Antony Walsh, who is very eager to help, not only with ships but with money and arms. So you see you must be ready when the time comes. Your father says so.

It is your duty to your father as well as to your King.'

And she kissed him goodbye, and left in a flurry of skirts and expensive perfume. Charles watched her go with some amusement. His father had written to him only last week, and had said nothing of this, and Charles knew, moreover, that even if his father was being active he would never ask Charles to do so, rather wishing to leave it to Charles himself to decide. But Karelia, he had come to understand, was ruthless, and would employ any means, even lying, to get her way.

He was sorry to see her go. Now that the Queen was dead – she had died eight years ago, long before Charles came to Rome – there was no female household and a very noticeable lack of young women about the Court. Charles regretted it for his own sake, but the cool, noticing part of him thought it a very bad thing for the young Princes, who were thus brought up in a completely male atmosphere. With Prince Henry it did not matter so much, for he had more of his father's temperament, and was, by very consequence of being second son, a more stable and levelheaded young man. But the Prince of Wales, tall, handsome, with a startling combination of blond hair and brown eyes, had his mother's wild, passionate, unbalanced nature. He was proud, vain and hotheaded, with a fierce and unpredictable temper, and these traits were not helped by being brought up entirely by male tutors who filled his head with his own importance as heir to the throne and with stories of heroic deeds, glorious battles, dashing charges, and noble last stands. All the energies of his youth were chanelled into those thoughts and feelings, and he seemed barely to realize that women existed, other than in the purely practical sense of laundresses and scrubbing-women. A love-affair or two, Charles thought, might well cool that hot blood a little; a languid dalliance around the gardens and fountains might be better for him than martial exercises on horseback and mock battles with his fencing masters.

Charles himself was managing quite nicely, with the daughter of a long-term exile, Lord Cutler, with whom to exchange sentimental sighs. The Cutlers had a tiny house in the Via Veneto to which they were always eager to invite Charles when he could be spared from the King's table. They approved of him, on the one hand as the handsome and well-mannered son of an Earl, and on the other, since they were great music lovers, as the talented grandson of Scarlatti, cousin of the great Karelia, and son of Maurice Morland. His dalliance with Molly was of course kept on the most public and decent of levels, and he had only to be careful not to lead any of them to suppose he wanted to marry her.

The other half of his love-life was also well taken care of in the shape of a buxom young serving-maid, Lisa, also from the Cutlers' household. She was two years older than Charles, and he was sure he was not her first lover, but that was so much the better. She took his virginity and then proceeded to teach him everything she knew, a process as delightful as it was informative. What he did not suspect and had no way of knowing was that Lisa told Molly all about it afterwards, when she came in early in the morning to make up the mistress's fire or empty her slops. It gave Molly plenty to think about during her otherwise tedious days of attendance on her mother, a Catholic of enormous piety and no imagination.

In December 1743 things seemed so promising that King James issued another of his proclamations to the English people, in which he promised to maintain the existing form of government and named his son Charles Prince Regent, to lead his troops in his absence. He promised that any foreign troops used in the regaining of his throne would be kept under strict discipline while in England and sent home as soon as Parliament judged public tranquillity would allow – in this, Charles thought, he knew the temper of his people. He also promised safe conduct to the Hanoverian royal family back to Hanover, promising not to harm a hair of their heads and adding, 'I thank God I have no resentment against anyone living, and shall never repine at their living happily in their own country after I am in possession of my Kingdom'. Knowing how much King George loved Hanover, and how little he loved England, he thought the Elector might even be tempted by the offer. But of course, as Charles knew, and the King apparently did not, it was not the Elector that had to be persuaded, but the politicians who could hope for far more material benefit and power under an indifferent George than an active James.

However, France was evidently willing to help, and in January 1744 the Prince of Wales and Lord Dunbar set off, in disguise, for Paris. They left in such secrecy that no one at Court knew of their going until they were well on their way; then the King announced that King Louis was assembling ships and twenty battalions of infantry along the French coast between Dunkirk and Gravelines for an invasion of England, and that the Prince of Wales had gone to join them and lead them in the King's name.

Ill-luck had always dogged the Stuart cause, ever since James II first fled from England; storms in the Channel wrecked a substantial number of the assembled transports and the scheme had to be abandoned. King Louis wrote to say that he had by no means turned away from the Stuart cause, but that the right time must be waited for, and that secrecy was of the essence. The Prince of Wales could stay in Paris, but he must remain hidden and therefore unacknowledged. King James saw the reason in that, for Hanoverian agents were everywhere, and surprise must be the chief element in any attack on them; but Charles, knowing the Prince of Wales's temperament, wondered how wise it was to leave that hot-headed and proud young man in Paris, in idleness, and in obscurity.

Jemima's thirteenth birthday, in May 1745, was one of those perfect early-summer days when the sky was such a pure, clear blue that is seemed almost to sparkle, like polished crystal. After early Mass, Father Andrews took her to one side to say that as it was her birthday he excused her lessons.

'You will have a last fitting for your dress this morning, I know, so why don't you take your ride early? If you go straight away you will still have time, and I think you ought to have the exercise, since you will be much confined later on.'

Jemima curtseyed dutifully, glad enough to obey though she thought it an odd way to describe her birthday dinner and ball – 'confined to the house'. She supposed as a priest he was above enjoying such things. As she left the chapel Allen caught up with her.

'If you are going to ride at once, I shall accompany you,' he said. Jemima looked pleased.

'Oh, thank you! It is so much better to have someone to ride with, especially—' She paused, her cheeks reddening, though Allen, who was looking elsewhere, did not seem to notice.

'Especially what?'

'Especially on such a lovely day,' she finished lamely. 'I had better go and change. Will you speak for the horses?'

'Yes, but don't be too long. Father Andrews may

have excused you lessons, but I do not. I have a book of poetry I wish to read with you, so we must not waste time.'

Jemima nodded and hurried away. Since she had become heiress, her life had changed, to her mind for the better, though there were times when she felt weary and frustrated with things. Father Andrews had taken over her education, and taught her all the things, according to Jemmy's instructions, that he would have taught her had she been a boy. But she had come so late in life to education that she often found it difficult – difficult to concentrate, difficult to understand, but most of all difficult to remember. Her own stupidity frustrated her, particularly with languages, for though she was given lists of words to learn almost every day, she could rarely remember more than a few of them, and those she did remember were generally ousted by new ones from the next list. She was stupid with figures, too – Father Andrews said she was careless, but she knew she was not, and in a way that was even worse.

Her lessons with Father Andrew were carefully arranged so that other things could be fitted into her day as well. Her mother had insisted that she should not neglect her music, dancing, and needlework, and the needlework in particular she found irksome, for it was a time each day when she must sit still under her mother's eye and suffer her mother's conversation. She did not understand why her mother insisted on supervising her sewing in person, since she evidently disliked Jemima, and often complained that her dog was better company. Jemima set her teeth and sewed to a litany of her faults, as Lady Mary criticized her looks and her posture and her character, all of which had undergone a change for the worse since Father Andrews had begun teaching her. She was idle, inattentive, clumsy, careless, dirty, disagreeable, and above all, worst of all, unladylike. Since no reply was possible to any of these charges, Jemima could only try to endure it in silence, whereupon she would be accused of being sullen.

'For Heaven's sake, Jemima, try to look a little more pleasantly,' her mother would expostulate. 'As you have so few personal advantages, it is more than ever important for you to try to cultivate a serene expression. I cannot imagine what sort of a man would marry a girl who looks so sour.'

Her father did not interfere with her life or education, except to insist that she take exercise each day, either walking or riding, so that had to be fitted in as well. She still rarely saw her father, for his life was busy; and she did not yet dine downstairs, so except for morning Mass her encounters with him were brief and accidental. He would smile pleasantly but vaguely as she dropped a curtsey when they passed in the hall or on the stairs, and sometimes he would pat her shoulder and say, 'And how is the little Mistress today?' or ask her if she was being a good girl, but his preoccupation was always elsewhere.

Her greatest comfort was in Allen, and she now regarded him as her only friend, for even had she felt inclined to be friendly with her cousins, she never saw them. William, Robert and Frederick all went to school, and Augusta and Caroline, of course, did no lessons. Allen, though he was nearly as busy as Papa around the estate, found time to interest himself in her progress, and it was to him she took her problems when she could not understand her work, for he had a better way of explaining things than Father Andrews. Often, in the evenings when they were sitting in the drawing room or the long gallery, he would look up from his book and catch her beseeching eye, and come quietly across to her to see if he could help. And though their clandestine lessons had ceased, he still sometimes accompanied her on her morning rides, and when he did he would often bring along some book, or instruct her out of his head as they rode along. He sometimes made a joke about it, as he had this morning, but he always expected her serious attention, and could be quite severe if he felt she was not giving her mind fully to what he was saying. Jemima always worked hard for him. He was the person she loved best in the world, and besides old Jacob and Jane Chort, the only person in the world who loved her.

Up in her room, Jane now helped her out of her linen day dress and sash, and lay it over her bed saying. 'Well, miss, this will be the last day you will wear a frock. When you put your best dress on for dinner, you will be a grown-up woman at last – and not before time, I say.'

'Do you, Jane?' Jemima said, stepping into the petticoat Jane held out. 'Why, don't you want me to be your little girl any more?'

'Little girl? Why, miss, you've got so tall in the last year, I wonder you can get in the door without bending. You're no little girl any more, and it's good and time you were put into grown-up clothes. No, I shan't be sorry to see the old frocks taken away.'

Jemima made a face. 'That's all very well, but sitting for hours at my studies in a corset and busk does not sound like fun.'

'You know what I think about that, miss,' Jane said, lacing the petticoat. 'You shouldn't be doing all that study. It isn't right for a girl.'

'But I have to be educated if I am to be Mistress one day,' Jemima said.

'Nor that isn't right, neither. Your father's a good man, I'm sure, and Morland Place is his to give away as he likes, but it isn't right to give it all to a girl, and deprive the young gentlemen. That isn't the way things are done.'

'It's the way they are done here,' Jemima said, holding out her arms for her jacket. 'And what about Shawes?'

'Shawes is Shawes, and nothing to do with us,' Jane said robustly. 'And though it's not my business, you make me say it, miss, that Lady Strathord is a horrid mannish lady, and I should be very sorry to see my young miss grow up like that.'

Jemima laughed and kissed her on her disapproving cheek. 'Too late, Jane, I've already grown, as you just told me. Oof, this bodice is tight!'

'Aye, so I see – you're growing other ways as well as up. You ought to have a corset under this, I'm sure, but I suppose you'll be getting a new habit after today, so once more won't hurt. Now, then, miss, don't go galloping about and getting yourself heated, and be sure and tell the groom to have you back here sharp at eleven. If you're late for your fitting your mother will have the vapours.'

'I'm going with Allen,' Jemima said carelessly. 'He'll look after me.'

Jane Chort studied the averted face carefully, and after a moment said, 'Aye, well. I suppose.' She looked thoughtful for a moment, and then dismissed the thought. 'Now take your hat, and keep those gloves on! It's bad enough having ink stains on your fingers, without blisters as well. Why God saw fit to make you a girl I don't know, but I daresay He had His reasons.'

'Oh He did, you'll see,' Jemima said, kissed Jane again and whirled out of the room and away down the stairs.

Everything was burgeoning that day. They rode beside the orchards, where the plum and cherry trees were heavy with blossom, and past the curdled milk of mayflower bushes and through patches of gleaming buttercups to the river at Clifton Ings, and then rode along the river bank under the trees, tender with their young leaves, the horse chestnuts laden with their fragrant white candles of blossom. Then they turned away from the river and hayfields and across the open fields, where already the oats were tall and green, and they cantered along the turf baulks between the cultivated rigs until they got to the fallows in North-fields, and then they galloped right up to Harewood Whin.

Where they pulled up, Jemima was breathless and laughing, her cheeks bright and her eyes brighter. 'Oh, that was lovely!' she cried as they waited for the groom to catch up with them. 'But please don't tell Jane Chort. She told me not to gallop and get myself heated.'

'Are you heated?' Allen asked solemnly. Jemima shook her head.

'Not at all.'

'Pity,' he said. 'I was going to suggest we sat down on the bank for a while to rest, but of course if you don't need to rest—'

Jemima laughed again, and without waiting for the groom she freed her foot, swung her leg up and over the pommel, and jumped down. 'I do, I do, I swear it! I'll rest all you like, if you promise to go on educating me.'

Allen jumped down too and took her reins. He handed both horses to the groom as he arrived, gesturing him to lead them away a little and graze them. Then he went to where Jemima had flung herself down on the bank and stood looking down at her. He realized suddenly that the little girl was growing up, that under the cloth of her uncorseted jacket were the soft mounds of growing breats. It made him feel tender towards her, and strangely sad, too, for when she was really grown up, there would be no place in her life for him. She would fall in love, perhaps several times, and then they would marry her to some suitable person, and she would be his no longer. Oh, he did not accuse her of having an ungrateful heart: he was sure she would always think kindly of him; but he would be Allen Macallan, the poor relation, the dependant, perhaps even 'Uncle' Allen – and she had not called him uncle for many years.

'Well, what have you got for me today?' she said, and he forgot about her age, for with her hat off and her hair tousled by the wind, she was Jemima the child again. He drew out the book of poetry from his pocket and sat down on the bank beside her.

'Father Andrews may teach you mathematics and Latin, but he neglects the more spiritual things in life,' he said. 'So I must make good the deficiency.'

'Strange to accuse a priest of being unspiritual,' Jemima said, and he frowned at her with mock severity.

'Be silent and attend. Keep your frivolity for the ball tonight.'

It was a mistake to mention the ball: he saw her attention fly away at once. She sat up and hugged her knees to her chest.

'Oh the ball! Oh Allen, I can't believe it will really be for me, my own ball, in my honour! And my dress—! And a new way of dressing my hair—!'

Allen sighed and shook his head. 'I see you are a woman after all, despite all we have done to make a man of you. Dresses and hair? Is that the highest level you can raise your mind to? When I am offering you poetry—'

'Oh I know, but just think,' she said apologetically. 'Do you really think anyone will want to dance with me?'

'*Everyone* will want to dance with you,' he said firmly. 'After all, you are an important heiress now.'

It was the wrong thing to have said, as he realized when he saw the smile disappear.

'Of course, I was forgetting,' she said dully. 'It will be the heiress to Morland Place they will be dancing with, not Jemima.'

He was stricken, and took her hand and pressed it between both of his.

'If I were a young man, the greatest joy of my life would be to dance with Jemima,' he said gently. Her fingers curled round his, and then she pushed her other hand in too, and looked earnestly into his eyes.

'Would you?' she asked. 'Will you? Will you dance with me?'

It was all suddenly too serious for him, coming so soon after his thoughts about her growing up. He avoided the full gaze of her eyes and said lightly. 'Oh, you wouldn't want to dance with an old man like me, especially an unimportant old man.'

Had she been a few years older, she would have been rebuffed, but at thirteen she still had some of the directness of a child. She said, 'You aren't old. And I would rather dance with you than with anyone else.'

'Very well then, I'll tell you what we'll do. When the minuets are over, I'll come to you, and if you have any dances still free, I'll take them, but if anyone else asks you afterwards, I'll step down. How would that be?'

'Oh, very well,' Jemima said, dissatisfied, without quite knowing why. Her mind jumped to her new dress again. 'Do you think Papa will let me wear the Countess's diamonds?'

Dining downstairs was exciting enough, with its new dishes, and so much more choice, although having to make conversation was uncomfortable, particularly as she was seated between an elderly lady who was deaf and a fat alderman who wanted to talk about the scandal of young men bathing naked in the River Ouse beside the New Walk, which made it difficult for Jemima not to laugh. After dinner everyone went to sit in the drawing room while the family gave her her birthday presents. Robert gave her a book of his own sermons; Edmund was away, but Augusta gave her a pair of tortoise-shell combs, which Jemima thought very kind. Uncle George gave her a pair of lavender gloves for riding, and kissed her cheek, whereupon he became more scarlet in the face than ever and retired hastily to his fireside seat.

Everyone's presents were typical of them, Jemima found herself thinking. Her mother's present was a needle-case with the comment that she didn't suppose Jemima would get much use from it: Allen, who had little money but was skilled at working in wood, had made her a beautiful cedarwood box in which to keep her handker-chiefs. Finally her father took her hand and said:

'Come to the window, chick, and you'll see my present to you.'

Jemima went with him, intrigued, noticing her mother's sour expression as she did so. It must be something her mother disapproved of, she thought. Her father flung open the casement and stepped aside, and Jemima leaned across the windowseat and looked out. On the opposite bank of the moat stood a groom holding the halter of a beautiful black colt. He had one white sock before, and a white star on his brow the shape of a dew-drop; the sound of the window had caught his attention, and he was looking towards it with his ears pricked, and when Jemima leaned out and cried, 'Oh he's lovely!' he whickered as if in reply.

She turned round and hugged her father. 'Oh, Papa, thank you! He is perfect.'

'He's called Jewel, and he's four years old, just the right age for you to mould him your own way,' Jemmy said, pleased with her pleasure. 'It was time you had a horse of your own. If you're old enough for grown-up dresses, you're old enough for a proper horse. I picked him out for you myself last year, and I've been schooling him, though I had to leave it to Allen to ride him – I'm much too heavy – so if he's any bad habits, you can blame your uncle.'

'I'm sure he hasn't, he looks perfect,' Jemima said. 'Does he—'

Here Lady Mary intervened. 'That's enough, Jemima. It is quite unsuitable to talk about horses in the drawing room. Remember we have guests. Mr Morland, will the tea be here soon, do you think?'

Jemima subsided, hurt, and Jemmy obeyed the hint by going to the door and calling for tea. It was brought at once, and after tea Jemima went upstairs to lie down before the excitements of the evening began with dressing in her new dress.

While Rachel dressed her for the ball, Mary was aware of feeling more miserable than at any time since the first terrible days of her marriage. Rachel did her best to cheer her mistress by admiring her dress – of her favourite harebell shade, no Lady Dudley now to make her wear pink – but it did no good. After a moment Lady Mary interrupted her.

'Thank you, Rachel, but you may save your breath. What pleasure can I have in a ball for my grown-up daughter? I am nearly forty years old; I am lame and cannot dance; and I certainly have no lover amongst the invited guests.'

Rachel was silent, blushing at the unexpected frankness, but Mary was beyond caring if she shocked her maid. Her sons were dead, and as if that were not enough, here was her daughter preparing to usurp everything she had ever had, her place as Mistress of Morland Place, and the regard of her husband which she had always wanted. She remembered so clearly the time when Jemmy had given her a horse, how afraid she had been, how Davey had taught her secretly to ride. Jemmy would not do as much for her now; she doubted if he even remembered giving her Leppard.

Tonight at the ball her daughter would become a woman. Her daughter who had crippled her, so that she would not be able to dance tonight; her daughter who, in growing up, was making Mary old. And her husband would dance with Lady Strathord, with the Princess, as he still insisted on calling her. When the Princess was a child, Jemmy had loved her more than he loved his own sons. And now, now that the Princess was a child no longer? She stared down at her blue dress, and hated it, and hated herself. Her restless, pained mind turned here and there, seeking relief, and fixed once more on her daughter, and her mouth turned down bitterly.

'Rachel,' she said, 'send word to Miss Jemima that I want to see her when she is dressed. I want to see how well she looks.'

'You look wonderful, Miss,' Jane Chort said, standing back to admire her handiwork. Jemima stood like a statue, hardly daring to breathe, looking at her upper half in the mirror, and longing, as she had done at Lyme, to see the rest. She could not claim to be comfortable: everything she had on seemed to be hurting her in one place or another. Her stockings of fine silk had to be gartered very tightly to keep them up, and the garters were biting into her lower thigh. Over her chemise, around her waist, the tapes of her pannier-hoops were gripping her tightly. Her corsets were stiffened with both whalebone and wire, to give her upper body the fashionable, smooth cone-shape, and to make her neckline convex. Her new, budding breasts were forced in and up into the neckline in a way that they, at least, found most unnatural, and the sachet of scented herbs that was tucked down between them was scratching her. Her shoes were pointed and high-heeled, and hurt her feet, and her head felt as though it was stuffed with nails, where the multitude of hairpins was holding her *tête de mouton* coiffure in place.

But all that was as nothing beside the pride and excitement of being dressed in her first ballgown. It was of satin, of a heavenly lilac colour, with the petticoat and robings a shade darker. The stomacher was frilled with silver lace, and petticoat was trimmed with layers of stiff silver ribbon, and there were silver rosettes on the shoes. Her hair was curled all over, and the bunch of ringlets behind was held with artificial flowers and silver and purple ribbons. And, best of all, she was wearing the Countess's diamond collar, which made her hold her head up in a way that all the deportment lessons she had had all her life had tried and failed to achieve.

'You're an absolute picture, miss. Now here's your gloves – you'd better go along to your mother's room. Be careful of your heels, and walk slowly, remember, and mind how you go through the door with your panniers. Have a good time, and remember all I've told you and be a credit to me.'

Jemima could only nod, carefully, for to have kissed Jane would have involved manoeuvres she was not sure she could manage as yet. As Jane held the door open for her, she walked slowly and carefully out and towards her mother's room.

Mary stared at her daughter bitterly. At a stroke, she thought, they had changed the child into a woman, and cast Mary herself back a generation. Jemima's cheeks were so bright she might have painted them, though Mary knew from experience it was the tightness of her bodice that was causing it. But her eyes were bright too, the curling hair was glossy, and her figure in the new stays was womanly. She was not pretty, but she was no longer, as she had been all her childhood, plain. She was – striking. Why are you alive, she thought, and my sons dead?

'I suppose you look well enough,' she said at last, 'though purple ribbons will put everyone in mind of funerals.'

Jemima's excitement was enough to make her

unguarded. 'I can't think how I shall manage to dance, in these corsets, and these shoes,' she exclaimed breathlessly.

Lady Mary made a dismissive movement of her hand and said harshly. 'No doubt you'll fall down and make a spectacle of yourself, but that's no more than to be expected. You always were clumsy. Leave me now.'

She saw Jemima's eyes brighten with tears and her lips tremble as she made her curtsey and left, and knew that just for a moment at least she had quenched her pleasure in the evening. It was very small consolation.

'You look very nice, chick,' her father said, and she had to make do with that, telling herself that a father would never notice how a daughter looked, not in any detail at least. He had already decided whom she should dance with for every dance until supper, and told her so, which rather took the excitement from the first part of the ball, but as the guests arrived she discovered that she was getting quite enough interested glances, the young women admiring her dress, and the young men admiring *her*, to satisfy her unpractised vanity. One good consequence of her father's policy was that when young men came to ask if they could dance with her, and she said she was engaged right up to supper, it made them very eager to secure her after supper, thinking that she must be immensely sought-after. She was to open the ball, of course, dancing the

331

first minuet with Nicholas French, the most eligible bachelor in York, but as he was twenty-two and very haughty, Jemima rather knew it to be an honour than felt any pleasure in it.

As soon as she and Master French had taken their places, her father led out Lady Strathord to stand beside them. There was a sprinkling of applause, and Jemima saw heads leaning together behind fluttering fans as the onlookers whispered comments upon the handsome couple. Lady Strathord looked magnificent, dressed all in white, white lace over white satin. Her stomacher and petticoat were sewn all over with pearls, her magnificent copper-gold hair was dressed high with pearls and white feathers, and at her throat she wore a necklace of crystal spars. All eyes were upon her and Jemmy, handsome in emerald green velvet and white silk breeches, and for a moment a resentment raised its head in Jemima. It's *my* birthday ball, and I am opening it: they should be looking at *me*. But it was only momentary, soon banished by simple admiration for the couple who looked so out-of-the-common they were more like a King and Queen than ordinary people. Then the music began, and Jemima had to concentrate on the proper sequence of the complicated steps.

'How pretty the child looks,' Marie-Louise said to Jemmy during their third dance together. It was gratifying to her that he should so openly prefer her to anyone else in the room, even though she knew some people would excuse it on the grounds that Jemmy could not dance with his wife, and was therefore taking his nearest female relative as a substitute. Marie-Louise's eyes were drawn, as they were every time she looked at Jemima, to the diamond collar. It was absurd that a thirteen-year-old child should be wearing such a fortune of diamonds when her own more appropriate throat was encircled by common crystal. Her only consolation was that Jemmy felt so too.

'You would look so much better in the diamonds than Jemima,' he said apologetically, 'but they were given to her, after all, and she so wanted to wear them to her first ball that I hadn't the heart to refuse.'

Marie-Louise felt she could afford to sound generous. 'She had better get used to jewels, I suppose. One day she will be very rich.'

Jemmy raised an eyebrow. 'One day! By one day, you mean when I am dead. How lightly you shrug off my death, Princess! You are quite heartless.'

'Great beauty is always heartless,' Marie-Louise said gravely. 'Besides, how should I not be heartless, when I gave my heart to you more years ago than I can remember?'

Allen caught up with Jemima as she came out of the supper-room after supper, and drew her hand through his arm in a friendly way.

'Are you having an agreeable time?' he asked. Jemima was hurt.

'You did not come to me as you promised, to ask for a dance.'

'I did not think it worthwhile. Your father told me he had arranged all your partners for you.' Allen said reasonably.

'Will you dance with me now?' she asked eagerly. 'I have saved the two first after supper for you.'

He smiled. 'Why, that was kind of you. But I'm afraid I have engaged to dance with Lady Strathord.' He saw her crestfallen face. 'Don't worry, we'll get you a partner for the two first with no trouble at all. Everyone wants to dance with you.'

Jemima swallowed her disappointment. 'Will you dance with me later on?' she asked in a small voice.

'I would be honoured, if you have a dance free.'

'The two third? I have the two third free,' she said at once, and he bowed his acceptance.

'Enchanted,' he said. 'And – why, this looks to me very like a young man come to ask your hand. Are you sure, Jemima, you want to waste a dance on an old man?'

Jemima made no reply, except to give him a reproachful look as she turned away to receive the approaching young man.

The Princess put in two extra steps at every half-turn, and Allen was partly amused, partly admiring.

'You are very gay tonight,' he said.

'Should I not be gay at a ball?' she said, smiling at Jemmy as he passed her going down the set.

'Indeed you should, when every eye is upon you.

334

You are out of place here, you know – the assembly is too dull for your extraordinary beauty.'

She bent her golden gaze on him curiously. 'You never used to say such gallant things to me. When we were children together, you used to shower me with such cold and critical looks, that I could only be glad you never gave them tongue.'

'Time wreaks many changes,' he said. 'You were a very unpleasant and arrogant little girl – though even then I was in love with you.'

She laughed, making the crystal spars tinkle with the movement of her throat. 'I am a very arrogant and unpleasant young woman,' she said. 'Are you still in love with me?'

'Of course,' he said. 'As you know very well. So tell me why you are so especially gay tonight? There is something about you – an excitement, as if you were planning some mischief.'

'Not mischief,' she said, becoming confidential. 'I have had news from my uncle Maurice, who keeps very poor company these days – a renegade slavetrader by name of Antoine Walsh, and a drunken, unfrocked priest by the name of Father O'Sullievan. The new Lady Chelmsford is not pleased with the acquaintance: they have made her sell her jewels, that she worked so hard to wear.'

Allen looked bemused. 'I suppose all this means something.'

'It means that my brother has been over-long in Paris, and has grown tired of waiting for the King

335

of France to give his sanction. He has determined to move, to go alone to Scotland if necessary, and I, I applaud him, with all my heart.'

'Scotland? Your brother?' Allen felt dim stirrings of understanding and apprehension, as if at the approaching of a storm.

'My brother the Prince of Wales,' she said superbly, lifting her head high as if she wore a crown. Allen had no words, and she said, 'Come, you must know the story of my birth – the servants tell you everything.'

'I—' He shook his head, realizing that it was far too late to begin denials. 'I didn't think you knew.'

'My grandmother told me. All through my childhood she told me about my father and grandfather and the Cause and what I must do when the time came. And now the time is coming. When my father has his throne again, I shall be a Princess of England.'

Allen looked at her with enormous sadness, at such delusion, at the head filled with romantic dreams that reality would prove so hollow. Was this how the Countess had thought fit to prepare Marie-Louise for life? It made him both sad and angry, and also afraid for her.

'What is it you plan to do?' he asked. She looked at him shrewdly, her head a little tilted, as if wondering how far she could trust him. When she spoke, it was not an answer.

'You should be glad too, Allen Macallan,' she said. 'When the King has his throne again, you

336

may have your estate returned to you. You will be a gentleman of means. Depend upon it. I shall speak to my father on your behalf, I shall do everything I can for you. And if you fight for him, as duty says you should, he may reward you with a title.' And she smiled, as if to say that things between them would be very different if he had an estate and a title.

'But what is it *you* plan to do?' he asked again. The dance was coming to an end, and he pressed her hand urgently to hurry her answer.

'I have to dance with Jemmy now,' she said. 'Come to me after the next dance, and we will talk.'

She met Jemmy by the screen that closed off the kitchen passage, and said, 'I have danced enough for now. Let us take the air somewhere. Can we slip out without being seen?'

'You should not go outside if you are heated,' Jemmy said, but she ignored him, looking round.

'The herb garden – we can get to it through the pantry, if I remember rightly, and it will surely be private at this time of night.'

She slipped round the screen, and with a shrug and a backward glance, Jemmy followed her. In the herb garden the air was warm and scented; having trapped the heat all day, the stones of the walls were giving it back into the still night. Marie-Louise stretched her arms wide and walked forward.

'Oh to be outside, to be in the fresh air, unconfined.' She turned to Jemmy almost reproachfully.

'You don't know what it is like to be a woman, to be always shut indoors, never allowed to do the things you want, to have always to be careful of the night air, of the rough ground, of the thorn hedge—'

Jemmy laughed aloud. 'I do not recognize this picture you are drawing. There never was a woman more unconfined than you! Why, I don't suppose you spend two hours of a day indoors, unless the weather is foul – and as for fearing the thorn hedge or the rough ground, even your grooms are afraid to follow you when you are hunting!'

Marie-Louise came up close to him and pretended fierceness.

'Don't you dare to laugh at me, or I'll—'

'You'll what?' Jemmy laughed, catching her by the upper arms and looking down into her face. It was intended as the sort of playful gesture that a man might make to a much younger woman he regarded as a daughter, but Marie-Louise at once put her arms up and round his neck, and the smile gradually faded from Jemmy's face.

'Or I'll make you sorry,' Marie-Louise said huskily. Jemmy struggled with his feelings, but not successfully enough to prevent him putting his arms round her.

'I wish *you* may not be sorry, Princess,' he said hesitantly. 'Please don't do anything you will regret afterwards. Please—'

'I regret nothing. I know what I want,' she said.

338

'Sometimes,' Jemmy said with difficulty, 'a thing once done is not what you thought it would be. Sometimes it is better to go on wanting a thing than to have it.'

'Do you want it too, then?'

Jemmy closed his eyes for a moment. 'God,' he said. 'God.' He opened them again, and she saw the lines of his face harden, and just for a moment, for the last moment before it happened, she was afraid. And then he was kissing her, and it was not like the last time, in the vinehouse, for there he had been tempted into madness, he had been like a man intoxicated. This time he knew what he was doing, he knew her, and his awareness made it a thing of brilliance, like adamant, like a knife-blade. She realized that he was being forced beyond his nature, and that there was danger in it, hurt and harm; that to survive it he would have to be hard, even cruel. She realized that the thing she had begun was no longer in her control, that she had wilfully broken down a barrier which had held back forces better under control.

But all her life she had had what she wanted; she lived to do, to act, she could not endure the dicates of caution. She gave up her mouth to his mouth, put her hands to the back of his neck and held his head closer to her own. When they broke apart, panting for breath, she said, 'Where can we go?'

His face was sharply defined against the light from the windows, and he looked different to her, no sign now of the soft, lazy, laughing Jemmy: he was keen and considering like a hawk. He said, 'There is a store room, over there, the end one, where we keep wool for the household weaving. It will make a soft enough couch. But are you sure?'

One last chance to return to sanity; but for her it had always been too late. She turned her back on it, and took his hand, and let him lead her. The store room was dark, and smelled of wool and candles and new wood. When he shut the door there was no light at all, and she could only feel him and smell him and hear him, so that it was like a dream, not like real life at all, until the last moment. Then it was real, and she knew it, and she cried out, as if she might hold it off: knowledge, which is the death of childhood; womanhood, which is the beginning of death.

Allen looked for her, as she had bid, at the end of the dances, and found her at last just coming in, alone, from the kitchen passage. Her cheeks were bright as if they had been stung by cold air, her eyes were brilliant as if with some madness.

'I was looking for you,' he said. 'Surely you were not outside? You know that it is dangerous to go out at night from a heated room.'

'It was warm outside,' she said, and her voice was high and fevered. 'I had to get out.'

'Do you wish to sit down, to rest?' he asked. 'You were going to tell me—'

'No, no, I must have movement, I must dance. Come, quickly, the music is starting!'

She seized his hand and almost ran with him to the set. Jemima, who had been waiting for him to claim her for their dance, saw them as they took their places, noted Lady Strathord's bright cheeks, her gay laughter, saw how Allen looked at her bemused, like a bird fascinated by a snake, and her happy anticipation drained away, leaving her feeling tired and flat. Her father suddenly appeared at her side. He looked hot and flurried, as if he had been running.

'Not dancing, chick? That will never do,' he said. 'We must see about a partner for you.'

'I don't want to dance,' she said sullenly, but he did not seem to notice her tone of voice.

'Nonsense, of course you do! Why it's your evening tonight, your birthday ball! You must dance every dance. Now who can we find for you?'

And he looked around as if searching for a partner for her, but Jemima noticed that though he turned his head, his eyes remained on Lady Strathord.

At the end of May 1745, Karelia was again planning a journey to France, to sing for King Louis, before going on to Spain, and Charles received a letter from his father in Dublin, asking him to go with her, both to escort her on the journey, and when in Paris to visit his Aunt Aliena, who has been unwell. Charles immediately asked for an audience with the King, to ask his permission for the journey, but though he did not say so to anyone, he thought the request somewhat odd. In the first place, Karelia travelled as regularly and confidently as a swallow up and down the world, and had never suggested to anyone that she needed or even wanted an escort. In the second place, Aunt Aliena's illness had been a slight one, not dangerous to her life, and was now over. If he had not been asked to visit her while she was ill, why had he been asked now, when she was well again?

The King, however, saw nothing strange in his request, and granted it readily.

'I hope you will find your aunt in such a state as to relieve all your alarms,' he said. Charles bowed.

'Thank you sire. I understand there is no concern for her life.'

'I am very glad. You perhaps know that I regard her – almost as a sister,' the King said a little awkwardly. Charles bowed again, not knowing what else to say.

The King seemed preoccupied, and did not immediately dismiss him. After a moment he said, 'I wonder whether, while you are in Paris, I might employ you about some business of my own.' He looked at Charles thoughtfully, with a little worried frown between his brows. 'My son, the Prince of Wales – perhaps you know that I have not been entirely at ease in my heart about him.'

This was an understatement, as Charles knew

very well. Since he had gone to Paris, the Prince had caused nothing but concern. He had been fretful and bored, complaining in his infrequent letters that he was neglected by King Louis and allowed no access to the royal family or acknowledged in any way. He had also been keeping very bad company, concerning which it was widely known the King had rebuked him a number of times, and he had been drinking and gambling heavily, overspending his allowance and running up debts which it was not in his power to pay.

The King's only reliable communication with the Prince's household was through the elderly Sir Thomas Sheridan, who was devoted to the Prince, and wrote long detailed letters to the King explaining their domestic circumstances, but not giving any information about what was really going on. The only thing the King did not suspect was involvement of the Prince with women, perhaps because it had never been a temptation to which he personally was subject.

'You perhaps know that the Prince has now gone to stay at Compiegne, with my brother Berwick's son, the Duc de Fitzjames? I feel sure that the Duc must know what is happening at Versailles, whether there is any progress in the matter of aid for the Prince in our attempt upon England. I wonder if—' he hesitated; it was obviously against his nature to suggest anything as underhand as spying or gathering information in a clandestine way. Charles helped him out.

'My uncle, sire, the former Earl of Chelmsford, was a close friend of the Duke of Berwick, as you know. I think it would be only proper, while I am so close to Compiegne as Paris, that I should request permission to make my devoirs to his son.'

'Yes,' the King said, eyeing him thoughtfully. 'I think that is quite right. Thank you. I hope you will also carry some letters for me, to the Prince and Lord Semphill and one or two others. When do you leave?'

'In the morning, if it please Your Majesty.'

'Very well, I will have them ready and sent to you this evening.'

Charles spent the rest of the day packing, and wondering whether he ought to take his leave of the Cutlers. They had been very kind to him; on the other hand, they were growing a little possessive of him, and referring to him in the same breath as their daughter Molly in a way which made him nervous. In the end he decided to take his leave of them by letter, pleading shortness of time as an excuse for not calling in person. The King's letters came round to his room in the evening, and Charles packed them carefully into the saddlebag which contained his immediate necessities for the journey. That way they would be always with him.

Early in the morning he joined Karelia at her lodgings, and they set off together. He was amazed at the amount of luggage she was taking, having expected an experienced traveller like her to be more thrifty of space and effort. But he supposed that she was now such an important person that she needed a large number of clothes and jewels and household items. She was not disposed to be talkative, though she cast him many a look when she thought he was not watching. It was not until they were halfway to Avignon that she thought it safe to tell him the truth about the journey.

'Well, little cousin Karellie, and what do you suppose is in all these boxes?' she asked him cheerfully.

'Why, clothes, I assume, madam.'

'Not a bit of it – it is guns.'

'Guns!'

'Indeed. And why do you think your father has sent you to Paris?'

'Not to visit my Aunt Aliena,' Charles said grimly. She smiled as she shook her head.

'You learn quickly. That is good. No, you are not going to Chaillot, you are going to Scotland, with the Prince Regent, the Young Chevalier. Your father is giving you the chance to take your place in history. I only wish I could go too, but my work lies in another direction. I have to speak to the King of France and the King of Spain and persuade them to give their aid to the scheme.'

'Surely it would be better to secure their help first?' Charles said desperately. 'Why must it all be done in secrecy? The King does not know about it, I gather? How can it succeed, if King Louis does not approve?'

'The Scottish people have invited the Prince, and he will go, whether any help comes or not. The time is right, and the King of France has hesitated too long. If the Prince goes, it may spur him to give the aid he promised. And if he does not—' she shrugged. 'A swift and bold blow may succeed without great force, if it is assured enough.' She studied Charles's gloomy face with some amusement. 'Why, cousin Karellie, you should be pleased and proud that such a great opportunity is been granted to you. You may be a hero soon! And think what rewards will await you, when the King is restored to his throne.'

Charles held out his hands helplessly. 'These have never handled a sword or a gun, madam. They are musician's hands. I am a singer, not a soldier.'

Karelia held her head high. 'I, little Karellie, though only a woman, *I* am both!'

The Prince of Wales wrote to his father in June to tell him of the scheme.

'I have above six months ago been invited by our friends to go to Scotland, and to carry what arms and money I could conveniently get, this being, they are fully persuaded, the only way of restoring you to the crown and them to their liberties . . . I have tried all possible means and strategies to get access to the King of France or his minister. Now I have been obliged to steal off without letting them so much as suspect it . . . Let

346

what will happen, the stroke is struck, and I have taken a firm resolution to conquer or die, and stand my ground as long as I shall have a man remaining with me . . . Your Majesty cannot disapprove a son's following the example of his father – you yourself did the like in the year '15 . . . I write this from Navarre, but it won't be sent until I am on shipboard . . .'

Charles felt obliged to send a letter of his own to the King, explaining that he had not known about the scheme when he applied to go to Paris, for he did not, above anything, want the King to think ill of him.

'It may seem a wild and desperate thing, Your Majesty, but His Highness has made great preparations, and with speed and luck it may well succeed. His Highness was convinced that the King of France would try to stop him if he knew, hence his desire for secrecy until this, the last moment. I know Your Majesty would approve the Prince's courage and resolution, if not his prudence, in this matter, and if I offend in assisting, I beg Your Majesty will attribute it to my love for you and not to any slighting of Your Majesty's wishes.'

Everything had moved too fast for Charles, who discovered that, as his father had so long been involved in the planning, it was assumed that he had known about it all along, and had come to give his help of his own accord. There were many things to be done and few people to do them, and he was kept as busy writing letters and seeing to details of the organization as anyone else in the Prince's household, so that he hardly had time to think or to object to being included, willy-nilly, in what he certainly thought of as a 'wild and desperate thing'.

The expedition assembled secretly at Nantes during the month of June. There were two ships: the *Du Teillay*, the armed frigate belonging to Antony Walsh, having eighteen guns and a crew of sixty-seven, and a warship, the *Elizabeth*, of forty-four guns which had originally been English but had been captured some years back by the French, and which had been given permission by the French Minister of Marine to patrol the Scottish coast. She would therefore be able to escort the *Du Teillay* without appearing to do so. The Prince had assembled 1,500 guns and 1,800 broadswords, along with gunpowder and balls and a quantity of small arms, and the *Du Teillay* would also carry twenty small field pieces. All that was lacking was the men: it was hoped that Scotland would provide them, and that when it was known the Prince had set sail alone, the King of France would respond by sending troops after him for his assistance. Like his father before him, the Prince had taken the title of Chevalier St Georges for the expedition.

They finally set sail on 15 July, intending to round Cornwall and sail up the west coast to the Isle of Mull. Charles, bemused and seasick, was aboard the *Elizabeth*, where he was supposed to be providing a liaison with the *Du Teillay*, but was in no condition to do so. On the 20th, just off Lizard Point, the two ships crossed the path of the English man-o-war *Lion*, patrolling there. It was no part of the plan to have a sea battle, and the two French ships tried to shake off the *Lion*, but she gave chase, and in the end the *Elizabeth* had to turn back to engage her, in order that the *Du Teillay* could make her escape.

Charles was certain that his last hour had come. Huddled below in his cabin, which, tiny and cramped though it was, he shared with five other officers, and already green with sea-sickness, he lay for what seemed like hours, hearing the thunderous rumble of the guns being run out, the shuddering explosions as they were fired, the tearing crashes as the enemy balls thudded into the fabric of the ship, the terrible screams and cries of men being wounded. He lay with his eyes screwed tight shut, praying that if he were to die it would be quickly, praying for the courage to endure this terror, wondering whether it would be better to die by drowning when the ship sank, full of holes, or by being smashed to pulp by a flying cannonball.

Eventually the terrible sounds of battle creased. The *Lion* had been beaten off, but not without cost: the *Elizabeth* was badly damaged, and 156 of her crew were dead or wounded. It was impossible for her to continue in such a condition, and she turned back for France, leaving the *Du Teillay* to sail on alone up the west coast towards Scotland. On 22 July the *Elizabeth* made Brest, and Charles was able, thankfully, to crawl ashore. The ship's arrival and her condition made it impossible to keep it any longer a secret that the Prince of Wales had sailed for Scotland, and before nightfall Colonel O'Bryen, the chief Jacobite agent in Paris, had written to King James, King Louis, and the French foreign minister. 'The Prince has embarked with no more than five or six gentlemen on a small frigate carrying eighteen guns,' he wrote. Charles, at last having the leisure to consider just how wild and desperate a thing it really was, could only be glad, however it might disappoint his father, that he was out of it; and by offering his services to Colonel O'Bryen as a courier, provided himself with both the means and the excuse to go back to Rome.

BOOK III

THE MERMAID

When thy beauty appears in its graces and
  airs
All bright as an angel new dropped from
  the sky,
At distance I gaze and am awed by my
  fears,
So strangely you dazzle my eye!

But when without art your kind thoughts
  you impart,
When your love runs in blushes through
  every vein;
When it darts from your eyes, when it pants
  in your heart,
Then I know you're a woman again.

Thomas Parnell: *Song*

CHAPTER 12

It was the middle of August when the news reached Yorkshire that the Young Chevalier had landed in Scotland, on a bleak western island, barely more than a rock in the wild sea, with his seven companions. It was at first not credited, dismissed as a rumour bred out of hopeful hearts, but by the beginning of September, there was no doubt about it.

'The clans are hurrying to his standard,' Allen told Jemmy eagerly. He had been out and about all day, gathering news wherever it was to be found. 'He raised the standard on 19 August at Glenfinnan – Cameron country. Cameron of Lochiel was one of the men who invited him to Scotland, and he brought his whole clan over. Now there are thousands of them. The Prince issued a declaration, signing himself Prince of Wales and Prince Regent. I haven't been able to get hold of a copy,' he added in disappointed tones, 'but I understand he offered a large reward for the capture of the Elector if he attempted to land in any part of His Majesty's Dominions.'

'That young man has a sense of humour,' Jemmy

said, 'even if it is a grim one.' The Elector had been on his annual visit to Hanover at the time of the landing. 'Well George is back in London now, and no one is likely to be claiming the reward, but it won't have done him any good. The people have never liked that habit of his and his father's of dashing off to Hanover every summer.'

'The whole of Scotland is behind the Prince,' Allen said. Jemmy looked thoughtfully at him, at the eagerness, the spot of bright colour on each cheek, the hands twisting together in excitement. 'No one there wants the Elector. A huge army is marching towards Perth at this very minute, and the King of France is certain to send help. Speed is of the essence—'

'You want to go?' Jemmy said abruptly. Allen looked at him half apologetically, half defiantly.

'I do, I admit it. It is my only chance to get back my estate. Aberlady, Birnie Castle, Braco – everything that should be mine, in the hands of the Elector and his cronies. I could be a rich man, an independent man. Oh Jemmy, I know you have been very good to me, given me a home, treated me like an equal, and I am very grateful, you must not think I'm not—'

'You have no need to be grateful,' Jemmy said. 'You have given Morland Place far more than it has given you, in your service and your care. I do not know how we should have managed without you, brother.'

Allen looked down. 'I am not really your brother. We share no blood.'

Jemmy laid a hand on his shoulder. 'You are more a brother to me than any that share my blood. I shall miss you more than I can tell you, but I do see that you must go. Go then, and with my blessing.'

Allen looked up, and laid his hand over Jemmy's. 'I will never be able to repay you—' he began, but Jemmy stopped him.

'Repay what? There is no debt, my friend. Now, you must tell me what you will need – horses, money, servants. When do you want to leave?'

'In the morning,' Allen said, almost shame-facedly. 'As I said, speed is of the essence.'

'So soon? Well, it shall be done. We'll prepare everything tonight, and you can leave at first light. I envy you, in a way.'

'Envy me?'

'The adventure. The excitement. When I was only a child, I ran away to fight for King James, in the year '15.'

'Yes, I have heard the story.'

'I didn't get very far, I suppose you heard that too,' Jemmy said ruefully. 'Brought back very bedraggled, with my tail between my legs. Oh but I remember how I felt the day I went! How high my heart was, how *alive* I felt. I don't think I have ever felt quite so good since then. You are lucky in that way, to have nothing to lose. I could not go now, however much I wanted to. Possessions are a privilege, but they are also a duty.'

Allen nodded sympathetically, and then said, 'If

we – *when* we come south, what will you do? Will you join us?'

'I don't know. I don't know. We must wait and see.' He smiled suddenly. 'I can imagine what Lady Mary would say about it. You had better keep your departure a secret between you, me and Clement, I think, until you are safe away. When you get to the Prince, I should be glad if you could try and send me word, that you are safe.'

Early the next morning, before the sun was up, Jemmy witnessed Allen's quiet departure. He was taking one servant with him, an eager young man named Colin, who was half Scottish and a Roman Catholic, and had a great interest in the restoration of the true King. They were both well mounted and well armed, and had a sufficiency of money with them, hidden about them and their packs in case of highwaymen. They had a mule to carry their baggage, which they were keeping to a minimum, together with some spare arms and powder and shot as Jemmy's contribution to the cause.

Jemmy clasped his brother tightly in his arms and bid him farewell.

'God bless you!' he said. 'I pray God keep you safe, and bring a good outcome to the venture.'

'I will send word when I can,' Allen said, and turned back as he was about to mount to add hesitantly, 'Jemmy, just one thing – Lady Strathord – Marie-Louise—'

'What about her?' Jemmy asked, hiding a smile. 'Do you wish me to make your adieux for you?'

'No – not that. But I wish you would keep an eye on her. She was talking – at the ball, you know – about going to join the Young Chevalier if he came to England.'

'Join him?'

'Yes – God knows what she meant, but I wish you would look after her, and make sure she does not do anything foolish. She talks about *her brother* in such a way – and you know how spirited she is . . .'

Jemmy looked a little alarmed, but he said soothingly, 'I will see to it. She shan't come to any harm. Now you had better be off, before the house is roused. God go with you, Allen.'

'With God's help, I shall be a rich man when next I see you,' he said with a grin, and in a few moments the two men had clattered away into the dawn mist, with the mule between them, its packs swaying.

Jemmy lost no time in riding over to Shawes, partly, he had to admit, because he had sooner be out of the way when Lady Mary discovered that one of her household had done such a shocking thing as to go to the aid of the Pretender. He was really more curious than worried about Marie-Louise, for he could not imagine what she, a woman, could hope to do to aid the cause. When he arrived at Shawes he was told she was with her priest – Father Renard still served the household – so he waited for her in the drawing room. The house seemed strangely silent, and he soon fell into a reverie, remembering the many evenings he had spent in this room with Annunciata and Aliena. Over the marble fireplace was a portrait, taken by Kneller in 1719, of Annunciata seated, with Aliena standing beside her and Marie-Louise, a baby of two, sitting in her lap. The baby was holding out its hands towards its mother and laughing, and Aliena was leaning slightly forward with her hand out, as if about to take the child from Annunciata's lap, but her eyes were looking outward, at the artist. It was a poor picture of the baby, and Kneller had painted Annunciata more as he remembered her than as she was then – Jemmy worked it out in his head that she must have been over seventy – but the likeness of Aliena was excellent. Jemmy gazed and gazed, and the dark-blue eyes of the painting gazed back into his, and the lips seemed on the brink of smiling, or speaking; he grew almost hypnotized, and the rest of the room grew dark, so that there were only the eyes, and her remembered voice speaking, saying . . .

'Well, sir, and what can bring you here so early in the day?'

No, it was not Aliena, of course, it was Marie-Louise, who had come into the room unseen behind him. Jemmy shook his head to clear it, and turned to see Marie-Louise, already dressed in riding habit, standing where a bar of sunlight from the window touched her hair. He had never been able to discover whether she did those things deliberately. He scanned her face eagerly, but her resemblance to her mother was a fleeting thing that came and went like sun-shadows over the grass, not to be defined or captured. She looked, he guessed, much more like her father: which brought him to the matter in hand.

'I wondered if you had heard the news from Scotland,' he said casually.

Marie-Louise raised an eyebrow. 'If you had been a more frequent visitor, you would have known the answer to that question; you would have been able to discuss it with me. But somehow or other – I don't know how it is – you have been a stranger here since the birthday ball. I could almost think you have been avoiding me.'

'You know that I have. You know why,' Jemmy said in a low voice. 'I thought it best for both of us if—'

'Yes, that is like you, to run away from the problem,' Marie-Louise said, but without malice. Jemmy frowned.

'It is not running away, to acknowledge that there is nothing that can be done, either to recall what happened or to make amends for it.'

She smiled and shook her head. 'Is that how you see it? Well, if things had been different, I would have shewn you what we could do. Your wife, for one thing, is barren, and you have no son. Good enough reasons, I would have thought, for putting her away.'

'Putting her away?' Jemmy cried in amazement. 'What can you mean? What . . .'

'Peace, Master Morland: as I said, things are different now. I have more urgent matters to attend to. My brother is at this very minute marching south; he is probably already in Perth, where he will gather the lowland tribes before moving on to Edinburgh—'

'That is what I wanted to talk to you about, Princess. Allen said—'

'Allen?'

'He has gone to join the Prince,' Jemmy said, a little reluctantly. He would as soon not have told her of Allen's departure, if her mind really was on going, in case it encouraged her. But, after all, she would very soon know anyway. 'Before he left he asked me to look after you. He said you had spoken to him of going to join the Prince when he landed.'

'Yes,' she nodded calmly. 'I did say that.'

'But you didn't mean it?'

'I never say things I don't mean,' she said, walking to the window and sitting down in the windowseat. The sun made her copper hair a nimbus around her head. Jemmy stared.

'But what for?' he asked. 'What could you possibly do to help?'

'What Allen is doing, I suppose.'

'But Allen is a man. If you were a man, I would

say, go to it, I would wish you luck, but you are not.'

'I am as good as any man you care to name,' she said, still calmly. 'I am young, strong, healthy, a fine horseman; I am rich, independent, and master of Shawes. I am a man in everything that matters.'

'You are not!' Jemmy cried, growing angry. 'You cannot fight for the Prince, nor lead his soldiers, nor even help to organize his camps. You cannot even ride that far – Good God, it is two hundred miles or more! It would be far too dangerous. You would never get even a quarter of the way before being attacked and robbed, or losing your way – there are no roads in the north, you know, nor sign-posts, nor houses and inns to rest in. Even if you reached the Prince, you would only be a burden. There is only one sort of woman that travels with an army. There is only one thing a woman can do in time of war.'

Now Marie-Louise grew angry. She stood up, her golden eyes blazing in her pale face. 'You are very free with your condemnations, sir. You are very knowing about what I can and cannot do. I should be glad to know, sir, on what authority you think to tell me my business.'

He spread his hands. 'Don't, Princess, don't be angry. You know why I am anxious – because I care for you and your safety. But you did not, I am sure, mean to try to travel to Scotland. You know that there is nothing you could do.'

She looked at him speculatively for a moment, and then said more peacefully, 'I know that there is nothing a feeble woman could do, of course. But there is my money. I am very rich, and the Prince will surely need all the money he can get. My jewels, for instance. Father Renard might take my jewels to the Prince, to be sold to buy arms.'

Jemmy almost grinned with relief. 'I knew it, I knew you could not be so foolish. Yes, your money could help the Prince, that's true. It is a pity Allen could not have taken it for you, but you did not know he was going. But would Father Renard be the best person to go? He is not a young man, after all. We could surely find someone else to take your jewels to Scotland.'

'I am sure you are right,' Marie-Louise said. 'We must think what we can do. Someone else, someone younger than Father Renard will go. My dear Jemmy, I have not offered you any refreshment. I am forgetting my duties as hostess! Let me call for something – some wine? Or a dish of chocolate?'

Jemmy let her change the subject, glad to have won so bloodless a victory. In the back of his mind was a nagging worry that she had given in too easily; but, as she had emphasized, she never said anything she didn't mean. Well, he would keep an eye on her, just in case, and ask Father Renard to do the same.

★　★　★

In the afternoon Marie-Louise had another visitor, a much more surprising one: Jemima, very pale in the face, and very anxious.

'I slipped out unnoticed,' she explained to Marie-Louise's surprised question. 'It wasn't difficult to do today – there is such a fuss about Allen's going away. My mother is furious. She says it is an insult to her brother, who is our patron, and she won't believe that my father didn't know about it, or that he couldn't have stopped Allen. But you can't stop people when they really want to do something, can you?'

'No,' Marie-Louise said. 'You can't.' Jemima's face cleared, and she almost smiled.

'I knew it! You are going, aren't you? Oh, it's all right, I won't tell anyone. Papa only told me because he thinks I don't count,' she said it sadly, but without bitterness. 'He told me that he'd been to see you and he'd persuaded you to give up the idea. But I didn't believe it. I knew that you would not change your mind just because he asked you.'

'It seems you know me better than he does,' the Princess said rather grimly. She was looking with new eyes at the thin, earnest child, wondering if grandmother had not been right after all in her assessment. 'So what is it you want? I cannot imagine that you have come here just to see if you were right. I hope you don't want me to take you with me.'

Jemima flushed. 'Oh no! Although I *would* love to go. I do envy you so, being free to do what you

363

want. It's so terrible being a girl. I mean—' she became confused, afraid she had insulted Lady Strathord, but Marie-Louise laughed.

'It's all right. I know what you mean. So you would like to come with me, eh?'

'Oh *yes*! To fight for the true King! I know I'm only thirteen, but Papa did it when he was not much older than me, and if I was a boy—'

'Is that what holds you back? That you are a girl?' Marie-Louise was curious.

'Not really,' Jemima said sadly. 'It's because – well, I'm the heir to Morland Place. There's only me, and Allen talked to me often about the estate, and how the Master is like a father to his people, and if I am to be father, or mother, I can't just go, can I? I can't just abandon them? It would be wrong.'

'No,' Marie-Louise said thoughtfully. There was a great deal more to this child than she had supposed. She found herself rather approving of her. 'Well, what is it you want, then?'

'He went – Allen went – without anyone knowing. I would have liked to say goodbye, and wish him good luck and – but I had no chance. I wanted to ask you, when you see him, to give him something from me. I suppose you *will* see him?'

'I don't doubt it,' Marie-Louise said, holding out her hand to receive the small object the child held out. 'What is it? Can I see?'

'If you like.'

The Princess unwrapped the small square of

cloth, and saw inside the gold locket that Jemima always wore, the locket that Jemmy had had made to enclose the lock of hair that Annunciata had left her.

'Your great grandfather's hair?' she asked, puzzled. Jemima blushed again, more deeply.

'No – I took that out. I wouldn't part with that. And anyway, it would not mean anything to Allen. I put in a lock of my own hair instead. As a – a sort of—'

'A talisman?' Marie-Louise asked. Jemima nodded. The Princess folded the cloth around it again and pushed it into her pocket through the placket-hole. 'I will keep it safe, and give it to him.'

'Thank you,' Jemima said, and turned to go, but paused and looked back, curious in her turn. 'The Prince of Wales really is your brother? As the servants say? You really are a Princess?'

'I really am.'

'And what will you do, when you get to Scotland?'

'I will give him the money I have brought, and I will fight for him, and for my father, the King,' Marie-Louise said simply. 'I will put on a man's clothes, and cut my hair. I am a better horseman and as good a swordsman as any of them, and who has a better right?'

Jemima sighed a sigh of pure satisfaction. It was better than any novel; and Marie-Louise reflected that the little girl, at least, did not see anything impossible in the idea.

'I shall pray for you, every single night,' Jemima said. 'And for Allen. Will you give him – give him my love?'

'What good do you think you can possibly do?' Mary cried, almost shouted in her frustration. Jemmy ran a distracted hand through his hair. He had already done it so many times that it was standing up like a bush.

'I must catch up with her and bring her back. For God's sake, Mary, surely even you can see that?'

'She has had more than a day's start on you. How can you catch her up? How can you even know which way she has gone?'

'She will have had to hire guides – she could not even get through the Forest of Galtres without a guide. It will not be difficult to pick up her trail. A woman, especially such a woman, will not pass anywhere unnoticed.'

'Do you not think she will have had the sense to cover her trail?' Mary said. 'And besides, if she wants to go, why should you risk your life following her to bring her back against her will? It is the height of absurdity. I utterly forbid it, do you hear? I forbid it!'

Jemmy stared at her, too distracted to be angry.

'What are you talking about, forbid it? You cannot forbid it. And you cannot seriously think that I would simply do nothing, shrug my shoulders and forget it? A helpless, unarmed woman, alone in a hostile country—'

'Helpless? Unarmed?' Mary came a step towards him, and actually lifted her stick as though she would strike him. 'She is a demon! She is no more helpless than a wolf or a lion! I pity any man who comes up against her, yes, and I pity you, you poor, bemused fool! You have run after her all your life, fetching and carrying, cringing at her feet, and now you would risk your life too, and for what? You are mad, you Morlands, mad and tainted, every one, tainted with the blood of that evil woman, the Countess. Generation after generation, mad and tainted. I never wanted to marry you, I never wanted to be allied to such a family of traitors, but at least I thought you might be grateful. It is my marriage to you which has saved this family, don't you realize that? My blood, my brother's intervention, that has kept you from prison or the rope. But you don't think of that, do you? You want to throw away everything I have given you, for that evil woman's progeny, for the bastard daughter of a bastard daughter of a whore!'

And now she actually did strike him, so beside herself with rage was she. She hit him a blow on the upper arm with her stick, and staggered off-balance in the process, so that he had to jump forward and catch her to prevent her from falling. It was a feeble blow, and hardly hurt, but he was more concerned for her than angry.

'Mary, calm yourself, for God's sake. You don't know what you are saying.'

She looked bitterly up at him, enduring his hands which prevented her from falling, sick with helpless rage.

'I know what I am saying. I know more than you think I know. I know *you*, my fine husband, and how you have wished me dead.'

'I never have, Mary, I swear it,' he said distressed. 'I care for you.'

'*Liar*!' she shrieked breathlessly. 'I know where your heart is, and it is not with me.' Jemmy turned white, wondering how she could possibly have discovered the truth and then she went on. 'But I have the laugh of you – she rejected you, didn't she, and not even for another man. She rejected you for her Saviour, for her faith. Whenever I think of her in that nunnery, I smile for joy.'

Jemmy set her carefully back on her feet, and said quietly, 'I shall send for your woman. I think you should rest, take a cordial. I am sorry it distresses you, but I must go after Marie-Louise and try to bring her back. She might be killed.'

'I hope you are killed,' Mary hissed. 'I should laugh at your funeral, yes, and dance at it, if you hadn't crippled me. No, leave me alone, I shall get to my room without help.'

Allen reached Aberlady on 10 September, and with a great deal of emotion, went to see Aberlady House. Part of it was still in ruins, but one wing had been restored, and it was evidently occupied. He sat on his horse at a safe distance for some time, looking at it. It was from this house that his mother had escaped, bringing him with her, when he was a babe in arms; it was in this house that his father had died, and his brother had been murdered; in this garden, his aunt and cousin had been hanged by the Hanoverian mob – perhaps from that very tree. There was a tightness in his throat which would have made it impossible to speak, even if he had known what to say, though Colin was looking at him curiously, wondering at his long reverie. Allen said a prayer in silence for the departed ones, and then with a nod to his servant, turned away.

'Is that the house that should have been yours, sir?' Colin asked after a while, and Allen nodded. 'It's a handsome enough place, sir,' the young man added obligingly. 'I daresay the King will give you a pension to help rebuild it, when he is home again.'

When they got near Edinburgh they stopped at an inn to get the latest news, and discovered that the Prince of Wales was camped at Perth, where he had been for almost a week.

'More people joining them every day,' the innkeeper said in a neutral voice, eyeing his customers carefully. In this part of the world, there was never any knowing with strangers which side they might favour, and it was best to avoid shewing sympathy either way. 'Lord Ogilvy's gone there, they say, and Lord George Murray's expected. There's a big army of them, though some say it's no more than a rabble.

You can't expect Highlanders to behave like German soldiers.'

That seemed to cover it either way.

'Now sir, some supper? I've a good mutton broth, and buttered eggs with spinach, and a rice pudding. Or should you desire something with a little more body to it? Some haggis, maybe, or cabbie-clow?'

'I am very hungry,' Allen said. 'I should like all you have mentioned, but what, pray, is cabbie-clow?'

'You're an English gentleman, I plainly see,' the inn-keeper said doubtfully. 'Cabbie-clow, that's salt cod, boiled up with parsley and horse-radish, and we serve it up with egg-sauce and the bottoms of rachetcocks.

'You may be forgiven for thinking I am English,' Allen said, 'but in fact I am a Macallan from Stirlingshire, though I have been out of Scotland since the year '16.'

'Is that right, sir? Well, Macallan's a good name, as good as any, I'd say. I'll bring your dinner by and by. Will you take a dram with it?'

The meal came, and the two men ate with appreciation. The mutton broth was so full of good things it was almost solid – a multitude of vegetables had gone into it, bread for thickening, and even prunes. Rachetcocks turned out to be artichokes, and were a delicious foil to the rich pungency of the cabbie-clow; and the rice pudding was unlike any that Allen had tasted before. The rice had been cooked in milk, to which had been added butter, eggs, cream, and sugar, a few raisins, a dash of brandy, and a sprinkling of grated orange rind and ground cinnamon and nutmeg, all baked in a pastry-case.

They finished off their meal with a few more drams, and then stretched out their legs before the fire, and Allen remarked to Colin. 'Well, I had heard that Scotland was a barbarous place, but if the food is always as good as this, I shall have nothing to complain of. I shall be proud to admit to anyone that I'm a Scot.'

'Yes sir,' said Colin doubtfully. He was too young and earnest to understand a jest. 'Anyone would be, sir.'

Allen looked at him, and sighed inwardly. 'Yes, of course. Well, we had better enjoy this comfort while we have it. Tomorrow we ride for Perth, and I doubt that the camp will offer us anything like the luxury of this excellent inn.'

They set off early the next morning, and rode inland to find a crossing of the great river Forth, and once across it promptly got lost. When they arrived at Perth it was to learn that the Young Chevalier's army had left for Edinburgh on the 11th, the same day that Allen and Colin had left Edinburgh for Perth.

At first, Jemmy found the trail easy enough to follow. She had followed the rivers on the early part of her journey, the Ouse and the Ure as far as Topcliffe, then the Swale and the Whiske to

Northallerton; but after Northallerton he could find no trace of her.

'She must have got a guide from somewhere. She *must* have,' he said again and again. The last guide had taken her to within sight of Northallerton, and then she had seemed simply to disappear, for all the news he could get of her. He tried a few casts northwards, for that seemed the most obvious option, and drew a blank. Then he widened his sweep, and tried along the bank of the River Swale, which led north-westerly, and at last at a place called Catterick he discovered an old shepherd who said he had seen two travellers going along the old Roman Road, Dere Street as the local people still called it, a day or two back. Two people on horseback, he said.

'A woman and a man?' Jemmy asked eagerly. The old shepherd shook his head.

'Nay, maister, it warn't a woman. Two men. Two men on 'osses, gentlemen's 'osses.'

Jemmy shook his head. 'No, no, it couldn't have been. A woman and a man, I'm looking for.' For the Princess had set off accompanied by a groom – at least she had had the sense not to go entirely alone. Then Jemmy had an idea. 'Did they have a mule with them? A white mule?' Perhaps it was Allen and Colin the shepherd had seen. He was old, after all, and might not have a very clear idea of how long ago he had seen the travellers.

'No mule,' he said. 'Just two men on two 'osses. Riding north up the Roman Road. Posting along

372

good, they were. If you wanted to catch 'em up, maister, you'd need to get on a bit.'

Jemmy ground his teeth with frustration, but in the end he decided that it must have been them. The old man's eyesight might not be all that reliable, and he had seen them from a distance, after all. In any case, it was his best – his only – lead. The Roman Road, if he stuck to it, would eventually lead to Edinburgh, and it seemed likely that the Princess would have known that too. Roads in this part of the world were few and far between, and of a quality better not spoken of, but everyone seemed to know Dere Street, and the line of it, running straight as an arrow as it did, unlike the winding, tortuous local roads, was easy to see and to stick to.

They had reached the place north of Willington where the road, after running due north mile after mile, made its abrupt swing inland, heading north-west towards Hexham, when the rain began. The sky had been growing more leaden for some miles past, and now it grew quite dark, and a cold wind sprang up just before the rain began to fall. It quickly grew heavier, falling like iron nails from the lowering sky. The horses laid back their ears resentfully, but Jemmy spurred on, hunching under his cloak and trying to turn his face out of the wind. Soon, however, it was hammering down, and the drops running off his chin and hair were making their way inside his clothes and soaking him clammily. Pask had borne everything so far with silent fortitude, but he felt this was too much.

'We'd better find shelter, master, or we s'll be drawned,' he yelled through the hissing of the rain. The horses shied as a gust blew directly into their faces, and Jemmy was forced, reluctantly, to agree. But where would they find shelter? It was an empty country, this, hilly, green and deserted. They had seen no houses for a long time, and there were none in view now, nor even a bit of forest to offer shelter. There was a tall hill to the left of them, and halfway up it a clump of trees and a bit of drystone wall. Perhaps there had once been a sheep byre there, or even a shepherd's hut. At all events, it was the nearest thing in sight to a windbreak, though the hillside was steep that led to it.

'Up there!' he shouted through the roar of the rain, pointing with a hand that channelled the cold water down his sleeve. Pask looked upwards doubtfully but it was evident to him, too, that there was nowhere else. They turned their horses off the road, and towards the slope of the hill.

'The next place we come to, we must hire a guide,' Jemmy said. 'There's no point in hurrying, now we don't even know if they are on the same road, and a guide will at least take us from village to village.'

He kicked Pilot forward, and the horse ducked his head and set his shoulder to scramble up the slope. The turf was greasy with the rain, and his hooves slipped a little, and he dug his toes in, snorting with the effort. They had climbed a good way up towards the little outcrop with the trees when a whole section of turf came away under Pilot's hooves, ripping away from the raw, slippery red earth as easily as one might skin a freshly-killed rabbit. The horse stumbled, slipped, tried to recover himself, and fell, rolling a couple of dozen feet down the hillside before he managed to stop himself. Jemmy was pitched off at the first stumble, but his foot caught in the stirrup, and despite his efforts to save himself, he was dragged after, and half under, the horse.

When Pask reached them, having flung himself from his horse and slithered and scrambled down, torn between haste and fear, Pilot was on his feet, trembling, and holding one forefoot clear of the ground, trailing his broken reins. But Pask had no time to see to the horse just then. He crouched down in the icy, hissing rain, to help his master.

Jemmy groaned, and then, rolling his head over, was sick. His face was very white and pinched with pain, and when he had finished retching, he tried to sit up, with Pask's help, to see to his injuries.

'My leg,' he gasped. 'I think—'

'Try not to move, master,' Pask said, and bit his lip in the endeavour not to cry from his fear and panic.

'Help me – sit up,' Jemmy said with difficulty. Pask got his shoulder behind Jemmy's and propped him halfway up, and Jemmy reached hands that trembled shamefully towards his right leg. It was twisted strangely, and when he tried to move it the pain almost made him faint. His breeches and stockings were ripped and through them he could see the horrible lacerations which were just beginning to bleed in pinpoints from the glistening white flesh where the skin had been torn away. His calf-boots had saved the lower part of his leg from similar injury, but as Jemmy cautiously, nauseously, felt around, he knew that the lacerations were as nothing.

'It's broken,' he said. 'In several places, I think.' Pask gave a cry of alarm, and Jemmy felt his consciousness slipping again.

'Get help,' he said desperately, trying to grasp Pask's arm to emphasize his words, but his fingers would not grip. 'Leave me, get help.' And then the roaring blackness overcame him.

On Tuesday 17 September, the Young Chevalier rode into Edinburgh at the head of his troops. The streets were lined with cheering crowds, to whom his followers distributed white cockades; the Prince, tall and handsome on his white horse, bowed to left and right, receiving the homage of his people. He wore a tartan coat with the star of St Andrew pinned to it, and red velvet breeches and on his blond hair a bonnet of blue velvet, edged with gold lace and decorated with a white satin cockade. It was a sight to overjoy the people, long starved of processions and handsome Princes and all the glorious show of kingship. At the Mercat Cross, the heralds proclaimed his father King James VIII of Scotland, and the Chevalier Prince Regent, and then he rode through the city to the Palace of Holyrood House, where his grandparents, James II and Mary of Modena, had last stayed as Duke and Duchess of York. The government troops were garrisoned at the Castle, a mile away on its great and brooding rock, but they made no move against the Young Chevalier or the enthusiastic townsfolk who proclaimed him.

Marie-Louise had been two days in Edinburgh, staying in lodgings in the Grassmarket, and as soon as she learned that the Prince had gone to Holyrood, she sent her groom with a message to him, welcoming him to Scotland, offering her services, her money and her jewels, and begging the favour of an interview. The groom came back with a civil enough message, though not in the Prince's own hand, inviting her to the celebratory ball at Holyrood. Marie-Louise was delighted, for it would give her the opportunity to dazzle, to make a grand entrance, though she regretted not having secured a private interview with the Prince first.

'What is he like? Is he as they have described him?' she asked eagerly.

'He is very handsome, my lady,' the groom, Simon, replied. 'A tall young gentleman, with a ruddy face and fair hair, and very striking dark eyes, my lady, just as they say.'

'Stuart eyes,' she cried at once. 'Like grand-mother's. My mother had blue eyes, I suppose that is why I don't have them.'

'His Highness does bear a very striking resemblance to your ladyship,' Simon said, and Marie-Louise was pleased, although she had sense enough to know that Simon would have said it whether it was true or not.

'You had better pack everything, and we will take it to the Palace when we leave for the ball. We will be staying there from now on,' she said.

She wore the same dress that she had worn for Jemima's birthday ball, the pearl-trimmed white satin and lace. It was the only rich dress she had brought with her, and she had brought it in antici-pation of just such an occasion. She dressed her hair as she had done then, with pearls and white feathers, and added a white satin cockade, in honour of the Prince. She had to struggle with her hair, for she was not accustomed to doing it herself. The sooner she cut it off, and dressed entirely as a man, the better. She had dressed in man's clothes on the journey here, to make travelling easier, wearing a dark wig over her own hair, but she had not wanted to part with her crowning glory before seeing the Prince for the first time. Simon packed all the rest of their belongings and took them and the horses to Holyrood, while the Princess made the journey in a hackney carriage.

She made her entrance, and was well-pleased with

the effect. She was certainly more handsome, more richly dressed, altogether more striking than anyone else present, and as soon as she walked into the ballroom all eyes were on her, some speculative, all admiring. She heard herself announced as the Countess of Strathord, heard the name passed from mouth to mouth as she walked between the assembled people, but her eyes were on the figure of the Prince, resplendent now in red coat with the blue sash and star of royalty pale across it.

Reaching him, she went down into a deep curtsey, and said. 'Your Highness.'

'Rise, Lady Strathord. I am delighted to receive you here,' said the Prince. She was surprised by his accent – she had not expected him to sound so like a Scot, though it would do him no harm this side of the border. She rose and looked into his face, and received his smile.

'I am more delighted than I can say to be here, Your Highness,' she said, 'and to see you here in your rightful home.'

'Thank you,' he said. She was scanning his face eagerly. Yes, he was handsome as they had said; and he resembled his father, as far as she could tell from such portraits as she had seen; but, despite his smile, he was so *cold*! She had planned to greet him as her brother, but she saw now that it was not possible, with this young man, to do anything so passionate and spontaneous at a public reception: it must wait until her private interview with him.

Still searching his face she said, 'I would be glad

to have the favour of private speech with Your Highness.' She saw a slight frown gather at the words, and hurried on. 'There are certain things I have to offer in the way of money and information which I feel Your Highness would be glad to have. My uncle, the Earl of Chelmsford, has been intimately involved, I believe, in the planning of this venture.'

His face warmed a little. 'Ah, you are Chelmsford's niece are you?' he said. That, and much, much more, she cried in her heart, but not aloud. 'Well, Lady Strathord, I will see you in the morning, if you would like to speak to Sheridan, Sir Thomas Sheridan, about it.'

It was a dismissal, and aware that there were others waiting behind her to make their obeisances, she curtseyed again and moved away. She was disappointed she could not deny, but tomorrow would see everything made plain; tomorrow her brother would clasp her to his bosom, and confide in her, and share his adventure with her. It was for this that she had come. For now she would enjoy the ball, and look for Allen: she had not forgotten that she had something for him, too.

Allen arrived in Edinburgh again at the same time as the news that the government's troops under Sir John Cope had landed at Dunbar, and had set up camp at the edge of a marsh at Cockenzie, a few miles outside Edinburgh. He was weary from his fruitless journey, but glad that he had missed nothing more material to the Cause than a ball. He found Lady Strathord at once, for she was in the anteroom when he went to report his presence and offer his sword to the Prince.

'I hope you receive a warmer welcome than I did,' she said crossly. 'He didn't believe that I was his sister. I shewed him my patent, signed in his father's own hand, which I said I supposed he must recognize, and he said that it didn't prove I was the King's daughter. So I asked him why he thought his father had written my name as "Fitzjames Stuart" and he looked very angry and said he had no idea, but still he didn't greet me as sister. I cannot understand it. I would have thought he'd be glad.'

'But what on earth are you doing here?' Allen cried as soon as she paused for breath. She looked exasperated.

'You know very well what I'm doing here – the same as you. I am going to cut my hair and fight for the Prince.'

'You *can't*,' Allen almost wailed. 'It isn't right, or proper, or decent. It isn't *safe*.'

Marie-Louise linked arms with him affectionately. 'Never mind all that,' she said. 'Just tell me why the Prince wasn't glad to see me. He took my jewels and my gold readily enough. I thought he would clasp me in his arms – it is what I've dreamed of for so long.'

'He is very proud, I have heard,' Allen said. 'He is the Prince of Wales and the regent of his father,

381

and from a stiff-necked and a Catholic family. I suppose he did not relish being told his father had sinned like any mortal man. Besides, even if you are his sister, you're only a half-sister, and illegitimate—'

'What do you mean by saying *if* I am—' Marie-Louise began dangerously, but he forestalled her.

'Now please, don't begin a quarrel. We've got to think how to get you safely away from here.'

She pulled her arm free and turned to face him firmly. 'I'm not going away, Allen, so you must make your mind up to it. I shall follow the Prince wherever he goes, even if he doesn't want me, and there's nothing you can do to stop me. I think perhaps he just doesn't like women. Sir Thomas Sheridan hinted as much when I spoke to him. It is to Sir Thomas, by the by, that you had better make yourself known. And then come and see me again. I have something for you that I promised I would give into your hands.'

The next morning, very early, the Prince's army marched out to make a surprise attack on the government's troops. Allen, suddenly very nervous, went with them, although he had managed to persuade Marie-Louise of the impossibility of her actually fighting in a battle. As it happened, he did not fight in the battle either, for it was all over in less than ten minutes. The government's troops, despite being veterans of Dettingen, dropped their swords and fled, great numbers of them being killed, while the royal army suffered few casualties, and marched back to Edinburgh victorious and not a little surprised. The Prince gave orders that there should be no public celebrations of the victory, for though he naturally rejoiced at the outcome, he deeply regretted the necessity of spilling the blood of his own subjects. But though there were no public celebrations there was great private joy, and the taverns of the town were full that night with singing, cheering Jacobites.

'So now,' Marie-Louise said, 'I suppose we march into England. How relieved I am that you were not hurt in the battle. And I must say that I am glad you have come – I was beginning to pine for a familiar face, though I daresay all the faces will grow familiar to me in time.'

'Are you really determined to do this insane thing?' Allen asked her wearily. She smiled.

'Of course. I shall certainly march with you. In token of which—' She pulled off the wig she was wearing to reveal her red-gold hair cut roughly short, ending just above her shoulders. Allen was shocked, and if anything could have convinced him how serious she was, it was this sacrifice of a woman's greatest asset.

'Your poor, poor hair!' he cried. Marie-Louise fingered her rough bob with tentative fingers.

'I must say there was an awful lot of it. It was quite difficult to cut through, which is why I made such a poor job of it. But it will come to good use – I shall use it to stuff a pillow, for when we sleep out.'

Allen's only reply was a groan.

The news of the rout at Prestonpans reached Morland Place, but there was no other news, not of Jemmy or of those he had been seeking. Jemima prayed nightly for their safety, to which she must now add prayers for her father's safe return. Lady Mary was calmly convinced, she knew not why, that Jemmy was dead, and though she did not speak of her certainty to anyone, she made her plans on that assumption. The duty of ruling Morland Place in Jemmy's absence fell to her, and it was a difficult task, with Allen gone as well. Of his fate and Marie-Louise's she had neither information nor curiosity, and she forbade speculation on the subject. In her presence, at least, the Young Chevalier and the Rebellion were never mentioned.

The government, meanwhile, had not been idle: two further armies, including 6,000 experienced Dutch soldiers, had been raised and put under the command of the veteran General Wade, who had commanded during '15, and Lord Ligonier. They marched north, and towards the end of October Wade was nearing Northumberland and Ligonier Lancashire.

Their numbers far outstripped even the highest estimates of the Jacobite army, which was reported to be still in Edinburgh, apparently awaiting rein-forcements; but the rout at Prestonpans had made everyone nervous, and there were many who thought the Highlanders were invincible, and not a few who hoped they were. At Morland Place such a sentiment was not permitted to be expressed, however strongly felt. Grim-faced, and with iron self-control, Lady Mary held the reins of government. Convinced as she was that Jemmy was dead, she did not speak of it nor put on mourning clothes: it was as near as she could get to keeping her promise of laughing at his funeral.

CHAPTER 13

The worst moment in Pask's life was when Jemmy fainted, leaving him, effectively, alone on the strange hillside in the downpour. For a while he gave way to his panic and terror, and he fell on his face and wept; but he loved his master, and awareness of Jemmy's hurt made his lapse a short one. He sat up and bent over his master, pushing his tears away ineffectually with a wrist sodden with rain. There seemed nothing he could do to ease Jemmy's position, except to try to cover him a little more from the rain. He pulled Jemmy's own cloak more closely around him, trying to straighten it underneath so that it kept his body slightly away from the ground; he put his hat under Jemmy's head for a pillow, and then took off his cloak and laid it over him.

Pilot whickered as he stood up, and he paused for a moment to pat the horse, who was still holding his foreleg clear of the ground. Pask felt it over, and concluded that it was strained in some way, but not broken. There was nothing he could do for the horse, and nothing to hitch him to: he could only hope Pilot would stay where he was,

386

for it would certainly be easier to find Jemmy again if the horse was near by. He looked around him once more to fix the place in his memory, and then caught up his own horse's reins and led him back down the hill.

But where to go? It was artificially dark from the rain-clouds, but true darkness would be coming soon, and he had no idea where the nearest dwellings might be. The last place they had passed, a village called Oakenshaw, was a long way back; on the other hand, he had no idea if there was anything at all ahead other than naked countryside. He hesitated, turned this way then that, and in his helpless frustration began to weep again. But his master lay up on the hillside there and would surely die if Pask did not get help soon. He braced himself and decided to go on, and prayed to God that he had chosen right.

The rain eased, and became only a tolerable light fall, but it grew no lighter, and Pask knew that night was coming on. He rode on along the turf line of the Roman Road, and peered through the gathering gloom to right and left for a dwelling of any sort. The country was utterly empty, not even a sheep in sight; it was the absence of sheep that Pask, who had never been more than a few miles from Morland Place in his life, found the most disturbing. He began to recite the twenty-third psalm, inside his head at first, but then out loud, to comfort himself, and when he got to the end, he began again.

The repetition must have hypnotized him, for he suddenly came to with a jolt to realize that it was full dark, and he could no longer see even the line of the road. His horse was plodding on uncaringly, but Pask knew that if there was to be a dwelling or settlement, it would be near the road, and if he strayed from it he would be utterly lost. He pulled rein and stared about him again in growing panic; and then he saw it, glorious, heart-warming sight! Away to his left, the yellow blossom of a light in the calix of darkness.

The Young Chevalier and his army remained in Edinburgh all through the month of October, awaiting reinforcements from France and from Scotland. The news of the government's troops under Wade and Ligonier had reached them, and they knew themselves to be outnumbered. Against that, the Prince had had a definite promise of troops from Louis, which were expected at any time, and he firmly believed that as soon as they entered England, men would flock to their banner. During the month volunteers drifted in, and by the beginning of November the Prince commanded 5,000 foot soldiers and about 500 horse.

Allen had been given command of a troop of cavalry, and had spent the month getting to know them and giving them some basic training. He had been glad of the respite, both on his own behalf, for he was not sure how he would acquit himself in battle, and for Marie-Louise, who so far had been able to live in considerable comfort in Holyrood House, though she insisted on riding out with him every day to his training manoeuvres. Nevertheless he was glad when the Council of War was finally called, for he could not help feeling that if they were to act, it must be swiftly.

At the Council, the Prince was for marching into Northumberland and tackling Wade straight away, sure that Wade's troops would run just as Cope's had. Others were not so sanguine, and some of the senior officers were for never leaving Scotland at all. Finally a compromise was agreed upon, whereby the army would cross the border into Cumberland and head towards Lancashire; that way they would be close on hand to join up with the French troops, which would land on the west coast, and Lancashire, being a Catholic county, would surely supply them with reinforcements. The Prince had no doubt about it.

'A great body will join, as soon as I enter the country,' he said.

On 3 November, therefore, the army marched out of Edinburgh in two sections, the first under Atholl and Perth to head directly for Cumberland, the second under the Prince and Lord George Murray to take an easterly route with the purpose of deceiving Wade into thinking the whole army was heading for Newcastle. Allen and Marie-Louise travelled with the Prince's army. Marie-Louise put on man's clothes and a man's wig for the first time, and rode her horse beside Allen's at the head of his troop. Allen was at first distressed and embarrassed by it, but his men thought it wonderful, and had already made her a kind of figurehead or mascot, and cheered her mightily, calling her La Chevaliere, or the Princess, revealing that tongues had been busy during the month in Edinburgh. It evidently made them happy to have her there, and Allen finally gave up the unequal task of trying to persuade her to go home or to stay in Edinburgh, or at least to ride in the baggage carts and wear a dress.

After Kelso they swung westwards and marched down Liddesdale to join up with the other army just north of Carlisle. The feint was successful, and Wade had not moved from Newcastle; moreover the snow had begun to fall in Northumberland which would hamper Wade's movements. The Jacobites settled down to lay siege to Carlisle.

Afterwards Pask always thought that God had guided him towards that particular light, for it was shining from the window of a house in which lived a Catholic priest. He was an eccentric, and perforce a lone and secret man, who served the Catholics of a number of tiny villages scattered over a wide area of that sparsely inhabited land. Consequently, he was only only too eager to help a man who had come to grief marching north for the Young Chevalier – which was what Pask told him when he discovered he was a Catholic – but also knew the area, having travelled it in all weathers for the last twenty years. Between them, he and Pask made a litter and, collecting together all the priest thought he might need for the journey, they set out at once. Pask had wandered quite far from the road, but the priest, Father Guilfoyle, said that he knew the place where Jemmy lay and would take him a shorter way back.

It was hard going at first, being so dark, and though the priest knew his ground, Pask stumbled and blundered, leading his weary horse and trying to keep a constant distance between himself and the horse in front. Between them was slung the litter, and as Father Guilfoyle said, it would be no great effort to pull the thing apart, so hastily had it been bound together. Pask, through weariness, anxiety, and strangeness, had lost all sense of time and distance, and he had no idea how long they had been walking when the rain stopped and the clouds parted and a great white moon sailed clear, flooding the countryside with a brilliant blue-white light. By contrast it was now as bright as day, and being able to see, they made better time. They came to the place of the trees round the flank of its hill, and at once saw the bulky shadow of Pilot, still standing beside his master, head down and ears out sideways. Pask gave a cry and tried to hurry forward, and Father Guilfoyle restrained him.

'Steady, boy, we don't want you going down the same way. This ground is like glass. Let your horse pick the way.'

He left Pask holding the horses while he went to look at Jemmy, and Pask heard Jemmy groan and say something, and relief that he was still alive flooded through him.

'He's in a bad way – I pray to God he won't get pneumonia,' Father Guilfoyle said. 'Bring me the splints and bandages, boy – we must try to fix this leg so it won't move too much.'

Pask slithered down the last few feet with the things, and hunched there, watching while the priest worked. It was evidently a painful business, for Jemmy fainted again, but the priest said that it was a good thing, as it would hurt all the more when they had to move him. Finally he was wrapped in a blanket, and then came the task of lifting him onto the litter. It was a most difficult business, for the hillside was steep and slippery, and the horses had to stand exactly the right distance apart so that the litter was flat on the ground while they lifted Jemmy on. Jemmy was a big and heavy man, but at last it was done.

Pask held his horse's head, and said. 'What about Pilot? We can't just leave him.'

The priest went over to the black horse and felt his leg, and then quickly pulled off his cravat and with sure fingers used it to bandage the horse's fetlock. 'He's not so bad,' Father Guilfoyle said cheerfully. 'I'll knot his reins round his neck, and he'll follow us. We shan't be going so fast. Now, boy, steady at your nag's head, and look for my signals. All right? Now then, off we go.'

So the strange procession started forward, Father Guilfoyle leading the way, Pask urging or slowing his horse as the ground demanded, his eyes constantly returning to the inert, rolling figure of his master, tied onto the makeshift litter, and Pilot limpingly bringing up the rear. It was no longer like a dream, he thought, but like a mild and bizarre nightmare . . . and like a nightmare it seemed to go on and on.

Carlisle surrendered without casualties, Wade was snowed up in Newcastle, and the Young Chevalier's army marched on southwards to Lancashire. There was no resistance – the militia prudently sloped off to their homes as soon as the Jacobites drew near – and they were welcomed with mild enthusiasm. But on the other hand, there was no rush to the standard. Allen observed it all sadly, seeing more clearly every day how the times had changed, how the people now were different – they were comfortable, prosperous, contented – they were civilized. To them fighting was something to be left to the soldiery, and soldiers and civilians were two different sorts of things. They liked the look of the energetic, handsome young Prince, they were perfectly happy to acknowledge that his father was the true King, and if he managed to get to London and get himself crowned, they would accept him with far better grace than that old German George, whom they had never liked. But as for leaving their homes, arming themselves at their own expense, and risking their lives in battle – why, it never crossed their minds.

When they reached Manchester on 30 November they were greeted more enthusiastically, with church bells ringing, cheering crowds lining the streets, bonfires and torches, and a banquet prepared for the Prince and his officers. The Prince led the conversation at the table as to whether he would enter London on foot or on horseback, and what he ought to wear; but Allen saw Lord George Murray shaking his head gloomily. Though Wade's army was still hampered by snow in the east, the Duke of Cumberland had taken over command of Ligonier's troops, and was known to be at Stafford, threatening to bar their way south. Moreover, there was no sign of the promised French troops, although some arms and fieldpieces had been landed, and the only volunteers to join them at Manchester were two hundred unemployed labourers who came forward cheerfully to say that they had planned to join up with whichever army reached Manchester first.

Marie-Louise put on a dress and her dark wig again for the banquet, and she sparkled in all the attention that was lavished on a beautiful woman who also happened to be the only woman in the company. Allen was profoundly grateful that there had been no fighting, and that she had not been put into any danger. He thought she seemed a little preoccupied, and from time to time he saw her give a curious little grimace, as though at a spasm of mild pain, but when he asked her if she was feeling well, she only laughed and said that she was in excellent health and spirits. The Prince seemed to have got used to her presence at last, and during the banquet he even addressed one or two remarks to her. She and he were the most cheerful and sanguine of the company, both believing that everything was going well, and that the march to London would be attended with ever more success.

'When we have got past Derby, we shall be in the south, and then my people will flock to my banner,' he said. 'I shall ride into London on a white horse – God has never wished me to spill the blood of my own countrymen, and he has seen to it that the necessity has not arisen. The people want my father back. They have a sense of justice and of right which cannot be perverted.'

They set off for Derby again in two sections, Lord George Murray making a south-western feint to draw off Cumberland's army by making them think they were heading for Wales. Marie-Louise, to Allen's surprise, rode sidesaddle after Manchester, and put on her own riding habit. He could not account for it to himself, except to suppose that being nearer the south and London had affected her vanity.

They reached Derby on 4 December, and Allen, as had become his normal routine, first found lodgings for Marie-Louise, to which she retired at once, saying she felt tired. She looked tired, he thought, and decided that on the following day he would again try to persuade her to go home. Derby was not so very far from York, though Manchester would have been nearer. The next morning another Council was held at Exeter House, where the Prince was staying, and Lord George Murray opened the debate.

By that night at the latest, he said, Cumberland would have discovered his mistake and would return to Stafford, between Derby and London; while Wade was still coming south, and a third army was being formed for the defence of London. These three armies together would number 30,000, as against the Prince's 5,000, and if they were defeated there would be no chance of escape for any of them, including the Prince. The Scots, he said, had done their part in marching into England to support either an English rising or a French landing, neither of which had taken place, and they should now retreat to Scotland while they still had the chance.

The Prince was furious, and a long altercation followed, during which the Prince declared that he could not think of retreat after coming so far, that he was certain that a large part of the opposing army would desert to his side and that the people would flock to his standard once he got nearer London, and that those who counselled retreat were set to betray him. But the Scots had been losing courage the farther they got from Scotland, and though Allen and one or two others supported the Prince out of love and hope, the majority of the Council, and all the older, more senior members, were for withdrawing.

The meeting broke up, and Allen went to Marie-Louise's lodgings to seek comfort. He found her still in bed, according to the goodwife of the house.

'Is she ill?' he asked anxiously. The goodwife pursed her lips.

'A benign sickness, sir,' she said. 'But what can you be thinking of, to let your wife travel about ahorseback in such condition?'

'She isn't my wife, good woman, she's my – sister,' Allen said, and the woman sniffed disbelievingly, and Allen realized too late that Marie-Louise might have told a different story. Blushing, he hurried up to her room, for a moment too embarrassed to realize what the housewife had said. Seeing Marie-Louise in bed, propped up on her pillows, her rough-cropped hair, already growing again, fiery against the white pillows, he remembered.

'Is it true?' he asked gently, coming to sit on the edge of her bed and taking her hand.

Her face seemed glowing, no longer tired; she laughed and shrugged, and said, 'I suppose you would have had to know sometime. It was getting harder to hide it every day.'

'You are with child?' he asked, still scarcely crediting it. For answer she lifted her arms, to shew him how the bedclothes were humped over her belly. He blushed again, but his brain was scurrying on. 'But – how?' When? Who – I mean – did you . . . ?' He could find no possible way of asking the questions, just as he could find no possible way of accounting for her state to himself. He had

397

been with her almost all the time since they met in Edinburgh, and she had not, to his knowledge—

Marie-Louise laughed again, having a fairly clear idea of his train of thoughts. 'No, no, my dear Allen, it is not what you think. I have not been disporting myself with the soldiery.'

'I didn't – I never thought—'

'Calm yourself, please. The truth is that I was – like this – before I left home. I am seven months advanced.'

Allen was profoundly shocked. 'But Marie-Louise, it is dangerous for you to be riding about the countryside so far gone with child. You are risking your life, not to mention the child's.'

'Oh, the child can take care of itself,' she said with a curious grimace. 'I must say I have been finding riding astride uncomfortable, hence my change back into woman's garb.'

'Well there is no doubt now that you cannot continue with the army. It would be as improper as dangerous.'

'But what is different?' she asked, amused. 'It is only what I have been doing all along. The only difference is that you know it now.'

Then Allen told her. 'It is not all that is different. The Council today decided against advancing any further. We are to retrace our steps, through Lancashire and Cumberland, to Scotland. So you see there is no reason for you to go on risking your life and reputation. You can either stay here, or go home.'

Marie-Louise looked profoundly shocked. 'Retreat? It is madness, madness! We must go on, march into London, now, while the country is with us! Surely the Prince does not—'

'Oh no, he was for advancing, of course. But he was outnumbered, overruled.'

'Then I certainly cannot leave him now. In success I might have done it, but never, never in retreat.'

Allen sighed inwardly, and settled himself for a long, wearying argument.

Jemmy was very ill for a long time. The priest did what he could with the leg, though he shook his head over it, and doubted that it would ever be much good; but the more pressing problem was the fever and the effects of having been soaked to the skin and exposed upon a cold hillside for so many hours. He nursed him with all his skill, brewing herbal decoctions and sitting up with him during his worst deliriums. Pask shared the tasks willingly, afraid that if he left his master for a moment, he would up and die on him. It was two weeks before he even thought of trying to send word to Morland Place, another two before he did anything about it.

Father Guilfoyle shrugged and said, 'Write a letter if you wish, but there's no one to take it. If anyone should come by, we can ask him to set it on its way – that's the best we can do.'

'But what about your people – the people you say Mass for? Wouldn't one of them take it?'

He laughed at that. 'My people? None of them has ever been further from home than the end of his outlying field. What could induce them to travel as far as York? It would be like asking them to go to Paris or Rome.'

'At any rate, you could ask them to pass it on, if a traveller comes by. They would be more likely to see a traveller than we would, out of the way as we are.'

'Certainly, certainly, write your letter if you wish, and I will give it to someone. But don't hold out too much hope. We don't have many travellers here, in this country.'

Pask wrote his letter, explaining what had happened, asking for help, and giving such directions as he could, and Father Guilfoyle took it with him to the village when he went to say Mass. Whether it was ever sent or not, Pask never knew, but by the middle of October, when Jemmy was pronounced to be out of danger, though still very weak and ill, nothing had been heard. Pask wrote again, and Father Guilfoyle, with a shrug, again took the letter to the village. When he returned, he beckoned Pask to the window of his cottage.

'Look,' he said, 'look at the clouds there, over the hill. What do you think that means?'

'Rain?' Pask hazarded obediently. The priest shook his head.

'If your people are coming to rescue you, they had better come quick. Those are snow clouds. By this time next week, we shall be snowed in for the winter, and you won't be able to get south, nor they north, until the thaws. If you want to leave, now is the time to say so.'

'I couldn't leave my master,' Pask said without hesitation, and the priest nodded.

'I thought you would say that. Well, it will be the first time I have had company for the winter, and I must say it will be a pleasant change.'

On Christmas Day 1745 the Jacobite army marched into Glasgow. Of recent years Glasgow had improved its status from that of small town to increasingly prosperous city, largely on account of the tobacco and shipping trades. The tobacco lords, as they were affectionately known, were often also shipping lords, and some of them were immensely rich. One of them entertained the Prince at his mansion in the Trongate, but it was to another of them that Allen, with some relief, conveyed Marie-Louise. Alexander McNab was known by name to Allen, as the friend and patron of his step-brother Charles. It was in one of McNab's ships that Charles had sailed to the New World on his last 'herborizing' expedition and it was McNab's tobacco and shipping money that had financed the trip. Charles had spoken a great deal about him on his last visit home, and to Allen particularly, who had been his childhood companion, he had talked of Miss Alice McNab, the shipowner's eldest daughter, whom Charles longed, though not with any great hope, one day to marry. Alice would be very rich, and was her father's pride and joy, and Charles, though an enthusiastic and increasingly respected botanist, was penniless.

Marie-Louise had, since leaving Derby, taken to riding in the baggage carts, much to Allen's relief, and he was aware that she was now feeling very tired and strained. He had great hopes that she would at last consent to leave off her pointless adherence to an already lost cause, and stay with the McNabs, if they would have her. Enquiries soon found out the house, and Allen paused a moment in respect at its size and newness: evidently Charles had not told him the half of it. They were received with a great deal of suspicion by the butler, who at first would scarcely surrender them the hall, and was determined not to disturb his master, and was sceptical about the rather bedraggled woman being the Countess of Strathord. But when Allen mentioned Mr Charles Morland's name, and affirmed with great confidence that he was his brother, things changed rapidly. The master was disturbed, and came in person into the hall to greet him.

'Charles's brother – you are Charles's brother? My dear sir – your name, I did not catch it. Brother Thomas I know – can you be Edmund?'

'No, sir, indeed, I am Allen Macallan, Charles's stepbrother, but—'

'Allen Macallan! I am delighted to make your acquaintance, sir, delighted. Charles has spoken about you a great deal, and with affection, sir, with affection I assure you. And this is your wife, I suppose?' He looked enquiringly at Marie-Louise, tactfully ignoring her enlarged condition. Allen embarked again on his embarrassing explanation.

'Not my wife, sir, but my cousin. May I introduce Lady Marie-Louise Stuart, Countess of Strathord.'

McNab's smile disappeared and his eyes sharpened as his ready wits began rapidly to work.

'I think I begin to understand your unexpected arrival here. You have come in with the Young Chevalier? I think you had better come into the drawing room and tell me everything, from the beginning. But do not be afraid, you will be quite safe here. Your brother's name is enough to secure you my attention and protection for as long as you need it.'

Allen could only thank him, feeling quite weak with relief, and grateful for a mind which grasped essentials so rapidly and did not waste time on useless surprise and expostulation.

'Angus, bring wine and have some food prepared for our guests. And ask Miss Alice to come down. And Angus, see that there is no gossip and no speculation in the kitchen. Our guests are here incognito. You may take their servants to the kitchen and make them comfortable.'

'Yes, sir,' the butler said with massive dignity, and led Colin and Simon away, though his eye was a great deal too sharp and observant to be reassuring.

'And now,' said McNab, 'come in to the fire, and make yourselves at ease. When my daughter comes, I will ask you to tell us both your story. I think you will need her help and advice as well as mine.'

Early in January the Jacobite army marched out of Glasgow. At Perth there was a force of French soldiers who had landed on the east coast, under Lord John Drummond, and the Prince had sent word for them to meet him at Stirling, where they intended to besiege the castle which was held by government troops. Allen went with them, still in command of his troop and glad to be relieved of the burden of worrying about Marie-Louise; she, having at last admitted she was too heavy with child to travel further, had remained in Glasgow, on the condition that Allen would come back for her as soon as the campaign was over or she was able to travel again. The McNabs were generosity itself, and Alice McNab, a plain, sensible woman past the first flush of youth, had proved so sympathetic and understanding that Marie-Louise had taken her completely into her confidence, and was now enjoying the first friendship with another woman that she had ever had.

Simon and Colin both went with Allen, and Marie-Louise watched them ride away from the window of the room she had been given, with Alice McNab beside her. She was filled with a mixture of relief and disappointment.

'They are going to fight for the Prince, as I meant to do when I left home all that time ago. All I have done is ride up and down the country uselessly.'

'You could not help that,' Alice said comfortingly. 'There was nothing more you could have done.'

'If I had been a man, there would have been,' Marie-Louise said morosely. 'My nature has betrayed me.'

On the last day of February, Marie-Louise had her child. It was a boy, and healthy, though the labour had gone hard with her. Alice McNab had attended her herself, along with a male midwife, not an unusual thing in Scotland since the Monros and William Hunter had began to study midwifery as a science. The child was laid wrongly, and had to be delivered with forceps, which was a great trial to Marie-Louise. When she woke from her first sleep late that night, the first thing she asked was for news of the campaign, which scandalized the nurse, though it only made Alice smile.

'No more news,' she said, gently wiping Marie-Louise's brow. 'The Prince and his army are still in Inverness, and the Prince is very cheerful. They say he dines and dances every night in great spirits.'

'I would I were there – dancing—' Marie-Louise murmured drowsily. Then she remembered, and opened her eyes a little. 'The baby? Is the baby all right?'

'A son,' Alice said, 'and healthy. We are looking

405

for a wetnurse for him this minute. Have you a name for him?'

Marie-Louise closed her eyes. She was silent so long Alice thought she had fallen asleep and turned away to leave her, but the murmuring voice called her back.

'Henry. That is a good name. A royal name—' And then she *was* asleep.

For the first few days the Princess was very weak, but on the fourth day she was able to sit up in bed and give directions about the christening. McNab was scandalized that she wanted the baby christened by a Roman Catholic priest, and refused to allow one to be sent for.

'It is bad enough having taken Jacobite refugees into my house,' he said, 'and God knows I did it for love of your young man, nothing else. And that woman upstairs, with the name Fitzjames Stuart – can you imagine who she might be? But to have a Popish priest over my own threshold – that is too much to ask.'

Alice talked to him calmly, and eventually persuaded him that liberty of conscience was everyone's right, and he finally agreed that the baby might be taken to a priest, if one could be found, but no priest might enter his house, and thus it was done. Alice's own woman, and a footman with romantic views, volunteered for the task, and the baby was conveyed away secretly one night to the house of a Popish priest only three streets away, and baptized Henry Maria Fitzjames Stuart.

On the next day Marie-Louise seemed a little low; by the end of the week Alice was growing concerned about her, and the midwife was called back to examine her. He shook his head doubtfully.

'It is always a danger, when forceps are used,' he said. 'The childbed fever seems more prevalent when there are difficulties about the birth.'

'Is it childbed fever?' Alice asked with a dry mouth. The midwife shook his head again.

'I cannot say for sure. Time will tell.'

'But cannot you do something? Perhaps if you bled her.'

'Bleeding cannot help in these cases. I will give you the receipt for a febrifuge, but other than that, there is nothing to be done but wait.'

It was the fever. Over the next week it developed, and in the way it had, it came and went; sometimes she was delirious, crying and tossing in her bed, the sweat rivering from her; at other times she was quiet, lying lethargically, staring at nothing; sometimes she was rational and spoke cheerfully about being well. But each bout left her weaker, and after the first week Alice had no hope that she would recover.

She lingered on three weeks, always asking about the campaign, asking for news of the Prince, sometimes wondering how Allen was, but never mentioning the baby – she seemed, indeed, to have forgotten his existence. Only at the very end did she remember him. Alice begged her father to allow the priest to come to give Marie-Louise absolution, and this time McNab relented. The priest came after dark, well muffled up, and gave the dying woman the last rites. When he had gone, Alice came back to the bed, and held the Princess's hand. She was failing now, her consciousness coming and going, her voice weak as she spoke out of the waves of darkness that were lapping over her. She spoke of her mother, and of Morland Place, and of Jemmy; Alice thought that she did not know where she was, or what year it was, and pressed her hand and murmured encouragement to her, wishing only to ease her departure from the world. Then she said:

'The baby. I have a baby.'

'Yes,' Alice said gently. 'A fine son.'

'Henry,' Marie-Louise murmured, and she smiled. Her eyes were closed, and it was difficult to hear her words. 'A good name. A royal name.' Sinking into her last darkness, Marie-Louise thought of the baby, thought of the Young Chevalier, and the King, her father, which was her pride. The baby should be taken to her father, she thought, to have a royal upbringing. 'Take him to my father,' she said, and Alice bent forward, unable to catch the broken words.

'What did you say?' she asked, pressing the hand, but Marie-Louise spoke no more. She died an hour later, without ever regaining consciousness.

On 16 April at Culloden, the Jacobite army met the vastly superior forces of the Duke of Cumberland in battle. Apart from the rout at Prestonpans, and the inconclusive skirmish at Falkirk in January, it was the first battle the Young Chevalier's men had fought. They charged bravely, fiercely, but this time they were facing not soldiers but cannon loaded with grapeshot on top of cannonballs, and they were ripped to pieces as they charged. Cumberland had given the order 'No Quarter', and the battle soon turned into a bloody slaughter. The Prince fought bravely, and tried to rally his men, though their companions lay dead three and four deep on the field, but when it was seen that all was lost, and those who were left began to flee, the Prince could do no more than escape. With a handful of companions, including old Sir Thomas Sheridan, who though he was over seventy had never left the Prince's side, he escaped southwards towards Loch Ness, and took shelter for the night at Aird.

Here, on the following day, Allen parted company with him. The Prince and his companions were intending to seek shelter amongst the wild country of the west, where there were loyal clans enough to shelter them until they could take ship for France; but Allen had a promise to keep. He had to go back to Glasgow, and he hoped that from there he might be helped by Master NcNab. Colin had been killed in the battle, and Simon, who had escaped with him, was seriously wounded. Allen left Simon at Aird, knowing he was too badly wounded to travel, and rode alone for Glasgow.

It was a long and terrible journey. His name,

and the fact that he was travelling alone, were what saved him, and he received such kindness as he would never forget and could never repay. His horse died under him south of Fort William, and from there on he went on foot, passed from man to man, hidden in huts or woods during the day and moved on at night. Some of the journey he made by boat, along the lochs. It would have been quicker by sea, but government frigates were patrolling the western waters, looking for the fleeing Young Chevalier. It was the middle of June when he was finally rowed down Loch Lomond to Tarbet, crossed the neck of land into Loch Long, and finally in a fishing boat from Strone Point sailed up to Glasgow.

McNab received him gravely, but did not hesitate to offer him shelter and help.

'And the Princess – I mean, Lady Strathord – how is she? Is she still here?' he asked eagerly. When McNab told him, he was too stunned to weep. He could not take it in, could not make it real in his mind. She was too full of vitality to be gone; his mind grappled uselessly with the concept of Marie-Louise, dead.

'You must escape,' McNab said. 'You will be a proscribed man now. You must go abroad.'

Allen assented to the necessity. 'If you can get me to Dublin, my kinsman Lord Chelmsford will help me.'

Nothing could be easier than to get him to Dublin, said McNab – all his westbound ships called in at Dublin. 'But the baby – what of the baby? Shall you keep him here. I imagine you would perhaps be embarrassed by his presence.' Allen looked at Alice as she said that, wondering if perhaps she might have taken a fancy to the child, born in such romantic circumstances, but Alice shook her head.

'His mother's dying wish was that the baby should be taken to *her* mother,' she said. 'Do you know where she is?'

'Yes, indeed,' Allen said. It seemed most suitable, that Henry should be put in the care of his grandmother, and Maurice would certainly help to get him there. 'I had better take the baby with me, then, to Dublin.'

He sailed at the end of June for Dublin, accompanied by the wetnurse and baby Henry, posing as a widower, an Irish seed-merchant taking his son home to be cared for by his mother. It was a good enough story for anyone who might be curious. He said goodbye with deep gratitude to the McNabs, and promised to write to them by way of Charles to let them know he was safe. It was only on the long sea-journey to Dublin that he had time to think about things, to feel and understand his grief and shock, and to wonder about Henry's existence. His mind went back to the time before he left Morland Place, and counting backwards he arrived at May, and a very disturbing conclusion; he became more eager, the more he thought about it, to hand over the responsibility

411

of the child to either Maurice or Aliena, so that he need never think about it again.

As to his own future, he could not imagine what it would hold now. He was a fugitive, and he did not know if he would ever be able to go home again. France or Italy would have to be his home, for the time at least: Maurice, he hoped, might be able to help him there. He could not regret what he had done, though the outcome had been so disastrous, but he longed with all his heart to be able to go home to Morland Place. Around his neck he wore Jemima's locket which Marie-Louise had given him, and he felt for it and closed his hand about it for comfort as the ship bore him over the grey sea into exile.

CHAPTER 14

One afternoon at the end of April, 1746, Father Guilfoyle came up the hill from having visited his flock in Esh Winning, and found Jemmy sitting on the bench outside the cottage, enjoying the first really warm sunshine of the year. He greeted the priest with a wave of the hand.

'I've been committing the sin of vanity this morning, Father,' he said. 'I've been looking at my reflection in the window, and I must say I rather like this beard. I think I might keep it.'

Father Guilfoyle came and sat down beside him to get his breath from the climb. Jemmy glanced at his face and saw that he was grave, and added. 'Of course, I know you have guessed the real reason for my liking the beard: it's because I cannot endure the thought of having to shave again. What news from the village? On such a sunny day I cannot believe that the roads are still impassable.'

The thaws had come a week ago, but the snow had been so heavy that winter that the melt-water had caused flooding, and the mud had made travel impossible.

'No, I think you might really set out on your journey now, if it is what you wish,' the priest said. 'How is the leg? Does it still pain you?'

'A little – not so much when I walk, but when I stop walking.'

The priest nodded. 'It will be long before you are really sound. If you do want to leave, you must be sure to take the journey in easy stages, and never overtax yourself, or you may end up unable to walk at all.'

Jemmy sighed. 'Yes, I know. I will be careful. Father, I have never really thanked you for what you have done for me. You saved my life—'

'There is no need for thanks. It is no more than you or anyone would have done. And I must confess that I have enjoyed your company. Winter can be very lonely here, when the snows are down, and this winter I have not been lonely. Where is Pask?'

'He went up the hill after a rabbit. I don't think the rabbit had anything to fear, though – I think he was running for the pleasure of it. It is so good to feel the sun's heat again.'

'You have a good man there. A devoted man.'

'I know,' Jemmy said. 'Pask was my father's man before me. My father chose him when he was only a young boy, and he served my father well. He is the cousin of our steward, back home at Morland Place. Oh,' he looked suddenly hungry, 'how I long for Morland Place.'

The priest had been watching his face carefully,

and now he said, 'I had some news down in the village today which I feel I must tell you, though I am loath to darken this lovely day for you.'

Jemmy's face seemed to become suddenly all bones, as it had been during his illness. 'What is it? What have you heard?' he asked, his mouth dry. 'Is it news of my people?'

'No – at least, not directly. I have no names for you, Jemmy. But the word has come down the valley that there has been a great battle in Scotland, in the far north, at a place called Culloden.'

Jemmy saw in the priest's eyes all he needed to know.

'Was it bad?' he asked at last.

'They are saying it was a massacre, a bloody massacre. The Duke of Cumberland wiped out the Jacobite army, and very few escaped. They are calling him "Butcher" Cumberland, because he gave no quarter. But the Young Chevalier escaped, along with a few of his closest companions. They say he is gone into the western isles, but I do not know if that is true. At all events it is certainly true that he has escaped. But it is an end, I am afraid, of the venture. Inverness surrendered and all in it taken prisoner.'

'And my kinsfolk? Allen Macallan? And—'

Father Guilfoyle shook his head. 'I have no names for you,' he said again. 'Consider how unlikely it is that I should. No one knows you are here.'

'No,' he said, and suddenly grew active, pushing himself up from the bench. 'I must go home, I must start directly. That is where news will be known. You say some people escaped? They may have gone there, they may be on their way there this very minute. I must—'

'Gently, my son, gently,' the priest said, standing also and steadying Jemmy as he swayed. 'You will start tomorrow – there is not sufficient of the day left today.'

At first light on the first of May they set off, Pask and Jemmy, on horseback, supplied with food for the journey and other necessities by Father Guilfoyle. He rode with them as far as the Roman Road, near the place of the trees, where Jemmy had fallen.

'You think you can find your way back from here?' he asked. Jemmy smiled.

'Does a bird know its own nest? I could find Morland Place if I were blind, I am so eager to be home.'

'Remember what I said – take the journey in easy stages. Rest that leg, if you want it to serve you at all.'

'I will.' He stretched out a hand, and the priest clasped it. 'Goodbye, Father. I can never thank you enough. I will come back one day and visit you, and thank you again.'

The priest screwed up his eyes against the rising sun. 'God bless you, my son,' he said. 'You will not visit me, but if you can, write to me and let me know if you have news of your people. Until then, I shall continue to pray for them.'

There was nothing more to say, and Jemmy and Pask rode away. When Jemmy looked back at the turn of the road, the priest was already a tiny and distant figure, cresting the rise of his bare hillside.

The journey took a week, though it could not have been above seventy miles, but Jemmy soon discovered that it caused him great pain in his damaged leg to keep it in the same position for any length of time, so they had to keep stopping and resting. Father Guilfoyle had told him that the bone had not just been broken, but also crushed, which had complicated the healing. He and Pask kept up a cheerful conversation during the journey, as much to take Jemmy's mind off things as from light spirits, but when, on a perfect May day, they found themselves once again on Morland land, they fell silent. Jemmy's heart was full as he rode through Ten Thorn Gap; Pilot suddenly pricked his ears and whickered excitedly, recognizing the smell of his home, and Jemmy had to restrain him from breaking into a trot, which would have jarred him painfully. Then they were at the drawbridge, and Jemmy, from sudden shyness, dismounted, feeling it would be somehow intrusive to clatter into the yard on horseback. He had barely gained the ground when something furry hit him fair and square, and he lost his balance and sat down abruptly, to find his arms full of Jasper, and the old dog's frantic, crying, licking, tail-waving joy.

And then came the uproar, people running, calling, crying; disbelief and joy; hands touching, faces grinning or beslobbered with tears. There was Clement, hardly knowing whether to embrace Pask or help his master into the house; Father Andrews wringing his hands and shaking his head; brother George, with, astonishingly, tears running down his fat, red face; Jemima, taller than he remembered her, flinging round him arms as thin and white as withies, and exclaiming over the beard. They were in the courtyard now, and Jasper was barking non-stop as if he had gone mad, setting off all the other dogs, and for a moment, in his confusion, Jemmy thought it was bells being rung to welcome him home. Then Mary appeared on the steps, and Jemmy looked over the heads at her, and there seemed a sudden silence, in which she came forward, leaning on her ebony stick, descended the steps, and walked through the parting crowd to stand before him. Her eyes roved over him, taking in the beard, the thinness, the awkward way he stood to save his leg – did the shadow of a smile touch her lips at the realization that he was lame, too? – but she did not speak.

'Mary,' he said, 'Mary.' And then he understood her trouble – she did not believe it. 'It really is me,' he said foolishly. 'I've come home.'

He held his arms out to her, and she stepped

forward and embraced him, and he felt her small, thin body, braced like a shell, brittle and unsubstantial, and her arms, light and powerless around his body. He held her tightly for a moment, and then released her enough to kiss her forehead.

She pushed herself away from him and said expressionlessly, 'I thought you were dead.'

And then her lips trembled, and for a moment her face seemed to waver as if it were about to break up into shards, and an extraordinary whimper broke past her clenched teeth. She was trying not to cry, he realized, and he hastened to put an arm round her and turn her towards the house.

'Let's go in,' he said, covering for her. 'I must sit down, or I shall fall down. And then you can tell me all the news, while I rest and drink some wine.' Mary walked with him, bracing herself for his ugly limp, and felt a warm and treacherous gratitude for his sympathy, and for his big, warm body in the cold place beside her.

It was long, long afterwards, when Jemmy had sought the solitude of the chapel to assemble his thoughts and feelings, that Jemima came to him. He was sitting alone in the Master's seat – alone except for Jasper, who would not let him out of his sight, and was sitting at his feet now with his head on Jemmy's knee, staring at his face. Jemima came silently up beside him, and said hesitantly, 'Papa?'

Jemmy turned his head slowly, and they exchanged a long, searching look, before he sighed and held out his arms, and she came slipping in onto his lap and put her arms round his neck and buried her face against him. Getting too big for this now, he thought, holding her tenderly; growing tall and womanly; he felt a surge of passionate regret for all of her life that he had missed sharing.

After a while she lifted her head and said shyly, 'I rather like you with a beard, Papa. I never saw a man with a beard before, except in pictures. Will you keep it?'

'Perhaps. If you like it, perhaps I will.' She stroked it with the tips of her fingers, and then met his eye.

'Papa, did you find them? Have you any news of – of Allen?'

'No. I never saw them. I do not know where they are, or even if they are alive or dead.'

'Oh,' she said, but he saw that it was only what she had expected. Then, 'Mama thought you were dead. She didn't say anything, but I could see that's what was in her mind. But I knew you weren't. I could feel it.'

Jemmy closed his eyes for a moment, and pressed her closer, and then said. 'Things will be different from now on, I promise you. I have not been – just to you.' She did not deny it, and he smiled a little. 'You are the heir, and you must learn all about your inheritance. I shall take you around the estate, introduce you to the tenants, shew you what they do, explain everything to you. You must learn about farming, about the stock, about cloth-making. I daresay you know nothing about cloth-making.'

'Well, a little. Allen used to tell me things—' she said, but Jemmy was not really listening.

'I'll take you to market – you must meet the merchants and agents. You will have to learn how to keep books and do accounts. I should have been shewing you these things, but – I was blind, Jemima, blind and foolish,' he confessed suddenly. She did not ask, about what, and he hardly noticed the omission. 'But you and I will be together now. I realize I know nothing about you, my own child. We'll be friends, won't we?'

A number of things ran through Jemima's mind in the second before she answered: she thought of her mother, of her dead brothers, of Allen, of Father Andrews's poor opinion of her; of the future, of being mistress of Morland Place, and of the time she would have to marry, and who would choose her husband for her – her father, or her mother? Did he really think that things were that simple? And she kissed his cheek, and said:

'Yes, Papa. Friends.'

Allen reached Paris early in August. A number of other fugitives had also arrived, but there was no news of the Young Chevalier; no news, however, was good news to the extent that he certainly had not been captured. Allen first made his devoirs to

421

the King at Fontainebleau, where he was kindly received and his immediate wants supplied. Then he had to face the difficult interview with Aliena at Chaillot. In a still and shadowy little parlour in the convent she came to him, her hands folded in her sleeves, her face, framed in the black veil and white wimple, like a carving in alabaster, calm, timeless, beautiful. She was approaching sixty, he was forced to remember; he searched her face for memory, but he had been a child when she became a nun. He had grown up thinking she looked like Marie-Louise, but of course she did not. She looked like Jemmy.

She sat in silence while he told her the whole, long, sad story, making no comment, even when he told her of the death of her only daughter, or of the desire she had had to send baby Henry to her mother, or of his suspicions as to Henry's siring. She listened, gravely, attentively, and when at last he had finished she was silent for a long while, before questioning him.

'Who knows of this? Have you communicated with the family? Has anyone?'

'Your brother Maurice knows, of course, and the McNabs. Otherwise, no one. I have not written, nor sent any message. I have not had time or opportunity so far.'

She said, 'I will write to Maurice and to these McNabs, and ask them to keep silence. Better that no one should know. Morland Place and Shawes will have to be told that she is dead, but better that she died of a fever, with no mention of the child.'

'But—'

'To what purpose? It can only wound, it can only cause trouble. Let him be brought up here in obscurity, let there be an end to all this—' She stopped abruptly, and he saw her make the effort to control herself. Then she said, 'Is he here? Did you bring him here?'

Allen nodded. 'The wet-nurse has him outside. Shall I bring him in?'

In a few moments, the baby was brought in, and Aliena freed her hands from her sleeves and held them out for him. He was awake, and his dark blue eyes roved unseeingly across her face. Allen watched her, wondering what terrible accumulation of emotions she must feel as she held her grandson, but her smooth face was unfathomable.

'So,' she said at last, 'the curse is not yet worked out. I had thought that I—' She looked suddenly, sharply at Allen. 'She paid with her life, don't you see that? It must not be in vain. If anyone learns who this child is, it will all begin again. You must keep silence for her sake. Did you love her?'

'Yes,' he said simply. 'But she did not love me.'

'No, I imagine not. She loved herself so much, there was no room in her heart for another.' It was not said bitterly. 'I shall take care of him – that is *my* payment. I shall have to give up my vows, leave the convent.'

Allen could only assent to it – he could see the necessity. 'I will help you. I will try to be—'

'A father to the child?' she asked, with a wry smile. 'No, I pray you, do not take *that* useless task upon yourself. You have done all you need in bringing him here. I have been happy here, these last twenty years. It was never a sacrifice, you know. I think I should have known a sacrifice would be required at some time, from someone. My mother knew it.'

Allen did not understand any of this, and said awkwardly. 'There are one or two things of hers – I have them here. Some jewels – she sold most of them for the Young Chevalier – and this.' He unfolded the thick paper. Aliena smiled without humour at it.

'Her patent,' she said at once. 'Yes, I recognize it. How like her to have taken it with her.'

'She was afraid the Young Chevalier would not acknowledge her as his sister if she did not shew it. But I don't think he did anyway, even when he had seen it.'

'No, I suppose he would not. A proud young man, from what I know of him. Well, Henry shall have her title, there is no harm in that. But not until he is grown up enough to laugh at it as he should.'

The arrangements took time to be made. In October the Young Chevalier, having wandered for five months about the lochs and glens of Scotland, fleeing the Hanoverian retribution, finally reached

France, and was received graciously, even affectionately, at Fontainebleau. A few days later he presented a list to King Louis, naming those Jacobite officers to whom he thought the King ought to offer financial rewards. Allen's name was on the list, and he received a gift of 2,000 livres, which he used to buy a small house in Clichy, a pretty little village on the slopes of Montmartre, near Paris. Henry, Duke of York, was living at Clichy and the Young Chevalier soon joined him, so it became something of a resort for Jacobites. To this house at the end of October came Aliena to set up home with the baby Henry, having given up her vows.

Maurice had agreed to keep the secret of Henry's existence, and pointed out, 'That as Marie-Louise will have thus died childless and intestate, the Shawes estate will pass to me as her nearest kin. It seems only just, therefore, that I should pay a pension to you and to the baby, but it shall be done anonymously, dear sister, if that is what you wish.'

The pension was enough to keep them in comfort in the house in Clichy; and Maurice also agreed to write to the McNabs, and to Morland Place to inform them of Allen's escape and Marie-Louise's death.

In addition to the monetary gifts, King Louis also offered all the loyal Jacobite officers commissions in his own army, and after some hesitation, Allen accepted. He was not, by nature or training, a soldier, but he had to do something and there

425

seemed no other alternative. Aliena, gently but firmly, was discouraging him from having anything to do with baby Henry, whom she seemed to regard as a kind of living infection which must be isolated, and so at the end of November he accepted a commission in the Royal Ecossais, who were going to Flanders to fight the Dutch and Hanoverians. There was a kind of irony in that.

It was still full dark when Jemima came down into the yard, shivering a little from being so newly awake one April morning in 1747. A boy stood near the door with a torch, which made the shadows darker, and Pask was standing in the middle of the yard, holding Jewel and Pilot, already saddled up.

'There you are, miss,' he said. 'Shall I help you up?'

'No, it's all right, Pask, give him to me. I can manage,' Jemima said, and led Jewel to the mounting block, pushing a crust of bread under his long, enquiring lips. One of the things she had been sure to teach him, because Allen had told her long ago it was important, was to stand still to be mounted, and she swung herself up nimbly and settled her skirts and stirrup while Pask led Pilot forward for her father, who appeared on the steps at that moment, pulling on his gloves, and sniffing at the air.

'It's going to be fine,' he said. 'Good. Pask, have you the cloth there? Are you ready, Jemima? Excited?'

'Interested, Papa,' she smiled at him. He used the block to mount – it was easier so, with his stiff leg. He grunted as he settled himself in the saddle.

'Of course, you are too much of a young lady to be excited by a cloth-market. Besides, your mother would not approve. It's bad enough that I'm taking you there, but far worse if you were excited about it.'

'You do talk nonsense,' Jemima said affectionately, and in a moment the three horses were clattering out over the drawbridge on their way to Leeds. Away from the torchlight and the yard, the darkness seemed less dense. Sunrise was still more than an hour away, but it would start to grow light soon; in the meantime, they all knew the path well enough not to need the light. They walked briskly, enjoying the freshness of the air. In a while they reached the place where the track turned off for Shawes, and Jemima glanced at it automatically as they passed. The house was all shut up now. A letter had come from Dublin last September to say that Lady Strathord had died of a fever in Glasgow, and the processes of law had been put into motion to transfer ownership, on her intestacy, to Lord Chelmsford.

Maurice had not enjoyed ownership long, for he had not even had time to consider what to do with the house when he, too, died, in December 1746. He was seventy-four, a good age, though he came from a long-lived family. In his youth he had once described himself as a citizen of the world, and there was a deal of truth in it. Exiled from England with his mother in boyhood, he had never again regarded any place as home. He had lived in many places, wandered Europe, written music for patrons of many nationalities, married four times and begotten many children; he had been poor and he had been rich and he had been many times in danger of his life. But he died in the end peacefully, in his sleep, in his own bed, with the slumbering bulk of his last and perhaps most contented wife beside him. Molly Estoyle wept, more than she had expected to, and remembered to send for a priest, and then sat quietly at the bedside to wait, contemplating the dark and noble Stuart face, and wondering where she would order her mourning clothes, and how Maurice would have left his property.

Ownership thus passed to his elder son Rupert, the new Lord Chelmsford, who had had no hesitation in shutting up the house and dismissing all the servants, except for a few kept on as caretakers. Rumour was that he intended to let the house, but nothing certain had been heard yet. Morland Place had taken one or two of the old servants from Shawes, and tried to find places for others, so that they should not be destitute. Jemmy had offered a home to his former tutor, Father Renard, but he had smiled a mysterious smile, and said that duty called him elsewhere, and a few days later he had left for France. Jemima had thought of asking him to take a letter for her, for

Allen, but in the end she had realized that she had nothing to say to him, nothing, at least, that he would want to hear. He had been with Lady Strathord almost until the end, and she did not like to think about that.

She rode up beside her father, and he began to talk about the cloth-market.

'When I was a child, a lot younger than you – I suppose I must have been about seven – my father took me to the cloth-market. I remember it very well. It was different in those days, of course, a lot busier. The white cloth was sold in the market as well then, but then they built the White Cloth Hall in Wakefield, and that got the merchants thinking how much better it would be to have a market indoors, out of the weather. So they built the hall on Kirkgate, and now it's only us coloured cloth merchants who have to brave the weather.'

'But why don't you build a cloth hall, too?' Jemima asked.

'It wouldn't pay us to. It would cost money, you see, and there's never been much trade in coloured cloth in Leeds – not compared with the white. Not enough trade to justify it.'

Jemima thought about that, and thought that surely if the hall were built, it would attract the trade from other places, and then it would be worth it. But she did not say anything, aware that she was the most green of novices to the business.

They reached Leeds just before five, and Jemima, who had expected to see a busy market scene, was amazed to discover the street, Briggate, completely deserted, and with no sign of a market except the bare boards laid across trestles which lined the street on both sides.

'But where is everybody?' she asked. 'Are we too early?'

'Oh no, my lamb,' Jemmy smiled. 'It's the rule of the market. No one may be in the street until the market bell rings, or they will be fined. They are all in the inns, where we shall go now and break our fast with a Briggshot.'

'With what?'

'A clothier's two-pennorth, my child – the ordinary they lay on for breakfast for all the hungry clothiers who have travelled through the night to get here. We'll go to the Eagle and Two Lambs – that I think will be the best for a young lady. Some of the inns, to tell you the truth, are a little rough – and some of their ordinaries are more ordinary than others!'

After the silence and emptiness of the street, the Eagle and Two Lambs was crowded, noisy and smoky. Jemima pressed close to her father, and felt herself being crushed by the press of enormous men with red faces who were all bawling at each other, in between cramming their faces with food and drink and sucking on noxious clay pipes that smelled like burning rubbish. Jemmy worked his way through the crowd, receiving claps on the back and cheerful greetings, some respectful, some boisterous, from his fellow-clothiers.

'Now then, Master Morland! How's the leg?'

'What hasta brought today, Master? Another bit o' thy fancy stuff?'

'Hasta heard about Norris, then, Master? He were set upon coming across t'moor, an' 'is cloth stolen. Tha s'd mind thy piece has no mud on it, or t'magistrate'll be axing questions,' said one man jocularly.

'Nay, lad, tha forgets – 'e *is* t'magistrate,' someone shouted, and a roar of laughter swept over them. Now someone noticed Jemima, clinging to her father's arm, and way parted for them, making some space for which she was grateful, for she felt as though she could not breathe.

'Make way for t'little lass,' someone said.

The jocular man peered at her and cried. 'Now then, Master Morland, is 'at little maiden thy daughter? Why, she's grown up into a right handsome little maid, and no mistake. Now lads, step back and let t'little mistress through. Eh, but she's bonny!'

He clapped a meaty red hand kindly on her shoulder as he passed, and his beery breath whistled around her ears. Grateful as she was for his obvious intended kindness, she was more grateful to slip into the haven of the booth her father had been heading for, where Pask quickly joined them, having taken the horses round the back, and a serving-girl came up at once to take their order. Safe in the booth, with her back to the high wooden partition, Jemima felt able to enjoy the scene, and

431

soon the Briggshots arrived to stave off the pangs of early morning hunger: for each of them a clay pot of ale, a wooden piggin filled with oatmeal porridge, and a wooden platter of cold roast beef and a roll of bread. The jocular clothier, whose name, it appeared, was most appropriately Michael Clothier, came and leaned on the end of the partition to smoke his pipe and exchange gossip with Jemmy, with more details of the accident that had happened to the unfortunate Norris, and a list of the merchants who were known to be coming to the market that morning. After a while he looked across at Jemima again.

'So, tha'st brought thy lass to learn trade?'

'That's right. I thought she ought to know how it's done, even if she has an agent to come to market for her,' Jemmy said. 'After all, I won't always be here.'

'You've said truth there, Master,' Clothier said, suddenly serious. 'Well, I shall keep my eye out for her, if ever the time should come. She's the properest little maiden I've seen for many a long year, God bless her.'

He nodded and moved away, and Jemmy turned and smiled at his daughter.

'I think you've made a friend there,' he said.

At six o'clock came the sound from outside of a church bell ringing, and at once the most extraordinary change occurred. Suddenly there was silence; everyone in the inn put down his ale-pot, picked up his bale of cloth, and hurried outside.

Jemmy got up too, saying. 'That's the bell for the market. Come on now. Keep your eyes open and your mouth shut.'

Outside the clothiers were setting out their rolls of cloth on the trestles, and Pask did likewise, finding a space on a trestle near the inn. Each clothier stood behind his own bale, and everything was done in complete silence, without the least fuss or jostling, in the strangest contrast to the noisy scene inside the inn. The bell was ringing all this while from the old chapel by the bridge, and when it stopped, from both ends of the market appeared other men, some of them richly dressed, all walking in silence down between the rows of trestles.

'The buyers,' Jemmy whispered to Jemima. 'Some factors, some merchants, some agents for foreign merchants. Look at that one – he's a Frenchman. See his patent?'

Others, Jemima noticed, were carrying small squares of coloured or patterned cloth which they were evidently trying to match. A rich-looking man with a huge fur collar to his cloak came up to the clothier standing next to Jemmy and fingered the bolt of cloth, and then leaned across the trestle and whispered something to the clothier. He whispered something back, and the man in the fur collar shook his head and walked on. All around her the scene was being repeated, everything being done in a whisper, as if no one wanted anyone else to know his business. After a while one or two people began to take cloth away. Jemima watched it all with fascinated eyes. The fur-collared man came back and apparently made a new offer to the clothier, and this time there was a nod and a handshake.

In half an hour the trestles were beginning to empty. Jemmy sold his cloth to a handsome grey-haired man who agreed his first whispered price. He nodded and walked away, and Pask at once rolled the cloth up, put it on his shoulder, and went off with it.

'He'll take it to the merchant's house, and get payment for it,' Jemmy explained. 'We can stay and watch if you like.' Jemima nodded.

At a quarter past seven the bell began to ring again, and everyone began to pack up their belongings, some to take their cloth away to the merchants' houses, others to take it back into the inn.

'Everyone has to be out of the market by the time the bell stops ringing, or pay a fine,' Jemmy explained. The buyers concluded last, hasty bargains, and hurried away. At half past seven the bell stopped ringing, and Jemmy took Jemima back into the Eagle and Two Lambs from a street which was as deserted as it had been at five o'clock.

'What happens now?' she asked.

'We wait for Pask, and then go home,' Jemmy said. 'The street will be open again at eight, for general provisions, an ordinary market – baskets, shoes, pots and pans, that sort of thing.'

'Did you get a good price for the cloth?' she asked. Jemmy smiled.

'I got the price I wanted. One always does. The agents know as much about cloth as we do, or they would not be agents. There is rarely much disagreement about the price – a few coppers this way or that. That was Thoresby's agent I sold it to. Thoresby's one of the great merchants hereabouts – you'll come to know his name. He buys a lot of my cloth. Sometimes I don't even have to send it to market – his man will talk to Harvey, and they'll come to an agreement, and Harvey'll take it over to Thoresby's house straight from the finisher.' He looked at her hesitantly, and then appeared to make up his mind. 'I had better say this – don't be too trusting of your agent. Harvey's a good man, I don't mean otherwise, but any man can be tempted, and an agent has great power. He'll work better for you if he thinks you are keeping an eye on him. Look over his shoulder from time to time, and it'll keep him on the straight path.'

Their eyes met, and the unspoken words 'when I am dead' hung between them to end the sentence. She went up on tiptoe to kiss his cheek. The thought that all he was teaching her was a preparation for when he was gone was always with her, and she hated it.

The family was gathering for Easter. Uncle Robert, recently widowed, came from London where he had been angling for a stall at St Paul's but without success. His sons Rob and Frederick arrived on the same day, Rob from Christ Church and Frederick from Winchester. Neither of them was in his father's good books, Rob because he had run up a gambling debt at Oxford which, for lack of funds, he had been obliged to apply to Robert to settle; and Frederick because he was already celebrated at his school for being the youngest pupil ever to be expelled for the dual sins of debauching the maids and smoking in the chapel.

'It's your own fault, father,' Rob argued. 'If you would only give me a decent allowance I would be able to settle my debts out of it and not trouble you.'

'If you did not have the debts in the first place—' Robert began, but Rob interrupted languidly.

'Gad, father, a man has to gamble, it's only what's done. The other men would think one a poor sort of fellow if one didn't. It's only because I didn't have enough to settle a month ago that I had to go on wagering more and more to try to win enough to pay it off, and that way lies ruin, because you know one has to try all sorts of lame bets to get the odds one needs. Usually I am the very soul of discretion, I swear it. Besides,' he narrowed his eyes, 'what Frederick has done is far worse. At least I haven't brought shame on you. A gambling debt is such as any gentleman might own to, but to trifle with female servants—!'

Frederick and Rob hated each other cordially, and never lost a chance to blacken each other with their father. Frederick, while bridling at his brother's perfidy, nevertheless shewed a more accurate knowledge of his father's character when he replied.

'I hardly call it anything to get myself expelled at the end of my last term. I should have left anyway – and at least I didn't cost you money, Papa.'

Aunt Augusta and the girls came from Scarborough, where she had been recommended by a new sort of doctor to try sea-bathing for her gout, and she was full of the excitement of having done something so new, so daring, so absolutely *fashionable*. She talked endlessly of the *beau monde* at Scarborough, and what she overheard about her own fashionable appearance from a very gentlemanly-looking man, who someone told her afterwards was almost certainly a second cousin of the Duke of Marlborough. Jemima was much more interested when she began describing the process of bathing itself, but when she described for the fourth time the wonderful sensation of immersing one's *whole body* in sea-water, Lady Mary, noticing Jemima's rapt gaze, felt obliged to rebuke her sister-in-law sharply for talking scandalously in the drawing room.

Uncle Edmund had only to come from Leicester, where he was stationed. He was much less unhappy with the army since he had been commended for his part in the defence of Fort Ruthven during the '45. He had been extremely reluctant to go, and once there had sulked and complained bitterly, until the Jacobite attack had taken him so much by surprise that he had fought like a tiger before he had even had a chance to feel afraid. Thereafter he talked so much about his part in beating off the rebels that a fellow officer had since claimed that it was largely in order to get away from Captain Morland that they finally surrendered.

Now, when he could break into his wife's Scarborough chatter, he retold the tale of Ruthven to his admiring family. He had told it many times before, but each time he told it, he added more detail, and it was becoming quite a polished recital. His son William, who was completing his first year as a gentleman-cadet at the Woolwich Academy, listened with open scepticism to his father's tales of military glory but, commendably, kept his mouth shut.

Uncle Thomas and Uncle Charles were not at home – Uncle Thomas was with the Channel Fleet, on blockade duty, and Uncle Charles was somewhere in South America. But the rest of them more than made up for it, and the drawing room came to seem unbearably crowded; even in the long saloon, it was all too easy to overhear Uncle Robert and Uncle Edmund arguing. They argued all the time, for whatever one said, the other was sure to disagree, and they would soon become heated and blackguard each other most unpleasantly. One evening Lady Mary decided she had had enough and called Jemima to her from across the room where she had been taking refuge in a book.

'Put your book away and play to us,' she commanded. 'What is it you are so deeply interested in, anyway? Give it to me.'

Jemima handed it over reluctantly, and Lady Mary read out the title in tones of withering scorn.

'*The History of Imbanking and Draining*, by Sir William Dugdale. Suitable reading indeed for a young lady in a drawing room!' Jemima shrank under her cold and contemptuous eye, and stumbled a justification.

'It was just that I – well, you see, madam – the land down near the beck is sour, and Allen used to say—'

Lady Mary silenced her with an upraised hand; her attention was with Jemmy now. 'You see what you are doing, sir? I wonder you do not bid her come to the drawing room in breeches and boots. What will you do next? Teach her to swear? Cut off her hair?'

Jemmy's eyes gleamed at this passing reference to Marie-Louise, whom the servants believed to have run off to Scotland dressed as a man, but he only said peaceably, 'It is right that she should take an interest in her own land, madam.'

'And when she finds that she cannot get a husband, sir, what good will her "interest" do her then? For what gentleman would marry a hoyden?

439

Go to the instrument and play, Jemima, if you still remember how. That is a proper pursuit for a young lady. And do not bring *this* into the drawing room again.' She dropped the book over the arm of her chair and it hit the floor with a soft, reproachful thud.

Jemima walked across to the instrument, her cheeks burning, aware of her father's eyes upon her. The exchange had been carried out quietly, so that only those involved and the priest, who always sat next to Lady Mary, had heard – unless Uncle George heard it in his sleep – but she felt horribly conspicuous all the same. She saw her mother and Father Andrews put their heads together, and guessed what they were talking about. Father Andrews had never really liked the idea of teaching her, and had always claimed that she was too stupid to learn, that she had a woman's brain which was not shaped to understand certain things. He was probably telling her mother so again now, and her mother would be hearing just what she liked. Jemima clenched her fists, longing for the day when she would be free of them, her own mistress, and able to do what she wanted: then she would shew them all!

As she approached the instrument, her cousins, who were watching her rather like three hungry cats watching a very small mouse, jumped up and made a great parade of pulling out her chair, handing her into it, opening up the instrument for her, finding her music, and then begging her to favour them with this or that song. Jemima suffered it all, remembering with a pang how quietly and kindly Allen used to do the same thing, with no parade, only a real feeling for her convenience. She began to play, choosing out of perversity a song Allen had always liked, ignoring her cousins' requests, but they hung around her anyway, leaning on the instrument and staring languidly at her face, murmuring their praise of her playing and her singing, and, she knew, not listening at all. She knew what a really attentive audience was, and how it looked. William, she thought, was thinking of his own beauty and cleverness and how he outshone the other two. Frederick was probably thinking that the two elder cousins were so dull she would certainly prefer a gay dog like him. Rob was looking more grimly determined than sentimental, and Jemima guessed he only joined in because he would not be pushed aside for Frederick, whom he hated, or William, of whom he was jealous.

And at the other end of the room Uncle Robert and Uncle Edmund saw what was happening, and paused to watch their offspring with approval, before returning to their quarrel with renewed vigour.

Jemmy's leg became inflamed during Easter, probably as a result of more exertion than usual, for he hunted three times, and he was forced to retire to bed where he lay white and sweating with pain. The doctor came and examined it, and said that there were splinters of bone loose somewhere under the tissue, and that the wound ought to be reopened and probed. Jemmy did not trust the doctor, and said he would not have it done, braving accusations of cowardice which he knew his brothers would level at him. He remained in bed for two weeks, and inflammation went down, and he was able to walk again, although not without pain, and not for very long at a stretch.

Uncle Robert had been thinking carefully during the respite, aided by his observations of the three boys and their attentions to Jemima, and the realization that William, who rather favoured his mother in having fair hair and regular features, was far more handsome than his own sons. On the day before Jemima's fifteenth birthday, he cornered Jemmy and, in spite of Edmund's and Mary's furious looks, asked for a private word with him in the steward's room, to which Jemmy could only assent.

There, after considerable circumlocution, he revealed the essence of his change of stance.

'I feel I have been unjust in the past, in my condemnation of your actions over the property. I have come to the conclusion that you were quite right in respecting our father's wishes, however unreasonable they were. Indeed, you could not have done any less, and I was unjust to accuse you of a lack of brotherly affection.'

'Thank you, brother,' Jemmy said ironically. Robert lifted his hand.

'No, no, you must not thank me. I should have come to the conclusion before. I should have known that you did what you did out of proper filial duty, and not because you did not value your family and your family's love for you. Indeed, I know that, given the proper circumstances, you would do everything in your power to see your brothers were comfortable.'

Jemmy said nothing, and taking silence for assent, Robert went on. His hands were behind his back under his coat, and he rocked a little on his feet as his love of oratory took over.

'Well, and good, but having taken possession of the property, you have done what our father wished. Now the property is yours, you can, and in fairness to yourself, you *must*, do what you want with it. It is yours, and yours alone, and no one else's wishes have any bearing on your action.' Robert paused for the prescribed dramatic second before his thundering conclusion. 'You have chosen to give everything to your daughter, Jemima.'

'I have indeed. You are quite right,' Jemmy said, feigning admiration. Robert frowned slightly.

'Ah! But have you considered, brother, that when Jemima marries, unless she marries a Morland, she will be a Morland no longer, and the property will pass, on her death, out of the family entirely. And that, I am sure, cannot be your wish, or your under-standing of our father's wish!'

'It follows therefore—' Jemmy prompted, eager to have this over.

'That she must marry a Morland, yes. I was sure you would see the reason of it. And there, you see, lies the remedy your own sense of justice seeks. If she marries one of her cousins, that cousin could then see to it that the others are provided for in a suitable way. In reason, in fairness, in justice, she should of course marry her eldest cousin, but that, of course, I should have to leave up to you.'

'That is very good of you, brother,' Jemmy said, not even bothering to hide his irony, but Robert only bowed.

'I am glad we have had this little talk, brother,' he said, smiling a satisfied smile. Even if Edmund came to him now, the ground would be spoiled for him. 'I am sure we understand each other better as a result.'

That evening, partly to get away from the atmosphere in the drawing room where Edmund's suspicions had been raised by Robert's smugness, provoking him to argue ever more fiercely with him, Jemmy took Jemima down to the strong room to shew her the Morland family jewels and plate, which would one day be hers. Jemima was fascinated by the jewels, for she had hardly seen any of them before.

'But why does not mama ever wear this? It is beautiful – or this?'

'I don't think your mother cares for Morland things, chick,' Jemmy said gently. 'Look, here are the Queen's Emeralds – they once belonged to Queen Katherine Parr. I remember my mother wearing these – she was fond of emeralds, having green eyes. These are the Percy jewels, too heavy and old-fashioned to wear nowadays. We ought to have them reset – look at the rubies in this cross! They are magnificent.'

'These are pretty,' Jemima said, picking up a pair of diamond clips in the shape of sprays of blossom.

'My mother's again – my father had them made for her. And this pearl necklace is very fine – Mary wore that when we were first married. It's over a hundred years old. Of course, the most precious jewel of all is missing – the Morland Black Pearls. All the Morland ladies used to wear them.'

'Yes, I have seen them in the portraits,' Jemima said. 'What happened to them?'

'No one knows. When King James II fled the country, Morland Place was besieged by King William's men, and it was eventually taken and sacked. The pearls disappeared then. Probably one of the attackers stole them, though there is a story that they were put away somewhere for safe keeping, and that they lie there still. But no one knows where. I wish you might have worn them, chick – they would have suited you.' Jemmy turned to look at her with suddenly noticing eyes. 'You are growing quite pretty, you know. Allen always said you would be a beauty one day, and I think perhaps he might have had more sense than the rest of us. Yes, my dear, quite pretty! If you would only put on a little more flesh, you would be very nearly a beauty.'

Jemima blushed with pleasure, and a natural

train of thoughts brought her to the subject that had been uppermost in her mind ever since the family arrived for Easter.

'Papa – I know I should not presume, but – what did my uncle want to talk to you about today? Was it me?'

Jemmy looked at her affectionately. 'You guessed that, did you, chick? You are a noticing little thing. Yes, it was about you, in a way.' And while he packed away the jewels, he told her what Robert had said. 'And he is right, of course, about the Morland name, and the justice of sharing the property that way.'

They began to walk up the cellar steps, and he put his arm round her shoulder, partly for support, but largely out of affection. 'I notice that they pay you a great deal of attention, your cousins. That must be agreeable to a young lady of your age.'

'Papa, I do not want to marry one of my cousins,' Jemima said urgently, fearing that she might never have such a private opportunity to talk to him again. 'I cannot like them, Papa, well enough to marry them.'

He looked at her kindly. 'You are very young, child, to feel strongly about it. You cannot yet understand what love is, and what sort of feelings a young woman should have towards her husband.'

'But Papa—' They had emerged into the hall, and at any moment someone might come along. She turned to face him urgently. 'Please, Papa, don't make me marry one of them.'

He put his hands on her shoulders soothingly.

'I would not *make* you marry, Jemima, but I am persuaded that you will feel differently as you get older. You will see the sense and justice of it when you get used to the idea. But rest assured, while I live you shall never be forced to marry anyone you don't like.'

He had said the words, while I live, as a mere commonplace emphasis, but in the light from the hall sconces she saw with a sudden chill of fear how old he had grown recently. His face was lined and drawn from the pain of his wound and from the sorrow he had suffered when Marie-Louise died, something which everyone, including herself, had underestimated. He was forty-six, and a hale man of forty-six might expect ten or fifteen more years of life; he came, indeed, of a long-lived stock, when you thought of the Countess and Uncle Maurice. But he could no longer be called a hale man, and his recent illness had evidently made Uncle Robert nervous, at least. While he lived, she was safe indeed – but if he should die before she was of age, her life would be her mother's to command, and her mother hated her, and everything she wanted to do.

'I love you, Papa,' she said desperately. 'You are my only friend.'

Jemmy smiled quizzically. 'Why, my sweetheart, I love you too, of course. Don't be afraid, all will be well. Did I not promise, you should not marry anyone you didn't like? For the time being, I only ask that you be pleasant to your cousins – let them talk with you and pay you attention – indeed, that should be no hardship! Young ladies like the attentions of many men before they marry, and that is only what is right. Now, go on back to the drawing room. I shall come later, I have some business to attend to.'

When she passed alone into the staircase hall, she saw Uncle George going up the stairs to bed. He always retired early, for he got up at the crack of dawn every day to go out riding or hunting; Lady Mary said contemptuously that he kept the hours of a farm labourer. When he reached the turn of the stair he saw her, and paused as she dropped him a curtsey. Having got so far up the stairs, having taken his bulk so high, he was unwilling to have done it for nothing, and Jemima was extremely surprised, therefore, when he reversed himself and came back down to the hall, evidently for the purpose of speaking to her. She waited for him, and looked politely up into his vast, red moon of a face, which seemed to be working with some unaccustomed emotion.

At last he said, 'It's your birthday tomorrow, Jem, a'n't it?'

'Yes, sir.'

'And you'll be fifteen?'

'Yes, sir.'

He thought for a bit. 'Getting old enough to be wed,' he said, almost as if to himself. Jemima felt a desire to giggle. Surely Uncle George could not be hatching secret plans about her? He thrust a large hand into his pocket and fumbled about for a moment, and then brought out a golden guinea, which he pressed into her hand.

'Buy yourself some ribbons, or whatever it is young ladies like,' he said. Jemima was touched, for Uncle George, though he lived comfortably at Morland Place, had very little money, and the guinea was probably all his pockets held.

'Thank you, sir,' she said, and on an impulse reached up on tiptoe to kiss his cheek. He bent his face towards her to receive her kiss, and she found he smelled rather nice, of leather and tobacco and, unexpectedly, of lavender-water.

As her lips touched his cheek, he said. 'Tha'rt a good girl, Jem, a good girl. Your mother doesn't like me. When your father's gone, she'll likely try to throw me out. But you wouldn't let her, would you?'

Jemima looked at him sadly when he straightened up. So it had not been an entirely selfless gesture, the giving of the guinea! But it was something to discover that there was someone in the house who had more to fear than she did, and it made her feel suddenly grown up and strong and protective towards him.

'While I live, you shall always have a home here,' she said stoutly, and he nodded and went away, comforted. But her own words were an unhappy echo of her father's, and she realized that Uncle George would not have said anything unless he,

449

too, thought that her father might not have much longer to live.

Her birthday ball the next day was a much quieter and more private affair than the one two years before, held in the long saloon, and with only a few outsiders invited. Despite what had happened at the previous one, Jemima enjoyed this one less. She hated to see her father sitting down instead of dancing; she did not even have the prospect of a dance with Allen to cheer her; and the fact that only a few families had been asked meant that she had no excuse for refusing to dance with her cousins, who were laying siege to her with an almost military grimness. She did not know which one she hated most – William with his self-conceit, his contempt of everyone else around him, and his father's brutality of mind; or Robert, with his stupidity and peevish jealousy; or Frederick, with his wandering hands and his shallow viciousness. When they danced with her they blackguarded each other in a manner worthy of their fathers, and tried to interest her in schemes to be alone with them or to do down their rivals. Oh Papa, she thought despairingly as she walked up the set with Robert, who hardly ever even looked at her because he was so busy glaring at his brother and cousin, and whose hand was both cold and clammy, like a week-old fish, oh Papa, why can't you *see*? You would never have left Marie-Louise to such a fate; you would have paid more heed to her wishes. Why can't you love me as much as you loved her?

She caught her mother's eye upon her, and had a rare moment of sympathy with her; for Lady Mary had hated the Princess too, and with some reason. Jemima did not so much hate Lady Strathord as envy her, for the two men Jemima cared most about in the world had both been devoted to the Princess, and had both destroyed themselves in her service. No wonder Lady Mary was bitter. For a sweet moment Jemima daydreamed about running away and taking ship for France, where Allen was an officer in the French army. That was another source of pain to Lady Mary, of course. If only she didn't hate me so much, Jemima thought, we might have a great deal to say to each other.

CHAPTER 15

The sight of the Master and the little maiden riding together along the village street on their matching black horses was such a familiar one that children no longer ran to the door to watch them go by, though everyone who saw them waved cheerfully and called out to them. The Master was a good man, and well liked; he always had time to talk, and remembered everyone's name. Besides, with his game leg he was always glad to stop and sit for a while, and chat, and take a little something. And his daughter, they reckoned, was another of the same cast – growing rare pretty now she was sixteen – quick to learn, and always asking questions, sensible ones that shewed she had her wits about her.

Tab Fuller was sitting outside the door, as it was such a fine day, with a basket of raw wool beside her, her leather hand-carders in her lap, working the wool between them. She was so skilful that she never needed to look, but was able to keep an eye on her two youngest bairns, one of whom was shelling peas into a basin, and the other of whom was just inside the doorway spinning his daily quota. The bobbin lying beside him shewed he was spinning for his father, and would later wind the spun yarn ready for weaving. She waved to Jemmy and Jemima as they approached and called out a greeting.

'Good day, Master – will you come and take a sup of something?'

They drew rein and Jemmy leaned over his saddle and smiled at her. 'Well, good day to you, Tab – keeping the bairns busy, I see. How's that leg of yours?'

'It's well enough, Master, while the sun shines. It's only the rheumatiz that aches me. And how's *your* leg?'

'Take your own answer for mine,' Jemmy laughed. 'Your Master's above, I can hear. Not working for me today, by the sound of it.'

'No, Master, he's weaving broadcloth today,' Tab said, and blinked against the sunlight up at Jemima. 'How did he know that then, miss?'

Jemima bent her mind to the problem. Lots of the people liked to test her in little ways – her education had become a kind of game in the village. 'He heard him weaving,' she said, hearing for herself the creak and thud of the loom in the attic which, as the cottage was so low, was on a level with her head while she was on horseback, 'but I don't know how he knows it's broadcloth.'

Tab cackled with glee at having bested her, and Jemmy said, 'By the rhythm, of course. Broadcloth is too broad for the weaver to throw the shuttle from hand to hand – he must pass it to a helper,

453

which is slower. Who's passing the shuttle for your man today?' he asked Tab.

'Our Billy,' she said. 'I can better spare him from the spinning than little Jackie here – he spins too soft, does our Billy. Lord knows how he'll get on in life – a good boy, Master, I don't say contrary, but slack-twisted.' She shook her head sadly, as if Billy, whom Jemima knew to be only five years old, or six at the most, was so hardened in sin he was beyond saying.

'Wouldn't your man like to have one of these flying shuttles?' Jemima said eagerly. 'I saw them using it over at the manufactory at Leeds, and it's much quicker, at least for broadcloth-weaving.

Tab's brows drew down, but she only said, 'Well enough. miss, but my John weaves mostly fancy-weave for Master here, so it'd be no use to him. We like the old ways best. That manufactory—' She said no more, but her lip jutted in clear disapprobation. Jemima saw from the corner of her eye that Jemmy was giving her a look of warning, but Tab was much more reasonable to talk to than the other women, and she really wanted to know, so she ploughed on.

'What's wrong with the manufactory, Tab? Why does everyone talk about it as if it were Newgate prison?'

'Well, miss, you've said it. It might as well be Newgate, when a person has to go at this time or that time, and stay till someone says he may go home.'

'But you all get up at the same time in the village anyway – the hornblower comes round at five or six o'clock, I know that.'

'That's as may be, but that's not to say we've got to get up, every day, whether we want to or not. And another thing, if a person's away from home, how's a person to tend their garden or their field or their beasts? Or keep an eye on the bairns? No, miss, it's well enough for work'uss children to go to a manufactory, but not for decent folk. I'll bid you good day now, miss, and Master. You'll want to be getting on, I'm sure.'

They were very firmly dismissed, and when they had ridden out of earshot Jemmy laughed at Jemima's crestfallen face.

'Well, chick, what did you expect? You mustn't tease them, you know.'

'I wasn't teasing, I really wanted to know. Why do they hate the manufactory so much?'

'I don't know that I blame them,' Jemmy said. 'You heard what she told you – at home they can work when they like, and fit in all the other tasks, the cooking and washing and tending their field and beasts. They have their children and their own familiar things about them, they can work at their own pace, and if one day they don't feel like getting up at all, or they want to go out and pick mushrooms in the wood, why there's no one to say 'em nay. A little freedom is as precious to a weaver and his family as to any man.'

'But they'd do more work and earn more money

at the manufactory,' said Jemima. 'The work is so ill-regulated when it's done at home, and it does seem silly to have the wool travelling about from one place to another to have things done to it.'

'Better the wool should have to travel about than the people, don't you think? The wool doesn't care one way or another. You've been listening too much to Ibbetson's complaints! Of course the manufactory system is better from the clothier's point of view, but the people don't like it. I'll tell you something, chick, why you shouldn't talk about it to people like Tab. The Morlands used to have a manufactory years ago, down by the water-mill.'

'Did we?' Jemima was astonished. 'I never heard tell of it.'

'Oh, this was long, long ago, a hundred, maybe two hundred years ago. Back in history, you might say. But the legend has never died. They tell it to each other generation after generation, and it loses nothing in the telling.'

'But what happened?'

'The river flooded, and destroyed it. People were killed, drowned; how many depends on who is telling the tale; but since then it's been looked upon as an act of God, or a curse, or something of the sort. You'd as well tell a Morland worker to go to Hell as to a manufactory. And now we must go and see how old Widrith is doing.'

'Must we?' Jemima wrinkled her nose. Widrith was a comber, and lived in an outlying cottage with his sister and their three sons. Combers' cottages were noisome anyway, but Widrith's wife-cum-sister was slightly mad, and sometimes forgot to use the privy. Jemmy was firm, however.

'We must – he hasn't been well. But we won't stay long.'

The cottage stood with its windows open, and the smoke and fumes from the charcoal stove billowed out into the clear air. It was stiflingly hot inside, as could be seen by the rivers of sweat running down the eldest son, but the stove was necessary for the job, for both wool and combs had to be heated. They did not have to go in, however, for Widrith himself was sitting on the bench outside the cottage. One of the combing posts was set up outside too, and the second son was working there, throwing the wool onto the comb that was nailed to the post and working it off onto another comb held in his hand. The third son was doing the same thing, but at the post inside the house. Watching him through the open door, Jemima wondered if they drew lots for, or took turns at, the favoured outdoor post.

Her father had dismounted to talk to Widrith, who was indeed looking very ill, his face an unhealthy cheesy white, with blue circles under his sunken eyes. Jemima remained mounted, for fear anyone should invite them in for refreshment. The second son gave her one shy look and smile before continuing with his work, and she thought he did not look so healthy either, but working in that atmosphere was hardly likely to produce rosy cheeks. Inside the house the older son lit up his pipe as he stirred the stove, as if the air was not already foul enough, and the youngest paused in his combing to re-warm the wool and to take a swig at a bottle which he then passed to his brother. Jemima looked away, and concentrated on the birds in the apple tree nearby until her father clapped old Widrith on the shoulder and came back to take his horse from her.

'He's in a bad way,' Jemmy said as they rode away. 'He could hardly catch his breath to speak to me, and when he did speak, his words were slurred – though that may have been the gin. The poor devils have little pleasure in life except gin and the garden, so I can't blame him for being drunk this early in the day. He'll be off to a better Garden by and by, God love his soul.' And he rolled his eyes upwards expressively.

'But he's quite an old man, isn't he? I mean, we all have to die one day.'

Jemmy looked at her sharply.

'He can't be more than thirty-five,' he said. 'It's the combing that kills them. Fortunately his sons are all simple-minded, or they would never have followed him into his trade. Let's go to Murrain's now. It's only a step, and he keeps a very nice cask of ale in his cool-house. I need to rest this leg of mine.'

As they rode towards the house of Murrain, the weaver, Jemima watched her father anxiously.

Earlier this year her Uncle Charles had finally got married, to Alice McNab, the daughter of the Glasgow merchant whom he had been in love with for years. Jemmy had insisted on going to Scotland for the wedding, despite all advice and protest from his wife and family. Jemima guessed that it was chiefly because it was at McNab's house that Marie-Louise had died, and he wanted to hear more about it at first hand; and there was no reason why her mother should not have guessed the same. He went, but despite travelling very slowly and with every comfort, he came back knocked up, which infuriated her mother doubly. Jemmy had spent most of the summer in bed, and for a time there had been some doubt whether he would be able to walk again. A large splinter of bone had actually worked its way up and out of his leg, and the doctor had said that there were certainly others, again urging Jemmy to have the leg probed. Jemmy had only shaken his head wearily and sent the doctor away. Since then he had spent more and more time at home, and when he did ride out with Jemima, they never went out of a walk, and he needed to rest quite frequently. He never complained of the pain, but Jemima saw him bite his lips sometimes when he thought she was not looking.

Later that summer Uncle Thomas came home on a visit, bringing Aunt Maria and little Thomas, who was five and already set on joining the navy like his father. Uncle Thomas looked very splendid in his uniform, which he had put on at the particular request of Jemima, who was interested because naval uniforms had only been introduced that year, and she had never seen one before, and little Thomas was so thrilled that he begged to be allowed to wear the hat for the rest of the day.

Uncle Thomas and Uncle Edmund argued a lot too, though it was at least a change from the interminable quarrelling between Robert and Edmund. The argument was generally about the peace with France which was being negotiated at Buda, which Uncle Thomas thought was disgraceful and humiliating. During the war the navy had been largely successful, while the army had been largely unsuccessful, so Uncle Edmund was obliged to defend the peace, and had the novel experience of finding himself on the same side as Lady Mary, for it was her brothers' doing.

Lady Mary was very proud at that time, for her half-brothers, Lord Newcastle and Mr Pelham, were in the ascendant, being Secretary of State and First Lord of the Treasury respectively, and therefore virtually in control of the government of the country. In October the peace was finally settled, the negotiations having been transferred to Aix-la-Chapelle, and Lady Mary decided that it was time for Jemima to be presented at Court, and brought to the notice of her brothers. As Jemmy's leg was still not sound, and as Uncle Thomas was still at Morland Place and Jemmy wanted to enjoy his company while he could, Lady Mary was to take Jemima to London without him, which pleased Jemmy but disappointed Jemima. She had no real desire to be presented at Court, though she did very much want to see London, and the thought of being so much alone with her mother was a terrifying one.

As it came about, however, it was much less disagreeable than she could have imagined. Away from Morland Place, in London where her consequence was her own and not her husband's, Lady Mary was a different person; as Jemima was doing nothing to arouse her ire or her jealousy, she was pleasant to her, and though never quite affectionate, she was kind even to the point of appearing to be proud of her.

They were to go for a fortnight before the date of the Presentation, so as to see what everyone was wearing and to order Jemima's Court dress. Cousin William was still in London, and made himself rather officiously useful by engaging suitable lodgings for them in The Strand, and by offering his services as escort for as long as they were required. Lady Mary received the offer doubtfully, but William certainly had London manners, and he looked extremely handsome in his uniform, and eventually, to Jemima's disgust, his offer was accepted.

Jemima hardly knew she *was* in London at first, for everything took second place to the making of her Court dress, and after the material was chosen she had to stand for hours while it was fitted and made up actually on her body. The material was beautiful, a white silk with silver threads woven in so that they formed a background pattern of silver diamonds; through the diamonds ran a twisting gold thread like a stalk, from which issued embroidered flowers of brilliant blue, yellow and red, and green leaves against the white background.

The style of the dress was dictated by Court etiquette: the stays were very tight and rigid, making a stiff bodice which came down to a point at the front; the hoop was very wide and oblong, and the skirt of the mantua was drawn back and draped up over the back, forming a train behind, so that the whole front of the wide petticoat was exposed. The sleeves were quite short, making a sort of cap from which tiered layers of silver lace came down to the elbows.

'At least you will certainly have some of the best jewels,' Lady Mary said happily as she watched the fitting. 'The diamond collar must be worth twelve thousand pounds.' It was the first time Jemima had ever heard her say anything that even approached approval of the late Countess. 'It's a pity,' she went on, 'that so many of the Morland jewels are in such unsuitable forms. The diamond cross for instance – the stones are magnificent, but a cross!'

She did however have a gold and amethyst brooch from amongst the Percy jewels for her bodice, and the diamond blossom sprays for her hair. A lace cap with long lappets pinned up was the official Court wear for the head, and the diamond sprays and some tall white feathers made a happy addition. She had no earrings, but Lady Mary said. 'The collar being so high, and the stones so good, you won't feel the want of earrings. Now you may turn round and see yourself.'

There was a long cheval-glass, brought in for the purpose, and Jemima turned carefully, for fear of knocking over anything with her wide-panniered skirt, and looked. Lady Mary, behind her, said, 'What do you think of yourself?'

Jemima couldn't decide. The dress was magnificent, the diamonds glittered at her throat with almost dazzling radiance; she looked unlike herself, she looked like a Court beauty, like a woman in a portrait. She didn't look like Jemima. Her mother's face appeared beside hers in the glass, and she almost smiled.

'You look beautiful, Jemima. You will be noticed at Court. I am very proud of you.'

'Are you, Mother?' Jemima asked shyly, and their eyes met in reflection. It was the tenderest exchange they had ever had.

Jemima did not enjoy being presented, nor did she enjoy the ball. The King was a stout, pop-eyed man, surly and impatient, and Jemima felt he hated having people presented to him as much as she was hating being presented. He listened indifferently to her name, and seemed about to elbow her away when something seemed to strike him.

'Morland?' he asked abruptly, turning towards Lord Newcastle. 'Maurice Morland?'

'The same family, sire,' Newcastle agreed. The King grunted, and nodded his head once.

'Good music, Morland's,' he said, and then he really did turn away, and Newcastle had to jump backwards to avoid being pushed aside. The ball was only interesting from the point of view of looking at the dresses and being told the names of the famous people, for Jemima did not dance – only the highest in the land actually danced at a ball. They merely sat, or paraded about the outer edges of the room, ate a little supper, sat again, and then went home.

Afterwards, however, there were more interesting things to do. She was able to see something of London, and Lady Mary took her to St Paul's on Sundays, and drove with her around the Park when the weather was fine. They went to the theatre, the opera, and to a concert, and to feed the ravens at the Tower of London. There was also a zoo in the Tower grounds, but Lady Mary would not visit it, nor take Jemima to the circus at the Ranelagh Rotunda. They were not suitable, Lady Mary said.

They were also invited to dinner and private parties of varying degress of formality, which Jemima enjoyed only because they freed her from the presence of William. William invited her and her mother to dine at his mess at college, and Lady Mary refused the invitation, to Jemima's relief. Not suitable, she said. 'You would meet no one of importance there.' Meeting people of importance was, Jemima understood, the purpose of being in London. To spend a season in London was expensive, but the goods had to be displayed if a sale was to be expected. 'Nothing less than an Earl,' Lady Mary stipulated, 'with your fortune and connections.'

Finally they were invited to Court again, for a masquerade, and Jemima felt that Lady Mary would have pronounced that, too, unsuitable, had it not been a royal invitation. The Master of Revels, an ugly man called Heidegger, had introduced them from abroad, and it was well known that the dressing-up, apart from being a means of relaxing rigid Court etiquette, was also an excuse for horseplay. Lady Mary took advice about the costumes, and was told that to be noticed they had to be either witty or magnificent, and that the basic costumes could be hired more economically than made, and personal trimmings added. She decided, since there was no wit in her nature, that Jemima should be magnificent, and struck upon Queen Elizabeth I as a suitable subject. Jemima could have wished for something a little less rigid: her mother, as a shepherdess, had much greater ease of movement.

But she enjoyed the masquerade much more than the ball. For one thing, anyone could dance at a masquerade, and there was no regard for etiquette in who danced with whom. Jemima, being new and pretty, was a popular choice, and though her mother was on hand to decide whom she accepted, she danced every dance, and had some very amusing conversations. At one point she was actually dancing next to the King, who was dressed as a sultan and partnering a very languid Mary Queen of Scots.

There was a great deal of horseplay going on, as she could see quite clearly from the vantage of the dancing floor, and she hoped her mother was not witnessing some of the kissing and pinching that she could see. It was after supper that Jemima danced with the Earl of Burlington, and thoroughly enjoyed their conversation, and was led back to her mother to find her talking to a man dressed as a pirate. Jemima made her curtsey, and was introduced to 'Your cousin Rupert, Earl of Chelmsford, who wishes to dance with you'.

Jemima, completely dazed, was led out, and stared at him, trying to make out the features under the false beard and moustache. He was extremely handsome, from what she could see, and though his hand was unpleasantly moist, he talked to her amusingly enough, telling her the names of the people nearest her and then repeating the latest and most scandalous gossip about them.

'That's Elizabeth Chudleigh, she's utterly, utterly wicked! And that man there, he's actually here in disguise, or at least more in disguise than the rest of us. He's a bankrupt, and banned from Court. That's Montague, and that's Pomfret – they share a mistress, you know—' So it went on. Jemima was fascinated but more fascinated than anything with the question of how he had managed to persuade her mother to let her dance with him, when he was chiefly famous at Morland Place for having 'killed' her brothers. At length she decided she had nothing to lose by asking. Chelmsford seemed not to find the question offensive.

'It is not hard to explain,' he said. 'She has a daughter to get rid of, and I am an Earl. But do not be alarmed, madam, I assure you I have no intention of marrying you or any woman.'

'Then why did you want to dance with me?' she asked. He shrugged.

'Because everyone is talking about you, and it is dull not to do what is fashionable. Besides, you will be very rich one day, and one always has need of money. There, the dance is ending, and I must take you back very quickly to your excellent mother, because there is a simply delicious nun that I have to dance with.'

During the next dance Jemima saw him with the nun, and was grateful that he had not behaved so intimately with *her*. There was one more surprise waiting for her, however. When they were in their coach queuing up to get out of the palace gates, another carriage passed them on her side, and looking in as it did she saw Chelmsford with the same nun. They were locked in a close embrace, and the pirate had his hand under the skirt of the nun's habit. They had gone by in a moment, but Jemima was very sure of what she had seen, because their own carriage was stopped right by a torch high up on the wall, which illuminated the scene; and however often she tried to make it different in her memory, she was absolutely sure that the nun was not a woman.

In the summer of 1749, the doctor recommended seabathing for Jemmy's leg, and since Jemima had also been mildly unwell, it was decided that she should go with her father to Scarborough. Jemmy's health had been declining all that year, and his leg was often so painful that he could not bear it to be touched. He walked little now, and that very slowly, with a stick, and on his worst days he did not rise from his bed. It had aged him, and his face, Jemima saw in the strong light of the seaside, was lined and gaunt, and the same unhealthy colour she had noticed long ago in the woolcomber. She was afraid for him, and was glad that they were to be allowed to go to Scarborough alone, and have a little time together.

The journey, though it was done slowly and in a coach, and though the roads were in reasonably good condition, since the weather had been fine, taxed Jemmy severely, and when they arrived at their lodgings at Scarborough, he went straight to bed, and Jemima, on her own authority, sent for a local physician. It was a Doctor Ross who came, a Scotsman, and Jemima was glad, for she had heard that the medical knowledge and training in Scotland was far in advance of the English.

He examined Jemmy, passing his large hands over him so gently that Jemmy hardly winced, and he sucked his teeth and shook his head, and said. 'Who was it that set this leg? He was a butcher, sir, a butcher, not a surgeon at all.'

'He was a priest, actually,' Jemmy said, and told the history of his injury. Jemima listened not to the story but to the sound of his voice, hearing with anxiety how he drew a gasping breath after every two or three words. His eyes, she saw, were shiny with fever, his expression almost glazed with pain.

The doctor listened attentively, nodding his head now and then, and meanwhile feeling Jemmy's pulse and laying his large hand over Jemmy's heart. When the story was told he thought for a while, and then said, 'I will be frank with you, sir, because I see you are an intelligent man, and a man used to making decisions. There are loose splinters of bone which should have been removed a long time ago. They have now caused an infection, which is making you feverish. I would guess you have had a low fever for some time, but your recent exertions have raised it to an acute level. I must recommend that you allow me to probe the site of the injury without delay. If you do not allow me to do this, you will certainly lose the use of the limb, and the infection, if it does not kill you in the next week or so, will spread to the rest of you body, and you will certainly be dead in a few months.'

Jemmy's hand crept across the counterpane and found Jemima's. 'And if – I do – allow you to operate?'

'Then you have a good chance of surviving,' the doctor said calmly. His lack of emotion was steadying to them both. 'Your condition is poor, it must be said, and if I had had the opportunity to work upon you earlier, I would have said that you had no reason to hesitate. As it is – it is the choice between certain death, and a chance of life. It must be for you to decide.'

He looked from one to the other.

'When—' Jemmy wanted to ask when he would want to operate, but his mouth dried up. The doctor seemed to understand, however.

'Tomorrow morning, early. It must be done as soon as possible. I will leave you now, sir, to think about it. I will return this evening for your answer.'

When he had gone, Jemima returned from seeing him off to sit with her father again, and hold his hand. 'It is my own fault,' he said at last. 'But I never could trust that fool of a doctor at home. Still, I could have found another doctor to do what was necessary. I always thought it would get better of its own accord.' Jemima said nothing, for the only thing she could think of was to ask if he would accept the operation, and she did not want to seem to press him. After a while he said, 'I looked forward to spending a summer with you, here by the sea, away from all the worries of home, and the accusing eyes. Away from your uncles and cousins.'

'Yes, Papa,' Jemima said, her voice husky. 'I have longed for it too.' The competition for her hand was growing stronger between the cousins, and her uncles and her mother made life hideous at Morland Place. Jemmy sighed.

'Well, there is no other possible decision. If I do not have it done, I will never be able to ride again, and I could not bear that. So I will have to say – yes.'

His voice wavered, and he looked up and met Jemima's eyes.

'Papa—' she said.

'I am afraid, chick, I have to admit it. I'm very afraid.'

She gave an inarticulate cry, and put her arms round him, and he pressed his head to her breast like a child, and they clung together wordlessly.

After the doctor had gone in the evening, Jemmy asked her to open the window.

'I should like to smell the sea air. Ah, that's better, that's good. Come and sit with me, chick.' She sat with him and held his hand, and for a long time they were silent, both looking out of the window at the pale dusk sky where the first star shone white and unwinking like a rose. From far away they could hear the strange cry of a seagull, and it made Jemima want to weep, except that her fear and sadness were too deep for weeping. She knew what was to come tomorrow – the doctor had explained it all most carefully – and the idea terrified and

471

nauseated her. But she had told her father she would be there with him through it all, holding his hand, and though he had at first tried to prevent her, when he finally accepted that she was determined, he was weakly grateful.

'It is good to have a little peace, before the storm,' Jemmy said at last. 'Or rather between the storms – a respite, eh, chick?'

'I wish we never had to go back,' she said, low and feelingly. He nodded.

'It cannot have been pleasant for you. But you know, I cannot keep your mother at bay much longer. You are seventeen, my darling, and you ought to be wed, and your mother and I are in agreement about that, if about nothing else. I know I promised you I should not make you marry against your will, but I wish you would consider taking one of your cousins.'

'Oh, Papa!'

'You must marry someone, Jemima, and we cannot wait for you to find someone you like until you are an old lady. Perhaps you will never see someone you like – few people, I suppose, marry for love. I keep making excuses to your mother, but they sound less and less reasonable. She wants you to marry a lord, but you don't seem to like that idea any more than the other.'

She shook her head, but said nothing. He turned his eyes from the window to look at her. In the late and rosy light, he saw how beautiful she had become; not pretty in the conventional way, the way her cousin Augusta was, but beautiful as a thoroughbred horse is beautiful, by her fine lines, the firm and sculpted features, the integrity and loveliness of her expression. There was decision and intelligence in her face, her eyes were full of feeling, her lips formed for passion; her glossy dark hair framed a face as innocent and pure as that one white glowing star. She looked very much the way he remembered Aliena, except that Aliena's serenity was one grown out of knowledge and suffering, while Jemima's was the unblemished bloom of maidenhood.

'Allen was right about you,' he said at last. 'I wish he could see you as you are now.'

'So do I, Papa,' she said.

The doctor came early in the morning, with his two assistants, in case Jemmy should need holding down; but he endured it all with immense and terrifying courage, hardly crying out, though he was conscious most of the time. Jemima held his hand, keeping her back to the operation for fear that the sight of it would make her faint, or sick, but her own imagination and her father's expression were enough to supplement the horrible sounds she could not block out. After it was all over, her father finally, blessedly, lost consciousness while the wound was being bound, and Jemima was able to release her hand and flee from the room. She went to her own room, and thought she would be sick, but though her ears rang and she sat on her bed with the blackness coming and going, she did not vomit. When the dizziness had passed, she felt the pain in her hand, and looked down at it, to see how red it was, and swollen. For a moment she was puzzled, and then realized that it was bruised from the strength of her father's grip.

She went back to the room after bathing her face and smoothing her hair, and met the doctor coming out, rolling down his shirt sleeves and putting on his coat.

'He has withstood the operation very well, but the shock to his body is great, and he is very weak. He will need careful nursing if he is to survive. Also, I must tell you, mistress, that the condition of his leg was much more grave even than I had anticipated. I am afraid there may be a recurrence of the infection.'

'And if there is?' Jemima asked hesitantly. Doctor Ross shook his head.

'We must pray that there is not,' he said.

For the first few days they both struggled, fighting for his life with his courage, her skill, and all the strength of their wills; but on the evening of the third day she came in to his room with broth, and found him weeping. She put the dish down and went to take him in her arms again, and he leaned against her and sobbed heartbrokenly, like a child. She held him in silence, rocking him gently, and after a long time the storm passed, and his weeping slowed and ceased. Still she held him, until he finally lifted his head and reached for a handkerchief. She looked out of the window, not to embarrass him, until he had blown his nose and wiped his face, and when she finally looked at him, they read in each other's eyes the knowledge that he was dying.

It was a strangely peaceful time that followed, as if the acceptance and understanding had removed both fear and sorrow. There was time for them to be together, and to talk, and to share a love which had been growing over the years since the Princess died; there was time for Jemmy to prepare himself, and for Jemima to prepare herself to lose him. For a week he grew gradually weaker, and the fever came and went, though he always remained rational. Now they did not talk much, only sat in silence, feeling each other's presence, glad simply to be together. Then one night he asked to see a priest.

'I wish it could be Father Renard,' he said. She had to lean close to hear him, because his voice was so weak now.

'Do you wish me to send for Father Andrews?'

'No. There is not time – and any priest will do as well. It was only Father Fox I loved.'

So as not to leave him, Jemima sent the landlady's girl on the errand, and she came back at last to report that she could find no Anglo-Catholic priest.

'Will you have the Protestant minister, mum, or

the Roman gentleman?' she asked. Jemima went in to her father, but he was asleep, and she was loath to wake him. She must make the decision herself. It was the use of the word minister that decided her; if the Protestant minister was very extreme in his views, he might not come to give the last rites, especially at night time, for there were some who regarded the sacraments as Popish and idolatrous. She asked for the 'Roman gentleman'.

He was a young man that came, with a soft Irish accent and a mild and anxious eye, but he listened kindly to Jemima's explanations, and said that there was no real difference, and God would manage to cope with the details. He gave Jemmy absolution, and anointed him, and then, since Jemmy did not seem to want him to go, he sat on, still holding his hand. It was thus, just after midnight, that Jemmy died, when the candles had burned low, holding the hands of Jemima and the priest, with a faint, contented smile and a small sigh.

CHAPTER 16

At Easter it was the custom of the Morlands to go to the Easter Sunday services at the Minster; all of York society gathered there, and after the service walked about the Minster gardens, displaying the first of the spring and summer clothes and exchanging the gossip. After the confines of winter, and the necessarily restricted social intercourse, Easter Sunday was a celebration and a heralding of the gay summer to come.

Easter 1750 also marked the end of the period of deep mourning for Jemmy, and for the first time on Easter Sunday his widow and heiress were able to put off their black bombazine and Norwich crape, and deck themselves in the black silk and charcoal-grey tabby of second-mourning, signalling to the world that they might now again be invited out. They went to the Minster accompanied by Edmund – who since the peace had scarcely been away from Morland Place – and Augusta and the girls, Robert and a very sulky Frederick, and Uncle George. Cousin William was in London, to Jemima's great relief, and Cousin Rob was staying

477

with a friend's family for Easter. Frederick was extremely cross that he had not been invited anywhere, and thus had to spend Easter under his father's eye. He was now at Christ Church too, where he was enjoying himself so much that only the threat of being taken away by his father curbed his excesses.

When they came out into the sunshine the whole world seemed to be gathered in the gardens to parade along the paths, and the blooming spring flowers and the pink and white blossom on the trees were hardly brighter than the clothes of the Easter communicants. Many people bowed or nodded to Lady Mary and Jemima, but there were few whom Lady Mary did not think too vulgar to be associated with, and for some time they walked alone. Frederick quickly sloped off to raise his hat to a party of giggling young ladies; Robert stopped to talk to one of the Cathedral clergy; and Edmund and Augusta fell in with a group of fellow-officers and their families; so for a time Mary and Jemima walked with only Uncle George stumping silently along behind them like a large, old dog. Jemima cast one or two glances at her mother, wondering whether to open a conversation, but Lady Mary's expression was cold and inward-looking, forbidding communication.

Mary was confused. She had expected to find Jemmy's death a release, and yet when it had happened she had been shocked, and worse, she missed him. There was an emptiness in her life, for everything she had felt and done for a quarter of a century had been directed towards him, either in love or in hate, and without him she had become purposeless. She was confused about Jemima too, for though she hated her still, she was dependent on her for her status. It was necessary for Jemima to be admired and respected, to reflect credit on Mary; to that end, it was essential that she make a good marriage, and Mary had so often said to herself that it must be nothing less than an Earl that she had come to believe her words as an unchangeable rule. But she did not want Jemima to be happy: if possible she would like her to be as unhappy as she had been all these years. Where to find a husband for her daughter who would appear to do her credit, yet would make her miserable?

More recently, the question had refined itself into, where to find a suitable husband, and soon? Jemima was almost eighteen, and in three years would attain her majority. Though Mary did not doubt that lifelong habit would keep her obedient to her mother in most things, she was aware that it would be hard to make her marry against her will once she was legally free and in possession of her fortune. Moreover, the marriage market was a fiercely competitive one. Even though they had been in mourning, Mary had made delicate enquiries in a number of directions, but had found titled bachelors hard to interest. They wanted to marry titled heiresses, not the daughters of

Yorkshire gentlemen, even though rich, and Mary's status as the half sister of Lord Newcastle, though it lifted her high in political circles, cut little ice with the nobility.

Since Jemmy's death, because of the period of mourning, nothing much had changed about the house. Mary had been, perforce, biding her time. Normal routines continued, except that where Jemima had assisted Jemmy in his duties as Master, she now performed them alone, with the aid of Clement, the steward, Cradoc, the bailiff, and Harvey, the agent. Father Andrews still cast the accounts and kept the coffers, making his report to Jemima. Fortunately there had not yet been any major decisions to be made, for it was a delicate point who would have been asked to make them.

Jemima was extremely glad, as they began their second circuit of the gardens, to be approached by Mrs Micklethwaite, who had been Miss Pobgee, the lawyer's daughter and once beloved of her brother Thomas. Jemima liked Mrs Micklethwaite very much, and as she had married the son of Sir George and Lady Micklethwaite, and was accompanied by her parents-in-law, whose acquaintance Lady Mary acknowledged, Jemima was able to walk and talk with her friend while her mother talked to the older people. Sir George was a magistrate and a member of parliament as well as a knight, which redeemed him from being too vulgar for Lady Mary's acquaintance, and as he and his wife were quite willing and ready to acknowledge Lady

Mary's superiority in every department, of birth, breeding, and consequence, she was even able to find them acceptable company. Talk at once veered to political matters, in which Lady Mary could enjoy all the consequence of a superior right of understanding; and as Mr Micklethwaite was loitering somewhere else in the gardens with his friends, Jemima and Sally Micklethwaite had soon linked arms and outstripped the others, and were having a comfortable chat.

Jemima could hardly have been more eager to hear the latest gossip than Sally to impart it.

'We have been shut away, you must remember, with none but relatives visiting,' she said when Sally expressed surprise at her ignorance of the details of Miss Hatter's elopement. 'Only my cousin Frederick has come recently, and he from Oxford, and with nothing but his own affairs to impart.'

'I doubt whether he would want to impart those in your mother's presence,' Sally said slyly. 'He has not been idle since he got home. Have you not heard that he is courting the Atkinson girls, and not even they can tell which amongst them he really favours.'

'I can tell you the answer to that one – it is none of them,' Jemima said. 'Frederick prefers to do his courting in the military style, by platoons. He thinks it is safer so.'

'Well it may be – he can hardly be accused of compromising one of them, if they are always all three present.'

'Surely their mother . . . ?'

'Oh certainly she remains in the room, but she is so deaf and short-sighted that it hardly counts as being chaperoned. Well, and what do you think of the news at Shawes?'

Jemima shook her head. 'I cannot tell you. I have heard nothing about Shawes. As far as I know it is empty.'

Mrs Micklethwaite raised her eyebrows. 'Well! I made sure you would have known that at least. Shawes is to be opened up again. The caretaker was in town last week hiring women-servants and ordering food and candles, but all the men-servants are to be brought down from London. We are all so looking forward to a little gaiety with Shawes opened again. The Earl will have all the London fashions to shew off, and his guests will certainly be people of fashion.'

'The Earl?'

'Why yes, the Earl of Chelmsford is coming to live at Shawes again, it is to be hoped for the whole summer. I cannot think he would open up the house for less. It was thought he was going to let it, and we have all been looking forward to a tenant, perhaps a rich young man in need of a wife, but this is even better. I cannot tell you, my dear, how excited the mothers of York have been at the prospect of an unmarried Earl from London living on their doorsteps. The moment he is known to have arrived they will be calling on him by dozens! Is not he a relative of yours?'

The question could hardly have been ingenuous, but Jemima treated it as such.

'A distant cousin, nothing more. The connection is very far back.'

'Well, but as your nearest neighbour, I am sure your mother will be calling, or rather one of your uncles.'

'Perhaps. My mother does not go out much, you know. She has never been fond of society. But tell me, did you not go to Harrogate last month? I have often wondered what it is like to take the waters. Do tell me all about it.'

Mrs Micklethwaite suffered the conversation to be redirected, though not without a thoughtful look. Jemima decided not to mention the matter to her mother, and wondered what could have brought the Earl to Yorkshire at a time when people of fashion were still in London: even those gentlemen accustomed to spending the summer on their estates did not usually go into the country before June, and this particular gentleman had never shewn any desire before to be anywhere but London.

York's curiosity was not suffered to be stretched for long, however, for the Earl appeared at the evening service at the Minster, having arrived that very morning. It was thought to be a great compliment to society that he had made a public appearance so soon, and there was immediate extravagant talk of the balls and suppers he was intending to give, and what a gay summer York

483

was going to have of it. There was no doubt that he would be a valuable addition, for he appeared in the very best of fashion, and smiled affably as he left the Minster, loitering outside as if he had no objection in the world to being approached. There was much less standing around and chatting after evening service but all the same Jemima heard enough to know he was thought extremely handsome, in need of a wife, the most charming man in the world, and come to Yorkshire for the racing.

'He will certainly be calling on you, Miss Morland,' one young man said slyly. 'I hope you have some good colts to shew him, for he is sure to want to race a few horses of his own. He spends a fortune at Newmarket every year.'

It was a new thought to ponder, and at least provided some sort of reason for his presence, albeit a slender one. Jemima caught her mother's frown and hastened to join her to walk out of the Minster, where they were at once approached by the Earl himself, who gave the most respectful bow to Lady Mary, and begged to be allowed the favour of calling upon her the following day.

Lady Mary was gracious, and Jemima could see she was pleased. If he had been anyone else, she would have been furious at his impertinence in suggesting to everyone that he was an old acquaintance, but as he was the man everyone was talking about, and an Earl, it was rather flattering than otherwise to be thus distinguished.

He made another bow, repeated more formally in Jemima's direction, and she responded with the slightest inclination of her upper body. In the carriage on the way home, Augusta chirruped and fluttered like a little bird about the handsome Earl and how he had approached them and no one else in such an intimate way. Social memories were short, Jemima reflected, shutting her mind to the chattering effusions; and in any case, Augusta had two daughters without dowries.

The Earl made his formal visit, and followed it up with another, and another, and then, in the most correct form, gave a ball, preceded by a dinner to which the best of York society was invited. As there were to be thirty at table, of whom seven would be Morlands, the compliment was very pronounced. Jemima was puzzled by it all, for the Earl seemed a different person. He dressed in the height of fashion, but with a restraint that made him acceptable to all the stuffier elements; his manners were impeccable, a nice mixture of graciousness, propriety, and affability. Had he been a famous actor asked to perform the part of a great nobleman who was free of all pride and hauteur, he would have behaved in exactly that way.

Lady Mary seemed curiously excited by the invitation, and insisted that Jemima should have a new dress for it, though she had two which would have done admirably. 'I shall not be able to dance, Mother, remember that. And I cannot be too fine, it would not be proper.'

'I do not think you need to tell me what is proper, Jemima,' Lady Mary said coldly. 'If the Earl is intending to entertain, there will be many occasions on which you can wear the new dress, and the two you mentioned are too close to undress to be complimentary to the occasion.'

Mildly puzzled, Jemima allowed herself to be fitted with a new sack. It was exquisite, more delicate than anything she had worn before. It was of dark grey lutestring, open both in bodice and skirt, with a wide stomacher and matching petticoat. The sleeves had treble ruffles of silver lace, which matched the handkerchief and ruff – ruffs were the coming thing, and convenient at a time when mourning made jewellery inappropriate – and the stomacher and robings were decorated with serpentine ruchings with trimmed edges, also of silver lace. It was a beautiful dress, one which Jemima would have been happy to wear at any time, though it would have been impossible for anyone to have pointed to it as improper for half-mourning. A small cap with violet ribbons completed the effect, and Jemima had to admit that her mother was extremely clever.

The ball was enormously well-attended, as was to be expected, and it was plain that the dressmakers of York had had a wonderful time of it in the past fortnight. There was so much and such relentless fashion being paraded in the room that

Jemima was actually glad that mourning had prevented her from being obliged to compete. As it was, when she entered the room there was a small and resentful silence that she should have appeared, even in mourning, so absolutely fashionable and so very elegant. A half glance sideways revealed to Jemima that her mother was smiling complacently as she accompanied Jemima to their seats.

The Earl danced with all the principal young ladies of York that evening, and the occasion was a great success, certain to be written up in glowing terms in many a journal; but he distinguished Jemima by sitting out with her during the two first after supper which, for a man who ought to be dancing every dance, was a compliment indeed. Jemima was again puzzled by him. He chatted to her and her mother easily all through the dances, and his conversation was witty and amusing, but not scandalous. His manners also were gentle and attentive, and she could see that her mother was affected by it: at one point she even laughed.

The ball was inevitably followed by others, and as spring turned into summer, Jemima found herself leading a gayer and more social life than she had ever anticipated. Raceweek was an extraordinarily jolly one, and Lady Mary, who had not attended a race for years, was in the grand-stand every day, and even learnt the names of the Morland horses. Jemima was in a difficult position that week, for as Jemmy's replacement she ought to have been in the paddock and amongst the breeders and owners, but as a lady, and a lady still in mourning, she had to be more retiring. She compromised by employing Pask as her go-between, and by dressing in a rather severe grey riding habit. The two colts she had highest hopes of did well, and she sold one immediately after the race at a good profit. The other she was keeping to put to stud, something which was very difficult to explain without using language which would have been indelicate in a lady in mourning.

And everywhere, there was the Earl. It was impossible any longer to deny that he was distinguishing Jemima: at balls and dinners he sat by her and talked to her, at the races he was always near at hand, asking her opinion, placing her bets for her, applauding her good fortune and mourning her bad. He behaved exactly as York wished him to, enjoyed everything, accepted almost all invitations, lost a large amount of money on the horses with a gracious laugh, danced with all the daughters of York at all the assemblies of York; but by the end of race week there could not have been anyone who did not consider Miss Morland his first object.

Lady Mary was confused. She knew she ought to have nothing to do with this man, who had killed her sons; she knew him to be a reprobate, suspected him of being vicious. Yet he was not only an Earl, but *The* Earl, York's darling, and his manners and behaviour were so impeccable that she even found herself liking him. Could it be that time had changed him? Could he have come to repent his former recklessness? Was he, even now, trying to make up to her for the harm he had done her? He never mentioned the past, yet she felt she detected a tenderness and solicitude towards her which suggested he thought about it. It was also balm to her pride, wounded over so many years of being neglected by Jemmy: he made her comfort his first concern in public.

And she had no doubt that he was also paying attention to Jemima in a particular way. It was this consideration which finally cleared her confusion: here was the husband she had sought for her daughter. It was a match to reflect credit on her and on the family, it would bring Jemima a title; the only danger was that it was too good a match, would not make Jemima unhappy enough. But at the back of her mind was the lingering doubt, the memory of what she had thought him to be. If there were a shadow on his character, he might make Jemima very unhappy indeed.

Jemima was married to the Earl of Chelmsford in October, two weeks after her mourning ended. The marriage took place in the Minster, which made Jemima a little uneasy, for it meant she was the first Morland heir to be married other than in the chapel at Morland Place, which she felt was almost ominous. Apart from that, she was not unhappy, only a little dazed, for things seemed to have happened so fast and so confusingly. It was after the races that Rupert, as she must now call him, had begun to pay serious court to her, visiting Morland Place more frequently and more informally until he was coming and going almost like one of the family. He identified himself with her interests, discussed the farming and the clothmaking intelligently, read the books she was reading and sang the songs she played on the harpsichord. He rode out with her when she went round the estate, providing her with a welcome companion and escort, and gave her some sound advice about investments.

He had become so popular with her mother as to lift the cloud of odium from Jemima by association. Her uneasiness about his character had faded until she forgot about it, for in the months he had been in Yorkshire, he had behaved so perfectly that she had to think she had been mistaken before, or that he had changed radically. No one could keep up a perfect pretence month after month, she told herself. Most of all, he had made himself indispensable to her. Since her father had died, she had had no one with whom she could converse sympathetically, as an equal; except for Allen, she had never had a companion before who was so interesting, so kind, so conversable, so understanding. Her life had always been lonely; now at last she had a friend.

When he finally declared himself, it was in the most proper manner. Her personal charms and merits he said, had rendered him so in love with her that he could not conceive of any happiness for him in the future unless it were with her by his side. He loved her almost to distraction; he begged her to allow him to speak to her mother for her hand. Jemima asked for time to consider, and in the most delicate way he consented and changed the subject, not pressing her for an answer. It was this which finally convinced her. Had he been in any way designing, he would not have been so patient, so unconcerned by her apparent hesitation.

She thought about it all night, hardly sleeping at all. He was handsome, he was charming, he was an interesting and sympathetic companion, he was an Earl which would please her mother, and he was not one of her cousins. As a final feather-weight in the scales, she remembered that his name was Morland, and that their children would therefore be Morland. The estate would not pass even nominally out of the family. She thought of beautiful Shawes, and of Chelmsford House in London, which she had passed several times when she had been staying in the Strand. And she thought of Allen.

If she married, she must never think of him again, for it would be a breach of loyalty to her husband, and so she indulged herself one last time, recollecting all his kindnesses to her through her childhood, recalling his face to mind; then she remembered that he had loved Marie-Louise, not her, and with a sigh she put him from her. Let Rupert replace him for her. She was not yet in love with Rupert, but there was nothing to suggest she would not be in quite a short time. The following day she gave him her answer, and he pressed her hand fervently, as if too overcome with his emotions for words, and then went straight away to speak to her mother.

The wedding was magnificent, and Lady Mary was inexpressibly glad that it was a public wedding in the Minster, which the whole world would take note of, not a dingy private matter in the half-Popish chapel, such as her own had been. Everyone who was anyone was there, and the ordinary people of York who had not been invited exercised their right of admission to the cathedral, so that it was packed to the doors, the crowd even spilling out onto the pavement outside. There were banks of flowers everywhere, candles, a red carpet and canopy at the door, and banners were hung up depicting the Chelmsford arms topped by the Earl's coronet, and the Morland arms with the Neville and Moubray quarterings.

Jemima looked beautiful, all in bridal white and silver. She wore the diamond collar, together with diamond earrings, a present from the bridegroom, and on her bosom the gold and diamond cross which was part of the Percy jewels. On her head she wore a coronet of gold, diamonds, rubies and pearls, which Lady Mary had had fashioned out of others of the Percy jewels which were otherwise unwearable, and over her dress a mantle of crimson velvet, laced with gold. Her husband to be looked not unworthy of her, and as he put the gold and diamond ring onto her finger she thought how handsome he looked, with a mixture of the looks of his beautiful mother and handsome father.

The wedding feast was held at Shawes, and on the following morning the couple were to set off for London on the first stage of their honeymoon journey to Italy. 'I have many relatives in Italy, and you will enjoy all the beauties of the place much better with someone to shew you them who is a native of the land,' he had said to Jemima. She had nothing to object to in the plan. Lyme, Scarborough, and London bounded her horizon so far: a foreign country would be exciting and new however she saw it.

The feast seemed to go on and on, and Jemima's sensation of being in a dream intensified. She had drunk rather a lot of wine, and it made her feel as though she were living inside her own body like a nut in its shell, and looking out of her eyes, an entirely different person to the one that everyone kept addressing as 'Your Ladyship' and 'Lady Chelmsford' and 'my dear Countess'. She wondered if she would ever get used to that. Rupert seemed to be enjoying the feast as much as he had enjoyed all the summer's activities: perhaps he was a little freer in his drinking than before, but after all, every man got a little drunk at his own wedding, didn't he?

It was very late when they retired to bed. There was no ceremony of putting to bed: Lady Mary was not the person to suggest such a thing. They walked alone up the stairs, seen off by the guests with cheerful blessings and no unseemly remarks, and as they turned the corner of the stairs Rupert muttered something which sounded like 'Thank God for that.'

'I beg your pardon?' Jemima said, and he shook his head. His eyes seemed rather bleary, and he stumbled slightly on one of the stairs. When they got to the bedchamber, Jane Chort was waiting for them, along with Rupert's man, whose name appeared to be Boy. He was a foreigner of some sort, with yellow hair and large blue eyes and a curious old-young face that made it difficult to say if he were, indeed, man or Boy.

'I'll use the dressing-room, madam,' Rupert said with a bow. 'Your servant. Come, Boy.'

Left alone with her mistress, Jane came forward with a shy smile and began to undress her to an accompaniment of chatter and compliments. It seemed to take a very long time to get her out of her elaborate clothes and take down her hair, and Jemima grew more and more sleepy from the long day and the unaccustomed wine, and she was glad when after a while Jane stopped talking and worked in silence. Of what was to come next, Jemima had a theoretical knowledge, from the breeding of horses, but she had grave doubts as to the practice of it in human beings. She had no idea how it was done, it being obvious that humans did not go about it in the same way as horses. She hoped it would not hurt too much, and that she would acquit herself creditably. Rupert, she was sure, would know what to do.

And then suddenly she remembered the time after the masquerade, when she had seen him in the coach with the nun. It was like a sudden splashing of cold water, rousing her from her sleepiness. But it could not have been true! she told herself. After all, it was late at night, and dark, and the coach had gone bowling by so fast. She had not seen what she thought she had seen. It could not have been Rupert in the coach; or if it was, he had not been doing what her fevered imagination had told her he was doing; and certainly not with another man. A man dressing as a nun? That would be shocking. Jane helped her into bed and arranged her nightcap becomingly, and then with a smile she left her.

The wine fumes rose once more in her head, and she struggled to keep awake. How long Rupert was taking! She began to drift off, jerking awake every few seconds as her head slipped over. By the time Rupert came to bed, she was really asleep. He got in beside her, and she half woke and stirred at the movement.

'Rupert?' she murmured. 'Husband?' She smelled the wine on his breath, and felt the heat of his body nearby, but she really could not keep awake. 'I'm sorry—' she began to say, but never got to the end of the sentence.

When she woke it was daylight, she was alone in the bed, and Jane Chort was coming into the room followed by a maid with a tray.

'Here we are, my lady,' she said. 'I've brought you hot chocolate and bread.'

My lady, Jemima reflected. So it had not all been a dream. But what had happened? She had fallen asleep when she should have been – did anything happen? And then she became aware that her night-dress was in disarray, and there was a certain strange smell in the bed, and the realization made her blush. Jane saw the blush, and smiled discreetly, and Jemima was all the more embarrassed, feeling the hot blood rush to her face uncontrollably.

'His lordship's up and dressed already, my lady. I'll have your bath brought, for when you've had your breakfast. You must get ready. An early start, my lady, you remember his lordship said. Off early in the morning. Becky, put that down, child, and stop gawping, and go and lay out her ladyship's dress.'

The chatter covered her confusion a little, and the blush subsided. When she had eaten and got up, and removed her bedgown to get into her bath, she began to blush again, finding a certain alien stickiness on her smooth belly which was certainly the source of the strange smell. She hastened to get into the bath and wash it away, hoping against hope that Jane Chort had noticed nothing.

An hour later she was walking out to the coach, where Rupert waited with evident impatience. It was still early, and none of the family was up, except Uncle George, who came out from the stables to bid her farewell.

'It was a lovely wedding, Jem,' he said shyly, and bent his head as she went on tiptoe, to receive her kiss. 'I hope you'll be happy,' he said, and turned away abruptly with a sniff to drag out his handkerchief and trumpet briskly into it. The boxes were already on, Jane Chort and Pask and Boy were inside, and Rupert dragged out his watch to consult it so Jemima hastily got in, and let down her window for a last look at her maiden home. The carriage rolled away through the barbican and turned out onto the track, and she looked back, thinking it would be three months before she saw it again. Clement and Uncle George stood alone on the drawbridge to see her off, Clement respectfully with his hands behind his back, Uncle George waving his white handkerchief for as long as the carriage was in sight.

There was silence in the carriage until it reached the main road and swung southwards, and then Rupert, whose eyes were very red, and who looked less handsome this morning, said quite distinctly, 'Thank God.'

'Sir?' Jemima asked. He grinned at her — a different sort of smile from any she had yet seen.

'Now it's done. I've got you, and we are safe away,' he said. Jemima smiled uncertainly. Out of the corner of her eye she saw Jane and Pask exchange a sentimental look at the young husband's eagerness; but Boy turned his head to look out of the window, and she saw his reflection give a smirk of altogether a different kind.

CHAPTER 17

Jemima loved Italy, and she loved her husband's relatives, his uncles, aunts and cousins, with whom they stayed in Naples, Florence and Rome. She thought it strange that while in Rome they did not visit his brother Charles, who was still with King James at the Palazzo Muti, but accepted it when Rupert said that there were spies everywhere and he did not dare to compromise himself. Surely, she thought, Charles could have come to them, or they could have met somewhere other than in the exiled Court? He had married the daughter of an exiled Jacobite lord, Mary Cutler, and they were expecting their first child, and Jemima thought it would have been proper to pay them a visit, but Rupert did not even send his card.

They spent Christmas in Naples, and in January went to Venice for the Carnival, where they stayed at the Palazzo Francescini. Jemima met the renowned soprano Karelia there, and discovered that her late father-in-law's music was held in great esteem. As a bride, she received a great deal of attention in Venice, and several parties and dinners were given for her, including a magnificent one at the Palazzo Francescini, at which Maurice Morland's music was played, and Karelia sang a number of arias which he had written either for her or for her mother. It was all very exciting and flattering.

All the same, she was puzzled about her husband. Since they had come to Italy, his manners towards her had become more offhand. He was not exactly cold or rude, but he seemed not to care very much what she did, or whether she was contented. Whenever he could, he left her with his relatives and went off alone, claiming that he 'had business' or that 'she would not enjoy what he wished to do – he had better go alone'. If she tried to press him, he grew annoyed, and so she quickly desisted. At Christmas he acted very strangely, drinking heavily and making odd remarks and laughing strangely, and Jemima saw that the Scarlatti relations exchanged glances as if they, too, found his behaviour strange.

And most puzzling of all was what she called in her mind, for want of any other term, their 'married life'. He never went to bed when she did, always staying up later, sometimes not coming in until after she had retired, so that she was usually asleep by the time he joined her in bed. She often smelled drink on his breath and suspected that he might be drunk, though she had so little experience of drunkenness that she could not be absolutely sure. At all events, there was no physical contact between them. He never touched her in bed in any way, except

500

accidentally, in his sleep, and there was certainly nothing in the way of 'married life', even though she was not entirely sure what that was.

In Venice things became abruptly worse. From the moment he arrived in Venice, he seemed strangely excited, and he had barely installed her at the Palazzo Francescini before he left her there and went out into the city accompanied by his strange manservant, Boy. Jemima did not mind at first, for she loved Venice, and had plenty to do and see, and her hostess was a kind and interesting companion. But after a week, she was hardly seeing her husband at all. Sometimes he did not come in at night, sometimes he arrived back, very dishevelled, as they were breakfasting, and when he did come home at night, he did not sleep even in the same room with her. He spoke roughly and rudely to her when she asked him whether they could not do things together, and she was no longer in any doubt that he was drunk a lot of the time. He also had some very strange friends, of whom she caught glimpses from time to time. Once, when she and Karelia were walking to St Thomas's, he came reeling out of a narrow side street with his arm slung over the shoulder of a young man in a mask. They were both dishevelled, their clothes awry, and drunk. Rupert was holding a bottle of wine by the neck and paused in the act of bringing it to his mouth as he saw them. There was a frozen moment, and then he straightened up and gave them an ironic salute, and whispered something to his masked companion. The man laughed and kissed his cheek, and the pair about turned and went back into the shadows, and Boy, who had been behind them, followed, after giving Jemima a very insolent stare.

Jemima's eyes filled with tears, and Karelia tactfully pretended not to have seen anything, and hurried her on, talking about the music they were going to hear.

A week became two, and things were no better. She began to notice the servants whispering and giving her odd looks, and Pask and Jane treated her with a kind of silent sympathy which she found both touching and irritating. Her own pleasure in Venice was marred by her husband's strangeness, and she began to wonder, dully, if he would be like this when they got back to England. Had he changed again, back to what he had been, or worse? She could hardly believe it, still feeling that his behaviour over the summer was too consistent not to have been genuine. Perhaps it was an evil influence? People did behave very freely in Venice, and she had once or twice been on the verge of being shocked by things which perfectly respectable people did. Perhaps being abroad, and on his honeymoon, and in Venice at Carnival time had made him relapse temporarily into his former ways. Apart from anything else, why would he have married her, if he were really a drunken reprobate?

She came into her room one day to fetch her gloves to find him standing at her dressing-table, and when he heard her he turned abruptly to look at her.

'Ah, the lovely Countess, my wife. How do you do madam?' he said. He swayed slightly as he spoke, his words were a little blurred, and she realized that he was drunk, though it was only ten in the morning. But more importantly, he was holding in his hand the diamond collar.

'What are you doing with that?' she asked anxiously. He gave her an unpleasant smile.

'Debts, especially gambling debts, must be paid,' he said. She stared with horror.

'You don't mean – you aren't going to sell them?'

'Absolutely correct, madam. I felicitate you on your acuteness,' he said carefully.

'But you can't! You mustn't!' she cried, coming forward a step. He snatched his hand back and held the diamonds high, out of her reach.

'What? You would not have me jailed for not paying my debts? Or called out – that would be worse. I'd never be able to shoot straight, and you'd be a widow, and you wouldn't like that, would you? Or would you?'

'But you can't sell those, you can't,' she cried in distress. 'They're mine!'

He laughed again, but this time quite a merry laugh.

'Yours? What can you mean? Do you not remember, dear Jemima, that you are my wife? All that was once yours is now mine, as the law allows and the state provides. It's all in the contract, my dear wife, all in the contract. I get all your property, and you –' he choked a little on his mirth – 'and you get *all my titles*.' And now he laughed so much that he had to sit down on the bed to indulge it. Jemima watched him, with a murderous rage in her heart which for a moment drowned out the terrible hurt. Through his laughter he spluttered, 'Oh my dear girl, if you could just see your face! *What a bargain*! All my titles for all of your fortune. A mess of pottage, dear girl, a mess of pottage. Lady Chelmsford! It is rich. You must see, it really is rich!'

The rage settled in her and became icy, as she watched him, and then, young as she was, a kind of wisdom came to her. She smiled. She felt her face might splinter and fall into shards as she did it, but she smiled.

'A good joke indeed,' she said, 'but all the same, my lord, you must not sell those diamonds. Everything else in the box, if you wish, but not those.'

His eyes narrowed suspiciously. 'Why not these?' he said, pulling them to his chest in a childish gesture. She forced herself to continue to smile.

'Because you would not get a good price for them here. In England, where they are famous, where everyone knows their history and therefore their worth, you will get twice as much for them.'

He nodded in a fuddled way. 'True. You are not without sense, Lady Chelmsford. Very well, I'll take this – and these – and these. That should do for now. And these – I return.' He dropped the

504

diamonds back into the box, put his booty into his pockets, and with a nod to her, strolled out. As soon as the door was shut she flung herself at the box, seized the diamond collar, and clutched it to her like a child snatched from fire. And then she fell onto the bed and wept with misery and frustration.

When the storm of weeping was past, she sat up, wiped her eyes and blew her nose, and fastened the diamonds round her neck, feeling that was the safest place for them. She thought about his words – all her fortune for all his titles. She knew that it was true, that a married woman's property became her husband's, but surely her mother must have made some provision in the contract for her to control the Morland estate – after all, she was the heir, the young master, except that she was female? Surely her mother would not have signed everything away without some surety? And what about her settlement? And in any case, Lord Chelmsford must be rich, and would not need her fortune. She could not believe he had meant to be so cruel and unpleasant. It was the drink, she told herself. He would be all right once they were back in England. In England! How she longed for it. The door opened at that moment, and Jane came in.

'I beg your pardon, my lady, I wondered if you—' She stopped abruptly at the sight of Jemima's red eyes and flushed face, and forgetting etiquette, rushed over to her and knelt beside her. 'My lady, what is it, what's wrong?' Jemima did not answer, and meeting her steady look, Jane frowned, and her lips tightened. 'His lordship was up here just now, wasn't he?' she said. 'Oh, my lady—'

'Jane, tell me what you know. I've seen you and Pask whispering. Tell me what you know about him,' Jemima said with a calm that wavered even as she spoke.

Jane shook her head, and then said. 'Only that he drinks a lot, my lady, and gambles a lot. The other servants said he lost a thousand pounds last week at some palace or other, where a friend of his lives. Has he been unkind to you?'

Jemima shook her head. Jane was not telling her everything, she was sure, but she could not imagine what the rest could be. Something worse? Something so bad she did not want to tell her? At all events, she could not confide in the maid what had passed between her and Rupert. That would be disloyal, and he was, after all, her husband. 'I'm homesick, that's all,' she said. 'Jane, go down and apologize to the Lady Karelia for me, and tell her I will be down very shortly, when I have bathed my face. Go on, now, do as I say. I am quite all right.'

Jane went reluctantly. Outside Pask was waiting for her with an anxious look of enquiry.

'She wouldn't talk about it. She's brave as a lion, that one – too brave.'

Pask's fists clenched themselves. 'I should like

506

to kill him,' he said fiercely. 'When I think – Oh, if only the Master were alive!'

'If only!' Jane said, and went off on her errand.

Jemima had been longing for home, but when they were actually on their way, she grew nervous, and wished they had stayed in Venice. After all, at least in Venice he was someone else's guest, and therefore bound to keep within the bounds of decency. Suppose she was wrong, suppose he behaved as badly in London? Then he would be entirely her problem, and what would she do then? And in London she would have no Karelia for company. And in London, if there was a scandal, everyone would know it. He was very silent on the journey, sleeping a great deal, and she was glad not to be the object of his attention. She looked at him while he slept and saw how the debauchery of the past weeks had marked him. His eyes were pouchy, and there were hard lines about his mouth, and he had a rash of little red spots along his cheek. But he was still handsome, although now – or was it her imagination? – she detected something strangely unpleasant about the handsomeness, a weakness, a softness, that ought not to be there.

He was very ill on the boat, especially in the Channel, which was choppy, and she sent Pask to help Boy take care of him, for Boy, though not actually sick, was also a little green and inconvenienced. Jemima found she was not troubled by the movement, and in fact stayed on deck as long as the sailors would allow her, enjoying the fresh-smelling sea breeze and the sight of the clean grey and white water and the strong, watchful gulls. Jane tutted at her for exposing her white skin to the weather, but she told her firmly she would not go below and Jane was forced to accept the inevitable.

When they got to London they went straight to Chelmsford House, where Rupert, still white and shaken, went straight to bed, leaving Jemima to unpack alone and to examine her new abode. She was shocked at its state. It was almost denuded of furnishings; all the pictures and mirrors had gone, as well as the plate, and anything that could have been of value. It was also extremely dirty, and in need of repainting, and the gardens were a tangled wasteland. There were only a handful of servants, too, and they looked an idle, villainous crew, evidently people who could not get work elsewhere and had taken the position for a low wage rather than starve. Jemima began to be seriously worried. Surely he would not live like this, if he had the choice, for she had seen how he liked luxury. In Yorkshire he had lived in great style – she remembered the numbers of candles, the great feasts, the excellent wines – so why would he be any different in London? Surely those evil-looking servants could not have laid the place waste in his absence? Four months was hardly long enough to have wrought such havoc. She tried to question them, but it was like trying to pin water to a tree, and when one of them discovered what she suspected him of, he grew abusive, and she was afraid. Explanations, she decided, would have to wait until Rupert was well again – but explanations there should be. She wanted to know exactly what had been going on, however bad it was.

Meanwhile, during his illness, she was embarrassed as to how to receive guests. With the help of Jane and Pask, for she was afraid to ask the other servants anything out of the way, they cleaned and polished the entrance hall as best they could, and took all the most decent furniture that was left into the smallest parlour. Pask washed the windows and the chandelier, and Jane went out to buy candles with Jemima's own money, of which she had a little left since her honeymoon, and picked some attractive leaves from the garden to arrange in lieu of flowers. And in this room Jemima, the new Countess of Chelmsford, received those guests who came to pay the usual wedding-visits. There were strangely few of them: one or two curious members of the younger set, who came to stare so that they could report back on her clothes and her looks – and now, she thought despairing, on the poverty of her furniture – and one or two kindly older people who had known her father or other members of her family. They sat a little while and chatted, and went away with sad glances, and Jemima was feverishly bright, and spoke of the wonders of Italy, and offered them wine, though she was not at all sure there was any.

There were also a number of visitors for Rupert, all of them young men, all fashionable almost to screaming-point, some of them very oddly attired, many of them heavily daubed with cosmetics and reeking of orange-flower-water. Some were gentlemen's sons, or scions of the nobility, some were actors or musicians or entertainers of other sorts, and some she could not place at all. They stared at her, and giggled, and asked after Rupert, and some asked to see him, and went upstairs, where they stayed for a very long time, though he had refused any visits from her, saying he was too ill.

Jane often urged her to go out, but she would not.

'You ought to take the air, my lady. You are looking quite pale and drawn,' Jane would say.

Jemima would reply, 'Where could I go? And how? There is no coach here, no horses. I do not know anyone in London, and I cannot bear to be stared at any more. No, I will not go.'

So Pask cleared a little of the garden, looking ruefully at the marks and blisters it made on his gentleman-soft hands, so that she could take the air there. There was a stone bench underneath a cherry tree where she liked to sit and watch the birds. She would sit there for hours, even in the winter cold, and try to imagine she was at home, riding darling Jewel across her own land, cantering up to the Whin with Allen beside her. At least, she thought, birds and trees and grass were the same everywhere, and did not change mysteriously in their properties.

She received a letter from cousin William, excusing himself for not calling.

'My duties prevent me, and I am sure at such a time you had much rather not be troubled,' he said. Then he began again, in a slightly different hand and ink, as though he had intended to end the letter, and had added something else on impulse, or on further thought. 'Well, you have cut us all out nicely, my cousins and I,' he said. 'I wish you may not regret it! You had much better have married me, but I dare say you enjoy your title.'

When they had been back two weeks, the servants told her there was no more money to buy food, and if she did not ask the Master for some, they would all starve to death. Jemima was angry. Rupert must surely have recovered by now from the journey, she thought – and he had had a visitor up there all morning, a young man who, by the equipment he was carrying, was a painter. If he was well enough to talk to a painter, he was well enough to talk to her, she thought angrily, and mounted the stairs with determination.

When she entered the ante-room to his bedchamber, she saw Boy just coming out from the inner room with a tray on which were empty food dishes, and the sight angered her still further. He had food from somewhere, but didn't care if the rest of them, including his wife, starved. Boy almost dropped the tray at the sight of her, and said. 'What do you want?' in a way that was made almost surly with nervousness.

'I want to speak to my husband,' she said firmly, walking towards the door. He stood against it, stretching out his arm as if to stop her, and she stared at him in amazement.

'Get out of the way, Boy,' she said.

'You had much better not go in, mistress,' he said. 'Let me ask him if he'll see you first.' For answer, Jemima grabbed his arm and pushed him out of the way. It was the first time in her life she had ever manhandled a servant, proof indeed of her outrage, and Boy shrugged, stepped aside, and said. 'Well, I tried to warn you.'

She opened the door. Her first impression was that here, alone in the house, was a comfortable room. It was very untidy and rather shabby, but it was fully furnished, and there was a large fire, which made the room quite warm. There was a huge bed with scarlet draperies falling from the central ball-and-crown, and at the foot of it stood an easel with a canvas upon it, while painting materials lay scattered about on the floor. The curtains were drawn across the window, though it was daylight outside, and the room was lit with candles, which reflected their light from several mirrors – the only ones in the house, to her certain knowledge. All this she absorbed in the brief second before her eyes went irresistibly to the bed.

Sitting up in bed, with a glass of wine in his

hand, was Rupert, and as far as she could see, he was naked, not even wearing a bedgown. His head was bare, and his hair tumbled loosely about his shoulders. She was surprised at that, for she had always seen him either in a wig or a cap, and had assumed that like other men he had his own hair cut short underneath for comfort.

His other arm was around the shoulders of a blond-headed, heavily-made up creature, who was also naked, and who was undoubtedly a man. Jemima's feet wanted to run away with her, but her eyes could not stop staring. Rupert, after a first start of surprise, defiantly drew the blond man closer, and lifted his glass to Jemima.

'Ah, my dear wife! are you enjoying life in London?'

'What are you doing?' she asked stupidly. The blond creature had been glaring at her with narrowed eyes, but at her words he laughed, and snuggled closer to Rupert.

'Why my dear, what do you think?' Rupert said. 'I'm having my portrait painted. Have a look at it, if you like.'

Their laughter followed her as she ran from the room, slamming the door behind her as if she was pursued by devils.

The following day, Rupert dressed and came downstairs. He was clean, shaven, sober, and serious, but Jemima looked at him, trembling, with anxious eyes, and was afraid she would begin to cry if she spoke. He stared at her for a while, and

513

then said. 'My little holiday is over. It is time to attend to business.'

'Business?' she managed to say. He sat down, still staring at her reflectively, like a man considering the value of a portrait he is about to steal.

'Business, Lady Chelmsford. You see, I cannot doubt, that Chelmsford House is in severe need of refurbishing. This is because, while my father left me his title and his houses, as he was bound to do, he left me very little money. There is no estate attached to the title. The old Countess left everything of value to her daughter, my aunt, who in turn left it to her daughter, Lady Strathord. And while the exigencies of fate have now reunited the fortune and the title in one person, I find that Lady Strathord, the Jacobite whore, sold practically everything of worth to give the money to the Young Pretender.'

'But—'

'There is an income from the Shawes estate,' he went on, cutting across Jemima's protest, 'but it is not enough to maintain Shawes and Chelmsford House and me, for you may as well know at once that I take a great deal of maintaining. I must have my little pleasures, madam, and pleasures do not come cheaply. I needed money. What was I to do? I would have to find an heiress, a rich heiress, and in spite of my repugnance to the idea, marry her. But where would I find an heiress who would marry *me*? That *was* a problem.' And he laughed. Jemima flushed.

514

'But when you came to Yorkshire – you lived at Shawes, in great style. You seemed to be rich.'

'I sold my last few valuables, and borrowed a great deal from some sporting friends, who were willing to bet that I would never get you to accept me, or your mother to agree. That was a hard task, I must admit, for she began with a prejudice I thought I should never be able to overcome. That was why my friends thought it a good bet. But it turned out to be easy,' he said with faint petulance, 'much too easy. It was hardly any challenge at all.'

'Then – you were not – you did not mean any of the things you said? You seemed – in Yorkshire – you seemed so different, so—'

'It was a good act, was it not?' he said, laughing gaily. 'The noble, the virtuous, gentle and good, paying court to the fair and innocent. Lord, what I would have given for my friend Garrick to have seen it! My deepest regret is that no one – no one who matters,' he amended contemptuously, 'saw my finest role.'

'But you couldn't have been acting the whole time,' Jemima said, clinging with fading hope to her own single comfort. 'No one could pretend all the time.'

'My dear girl, you underestimate me. Consider what a grounding I have had! The great Garrick! He has revolutionized the art of acting, and I have drunk from the fount. I know as much about the art as any of those who practise the profession – a great deal more than some of them, I may say. And you also underestimate the incentive I had to give that one, great performance. You were going to be very rich, and you were going to be mine. And now you are, dear girl, and so today I must attend to business. Apart from refurbishing Chelmsford House, I have a large number of most pressing debts to settle, and I must look over my new assets and decide what to sell.'

'You mean to sell my property to pay your debts?' Jemima said in a low voice.

'No, Jemima, I intend to sell *my* property. You are forgetting the marriage contract. I can let you have a look at a copy of it, if you like.'

'You can't! I won't let you!' she cried in frustration. He looked at her almost with sympathy.

'I'm sorry, but there is nothing you can do to stop me. You are trapped, fair and square. You are my wife, and your property is mine to do as I like with, and there is nothing in the world to be done about it. You must simply get used to it.'

Jemima's mind revolved sickeningly as she tried to find a way out. Frustration and anger boiled inside her, and she clenched her fists, and turned her head from side to side as if physically seeking a way of escape. 'I won't let you destroy my estate,' she cried. 'There must be some way. I'll divorce you.'

'You can't. You would need an Act of Parliament, and you have no grounds, even if you could find the interest to put it through Parliament; and even if you did divorce me, you would not get your property back. You would get only your settlement, which is a cash income, which I would have to pay you out of the profits of the Morland estate, which is now mine. So you see?'

She was thinking now, fast and frantically. 'What if I got the marriage annulled? Wouldn't I get my property back then?'

His eyes narrowed. 'You have no grounds.'

'I think I have,' she said, but her uncertainty shewed in her voice. 'What about non-consummation?'

'The marriage was consummated, on that first night,' he said.

'I don't think it was,' she said uncertainly. 'I don't think what you did counts.'

He shrugged. 'I can always do it again, and will,' he said, adding as she took an involuntary step backwards, 'by force if necessary. I need your property Jemima, and I will not let a small thing like that stand in the way. I can get to you much more quickly than you can get to a lawyer, so don't threaten me, unless you want another taste of married bliss.'

She turned away, and said with weary disgust, 'I hate you. I want nothing to do with you.'

'I dare say you do. But you are my wife, and for the time being, you will stay here with me, and behave nicely in public, and make me respectable at Court. I need that, you see, to counterbalance my little – pleasures. And if you are good, and behave nicely, I will let you go back to Morland Place.'

Her head came up eagerly, and he added. 'Eventually.' Her head went down again. 'Cheer up, dear girl, you will enjoy some of your new life. Being at Court – parties, balls, playing cards with the Princesses. Living in London – the theatre – well, no, perhaps not the theatre in your case – but the concerts, the opera, the entertainments, riding round the park, the *beau monde*! Think of it, Jemima, it's an opportunity most Yorkshire girls would give their eyes for. You might as well enjoy it.'

It was two years before he let her go home. They were strange years, not entirely without pleasure, but years in which she felt lost, cut off from the world, as though she were living inside a glass case, seeing and hearing but never a part of what was going on around her.

Rupert sold various things and paid off his debts and gradually refurbished the house. He did not ask her permission or opinion, but he always told her what he was doing with what she still insisted on thinking of as her estate, though whether this was out of courtesy or in a sadistic desire to cause her pain, she never knew. Reluctant though she was to part with Pask, she sent him home to Morland Place, so that she would have someone she trusted absolutely with whom to communicate. He was to help Clement run the estate, and to be the liaison between London and Yorkshire. Rupert let Shawes on a short lease, and the income was enough to maintain the house and to produce a surplus. To her surprise, he did not close down Morland Place, nor evict all her dependant relatives, though he would have had a perfect right to do so. She did not know whether he realized how many people were living at his expense; or whether he did not care; or whether it was his sop of convention and public opinion; or whether it was a curious, renegade streak of kindness in him.

She did consult a lawyer, secretly, about the marriage contract, and was told that what Rupert said was right. If Rupert died before her, and they were childless, her own property, the title, and the Chelmsford inheritance would go to his brother Charles and his children, though she would have the right to the title of Countess dowager. When he is dead, she thought to herself fiercely, I shall *never* use his title.

She was puzzled at his evident desire for the outwards trappings of respectability. Though he was not prepared to give up his vices, he seemed to want to carry them on with a certain amount of discretion, and to be received in the best places and at Court as a respectable married man with a beautiful and charming wife. She considered refusing to play the part, but he had too much power over her, and he had told her again that her being allowed to go home depended on her pleasing him. So she appeared with him in public, both of them beautifully dressed, and though she could not pretend to like him – she was not a skilled actor like him – she treated him civilly, and

519

never let anyone see her true feelings about him. He, in public, treated her respectfully and attentively, though he did not try to pretend the warmth and gentleness he had shewn her in Yorkshire, and few people could have thought she had any grounds for complaint. He allowed her no money, but denied her nothing in the way of comforts and clothes, though he still shewed a desire to sell her family jewels. But she persuaded him to sell other things first, and hoped that it would not become necessary.

Her life in London would have been a happy one, if it had not been for her loneliness. There was a continuous round of public and private engagements, and when they were not being seen together, Rupert left her in peace. She often sat in the garden under the cherry tree when she was alone, and thought about her childhood, and about Allen, whose image was never far from her mind. His kindness, compared with Rupert's cruelty, seemed a golden and distant thing, like a vision of Paradise, granted once and snatched away.

They were a strange two years in other ways. In March, shortly after their arrival in London, Frederick, Prince of Wales, died, and King George ordered six months' public mourning, which meant slight mourning on informal occasions and full mourning for public and Court appearances. Jemima found it odd to be back in mourning, after such a brief respite, and for a man she had never known nor ever seen in her life. Rupert was evidently affected by the Prince's death – he had been one of 'poor Fred's' Patriot Boys since the early days, and had shared many a debauch with him. The Princess of Wales, Augusta, was pregnant when her husband died, and in July gave birth to a posthumous daughter, which gained her great public sympathy: it was her ninth child, all surviving. And hardly were they out of mourning for Poor Fred than they were back into it for his sister, the Queen of Denmark, who died in December 1751.

Apart from the royal death, the talk in December was all about Lord Chesterfield's plan to change the calendar. England and Russia used the Julian calendar, while the rest of Europe used the Gregorian, and on official papers both dates had to be recorded. Now there was an Act before Parliament to say that the new year was to start on 1 January, instead of 25 March, Lady-day, as it had from time immemorial, and after 31 December 1751 the next day was to be called 1 January 1752, not 1751. It caused enormous confusion, and even more enormous resentment, amongst the people. In vain did the government point out the convenience of having the same system as the rest of Europe: still the pamphlets raged about the ungodly tampering with ancient law, and still the people said they didn't want to be like the rest of Europe. They were English, and English ways were good enough for them, and if the rest of Europe wanted to be the same they could change to English ways. It was widely called a Popish plot, the first stage of a ploy to place England under French sovereignty, and they were convinced that England was done for.

Later that year there was even more confusion when the second stage of the Act came into force. The Julian calendar had been eleven days behind the Gregorian, and so it was necessary to advance the date to catch up. Thus the day after 2 September was to be called 14 September, the eleven days in between being dropped, and at that there was open rioting in the streets, and people marched on Parliament with banners crying 'Give us back our eleven days!' They had lost eleven days of their lives; they were eleven days nearer the grave; they were horrified and outraged.

Only two days after the new 14 September, Jemima learned that the other Prince of Wales, Prince Charles, the Young Chevalier, had landed in England: not this time to lead a rebellion, but to visit friends in London and to convert from Roman Catholicism to the Church of England, which he felt was the best way to aid his plans to regain his father's throne. It was an extraordinary thing to do, and the public reaction to it was even more extraordinary. Everyone knew he was in London – he was staying at Essex House, just off the Strand, with Lady Primrose, widow of a Jacobite who had been executed at Carlisle in '46 – but nothing was done to arrest him. The Court, the King, the government, simply ignored the fact, even though he was walking quite openly about London, seeing the sights – for it was his first visit to his father's capital. He was received into the Church of England at St Mary-le-Strand a week later, and afterwards a dinner was given for him in the house next door to Chelmsford House by the Duke of Beaufort and the Earl of Westmorland. Jemima and Rupert were invited, partly, she thought, because they were neighbours, but mostly because Rupert's father had helped the Prince in the '45.

'Ironic, isn't it,' Rupert said as they prepared to leave for the dinner. 'I'm being asked to honour the man for whom my inheritance was sold. But for him and his attempt, I would have inherited a handsome property, and I should never had had to marry you, and you would never have had to part with your estate. I hope this dinner does not choke us.'

'But if it hadn't been for him, Lady Strathord wouldn't have died, and then you wouldn't have inherited anything. She might have had children herself, and then you would only have inherited the title and Chelmsford House.'

'True,' he said. 'In that case I shall eat all I can.'

Thus it was that Jemima met Prince Charles, the Young Chevalier, something she could have looked forward to telling her children about one day, if she had been able to anticipate ever having any. He was tall, very handsome, with brown eyes, wearing a blond wig which, it was said, matched his own hair.

He looked faintly familiar, but she could not quite think who it was he resembled. Perhaps one simply grew up knowing what a Prince looked like. His manners were charming and courteous, and he made himself very pleasant to Jemima, but she found him cold. She was amused that before the evening was out he was making up to Rupert in the hopes of borrowing money from him, and indeed Rupert did look as though he was very rich, and he was Maurice Morland's son. The Prince's money-problems were very pressing, Jemima had heard, but she did not think he had the least chance in the world of getting money out of Rupert.

She did manage to ask him in the course of the evening if he had any news of Allen Macallan, and the Prince said that as far as he knew he was still serving with the Royal Ecossais.

'I do not, as you know, go to France any more, and so I have no closer news of him. But he must be happy, must he not, madame, or he would come home?'

'Come home?' Jemima stammered, staring at him. 'How could he come home?'

The Prince raised his eyebrows. 'There has been a general amnesty, surely you knew that? It does not, of course,' he added, shewing his teeth in a grin that was part ironic, 'extend to me.'

'Perhaps he does not know about it,' Jemima said. She could not believe that he would stay in France, if he could come home. 'Perhaps I should write to him. I wonder—'

The Prince bowed to her. 'If you wish to write, madame, I may be of service to you in sending the letter. I have communications with some ladies in Paris, loyal ladies, who would pass the letter on for you.'

She wrote that evening, telling Allen about the amnesty, about her marriage, and adding that there was a home for him at Morland Place, even though she herself was not living there at present. She gave the letter to Jane to take round to Lady Primrose's, for she could not trust anyone else. A few days later, the Prince left for Antwerp.

For a time Jemima lived in hope. Surely he would come back – and if Allen were in England, she would have a friend. Even if she could never see him or speak to him, the knowledge that he was there would comfort her. She thought she could persuade Rupert to let him stay at Morland Place, since he knew more about running the estate than anyone, and would be of the first usefulness. But he did not come, nor reply, and she had no way of knowing if the letter had reached him, so after a while she let the hope quietly die.

In the March of 1753 she asked Rupert if she could go home.

'I have done everything you asked,' she said.

'True,' he said, 'but you are useful to me here. I need you to come to Court functions with me.'

'I can be more useful to you at home,' she said persuasively. 'You need a good, steady income, and Morland Place can be run more efficiently with its mistress there than it ever can through hirelings. You *know* that is true. I am needed more at Morland Place than I am here.'

Still he hesitated, and finally she said, 'Let me just go home for the summer. I find the summers in London trying, and my health is suffering.'

Finally he agreed. 'You can go at the end of April. I need you until then – there's the birthday ball, for one thing, and that party at the Warwicks' – but you can go home for the summer, and to check that everything is all right, and I shall even join you later on, perhaps in July. You are right about London being trying in the heat, and I have a fancy for some country air and some good racing. Yes, a happy thought of yours. I shall have the summer months on my country estate!'

He evidently liked the sound of the words, and could already hear himself saying them to his friends. Jemima's heart sank a little – she had not wanted him to come with her when she asked to go home – but nothing could quite extinguish the joy at the thought of seeing Morland Place again. On the last day of April, in spite of the most inclement weather, she set off, her heart lifting with every mile she travelled northwards.

Her mother seemed somehow smaller than she remembered; grim, but not so frightening. She and Father Andrews seemed, in the confused memories of that home-coming, always to be standing together, side-by-side and silent; oddly faded, as if the strength of their colours had bled away in the darkness of their oblivion in Jemima's mind. The people who were vivid were dear Pask, and Clement, whom she greeted with real affection.

Uncle George was pleased to see her too, and his watery old eyes grew more watery still as he attempted to lower his bulk into a bow over her hand. Robert and his sons were not there, and Edmund was from home, but Augusta and the girls welcomed her with mild enthusiasm. Young Augusta was eager to boast about her betrothal to a cornet of horse, and Jemima listened gravely and then congratulated her cordially.

'I hope you will be very happy,' she said, and added in her heart, happier than I am. The odd thing was that no one knew she was unhappy. Pask, of course, had not revealed anything of the true state of affairs, and for everyone at Morland Place, the Rupert they had seen that summer was the only one, and they still thought her lucky to have married a man who was not only rich and titled, but handsome, kind and pleasant into the bargain. Her mother, indeed, was sourly convinced of Jemima's good fortune, which she equated with her luck in becoming her father's sole heir against all the odds; her only relief was that there was evidently no sign of a child coming. Perhaps Jemima's perfect fortune would fail her in that one respect, at least.

As soon as she decently could, Jemima escaped to the stables, where William, the groom, had Jewel waiting for her, groomed so that he shone like black glass.

'He's been turned out since you went away, m'lady,' William said, 'but as soon as I heard you was coming home, I fetched him up, and I've been working on him every day since then.'

'I can see that you have,' Jemima said warmly as her horse investigated her hands and pockets with his soft, enquiring lips. 'He looks wonderful.'

'You might find him a bit fresh, m'lady, after so long turned out, but you should manage him all right, you being such a fine horsewoman, if you'll excuse me saying so, m'lady.'

In a very short time, she had had him saddled, and with Pask to accompany her, she rode out to look at her country. They ranged far afield, galloped the fret out of the horses' feet and their own minds, and then walked and trotted more quietly back towards the house. At the top of the last rise Jemima drew rein, and they both sat for a while looking down towards the house.

'It looks so timeless,' Jemima said, 'as if it grew up out of the ground. It is hard to believe that men built it, that there was a time when there was nothing here but green fields.' Jewel sneezed, and thrust his head down to rub his muzzle against his knee. The clink of his bit was a sound that blended so naturally to her ear with the sound of the wind in the grass, a distant dog barking, a lark shrilling far, far up in the blue heaven, a collar-dove cooing throatily in the chestnut tree behind them, a bee working somewhere near Jewel's feet. In the stifling London nights she had been able to close her eyes and conjure effortlessly the sounds of her own place; and the smells – the warm, chalky smell of earth, the ripe greenness of grass and trees, the sweetness of horses, the tang of sheep, the thousand different delicacies of flowers; the smell of apples in autumn, and woodsmoke, and cooking blackberries. The pleasures of London were many, and exciting, but what could compare with the pleasure of eating a plum warm from your own tree, or throwing a stone into your own moat and watching the silvery ripples spread and rock the exotic gold-and-white boats of the waterlilies?

'It is so hard to believe that it is not mine any more,' she said at last. 'I love it so – surely that ought to count for something? Surely—' Pask gave her a swift look of sympathy, and she could not go on, for fear of being disloyal. That her home should be drained, perhaps even destroyed, to finance his luxury, his vice, that it should be drunk away and gambled away by a man who cared nothing for it, seemed so hard that she could have cried out with frustration. 'Oh Papa,' she said aloud. Why had he died when he did, leaving her helpless? Pask bit his lip. He had been servant to her father and her grandfather, and whatever their faults as men, as husbands, as fathers, they had loved Morland Place, they had been its servant as well as its master, and faithful to it.

'All I can do, is endure,' Jemima said. She was

like someone marooned on a rock, waiting to be rescued – but there would be no rescue. A maiden, marooned on a rock – the mermaid should be my badge, she thought with bitter irony. Pask longed to comfort her, and dared to offer what brinked on an impious remark.

'They say that people who live – irregular lives, don't live long.'

Jemima met his eyes, and he blushed. 'But then it will all pass to his brother,' she said.

After a silence he said, 'I never heard any ill of Mr Charles, my lady,'

'No,' Jemima sighed. 'At least he will be a Morland.'

CHAPTER 18

In 1760 King George II died. His death was as bizarre and horrible as his wife's had been, for he collapsed of a stroke one morning while straining in his water-closet. In his will he ordered that his body should be buried next to that of his wife, and that one side of each coffin should be removed, so that his remains would mingle with hers in death. She had died twenty-three years ago, but he had never stopped loving her which, Jemima thought, was the best, the only good thing you could say of him.

He was succeeded by his grandson George, who was twenty-two, and had lived a life of such retirement that nothing was known about him, either good or bad. There was no question about the succession: the Jacobite cause was lost for ever. King James still lived in Rome, Prince Charles still wandered round Europe in search of a pension or an army, and Prince Henry had entered the church and was a well-loved and well-respected cardinal. Neither Prince had any legitimate offspring: the sad and unlucky Stuart line would end with them.

The past few years had been lucky for England,

for Mr Pitt was now at the peak of his career, and his forcefulness counterbalanced Newcastle's wavering. The name of Morland had had its share of the glories. William had been at Quebec with General Wolfe when the resounding defeat of the French had settled Canada's fate. The richest of the French sugar islands, Guadeloupe, which was also a rendezvous for French privateers, fell to the West India fleet, in which Thomas was still serving, a captain of twenty-five years' seniority now, and close to the top of the list: it would not be long before he hoisted his flag as an admiral. Even Edmund, lazy, cowardly Edmund, had found his glory at last: he had fallen at Minden in 1759, when the army's victory over the French had wiped out the memory of the defeat at Fontenoy back in '45.

Both of his daughters were married, young Augusta to her cornet, John Akroyd, in 1755, and Caroline, shortly before her father's death in 1759, to a distant cousin, Captain Ernest Pratt, a more senior officer than young Augusta's husband, which caused a coolness between the sisters. Their widowed mother divided her time between the two households, but infinitely preferred Mrs Pratt's boasting to Mrs Akroyd's complaining. She mourned her husband sincerely, and comforted herself with the knowledge that he and his children, though not inheriting Morland Place, had at least done better than Robert and *his* children.

Robert had still not gained his preferment, and was still living at Shelmet Rectory, where he vented his frustration in blistering indictments of his flock's wickedness. It had made him very popular locally, where his fierce threats of hell-fire made a refreshing change from the usual restrained and languid preaching; his services were always well-attended, and his congregation went home stimulated and agreeably scathed to their little sins, which seemed far more important and enjoyable for his condemnation.

His son Robert had also gone into the church, and had succeeded to a stall at Westminster where he drowsed and dined away his days in a manner which irritated Robert into fresh sallies of rhetoric. His son Frederick was still at home, living at his expense now since Morland Place had been banned to them. Frederick had reached the age of twenty-eight without ever doing anything useful or praiseworthy, and he spent his days in idleness, hunting five days a week, drinking too much when his father could afford it, and making himself an unparalleled reputation amongst the female servants of the neighbourhood.

It was Jemima who had forced Robert and Frederick to live upon their own resources, and had discouraged Augusta from living out her widowhood there, and it was not from spite, but from necessity. The years which had been so good for England and satisfactory for Edmund's progeny had been hard for her and for Morland Place. Rupert's expenses grew year by year, and he was a more and more careless gambler, capable of losing a thousand pounds in one night. He would gamble on anything: which of two rain-drops would reach the bottom of the windowpane first, which spilled drop of wine a fly would land upon, what day a mare would drop her foal. And all his expenses had to be met from the income of Morland Place, or from selling some one or other of its assets. Shawes was still let; Chelmsford House, too, was let, and for the past eighteen months Rupert had been living in lodgings in Drury Lane – an advantage from Jemima's point of view, since it had meant she had been able to go home to live permanently at Morland Place. It did mean she was no longer able to exert any kind of restraining influence on him; but in any case her influence had been growing more and more negligible, and she had come to hate him so much that she was glad to get away from him.

There was no longer any doubt amongst the denizens of Morland Place about her husband's true worth – the last two summers he had spent in Yorkshire had revealed the truth to them, at least about his drinking and gambling, if not about his more vicious propensities. Lady Mary had witnessed the truth before she died in 1758. She had achieved her ambition of seeing her daughter more wretched in marriage than she had been, but had failed in her ambition to rejoice at it. She had been ill for some months, and the truth only wearied and disgusted her. Jemima had been too hard-pressed by other worries to grieve much at her mother's death. It was becoming daily a harder struggle to keep Morland Place together, which was the task that obsessed her, even though she was doing it, ultimately, for someone else. But she was the servant of her inheritance, and she could not abandon it. Economies had to be made, the dependant personnel reduced. Gradually the staff shrank, though she never turned a servant away against their will or with no other place to go to. Robert and his family she turned firmly away, to live upon their own. Uncle George stayed – she could not send him anywhere else, and he was so much a part of the background of her life that she hardly noticed him. In any case, he was little expense: he ate, drank, and rode her horses, and that was all. He even, in his silent, shy way helped her, for when he rode out now, he hardly ever came back empty handed; understanding, at least dimly, her predicament, he would ride not simply for pleasure, but for the pot, and would come home with pheasants or wood-pigeon or rabbits or even, occasionally, a deer, and then stump, red-faced, up to his room before she could thank him.

Morland Place, increased over the years by the purchases of the generations, shrank back closer and closer to its original dimensions. The land in Northumberland was sold to Viscount Ballincrea, who gave, she suspected, a better price than it was worth, for kinship's sake. The outlying farms at Healaugh and Crockey Hill were sold. All the family plate, and many of the family jewels went, though she refused, doggedly, to part with the major family heirlooms.

She worked, and the reduced staff worked, to wring the best income possible out of the estate. She sold horses, unbroken yearlings, half-broken two-year-olds, promising four-year-olds, proven brood mares, one of the stallions. After the races, she sold the best and most successful of the geldings and colts, and raised the stud-fees. She sold wool, she sold farm produce, she sold Morland Fancy cloth, going herself to market to be sure of the best price, glad of the experience her father had given her. In 1756, when the market in Briggate was disturbed by the widening of the road, she and fourteen other clothiers got together to raise subscriptions to buy a piece of land and build a Coloured Cloth Hall, where their markets could take place under cover, just as the broadcloth merchants had built their White Cloth Hall back in 1711.

Jemima was so convinced that this was a good thing to do that she sold her finest breeding mare in order to be able to invest in it herself. They bought a fine piece of land near the centre of the city, and building began at once, and in April 1757 the hall was opened for business. Each subscriber received one stall in the new hall for every £2.10s he subscribed, and could either use, sell, or hire out the stalls. The hall was divided inside into five 'streets' around a central courtyard, and the streets were lined with stalls, each 22 inches wide, with the

536

owner's name painted on the front, there being 1,770 stalls altogether. Jemima kept the best stall on Mary Lane for herself, and hired out the other two. Her faith in the venture was amply justified by the immediate expansion of trade, the brisk demand for stalls, and the amount that could be obtained by selling or hiring the stalls. The hall was strictly controlled by fifteen trustees, of whom Jemima was elected one for the first period of three years, and was to be used only for the sale of coloured, mixed, or fancy cloths, and only by those who had served their full apprenticeship in the trade.

The scheme gave Jemima an interest, and she worked at it with a passion that made Pask and Jane shake their heads, and Jane to murmur that she ought to be having babies, poor lady, to devote herself to. But of that, they at least knew, there was no chance.

Then in October 1760 King George died, and Jemima was just congratulating herself that, now she lived in obscurity in the country, she did not need to put on mourning, when an Express arrived from London. She opened it with a sigh, expecting it to be another demand for money; but it was from Boy, to say that Lord Chelmsford had collapsed and was seriously ill, his life was despaired of, and that she should come at once.

Jemima stood looking down at her dead husband's face with a curious detachment. She had not been able to guess what she would feel when he died,

537

but in fact what she did feel was nothing. She felt unconnected with him or his demise in any way. His handsome face was ravaged by his lifelong debauchery, and by the illnesses he had suffered during his last two years, but the suddenness of his death had smoothed away many of the lines, and he looked younger than she remembered. His hair was still luxuriant and still untouched with grey, and it lay across the pillow looking curiously springy and full of life, when you considered it was growing out of a corpse.

Boy's face was beslobbered with tears, his eyes red, his mouth shapeless with misery. Jemima looked at him curiously.

'You really loved him, didn't you?' she said. He nodded wordlessly, and flung himself on his knees beside the bed, catching the cold, dead hand in his and pressing it to his wet face. Jemima watched him with detachment. It was right, she thought, that someone should have loved him. All human creatures should receive love from some source, even if it was only from a dog, or from a creature such as Boy, who was less than a dog. She looked again at Rupert, and wondered whether he had appreciated the devotion, or returned it.

'He should have lived many more years,' she said. 'It was the manner of his life that shortened it.'

He had left no will, and his personal possessions in that poor and shabby house were few and unimportant, and she did not think the new Earl would mind if she gave them to Boy.

'What will you do now?' she asked. He shook his head miserably.

'I don't know. I must find another place, I suppose. There is someone, a friend of my master, who might help me.'

'I wish you luck,' she said, and Boy looked at her with a doubtful frown. 'Yes,' she said, 'I do. It was none of it your fault.'

'Thank you, mistress,' he said. 'I wish you luck, too.'

Jemima smiled a little grimly. 'My luck ended the day I married him. I am now as homeless and penniless as you, and I have no friend to find me another place.'

She wrote to the new Earl, telling him of his brother's death, bidding him come home to take up his inheritance. She ordered her mourning clothes, gave orders for Rupert's burial, instructed the solicitor to gather together a record of his debts to give to the new Earl on his arrival, and then there seemed nothing more to do but go home to Morland Place and wait. There was an air of quiet nervousness at Morland Place. No one knew what was going to happen to them, and though Jemima tried to comfort them by saying that she was sure the new Earl would not turn them out to starve, she knew she had no right to say so, and knew that they knew it too. No one knew any harm of her brother-in-law, but no one knew any good either. She promised Jane and Pask a home, at any rate.

'He is obliged to pay me my widow's portion out of the estate, and that should be enough to keep us, if you don't mind living in a very small way.'

They hastened to assure her that they didn't.

'As long as we can be with you, my lady,' Jane said, and Jemima looked up sharply.

'Don't call me "my lady". I am Miss Jemima Morland. I have my name – no one can take that from me, at least.'

And besides her name, she had her clothes, her horse, and the diamond collar the Countess had given her. 'I have money saved, mistress,' Pask said. 'All of it is yours, if you want it.'

'That is a new departure,' Jemima said. 'The servant shall keep the mistress?'

'Don't despair,' Pask said. 'Maybe your luck will change. Something may happen.'

The new Earl arrived in November, with his wife and their five-year-old son, the only one of their children to survive. Jemima travelled to London to meet them. She found her brother-in-law a small, heavily built man, with the distinctive Morland looks, but with his mother's dark Italian eyes. He spoke English with a slight accent from his long sojourn in Italy, but his manners were perfect, and his mein kindly. His wife was jolly and freckled and rather flamboyant, evidently devoted to her husband and doting on the chubby boy to the extent of wishing to do everything for him herself, despite the nursemaids' protests.

In a toneless voice, Jemima told Charles of the death of his brother, and of the state of his fortune.

'Your inheritance, I'm afraid, is much reduced. You still own Shawes and Chelmsford House, but only just; they are both let, Shawes on a long and Chelmsford House on a short lease. The Morland property is reduced to the house and home estate. The city property was sold, I'm afraid, as well as the Northumberland estate, all except the houses on Goodramgate, and they bring in so little I didn't think it worth while selling them.'

It was Lady Chelmsford who answered, irrepressibly, before her husband could gather his words.

'Oh it doesn't matter in the least,' she said. 'I'm sure you have done wonderfully well, because, believe me, Charles knows what kind of a man his brother was, and the wonder of it is there is anything left at all. But we have the title, which is wonderful, and a home to come to, and as for money, we have plenty ourselves, quite apart from what my father left me.'

'I am sure no one was ever sorry to have more,' Jemima said drily. Molly smiled.

'Why, no, but we are so glad to be home that nothing could trouble us less. I want to live in London, and I'm sure little Charles ought to be brought up here, as he will be Earl one day in his turn. We shall take Chelmsford House and give the most wonderful balls, and you must stay here for as long as you like. In fact, Charles and I would like you to regard it as your home.'

'Thank you, my lady,' Jemima said. She beamed. 'It is only what is right.'

'And what about Morland Place?' Jemima asked, trying to sound casual, and failing. Molly glanced at her husband, exchanging some message with him, and he shook his head slightly, and she answered the question.

'We think of selling it.' Jemima heard the words with a dull shock. She had not thought of that.

'Do you not want to have a country estate? London is very tiresome in the summer, you know.'

'Oh yes, but Yorkshire is too far away,' Molly said, anxious to justify herself. 'We should like to have an estate nearer to London, in Hertfordshire or Oxfordshire – Charles favours the latter. He has very happy memories of Oxfordshire.'

'I do not think you would raise sufficient from the sale of Morland Place to buy an estate of any note in Oxfordshire,' Jemima said in one last attempt to save her home.

Molly said gently, 'As I mentioned before, Charles and I have plenty of money, enough to supplement the price of Morland Place. Indeed, we would be happy to sell it to you for a very reasonable price, as it is your home and you are fond of it, but—'

She did not need to finish the sentence. Jemima nodded miserably. She could not meet even the most reasonable price Molly might name, and Molly knew it.

★ ★ ★

A few days later Jemima went back to Yorkshire. Molly had offered her every accommodation in London, but she said she preferred to go back to Yorkshire for the time being.

'You will find it convenient to have me there until it is sold,' she said, and they agreed, gratefully, that they would.

'And afterwards, you will come and live with us at Chelmsford House,' Molly said. 'Perhaps you could be governess to little Charles.' Jemima could only be grateful that she would have a home to go to. She knew that in many ways it would be better for her to make a clean break and stay in London, but she owed it to the servants to tell them the news herself, and to be on hand until the sale was completed, to make sure that they were suitably provided for. It would certainly be some months before a sale of such magnitude could be completed, so she would have a little time more to say goodbye to everything. I shall have Christmas there, she thought, and the idea was both attractive and heartbreaking.

She knew as soon as she rode into the yard that something had happened in her absence by the number of lights that were blazing and by the air of suppressed excitement. There were torches in the sconces on either side of the great door, and they flared so brightly that they dazzled her, and as she dismounted she could not see who it was that came out to stand on the top step to greet her. Then she handed Jewel to William, and at the foot of

543

the steps looked up to see Allen standing there, smiling at her.

She felt dazed, she thought she was dreaming, and she rubbed her eyes in a bemused way that made him laugh aloud.

'No, it is me, it really is,' he said. 'I've come home, my dear Jemima. Aren't you pleased to see me?' And he held out his arms, and a moment later she was pressed close against him, not knowing whether to laugh or cry.

'Allen, Allen, is it really you? How did you get here? What are you doing here? Have you – why did you not come before? Did you—' Her questions tumbled out in disarray, but her arms were round him and never for a moment relaxed their grip. He hugged her and set her back a little to look down into her face.

'Dear Jemima, I will tell you all in a moment, but first I must look at you, and look at you. You cannot imagine how often I have thought about you and dreamed of seeing you again; but I never imagined anything as beautiful as you are in reality. You have grown up while I've been away, and grown very, very beautiful. But you aren't really any different, are you?'

'No,' she said, meaning it from her heart in a way he could not know of. 'And you haven't changed either.'

'I am older and sadder, but I hope I haven't changed in appreciating your worth. I still wear your locket, you know, round my neck under my cravat. Here, you can feel it through my shirt.'

He took her hand and pressed his fingers to his chest so that she could feel the hard shape of the locket underneath the linen. But the gesture, begun jokingly, changed at the touch of their hands. He looked into her eyes, and there was a moment of stillness and strange intensity. Then he released her gently and said, 'Come inside. You must be cold and hungry. There is a good fire in the drawing room. Come and warm yourself, and eat, and I will tell you everything.'

For a long time he only spoke of his life in France, telling her amusing or interesting stories of his soldiering or of the French Court, while she ate and drank and held her frozen toes to the blaze. Then when she had finished eating he slipped from his seat to crouch on the hearth beside her, and took up her hands from her lap, and held them in his own.

'You have changed in some ways, Jemima. You are older and sadder too. I know about your marriage to Lord Chelmsford. When he died, Pask wrote to me and told me everything, and that is why I came home.'

'Why did you not come before, when I wrote to you about the amnesty?' she asked, holding tightly onto her senses, afraid they would run away with her. She must not hope for or expect too much, or she would be hurt.

'Can you not guess? You wrote telling me you

had married, and for all I knew, had married for love. And even if you had not – what good would it have done me to come home? There was nothing for me in England. But when he died, and Pask told me – I thought – I hoped—' He seemed to find it difficult to phrase, until he looked up into Jemima's eyes, and cut through his hesitation with straightforward words. 'I have thought about you so much in France. You have become so precious to me, precious as you always were, only I was too blind to realize it. Hearing you had married opened my eyes when it was too late, but I have never stopped loving you. I came home hoping that perhaps you might be glad to see me, perhaps you might love me too. I know that you were fond of me, years ago, and I hoped that the fondness might still be there, might be capable of growing into something more tender.'

Jemima wanted to cry, except that there was suddenly, miraculously, nothing to cry for. Her hands were safe in his strong, warm ones; his gentle eyes were looking into hers with such love, such promise of cherishing; here at last was her friend, the one perfect friend, whom she could trust and confide in, care for and depend upon.

'I love you,' she said. 'I have loved you all of my life. Did you really come home for me?'

'I came home to ask you to marry me, and if you would not marry me, to offer you my service for the rest of my life. You have been shamefully abused and neglected, but while I have life, you shall want for nothing that one man's energy and devotion can provide.'

Her answer was to place herself in his arms, and he held her close, and after a while she slipped down from her chair onto the hearth with him, and turned her lips to his to be kissed. Neither of them heard Pask open the door and look in, only to close it discreetly and go away again. In the circle of the golden firelight time stood still for a little while. Jemima, dazed with joy, giving and receiving love, thought only how happy and lucky she was, and, inconsequentially, how glad she was that she was still a maiden, so that Allen would be her first true husband, her only husband. Some time she would tell him that – but not now, not now.

The next time Pask came in, he made enough noise at the door to rouse them, and they got up from their absurd position on the floor, flushed and smiling, and sat correctly on chairs as he came in with candles, followed by maids to make up the fire, and footmen with trays.

'I have brought you supper, madam and sir. I thought you would prefer to eat here, where it is warm.'

'Supper? Is it so late?' Jemima said. 'I had not imagined.' Irresistibly her eyes went back to Allen, exchanging smiles and secret thoughts.

'It is past eight, madam.' The footmen put down the trays and Allen lifted the covers and smiled at the contents.

'Venison pasty, veal collops, celery salad – cold pigeon – and what's this? Eating posset? And champagne! All this for supper, Pask? You must imagine we have something to celebrate, your mistress and I.'

Pask, busy lighting candles, only grinned.

Jemima said, 'It seems I have something to thank you for, Pask. I never knew you were such a renowned correspondent.'

'Perhaps we might have a merry Christmas after all, madam,' he said, and chivvied the maids and footmen out of the room to leave them alone.

Some time later Jemima said, 'You know that I am penniless? I shall have nothing but my widow's portion. You know that I am no longer mistress of Morland Place? The new Earl owns it, and he is going to sell it, as soon as he finds a buyer.'

'Did you think I wanted to marry you for your inheritance?' Allen said. 'I am sorry about it for your sake, but we shall live somehow, don't fear. As an officer in the French army I had a good income and nothing to spend it on. If we had succeeded in the year '45, I should have had an estate to offer you, but as it is . . .' He shrugged, a very French shrug . . . 'we shall not starve.'

Jemima smiled and touched his hand. 'If I can be with you, I shall not even very much mind losing Morland Place,' she said.

They did have a happy Christmas, and the servants gave themselves wholeheartedly to the celebrations, and Uncle George even stayed awake to enjoy the games, and organized the hunt on St Stephen's day, the first thing he had ever organized in his life. Jemima, in one of those long conversations that she and Allen had, sitting up late by the fire when everyone else was in bed, said, 'We shall have to take Uncle George with us when we go – wherever it is we are going to. I could not abandon him.'

'Uncle George will be provided for,' Allen said. 'Don't worry about anything.' And Jemima sighed and put her head on his shoulder.

'I must say that at the moment I am so happy I am finding it hard to worry. I ought not to let myself get out of practice.'

After Christmas Allen said he must drag himself away from her for a few days to go to London on business. 'I shall be as little time as I can,' he said. 'Don't fret about anything while I am away.'

She clung to him when he went away. 'I am so afraid I shall wake up and find it was all a dream, and that you are still in France, and not in love with me.'

'It's real,' he said, kissing both her eyes, the end of her nose, and her lips in rapid succession. 'When I come back from London, I shall never leave you again. You may grow to be sick of my company before you die.'

He was away a fortnight, and Jemima thought it the longest two weeks of her life. She spent the time putting things in order for the forthcoming sale, packing her personal possessions and making lists of the household possessions for the new owners. When she was not working thus, she rode out a great deal, saying goodbye to all the places she knew so well, the favourite haunts of childhood and young womanhood. Allen had not said where they would live, but she supposed they would go abroad, where he could earn a living more easily. Perhaps they would live in Italy. She had liked Italy.

He arrived back one afternoon at dusk, just before the outer gates were closed for the night. It was a day of grey sky and raw cold, and she hurried him in to the fire and herself drew off his boots and chafed his feet, despite his protests.

'Well, did you get your business done?' she asked. He nodded.

'And I have brought you something,' he said, pulling a roll of paper from his breast and handing it to her. She unrolled it, and read the words at the top 'Bill of Sale' and further down her eye jumped to the words 'Morland Place'. She felt a stab of pain in her heart, and looked up at him reproachfully, wondering why he had done something so needlessly cruel as to bring her this paper that marked the end of her home. 'Read it,' he insisted, smiling. 'Read it all through.'

Reluctantly she read it, finding it hard at first to take in the words and the strange, legal phraseology. It said that the house known as Morland Place together with all its appurtenances and furnishings, its demesne, its outbuildings, and its stock, its rents and revenues and tithes and all other benefits belonging to the estate, were now the property of Jemima Morland, Countess Dowager of Chelmsford, of Morland Place in the County of Yorkshire.

She could only stare at him, wordless and bewildered. He smiled triumphantly.

'I bought it,' he said. 'That was my business in London.'

'But—'

'I didn't say anything to you before, because I did not know how much your brother-in-law the Earl would want for it, and I did not want to raise your hopes only to have to dash them. But he was kindness itself. He seemed very glad to sell it to me, and I'm sure the price he asked was not all that it is worth.'

'But – if you bought it, why does it have my name down here?' she managed at last.

'I bought it for you, of course,' he said. 'It is yours by every right, left to you by your father. It is your home, your inheritance, and now it is yours absolutely and nothing can ever take it from you.'

She shook her head, astonished by such generosity. 'I can't believe it.'

'Dearest Jemima, Morland Place is yours. Of course, I did hope that you would let me live here with you. I hope I was not mistaken?'

She took both his hands, and said, 'I have nothing to give you in return for this gift, which is like the gift of life to me, too precious to comprehend. I love you, and to marry you would be the greatest joy of my life. And,' she felt herself reddening but forced herself not to lower her eyes, 'I want you to know that I – that you will be my first husband. I was not really married to Rupert. Do you understand what I am saying?'

He lifted her hands to his lips and kissed them, first one, then the other. 'I understand,' he said. It was a gift beside which the whole of England would have been a mere trinket.

They were married in April 1761, a month before Jemima's twenty-ninth birthday. It was an occasion of such perfect and universal happiness that the servants and estate workers talked of it for months afterwards, and used it as a standard of joy for the rest of their lives: 'It were near as good as Miss Jemima's wedding,' they would say of some high point in their lives. The couple did not go away, for as Jemima said, there was nowhere on earth they could be happier than at home. She was glad that it was Allen's home, too, that he knew it as intimately as she did, had the same memories of it, and loved it as much.

'It is terrible to see it brought so low,' she said at the wedding feast. 'Everything sold off, only the home estate left. And you know, now that you have spent your fortune in buying it, we have nothing left in the coffers at all.'

But he said, 'Don't worry, there are lots of ways

in which we can improve it. There are new ways of farming – fertilizing the ground, draining, planting new crops, root crops and artificial grasses, which will actually improve the soil. I have always wanted to be able to put my ideas into practice. I have been reading of these new ideas for years, and now I can shew you what land can really do.' She laughed, and he said, 'Yes, you see now I did not buy Morland Place merely to please you. Then there's stock-breeding – did you know you can improve the weight of a sheep and its fleece simply by breeding with the best rams and the best ewes?'

'And the cloth-making side *I* can tell *you* about,' she said eagerly. 'There are improvements to be made there, too.'

'And there is always a good market for our horses,' he said. 'Oh Jemima, in a few years we'll be able to start buying our property back. We'll have a wonderful estate to leave to our children.'

'Our children,' she said, and thought of the night to come. She was not afraid; she loved him, and all her senses clung to him. 'I hope we have lots of children.'

And much later that night, when the feast was over and they had danced the soles out of their shoes, they simply linked hands and walked up the stairs to bed, with no ceremony, or formality, or embarrassment; as if it were the most natural thing in the world.